HORSES IN WONDERLAND

Book 2:

Show Barn Blues

Natalie Keller Reinert

This is a work of fiction. Names, characters, businesses, places, events, locales, and incidents are either the products of the author's imagination or used in a fictitious manner. Any resemblance to actual persons, living or dead, or actual events is purely coincidental.

First Edition Copyright © 2015 Natalie Keller Reinert

Second Edition Copyright © 2020, 2021 Natalie Keller Reinert

Cover Photo: negelb10/depositphotos

All rights reserved.

ISBN: 978-1-956575-03-3

Also by Natalie Keller Reinert

The Grabbing Mane Series
Grabbing Mane
Flying Dismount

The Hidden Horses of New York

Catoctin Creek
Sunset at Catoctin Creek
Snowfall at Catoctin Creek
Springtime at Catoctin Creek

The Show Barn Blues Series
Show Barn Blues
Horses in Wonderland

The Alex & Alexander Series
Runaway Alex
The Head and Not The Heart
Other People's Horses
Claiming Christmas
Turning for Home

The Eventing Series
Bold (A Prequel)
Ambition
Pride
Courage
Luck
Forward
Prospect
Home

Chapter One

SUMMER WAS IN the air, and in Florida, that feeling was more like a warning than a promise.

The morning's heavy humidity had settled onto my skin like a cloak the moment I left my little bungalow. The wooden porch steps, gently rotting into slivers and chips after living through eighty seasons of dry winters and wet summers, squeaked a good morning beneath my boots. All of the wood—the floorboards, the porch, the stairs—had more give on humid mornings. More pliable, more squeaky. I could tell the new season had arrived from the moment I put my feet on the floor this morning. The longer you lived somewhere, the more you became aware of the barometers all around you. Nature forecast the weather every day, in chirps and frog-song, in locust chorals and soft westerly winds, in spiraling leaves and creaking wood. I paused at the foot of the steps and stretched, dew-drops clinging to the hairs on my arms. A spiderweb glittering from the little crooked light by the front door. A dark early-May morning at the end of a short spring. Perhaps my last spring here, in the house my grandfather built. I paused at the bottom step, swept my gaze around, and soaked in my surroundings.

The pre-dawn sky had just lightened to cobalt, a blue growing richer with every passing second. A swirl of fog wound its way through a small glade of live oaks. Just beyond it, the blue-white light over the barn's side-entrance hummed away, swooping moths orbiting its moon-glow. I pointed the toes of my well-worn paddock boots towards the barn, brushed a few unruly strands of gray and brown forelock from my eyes, and started off to work. My footsteps were softened by the wet leaves piled up on the sparse grass and sandy patches beneath the trees, but the horses would still hear me. I imagined them turning their heads all at once, ears pricked, gazing into the darkness, ready to turn on their whinnies and neighs at precisely the right moment.

My gaze shifted to the right, towards the construction site next door. There was a model villa going up over there, with just a thin belt of pine trees left to shield the future residents from the smelly, noisy reality of equestrian life. Just wait until the first morning someone left their windows open all night and heard my barn's wake-up song, belted out in three dozen or more untrained voices, each more shrill and lusty than the last.

A tree frog peeped in the gutter above the open barn door as my feet hit the pavement, but he was quickly drowned out by those thirty-some roaring horses. From across the driveway, the night turn-out horses neighed and pushed at their paddock gates, adding the rattling of chains to the morning music recital.

"How quickly you forget," I announced to the barn at large, flipping on the lights. "Twelve hours ago you were a herd of cows in clover."

The barn's overhead lamps were huge, the kind you saw in school gyms, and they'd take a good fifteen minutes to warm up to full capacity. For now, the broad barn aisle ahead of me was washed in a cool dim glow. The horses blinked at the sudden shift from nighttime to twilight, and then went straight back to whinnying. A few kicks were added here and there, fore-hooves shoved against stall doors, hind hooves slammed against side walls to prove some point to the neighboring horse.

"Your percussion section is out of rhythm," I observed.

No one listened to me. They never did.

"Good morning," I continued the greetings to my left and my right as I proceeded down the wide concrete aisle, horses on either side of me stamping and shouting for my immediate attention. I alternated between pleasantries and protestations. "Good god. Yes, I get it. Hello, Ivor. Yes, you're hungry. Good morning, Splash! Oh, please, all of you shut up, it's too early for this."

No one listened. Two long aisles of horses sang the song of their people. It was me against the herd, and I'd given up trying to shout them down years ago. Everything I said these days was for my own benefit.

At the end of the aisle, just past the school tack room where the heaps of battered riding lesson tack and brush boxes perched on top of weathered old tack trunks, I turned left and unlocked the feed room door. It was odd, and a little pleasant, to be here alone. Usually there would be grooms here throwing down hay and getting everyone's bellies settled with some roughage before their grain, but this morning I'd started early, so it would be just me out here for a while. I didn't feel like listening to the barn complaints for the next twenty minutes while I went out to the hay-shed and loaded up the Gator with bales of timothy, so they could eat their grain first for once. The magazines promised dire consequences for horses who were fed grain on empty stomachs, but I was already several decades deep into housekeeping before those veterinary studies had come out, and I felt comfortable breaking their rules from time to time.

I had to rummage through two trash cans full of pellets and sweet feed before I found the feed scoop in its shallow grave, buried under the alfalfa pellets. One of my employees, Kennedy, had been in charge of refilling the feed bins last night, and she could be a little scatterbrained. I dug it out with a sigh, glad she wasn't around right now. I wasn't up to Kennedy's bright-eyed enthusiasm at this time of morning.

Six o'clock was early for me, but I would be short on help today and figured I'd better get a head-start, because the afternoon tumult of riding lessons and trail rides was not going to take a vacation just because my groom head-count was down by three. Not so many months ago, there had been enough grooms for the endless work of keeping a massive show barn ticking over smoothly, but the threat of moving properties was hovering over our heads, and grooms were not known to stay aboard sinking ships. As they went on to greener pastures, one by one, I waved *bon voyage* to the tail-lights of their pick-up trucks, then trudged back into the barn to take on a few more of their abandoned responsibilities. There was no point in trying to hire people when I couldn't promise whether their job would be here or an hour away in six months.

Beneath the sterile gleam of fluorescent lights, I pulled out the morning supplement packs, individually packaged for each horse, and stacked them in order on top of the grain cart. I dumped what was left of the pellets in the trash can into the grain cart's well and topped it off with most of another fifty-pound bag. I grabbed a couple of old Strongid buckets' worth of alfalfa pellets and sweet feed from the other trash cans. Then I threw the feed scoop on top of the whole pile, dragged the heavy cart into the aisle, and stopped immediately at the first stall on my left.

A bay Hanoverian mare named Catarina eyeballed me, and then the grain cart, with barely contained excitement. She whinnied explosively and kicked her door. *"Stop it,"* I snapped, the words blended into one fierce command, and reached down for the first supplement pack.

Moses, the name on the pack read.

At this moment, I realized I'd stacked the supplement packs backwards. I redid them. There were thirty-seven in all. The horses were not amused with this delay. Catarina, with her front-row seat to the proceedings, nearly had a fit. "Here," I sighed, throwing a scoop of grain through the little feed door above her bucket, and dumping the supplements on top of it. She dug in with her mouth wide open, like a lion going for the kill, before I had even pulled back my hand. I whacked her with the plastic supplement pack for being so rude, but she ignored me. Food was more important than a puny slap from a puny human.

By six forty-five every horse was finished with grain and nosing through fresh hay, and I was exhausted. Well, not exhausted from the work I'd done, precisely, but at the thought of so much more to come, with the same routine yet to come tomorrow, and the next day, and the next, forever and ever. I'd been the manager for so long, and I'd done precisely that: I'd managed. *You, go handle feed. Carole, go handle hay. Mike, start filling water buckets. Liz, pull off blankets. Me, I'll be in the office, going over the day's schedule.* Carole, Mike and Liz were all part of the past now. Tom had been gone even longer, off to work with his first love, marine mammal rescue. I had Margaret, Kennedy and Anna full-time still, and part-time help from some Ocala castaways. Ricky and Nadine were young but battered, in that way a poor Southern upbringing can mark a person. Ricky drove a rock truck most days, hauling dirt to the construction site next door. Nadine worked part-time at a Hair Cuttery. Both of them spent Saturday through Monday here, mucking stalls and being generally useful while they gave the full-time grooms a much-needed day off.

I looked up over the central rank of stalls to the windows overlooking the barn floor. My dark office window looked blankly down, useless without me peering out of it, watching the barn live its own measured life.

My phone rang from somewhere down the aisle and I ran for it.

"Kennedy?" I answered, breathless from my sprint to the feed room where I'd abandoned my phone on a shelf next to a tub of bute. "Please tell me you're coming today. We have six horses going out at two and—"

"Of course I'm coming," Kennedy laughed. She was always so awake. Kennedy was twenty-six and had a naturally chipper attitude which had made her perfect for the role of princess at a long-running dinner show on the other side of the theme park district. This also made her perfect for teaching little girls to ride and for leading trail rides. She put on a very convincing cowboy-themed ride, which was especially impressive when you considered we were operating in a rapidly developing section of Florida and the trails were based out of an English show barn, about as far from the Wild West as one could go. "I just wanted to know if you needed help early this morning. I'm up, so..."

I looked outside, across the empty parking lot towards the pine woods at the farm's eastern border. The sky was just turning pink above the stark longleaf pines and the spike-edged palmettos, and a hint of morning light was creeping into the barn, brushing the stalls closest to the end, inching across the feed room floor towards my boots. At my far right, the hay shed stood dark and forbidding, stacked high with bales. I still had to throw down bales and get everyone fed up. The night horses had to be brought in, and the day horses turned out. The night horses were watching me steadily over the dark fencing, occasionally belting out a fresh chorus of whinnies in case I'd forgotten them. Behind the paddocks, along the farm's southern fence-line, a red-tiled villa was catching the first glints of orange sunlight, a morning glow highlighting its fanciful arches and mosaic tile-work around the windows. The model home for the new resort village going in next door, somehow closer to my barn than my own house was. The sight of it was enough to make me droop.

"I need help," I said honestly, and I remembered that not long ago, I couldn't have admitted that, not to Kennedy, not to anyone. As more years went by, the more thankful I was for people like her. People who got up at six-thirty for no apparent reason and thought, *I should go into work early today.*

"I'll be right over," Kennedy promised. "With breakfast. Hey, when is Anna coming back?"

"This afternoon, I hope," I said. "I haven't seen her car here yet."

"I hope so. I miss her so much."

Something about Kennedy's tone made me pause. She was given to extravagant emotions, so I would always expect her to react just a little over-the-top when someone close to her did something basic and expected, like go home and visit her parents for a week as Anna had done. I missed Anna, naturally; my sweet and unruffled barn manager had been part of my barn family for years, and she was certainly the calm glue that held us together when ridiculous situations—hurricanes, wildfires, a skunk in the feed room— threatened our sanity.

But Kennedy sounded as if she was absolutely *pining* for Anna to come home.

"Look for her when you're back from your trail ride," I suggested. "I better get back to work now. There's a lot on this morning and just me right now."

"Okay, I'm leaving now. And I'm bringing breakfast," the optimist said. "Just relax."

I slipped the phone into the back pocket of my jeans. Just relax. Just *relax*. Kennedy was out of her mind if she thought I had the luxury to relax for one damn minute. I hadn't spent all these decades running a show barn for my health and mental wellbeing.

I hustled out of the feed room and up the barn aisle, ready to start swapping turn-out horses with stalled ones before the construction clamor started up next door. I'd gotten through two paddocks and had two horses in hand, just leading them through the gate of their paddock, when the first rock trucks started roaring by on the other side of the back fence. The horse on my right spooked forward, the horse on my left spooked backward. I was splayed out like a scarecrow, hauling on both lead-ropes in an effort to reel them back in.

"That noise is hardly new," I scolded, tapping a wide-eyed warmblood on the nose once I had him heading in the right direction again. "Why don't you get a grip?" With that, I released them both into the paddock so they could bolt around like idiots, snorting and snapping their tails, as if they hadn't been living next to a construction site for the past six months.

"Might as well get over it," I advised, snapping the gate closed. "Because it's not going to change any time soon."

I walked across the driveway and back inside the barn for the next two horses, thinking again that it was time to get over myself, get a new farm, and get out of here, forever.

It hadn't always been like this.

Really, it was just the past few months that things had gone so far downhill, and when I considered I'd been running Seabreeze Equestrian Center on this property for the past twenty-some years, that kind of a track record wasn't too bad. Even as the rest of the neighborhood was slowly transformed from farmland and equestrian centers to subdivisions and resorts, I'd always resolved to never be one of the ones who would leave.

Sure, life wasn't as good here as it used to be. The scent of orange blossoms no longer filled the air when the groves were in bloom, because the groves were all gone. The flock of sandhill cranes who used to winter on the farm, dividing their time between picking up bugs in the sandy grass around the property and having noisy family disputes in the palmetto grove behind the barn, had picked up and moved to presumably quieter digs. The roar of the rock trucks as they poured onto the neighboring property, day in and day out, dumping unbelievable quantities of rich red Lake County soil to build the false hills and pretend vistas of yet another Tuscany-themed resort, could sometimes drown out the multiple-personality concerts of mockingbirds and the pulsating chorus of frogs peeping during the humid run-up to an afternoon storm. Tuscan Hills, they'd called it, until they'd decided that wasn't luxurious enough and renamed it Bella Tuscany. Absurd, of course—this was Florida, not Italy, and the two places had almost nothing in common. They made me crazy, those resort people.

Still, I'd never thought they'd truly make me want to leave. This was my home.

Then one cool January day, with smoke hanging in the air from the endless fires burning up all the cypress and pine trees they'd uprooted and piled into pyres, and the rock trucks downshifting on the highway right next to my arena, their brakes squealing and spooking my lesson ponies, my phone rang and I answered and it was a realtor I'd hung up on before, and this time I listened. I nodded, although she couldn't see me. I traced figures in the air. My students looked at me. I looked away. I couldn't meet their eyes. "Yes," I said. "I'll come into your office next week."

Then I brushed the clay off little Allie Lewis, who had toppled off one of my most bombproof ponies when a truck clattering past hit a pothole with a sound like an explosion, gave her a leg-up back into the saddle and told them we were all going to ride in the covered arena, away from the road.

That was the last day I'd used the outdoor jumping arena this year. That was the day I started to accept that it was over. It might have been the day I'd decided to sell.

Four months ago, I thought now, taking a long drink of the black coffee Kennedy had brought me. The contract gave me six months to find a new property, although I'd told the developers it was going to take much longer and they'd agreed to extend month-to-month. The property value was only going up, but our price was agreed upon, so they had nothing to lose in letting me sit here awhile longer, considering my options. I'd thought about Ocala, then discarded the idea, a hundred times. There was no lesson business for me in Ocala. Too many trainers were already there. My business was here, in Orlando. "They're not following me to Ocala," I said aloud now, deciding once again to accept my fate. I'd pushed back against it so many times.

Kennedy looked up from the stall she was mucking and made a face at me through the bars. "Are you being a pessimist again?"

"I can't ever be myself around you," I complained.

"It's not good for you."

"You don't appreciate the real me."

Kennedy laughed and pushed her frizzy hair behind her ears. She'd dyed it a sort of maroon color last week and it made her round face look even younger. She looked like she had a high school drama club meeting to get to. "The real you is an optimist. You just have to find her."

"Let's not do this," I begged. "Let me wallow for a little bit. It's how I get my best ideas."

"From the depths of despair," Kennedy orated, and dumped a forkful of manure into the wheelbarrow. "I heard about a place in Sorrento for sale," she said from the back of the stall, flipping over shavings to look for the wet spot. "That's only like forty-five minutes away from here. Fresh students to make up for the ones who don't come. But I still think a lot of people will make the drive for you. Especially if there's no one left around here to ride with."

I'd heard this argument before. The last stand of central Florida's equestrian community was in the hills northwest of Orlando. It was a long drive up toll roads for the people who lived here, though. I'd lose kids who didn't have horses yet, and I might lose some boarders who decided they couldn't handle the commute, and chose to sell their horses instead. To give it all up and pack it in, just like I was doing—who could blame them? "The point of trying to stay in Orlando was to keep my same clients. I just don't see them driving all that way on toll roads every night, when they're already dealing with tolls and traffic just to get to and from work. Especially not the kids. Their parents aren't going to be able to handle it."

"Maybe we could organize a Saturday car-pool," Kennedy the innovator suggested. "Set up a Facebook group, then they can all help each other out."

"That's not a terrible idea." I leaned against the stall door and watched her smooth out the clean shavings. "You're smart. Did anyone ever tell you you're smart?"

Kennedy laughed. "So you'll look at this place? It's really cool."

I shrugged. "What the hell. I'll look at it."

"I'll call the realtor," Kennedy offered, coming out of the stall. "Are you going to clean any stalls today? Or just watch me?"

"You know, for an employee you are really smart-mouthed," I griped, pushing off from the door. I started off in search of another manure fork, the coffee she'd brought me still in hand. I might send her out for more when this was gone. The tack room coffeemaker had died tragically in a thunderstorm, and no one had offered to replace it yet.

"I learned from the best," she called after me.

"Charmer."

Sorrento, I thought morosely, rolling a wheelbarrow down to the next stall. How many of my twenty-two boarders would come with me? How many of my thirty-odd more students? The car-pool idea might be a winner, but there would still be losses. Not that I wasn't already losing boarders left and right. Since January, five owners had pulled their horses out of the barn, a couple for sales, the rest to go to expensive show barns on the east side of Orlando. I was out of east Orlando residents amongst my owners, though, so that particular escape route seemed closed to them now. Still, it was possible I was losing horses precisely because I was unable to make a decision about when to leave and where to go.

I wasn't usually indecisive, but I'd never expected to make this decision. I'd been here for half my life. I thought I'd be here until I dropped in the traces. I hadn't counted on this little patch of Florida turning against me. I'd thought we were *friends*.

"Oh! I just remembered. I had a call from a friend last week," Kennedy said as she started on the stall next to mine.

"Oh?"

"Louise Brinker, from Wonderland Horses, do you know her?"

I wrinkled my brow. At various points in my career, I'd known *everyone* in the central Florida hunter/jumper, dressage and eventing circles. But I'd never heard of this woman or her barn. "No... who is she?"

Kennedy came out of her stall and peered through the stall bars. "She trains horses for the theme park business. You know, parade horses, trolley horses, that kind of thing."

"I thought they did that themselves." Disney kept their collection of parade, carriage, and trail horses at their Fort Wilderness resort, just a few miles away from Seabreeze. I'd never been there, but sometimes we shared a farrier or a vet and they always had some stories. Apparently in addition to their run-of-the-mill Belgians and Percherons, they had six white ponies who could be hitched to a glass pumpkin coach for parades or high-dollar weddings for would-be Cinderellas. Nothing was too fantastic for the folks at Walt Disney World.

In the distance, a train's steam-whistle echoed, as if to punctuate my thoughts. The parks were gearing up for the day. In the morning and evening, when the air was wet and heavy, the toots and whistles of the Magic Kingdom's boats and trains could sound like they were coming from the dressage ring.

"They do, but Louise sources the horses and gets them started. She finds horses with the right temperament for the job. They go all over the country, not just to Disney."

"Okay." I dug wet hay from under the water buckets. This horse was a dunker. He left a soggy mess in his stall every day, but at least he was always hydrated. "So what's she want?"

"Stalls to rent," Kennedy said. "And some training space."

I stopped what I was doing and looked her in the eye. "Someone wants to give me money and you saved this for now because?"

Kennedy shrugged. "I just remembered."

"I will never understand you."

"I know."

"Call her back."

"And tell her…"

"Ask her what she wants to pay and don't take anything under twelve dollars a day, dry stall. But try to get fifteen."

Kennedy grinned. "I'm so excited! Draft horses! This is going be fun." She disappeared back into her stall.

I went back to digging out wet hay. The steam whistle piped up again, followed by a longer, lower whistle I knew belonged to a ferry boat. *Theme parks.* They were what had eaten up central Florida, kicking out my neighbors one by one, replacing their barns with condos and resorts and houses. But they could coexist with equestrian life in some ways. Kennedy came from their world, with her dinner show princess routine and trick riding. I wondered if all entertainment equestrians were all as high-energy as she was.

I hoped not.

Chapter Two

THERE WAS A knock on the office door and my head shot up. Had I been asleep?

I'd definitely been asleep.

Clouds had rolled in around lunchtime, unexpected but appreciated, and apparently the shift in sunlight had been enough to let me nod off over my boring bookkeeping. I remembered hearing some footsteps and drawers closing in the apartment next door—that would have been Anna coming home from her trip and getting changed for barn work—but other than that, the afternoon had slipped away from me.

There was another knock. I blinked into the dim office and considered the scatter of papers in front of me. A long time ago, I'd learned it was best to keep clients from seeing your business in full. Too many pro-rates and barters and deals done under the table; no one was paying the same thing for the same services, despite the publicly posted rate sheet on my website.

I pulled my lesson binder, the evening's schedule full of children's names matched to ponies and horses, over top of the invoices I'd been running through and the notepad I'd been using to scribble numbers. There was a wet patch on the collar of my polo shirt, but nothing to be done about it. Sometimes I missed having enough hair to pull a braid over my shoulder and cover green splotchy hay-stains from enthusiastic horses, let alone a little splotch of nap-time drool.

"Come in," I called, my voice a froggy croak. I glanced at the clock as I did so. Nearly three. Kennedy would be out with the afternoon trail ride, and Margaret would be with Anna, getting ponies ready for the after-school lessons. Neither of them would have bothered knocking at my door, anyway. Maybe it was one of the older high school girls. They got out of class early and were always after me to give them part-time jobs. I told them the truth every time they asked: I couldn't afford them. Also, Margaret would probably kill them after the first unlatched gate or forgotten hay-string. I'd considered bringing one or two on as a working student, but the best candidates always seemed to be too busy on the weekends, only making it out to ride between their other commitments, their tutoring and their tennis and those other important social pursuits. High-power career parents were loathe to let their daughters sign away their weekends for free labor at the farm, a pursuit which could only lead to dangerous ideas like becoming a professional trainer instead of getting into law school.

The door creaked open, letting the pearly afternoon light wash around the office, touching up the dust coating the bookshelves and clouding the glass frames of the show photos crowding the walls and tipping against the riding manuals. My old horses, my old friends, their coats and faces now pale as milk from my neglect. I should get Margaret up here to dust, I thought, though she'd probably be outraged if I pulled her from barn duties. Maybe I should get another full-time working student, an adult who had already broken her parents' hearts by ditching higher education for horses. That apprenticeship arrangement with Rockwell Bros. Saddlery last summer had been a real doozy, with them sending me Jules Thornton, problem child extraordinaire, for three months of boot camp. But there was no doubt I'd gotten some good work out of her, and made a valuable contact in the eventing world, besides. I'd let the eventing community get away from me, buried up to my neck in hunters and jumpers for all these years, but there was money in eventing now. How times changed! There was money in every horse sport now, if you could find the owners with enough to spend.

I shook myself, physically and mentally, to get a hold of my wandering thoughts. The woman in the doorway hesitated. She closed the screen door behind her, blinking at me as the light dimmed again. Not a teenager after all, but a slightly round woman somewhere in her fifties, and dressed like a horsewoman, in jeans and paddock boots and a loose-fitting, shaped riding tee. Her hair was short like mine but missing the gray strands, tight dark curls fiercely jutting from her head, and a little pair of diamonds peeped from her small earlobes like a hint of some inner flair for dressing up.

"Hi," she began, her voice a little uncertain. "I'm Louise. Louise Brinker? I met Kennedy and she said to come over..."

Well, *she* works fast, I thought. I stood up, held out a hand. When her hand grasped mine, I felt like I was shaking hands with myself. Our palms were rough in the same places, our nails were the same short cuts, our skin was tan and spotted. If you'd held our two hands together and put the rest of us behind a curtain, you couldn't have picked which one belonged to which of us. I liked her immediately — or I liked how alike we seemed. "I'm Grace," I replied warmly. "Kennedy just brought you up this morning. I thought she was going to work out the details herself, but I'm glad you're here. More personable in person." I grinned.

"But if I'm intruding—" she let her eyes cast over my desk, the sea of invoices and notebooks and binders, the open laptop that had gone to sleep an hour ago, right around when I had.

"You're definitely not. There's no such thing as intruding on paperwork. Please sit down, let's talk and then we can go look at the barn." Behind me, I knew without looking, there were ponies and horses lining the bay of cross-ties in the center of the barn, getting the sand swept from their haunches one by one. Shortly, Kennedy would be back with her trail riders and I'd have to step in to help untack and give showers. Then the afternoon lessons would descend. These were the final free moments I'd have today. "I've got about an hour before my evening rush," I added. "We're on school hours here."

Louise slung herself into a cracked leather chair and sighed. "I feel like this is the first time I've sat down in an actual chair all day, not a truck seat or a saddle."

"I know the feeling." We allowed ourselves a moment to grin knowingly at one another about barn life. "So you're training the Disney World horses?" I asked finally.

"I find them horses," Louise said. "I specialize in sourcing really bombproof horses, for riding and for driving. Theme parks, petting zoos, historical parks, they all need horses. You've got your Colonial Williamsburg-type places, they have carriage rides, they do pony rides. I give them basic training to make sure they'll suit the job, then the client finishes them up."

"How interesting," I said encouragingly. "I've always been in show horses, so this is totally new to me."

"I started out showing, too," Louise said. "I just kind of stumbled into this about twenty years ago. It's changed a lot over the years, so you have to stay on trend. Everyone wanted Friesians for a while. Now they want draft crosses, especially spotted ones. You have to totally change your suppliers, the auctions you go to, every couple of years."

"What on earth do they want spotted drafts for?" I'd had a few draft crosses around the barn from time to time, but I wasn't their biggest fan. A little too much cold blood, a little too bulky, a little too slow in thoughts and movement. When warmbloods had been like that, everyone had ridden Thoroughbreds. Then the warmblood breeders got wise, bought up a bunch of Thoroughbred breeding stock, and lightened up the gene pool.

Louise laughed at my skepticism. "Partially because they look impressive, partially because they're easy keepers and help save tight budgets. And they can carry a heavy rider. That's coming up more often. I run into program managers who've started worrying about the aesthetics of putting a big actor on an average-sized horse. The thing about exhibiting horses to the public is that there's always a percentage of the audience who thinks the whole business is cruel. So we have to find ways to play to these folks' conceptions of what a horse can and can't do comfortably."

"Even though they have no idea." I rolled my eyes.

"Exactly." Louise chuckled and then sighed, considering the ignorance of crowds. "You know what it's like. You get any crazies with your trail rides?"

Any crazies? I bit back laughter. *You bet your life.* Half the time, it was just because they'd been drinking. Even when the groups were totally sober, there was always a loose cannon who couldn't just get on the horse, go for the walk, and get over it. Last month a lawyer from Boston threatened to call PETA because I kept my horses in stalls, or "horse jail" as she called it. Back in December, a young woman with a group of accountants accused me of cruelty for using leather bridles. Apparently I should be using "vegan" fabrics. "She was particularly annoying," I remembered. "For some reason it's always women doing the shouting about abuse. The men have to be drunk to act out."

"What did you do with her?"

"I took her to the tack room and showed her just how much leather we had. She nearly fainted. Later Kennedy came back from the trail ride ready to scream. Apparently the entire group just argued about artificial fabrics made from oil versus actual leather for the whole ride."

"The joys of horses and the general public," Louise observed with a knowing smile, and I nodded along. Louise got it, I thought: the hazards of trying to introduce the ancient lore of horsemanship to a reactionary populace ready to believe whatever rumor they'd last seen on Facebook. That was encouraging. I could always use an ally in this fight.

"They're like oil and water. So, want to come see the barn?"

"Of course!"

We trundled down the steps, which still needed replacing and probably always would. The staircase waved and thrashed against the barn wall as we went. I glanced sidelong at Louise to see her reaction at the size of the place, and I wasn't disappointed. *Everyone* loved my barn. Two aisles lined with stalls, huge doors at each end to let the breezes blow through, a central aisle with a bay of cross-ties and wash-racks, tack rooms, windows, a paved walk right out to the covered arena: it had been the best show barn in the county for decades, and that wasn't going to change anytime soon.

The paved aisle had been blown clean of loose hay after the lunch feeding and it was still gleamingly tidy. Anna was leading a pony out of a stall, and I could hear the horse vacuum rumbling from the cross-ties, where Margaret must be handling a particularly messy mount, but otherwise the barn was deserted, free of clients, free of students, free of owners—just the way I liked it, really.

I showed Louise around, from the school tack room to the gleaming feed room to the empty stalls in the north aisle, closest to the outdoor arenas, where I proposed we'd put her horses. She walked through the dry stall in the corner and peered through the window bars. "Looks out at the riding rings," she observed. "That's nice, gives them something to look at."

"I haven't been using the jumping arena," I confessed. "But the dressage ring still gets use. They'll definitely have some entertainment."

"They eat their hay like machines, so they'll appreciate that." She ran her hand over the bars again, then turned and nodded at me. "When can we move in?"

Margaret received the news about the incoming eight horses with a short nod; Anna with bright eyes and a wide smile. In fact, I thought she was going to hug Louise—Anna's actions were forever reminding me she was too kind and sweet for this business. But she managed to contain herself to holding out a hand (after rubbing off the worst of the dirt on her khaki shorts) and saying how much she was looking forward to meeting Louise's little herd.

"I love seeing horses in parades," she admitted, as if it was a weakness—and maybe it was. "Maybe I can watch some of your training sessions, learn more about it."

"Of course," Louise agreed cheerfully. "Anytime I'm here and you have the time, come out to the ring with me. I'll be using the outdoor jumping ring, since Grace tells me y'all aren't using it anymore."

I narrowed my eyes. I *had* said she could use the outdoor jumping ring. I hadn't said she could lure my assistant from her duties.

Margaret, standing across from me, gave me a wink and trudged off to finish tacking up Douglas, who was dozing in the cross-ties behind us, a droplet of drool hanging from his lower lip. "Trail ride should be back by now," she called over her shoulder.

I flicked my eyes up to the clock hanging over the tack room door. "They're late," I said, surprised. Kennedy was always punctual with the trail rides. She liked to say if the corporate bigwigs wanted more of her time, they could pay her for it. She had a tidy bit of resentment left over from the period of time she'd spent between horse jobs, pushing paper and making money without getting soaked in sweat, mud, or other things best not mentioned. I'd tried to talk her out of coming back to the horse business, but I could see now she had been falling apart as an office drone. She was better off out here in the barn.

"How have the trail rides worked out for you?" Louise asked brightly as we walked down the aisle towards the back parking area, where the trailhead was located across a short expanse of pavement. "It's so unusual to see a boarding and lesson barn diversify like this. Especially an *English* barn."

I shrugged. "They started out promising, but it's a seasonal business. The big conferences dry up this time of year and they don't come back until fall. They're where we get all our business from. Summer was pretty lean last year. I don't know if I can afford to keep it up."

"Kennedy had mentioned you didn't do families or advertise at the hotels. Do you not feel you're losing some business there?"

"I'm sure we are." We stopped at the end of the aisle and I pointed out the palm tree that marked the trailhead. "We were considering our boarders and what they expect from their barn. And a bunch of tourists running around at all hours of the day won't fly with them. So we just take in the corporate groups. They book all of our horses for one ride, they ship them in on their own vans, they take them away. No kids, no fuss, in and out before boarders and students even get here." I paused. "Maybe it wasn't the right strategy, but we were flying kind of blind."

"I hear that."

I glanced at my watch.

"Well, they might overlap today, because our first student will be here in twenty minutes. Where the hell is Kennedy?"

Margaret appeared next to us with a phone in one hand and a set of keys in the other. Her bony jaw was set, her expression even more morose than usual. "I'm going to take the Gator out and look for them," she said grimly.

I started to nod, then heard a sound that made me put a hand on her shoulder, holding her back. "Listen."

Someone was shouting in the woods. More shrill than a shout—a scream? Margaret's entire body tensed beneath my palm.

Not screaming—whooping.

"Hi-yi-yi-kay-yay!"

"Drunks," I realized aloud.

Louise looked at me, startled. "The riders? Where did they get drunk?"

I shook my head. "Here's the thing about business trips for non-horsepeople, Louise—they put it away like they're at an all-inclusive in Cabo. These guys clearly came prepared."

"I told you not to allow backpacks," Margaret croaked.

The whooping gave way to crashing foliage as horses plowed through the palmetto fronds at the edges of the trail, and then all at once the woods erupted and spilled forth my missing trail ride, the clueless riders swaying from side to side, loose fingers slipping the reins, laughing hysterically.

As I did a rapid head-count, I felt a growing sense of alarm. There were five riders circling my parking lot, all of them customers. But six riders had gone out. Seven, when you counted Kennedy.

"What the hell's going on here?" I shouted, abandoning professional courtesy, and the closest rider, who had somehow lost his hard hat, spun his horse around with a hard yank on the bit. My eyes narrowed and I sprang forward, snatching the reins just below the horse's chin. The horse, a stoic chestnut mare named Honey, gave me a tired look which clearly said, *not this again.*

"We just went out on some *trails!*" The rider, a thirty-something, clean-cut looking guy who looked like someone out of a toothpaste commercial, leaned back in the saddle and cackled. Sunlight sparkled on something metallic peeping from his shirt's chest pocket. Did I have to start frisking these idiots for flasks before they went out? "We wanna be *cowboys!*"

"Yeehaw!" a disheveled woman agreed, kicking her horse with

both heels. She was riding Frank, a patient Appaloosa who would rather be sleeping. I watched him gape his mouth against her wrenching hands and felt a surge of anger. These were my horses, and a bunch of putz pharma salesmen were not allowed to manhandle them!

"Everyone get the fuck off my horses, now, or I'm calling the police."

Alarmed faces, red with sunburn and booze, circled my way. Eyebrows went up. Tongues began to stammer.

"I don't... uh... I've never... let's just take it easy..."

I looked up at the idiot sitting on Honey. "You wanna be a cowboy? Take your feet out of the stirrups and swing off, asshole. Cowboys don't need ladders to climb down from a horse. That goes for all of you," I added, raising my voice to be heard above their worried protests. "Feet on the ground, *now.*"

Some of them hit the pavement on their asses, some of them on their feet, but I wasn't too worried about anyone getting hurt. That's the thing about being drunk when you land... you bounce when you hit the ground.

"Where's Kennedy?" I snapped as Honey's rider pushed himself back to his feet after his ungraceful landing back on earth, brushing at his pants as if he'd landed in a fire ant hill. "And the other rider in your group?"

He looked around in a slow arc, left to right, and then back at me. Then he laughed hysterically. "I don't *know!*" He looked at the others, in various stages of picking themselves off the ground, handing their reins to Margaret, Anna and even Louise, who had run outside to help collect the horses. "Do you guys know?"

The woman who had kicked Frank swayed on her feet. "Rita

didn't want to run with us so she stayed back with the leader-lady." She put her fingers to her lips and burped gently, then giggled. "We wanted to *run*."

"Go find your driver and get the hell out of here," I told the idiot standing in front of me, and then I swung into Honey's saddle without waiting to see if he had listened to me. I glanced over at Louise apologetically—this wasn't the farm I'd wanted to present to a new client today—but she waved me away. I knew she'd seen her share of idiot civilians around horses, too... training horses for amusement parks couldn't be for the faint of heart.

"I'll be right after you in the Gator," Margaret shouted, but I was already jogging away, ready to hit a canter as soon as Honey's unshod hooves reached the soft sand of the trailhead. My hand brushed the chest pocket of my polo shirt, making sure my phone was there, ready to call for help.

Nobody had better be hurt out there, or there'd be hell to pay.

Chapter Three

WE WERE GALLOPING along the white-sand trail between endless acres of palmetto scrub pierced by skinny long-leaf pines, Honey's breath coming so hard I knew I'd have to pull her up soon. Her neck was dark with sweat, and more was rolling down in dirty beads from under the crown of her bridle. But my reins were loose and my legs weren't even touching her sides; she was running with pricked ears and bright eyes, as intent on the job as I was. A flight of ibis startled from a pine, white wings flashing against the road ahead of us as they scattered into the sky. Honey didn't spook like another horse might have. She just swiveled an ear in their direction, deemed them unthreatening, and galloped on.

"You're a saint," I told her. I wished I'd recognized that before. I'd never given any of the trail horses much attention besides making sure they were healthy and well-fed. Honey had been in my barn for a year, and this was the first time I'd even been on her. She had a lovely disposition and a comfortable, long-striding gallop which I'd been sleeping on all this time. Why was I such a horse snob? Heavens knew I hadn't been raised that way. My grandfather might have bred Thoroughbreds, but he was happy to take on any horse who was a pleasure to ride. "Good brains can trump good breeding," he used to tell me.

Honey suddenly stumbled and caught herself in one smooth motion. I immediately glanced back to see what had tripped her, and realized the hoof prints left behind by the trail horses on their hurried gallop back to the barn had changed pattern. Their galloping hooves churned up the dark sand underneath the scrub's top-layer of white, but their sedate jogging and walking gaits left only pale half-moons in the road, and that's what I was seeing now. So I'd gone past the point where they'd decided to play cowboys and taken off at speed. That meant Kennedy and the missing rider had to be nearby, right?

I gently pulled Honey up and peered out across the palmetto, looking for some sign of horse or rider above that endless thatch of green. It was nearly impossible to forge a trail through the scrub without a machete, though. They had to be *on* the trail with me. There was a bend up ahead, the trail curving through a thicket of oak trees, so maybe I'd find them on the other side. I urged Honey onwards. Her walk was more of a trudge now that we'd slowed from the canter; the effort had caught up with her. I hoped I didn't have to get home in a hurry once I'd found them.

Suddenly Honey's head shot up so fast, one of her fuzzy ears nearly collided with my chin. She had come to a screeching halt, and puffed out a loud blast of air from her nostrils. My hands raced up the reins, ready for a spin and run. Mares usually only made that sound when they were warning of danger or trying to frighten something away.

There was a moment of silence while Honey waited, every muscle taut. A tiny lizard scurried into the palmettos, causing more ruckus than could possibly be expected. She followed its progression with one ear, before swinging it back to the road ahead.

Then Kennedy and the missing rider came ambling around the bend ahead, heads turned to one another, clearly chatting the afternoon away.

Honey nickered and started forward of her own accord, happy to find her friends. I let her go. There was no point in making her wait to prove some point. Trail horses hated being alone—their need to stick together was part of the chemistry of a good trail ride.

Kennedy and the trail rider looked fine at first, but as the distance between us closed, the smudges in the pretty picture became clear: the unkempt hair falling from previously tight pony tails, the jeans streaked with mud, the rip in Kennedy's flashy red shirt, the dirty tracks of tears on the other woman's face. Two broken leather straps dangled from the trail horse's bit. Kennedy had unfastened a leather strap from her saddle and slipped it through his bit, ponying him along.

She grinned as our horses met and Honey swung around to walk alongside Kennedy's horse, Sailor. "Another day, another set of broken reins."

"I can't afford you." I looked around her at the other rider, a rather shattered-looking young woman. "Did you come off?"

"No," she said, her voice cracking. "I *wish* I had. That would been less terrifying."

"There was a whole circus up a-ways," Kennedy explained, nodding at the trail ahead of us. "They went galloping towards home, and Rita here held back, *sensibly,* I might add," she told the shell-shocked looking girl. "I was trying to decide if I should go after the rest or stay with Rita, when a fox squirrel came out of the brush like a damn jack-in-the-box and Remy here blew his top." She nodded at the bay gelding Rita was mounted on, who looked too tired to ever consider spooking again. His head was nearly at his knees; I suspected the only thing holding him up was Kennedy's hand on the strap. "So that made it easy—I went after Remy. Caught up with them at the Indian mound. His reins were already long gone. He stopped short and poor Rita only had the saddle to hang onto... she tumbled right over his shoulder."

"I'll pay for the broken parts," Rita said sheepishly.

"No, you won't," I decreed. "Your idiot coworkers will."

"Are they all okay?" she asked.

"Fine, but I already kicked them off the property, so I'll drive you back to your hotel."

She blushed. "I'm sorry. I can get an Uber."

"Don't be sorry. You were the *good* one."

Kennedy held up a hand and reined back. "One moment, please." She dismounted and left her horse Sailor standing alone while she walked ahead a few paces, Remy staying at his side obediently. She ran her hand through the yellow wildflowers pushing from under the palmetto fronds and then closed her fingers around something. "Aha!" She held up her phone in triumph.

"That explains why you didn't call me," I said dryly.

"Came right out of my pocket when I turned Sailor after Remy," Kennedy laughed. "You should have seen us. Like outriders at the track!" She put a foot in the stirrup and hopped back into the saddle.

That was the thing about Kennedy... she always laughed. Horses ran away and broke their reins with rank beginners on their backs, and I could see only the averted disaster and all the mistakes that led up to that moment, but Kennedy found a way to laugh.

I'm sure some people would find her easy laughter an admirable trait, but at the moment, I just couldn't. I was always afraid Kennedy was going to get herself into trouble... and by extension, me.

The driver was waiting for Rita when we got back to the barn, having loaded all of his drunk charges into the shuttle-bus and firmly told them to stay in their seats or he'd call their bosses and explain the whole situation in the least flattering way possible. He explained to us that he wouldn't have felt right leaving her behind. Rita clambered up into the bus looking miserable, while everyone within cheered at the sight of her. I suspected she would have preferred the privacy of an Uber to a shuttle ride with her drunken coworkers, unchastened by the near-disaster they'd caused for her.

"She's going to quit that job." Louise had her hand on her truck's door handle. "I've seen that look on a face before."

"Thanks for your help, Louise," Anna called. "She helped get everyone untacked and cooled out," she told me quietly. "Margaret said we had it handled, but she insisted. I really like her."

"Seems promising," I agreed, waving as she pulled out of the lot. "Do you think I have five minutes to sit down before lessons? That little adventure took it out of me."

"Sure," Anna said. "I'll go tell them."

We turned for the barn just as a small girl peeped around the doorway. She pushed back her hard hat from where it was tipping over her big eyes. "Is Kennedy coming or what?"

I raised my eyebrows and was about to give a lecture on the *polite* way we asked questions about our riding instructors when a taller version of the little girl appeared behind her. Her mother's riding helmet fit her better, but her face was just as impatient. "Grace, we're all tacked up and ready to go. Are you coming or what?"

"We're coming," Kennedy called sweetly. "Monica, you can mount and start to warm up! You too, Elsie," she said to the small girl. "Margaret will help you mount if you ask her."

Mother and daughter made spookily similar versions of the same exasperated face and turned into the barn.

"I was just going to end the trail ride business, but now I think I want to end everything," I muttered. "Like spoiled mother, like spoiled daughter."

Kennedy put out a hand, stopping me. "Wait... you're not *really* going to cancel trail rides, are you? Because I—"

"Can we not do this right now, Kennedy? We have lessons."

Her face was aghast. "You can't just end the trails because of this. No one got hurt."

"Kennedy, the season is over. It's almost June. There are only a couple more rides scheduled. Let's just call it before someone *does* get hurt. The groups have just been getting worse and worse, anyway." I brushed past her and went into the tack room for a bottle of water, but she stayed close on my heels. I plucked two water bottles from the fridge, and held one out to her. "Drink this and think about your lesson, please. You need to focus."

"Don't put on your teacher voice with me," Kennedy bristled, but she took the water bottle anyway.

It's my boss voice, I thought, but I didn't say anything else. I knew she loved the trail rides, but if I'd been waiting for the right moment to call time of death, this had to be it. A drunk group running away from their trail guide, leaving behind one of their own riders to get run away with and get dumped, all in front of a new client with *eight* horses to come into the barn? When we'd started up, we'd been assured corporate groups was the safest bet. Now, for a business that wasn't making me any profit, they sure seemed like a pointless risk.

All of which I knew I'd be explaining to Kennedy later, after the next three hours of shouting at students.

I swallowed half the bottle of water, dropped the rest on my desk, and headed out the door.

Chapter Four

LESSONS SEEMED TO drag on and on that night, and all the more so because every time I glanced into the covered arena at the pony lessons, I saw Kennedy ignoring her students. Sure, she was facing them, turning slowly as red-faced children huffed and panted their way through walk, trot, canter drills, shouting the occasional command which they hastened to try and follow with sometimes hilarious results—kicking in hopes of a canter and ending up sprawled on the pony's neck when they got a halt instead, for example—but there was none of her usual banter, none of her cheerleader-like enthusiasm, which was what made her one of the most popular riding instructors I'd ever seen. When it came to teaching engaged, happy kids, even when Kennedy was having an average day, I couldn't compete with her. My riding lessons were more of the bark orders, find fault variety. I was not supposed to be proud of the number of strong, confident women who blinked away tears during my lessons, but if pressed, I'd have to admit I wasn't upset about it, either. If I tried to teach a group of kids, there'd be weeping in the arena before the ponies were even warmed up.

In between teaching Gayle, who was still locked in an eternal struggle with her big bold mare, and Patrice, who was cheerfully ignorant of every principle of dressage that her perfectly-behaved gelding knew by heart, I went into the tack room for a bottle of water and found Kennedy curled up on a tack trunk, her knees at her chin, staring at the polished concrete floor as if the smooth pavement held all the answers. Next to her, Anna was sitting, perched on the trunk so close their thighs were touching. I paused at the sight, remembering Kennedy's rather emotional outburst this morning. *I miss her so much.* The "so much" was what rang in my ears. A person *missed* a coworker. You missed a member of your family—or a loved one—*so much.*

Anna glanced up first, her eyes wide like a frightened deer's, but I thought nothing of it—that was just Anna, she always looked like she had some unwanted emotion threatening to spill over. Kennedy was slower to look up at me, and when I saw her red eyes, my premonition was quickly forgotten.

"Did you get hurt?" I asked quickly, running my eyes over her shirt (she'd changed back into a hunter green polo after the trail ride debacle came to an end) and her jeans, looking for rips or blood or muddy streaks which would give away a close encounter with hooves or teeth. There was nothing unusual to see, though. Just a little slobber mark, pale green and white, across one shoulder, obviously left behind by an itchy pony-face. "What is it?"

Kennedy sniffed and looked down again. "It's nothing," she mumbled.

Anna put an arm around her shoulders. "It's okay to tell her," she said encouragingly. "Grace always listens to me when I'm worried about something."

If that's what you believe, fabulous. I supposed my *I'm Absolutely*

Listening to Your Concerns Face was close enough to my *I Know You're Talking But I'm Still Working Here Face* to give me a lot of undeserved credit. "I have to go meet Patrice in the ring," I said urgently. "So if you've something to tell me, let's hear it."

Anna looked abashed at my sharp tone, and squeezed Kennedy's shoulders a little tighter even as she frowned at me. "We'll talk about it after lessons, won't we, Kennedy." There was a proprietary note in her voice I had only heard her use with her horses before. She had two—one in my lesson program, one a young novice she'd bought to train through the levels. Both of them got substantially more affection in the forms of hugs and carrots than the rest of the horses in the barn, and that was saying something when you considered how ridiculously spoiled some of the boarders were. The horses *and* the people, if I'm being honest here.

Kennedy just nodded and rubbed her face very energetically with her hands, which resulted in a lot of streaky dirt smeared up and down her round cheeks. I started to say something and thought better of it. Dirty faces were normal around here. Maybe she'd get over her drama by the time lessons were over if I just didn't say anything else. I left them to it and marched back out to the covered arena.

Patrice was trotting in circles at the far end of the covered arena, well away from a collection of beginners who were poking around with ponies, wondering where Kennedy could be and fumbling with their reins as they endeavored not to crash into one another. Margaret was watching over them with a pained expression on her face; she was not a fan of children, but she had a dedication to safety which wouldn't allow her to send anyone inexperienced out to the arena, even with these bombproof ponies dragging their heads at the ends of their reins. "Kennedy's coming," I called as I passed her by, my paddock boots sinking into the red clay furrows of the ring. "Thanks for holding down the fort."

She responded with a shrug and a grimace.

Patrice was a recent addition to the barn who had brought her good-looking French gelding with her when she moved to Florida from Philadelphia. She was a bit of a dressage queen, and she definitely had the style down pat—I could never complain about her turn-out, and I liked my riders to show up for lessons in breeches, boots and a nice shirt at the least. George Morris would have nothing to complain about in my barn. The part Patrice was missing was... well, it was the riding part. She bounced. She bounced *terribly*. She bounced like her poor horse was a trampoline, and I couldn't seem to fix it.

Now, Patrice bounced in a circle around me, Winter trotting with a look of great forbearance on his white-striped face. "Tighten your core," I tried, and Patrice did nothing. I thought up some elaborate metaphors, drawing on my memory of the bizarre-but-effective illustrations in *Centered Riding* involving accordions and such. I doled those out in succession during the lesson. Patrice smiled and nodded and bounced on, her seat unchanged.

After her ride she patted Winter elaborately and smiled at me. "That felt great! I can really feel all that work in my seat bones!"

I bet you can, I thought. "I think we should consider working without stirrups for a while," I suggested. "When's the last time you had a lunge lesson?"

Patrice's smiled faltered. She was wearing red lipstick, like a good dressage queen, but she had smeared it just a little when she'd flicked at a fly buzzing around her sweaty face. It made her look like a disappointed teenager after a bad first kiss. "A lunge lesson? Not since... since I was a kid. They're for beginners, I thought."

"No, no, no," I said hastily. "Everyone benefits from lunge lessons. *I* could benefit from one. They let you just concentrate on yourself. Everyone needs that sometimes."

Patrice still looked uncertain, but she agreed to let me pencil in *lunge* next to her lesson the following week. As she moved off to cool Winter down in the outdoor dressage ring, I turned back to see Kennedy's lesson wrap-up. She was standing in the circle of walking children, hands on hips, watching them practice rising in their stirrups into two-point position. "Good," she said woodenly. "That's enough for tonight."

"We didn't canter," someone complained. "You said we could canter this week."

"It's too hot to canter tonight," Kennedy said shortly. "All the ponies are hot."

"It's *always* hot," a little girl whined. "That didn't stop *her.*" She pointed at me. *"Her* lesson got to canter."

I waited to see how Kennedy would get out of this.

"We're not cantering," Kennedy snapped. "We're done tonight. Everyone whoa and dismount!"

It was the sharpest tone I'd ever heard Kennedy use. The children were equally shocked. Everyone pulled up their ponies and clambered down without grumbling. That would come later, I figured. First, to their parents. Then their parents would pass it on to me.

"Kennedy," I said back in the barn, as she surveyed the children handing off their ponies to Margaret and Anna. "A word?"

Kennedy looked at me and shrugged. Wordlessly, she followed

me into the tack room.

"You *knew* the trail rides wouldn't go with us when we get the new barn," I told her, once the door was closed behind us. "We're not making enough money to make it worth our time," I went on, "and we'll be too far away from the hotels to make it work, anyway. When you add in the disruption and the danger, I just see no reason to continue after the slow season. There will still be plenty of lessons and sales ponies, Kennedy, your job is safe! So what's all this drama?"

Kennedy shrugged. "I just like them, I guess," she muttered, her eyes on the concrete floor. "Maybe I like them better than lessons."

I had a flashback to two years ago, listening to Kennedy trying to justify giving up her corporate job to come back to riding and teaching full time. I'd tried to stop her. *If you'd really wanted this to be your life, would you have quit the first time?* But she was determined.

I couldn't escape the notion, time and time again, that Kennedy wasn't committed to a life sentence as an equestrian the way I was. She might be happier here in the long run, but she couldn't quite stick it year after year. She'd tried to escape before, and she'd come back, but when was the next breakdown? When was the next retreat to a simpler life, with office hours that never changed and the chance to ride on weekends?

Out loud, I tried to keep my voice less skeptical, more comforting. "You are a fantastic teacher, and your students love you. Think about that."

"But, Grace, we could still run trail rides when we move barns. Listen," Kennedy's voice lifted, started to pick up that excited tone she took on when one of her big ideas struck. This was a woman who had been a princess in a spangled crown, cantering under spotlights as families cheered over their dinners. She was not afraid to try new things, break traditions. "We could have family-style trail rides, with a picnic area and catered lunches. Families would come out on a Saturday, discover horses, get their kids in lessons—instant pipeline of new students! And I think one or two of these guys can drive... we could get a cart and do hay rides in the fall, maybe take everyone out to a pumpkin patch... sell the pumpkins... if there was enough room we could do a whole petting zoo thing away from the barn, right? Chickens and pigs? It would be so easy to set up a little farm park, and it would keep our income diversified, which was the whole goal of starting trails in the first place—"

"We are *not* opening a petting zoo."

Kennedy stared at me. I already felt bad about the sharpness of my tone, the finality of my words; it was never fun to pop someone's balloon. But Kennedy needed to be brought back to earth, and quickly. If she crashed with a rather painful impact, so be it.

"Kennedy, this is an English show barn. I've tried playing this game with trail horses. I've added ponies and children's hunters to the lesson program. I've diversified and brought in eventers and dressage students. But I'm drawing the line at turning it into some kind of family park. We have show horses here. We do serious work."

Kennedy's face soured. "Remember when I first brought Sailor here?"

Of course I did—she deposited a Quarter Horse and a pile of Western tack amidst a herd of imported show jumpers, and turned our tranquil barn life on its head. "What about it, Kennedy," I said tersely, my hand on the door-knob.

"You didn't like us because we rode Western," she said, running her fingers over the gleaming jumping saddle on a stand next to her.

"I didn't like you because you weren't going to add a single dollar to my bank account besides paying your monthly board." I rolled my eyes. "When have I ever done anything because of prejudice, Kennedy? Everything I've done here, I've done to keep the barn open."

I went out the door. It was true, at first I'd hated the mounds of Western tack in my cross-ties, I'd hated the long manes on the trail horses, and the flashy cowgirl blouses Kennedy took to wearing. But I'd gotten over it. There was nothing inherently wrong with running trail rides out of my barn. It just felt like a distraction that wasn't worth the investment or risk anymore. I had to make decisions, and hard ones. I had to find a new barn, I had to convince the business to come with me. Kennedy had to understand that the transient trail riders were the very least of my concerns right now.

The barn was closing up now, as the early summer sun set in its parched spring shades of yellow and orange, casting a harsh golden glow down the aisles. Margaret was already gone; Anna was walking stall by stall, checking water buckets, topping them off as she went. I went down to check the latch on the feed room door. When I came back, Kennedy was walking alongside her, their heads bent close. When Anna reached the staircase to the apartments at the far end, she put one foot on the step, then reached back with a hand.

Kennedy took it.

They went up the stairs together.

I ducked back into the feed room before they reached the landing, so neither woman would turn around and see me spying. *Was* it spying? I was in my barn with my two employees, so it shouldn't have been... but that had certainly looked like a private moment to me. I settled onto the lid of a feed bin to wait for the coast to clear.

A tabby-cat with white paws came around a corner and writhed around my legs for a few moments, desperate for a little attention. There were always random cats showing up now that we had so many houses and resort kitchens with tasty dumpsters in the neighborhood. Anna faithfully named each one, and mourned when they moved on to new hunting grounds, but I couldn't keep up with them. "Go back outside," I commanded, but the cat listened about as well as one would expect.

When she jumped onto the feed bin next to me, I relented and gave her a few absent ear-rubs until her purring revved up to rusty motor-boat status. *Ginny*, I recalled. That's what Anna was calling this one. "Kennedy and Anna," I told the tabby, "did you know about this?"

But the tabby-cat kept her secrets.

Chapter Five

"I DIDN'T EXPECT them to be so big."

I glanced at Gayle; that was a bit funny, coming from this small woman who regularly rode a fairly strapping warmblood mare. But she was staring through the stall bars at the Clydesdale within who was, admittedly, large enough to cause a total eclipse every time he stood in front of his window. Seriously, there was an actual shift in the barn aisle's light when he paced his stall.

Maybe they *were* pretty damn big.

Louise was fussing with a chestnut Belgian down the aisle. I admired her ability to dance around his foolishness like a ballet dancer evading a sumo wrestler. The Belgian had hooves like Frisbees and her tiny booted feet were in constant risk of being trampled as he spun and fretted, unwilling to walk past the center aisle where all the ponies were lined up in the cross-ties, waiting to be tacked up.

"What's his problem?" I asked, heading down the aisle to show Louise I was available and ready to assist, but still stopping a cautious distance away. The Belgian was Louise's horse and it was up to her to ask for help. No one liked a pushy barn owner. And anyway, what did I know about draft horses? I'd spent my entire life with ponies, Thoroughbreds and warmbloods. These old-fashioned cold bloods required a different approach altogether, as far as I knew.

"He's afraid of *ponies,*" Louise grunted, stepping away from his fore-hooves sharply as the massive horse spun around her, his hock-length blonde tail brushing the bars of the stall beside him. The horse inside, an easily offended bay gelding, took the opportunity to kick the wooden walls in retaliation, squealing to show what a big, tough beast he was.

"Knock it *off,*" I snarled, my voice descending into my chest, and the gelding grouchily retreated to the back of his stall, keeping a wary ear on the situation in case he should need to go on the defense again. I turned to look at the ponies, lined up in their cross-ties. They blinked back at me charmingly, innocent and unfazed by the cavorting of one giant horse who wouldn't walk past them.

"Maybe you want to take him around to the other end, and then let him see the ponies working out in the ring this evening?" The draft horses were stalled at the quietest end of the barn, away from the central hustle and bustle, but closest to the outdoor riding rings, and their windows overlooked the covered ring. "He'd have a better idea of what they are if he sees them moving."

Louise sighed, one hand on the big chestnut's quivering neck as he stood still for a moment, his ears pricked and his eyes still trained upon the ponies. "If I can just get him to take a few steps without anyone else doing anything—"

I obediently stood still and so did Anna, who was brushing off one of the ponies. Gayle, still standing about six stalls away, gazing at the Clydesdale within, was the oblivious sort who might make a sudden wrong move, but she seemed pretty mesmerized at the moment. I watched Kennedy slowly reach a hand over to Gayle's shoulder and place her fingers there, telling her to be still. We all waited for Louise to get the horse moving. I wondered if Belgians could explode from a stand-still with the same incendiary quality Thoroughbreds possessed. I wasn't sure my barn aisle was set up for that sort of explosion coming from that giant a horse.

"Come on, you big dummy," Louise said affectionately, but I could hear the notes of exasperation and embarrassment, in her voice. I could sympathize. No one wanted to be shown up by a naughty horse on move-in day. "Let's go, papa, those ponies won't eat you..." Louise gave the Belgian a tug on his halter, an encouraging pat on his shoulder.

One of the ponies sneezed.

The Belgian plunged forward, and Louise had no choice but to follow—it was that or drop his lead rope altogether, and Louise didn't strike me as the sort of person who would let a horse go unless there was a prospect of serious bodily harm. She ran beside him at his shoulder, then his barrel, then she was at his hip—and she was running out of lead-rope. My breath caught. Why was Louise still running? Not only was she almost out of rope, she was entirely too close to his plunging hindquarters. I was starting to worry he might decide to cow-kick to get rid of her, and a blow from one of those hooves might easily prove fatal. How tough did Louise think she needed to be to impress us?

For all his power, there was a lot of mass in that body to get moving, and it took the Belgian rather longer to get towards the end of the aisle than it would have taken a Thoroughbred or a warmblood. So he had barely reached a quick canter when Gayle and Kennedy both shot out their arms from their sides like a crossing guard keeping children from darting into traffic, and shouted *whoa!*

There were sparks flying from his front shoes as the Belgian came skidding to a halt, astonished by the two road-blocks which had appeared out of nowhere in his path. Their movements had been so in sync that he couldn't quite determine if they were human or not, so he decided not to risk it and hung a very determined right—directly into the open doorway of the empty stall awaiting his presence.

Louise came out a moment later, lead-rope in hand, and slid the heavy door closed. The latch came down with a rattle, locking the massive horse inside, where he stood staring through the bars with a bemused expression, not certain what had happened.

"Exciting," I observed, walking up to Kennedy and Gayle. "You two looked like those little jack-in-the-box guys who pop up in haunted houses. Have you been practicing synchronized horse-stopping?"

Kennedy pushed her maroon curls out of her face, laughing. "I just said 'Gayle, copy me,' and she did! Really nice work, Gayle. We make a good team."

Gayle blushed. "I think it was instinct, really."

"Jumping in front of a seventeen-hand horse is never instinct," Louise sighed, looking at her wild-eyed charge. "That's just your horsemanship getting the better of your sense of self-preservation."

Gayle gazed through the bars at the Belgian, who was now walking the stall with great purpose, his head high and his ears swinging. "He's really beautiful. What's his name?"

Louise snorted. "Adonis."

Kennedy and I both laughed. Gayle just kept watching him, her eyes shining.

Uh-oh, I thought. *Not good.*

Louise apologized profusely for the incident with the Belgian. I brushed her off, saying it could happen to anyone, but I was starting to see that having the big parade horses here might be more of a disruption than I'd anticipated. As the students started to arrive for afternoon lessons, they were drawn to the draft horse stalls as if by a magnet, and soon there was a crowd of children and assorted mothers and nannies gathered around the end of the barn I'd previously called "quiet." They buzzed with questions, asking Louise excitedly about what the draft horses ate, what kind of work they did, how big their hooves were. Consequently, the first lessons of the day started twenty minutes late, which meant by the end of the evening we'd be leaving late by an hour or more. That's just how the dominos started toppling when you had back-to-back-to-back lessons.

Once we had the first groups out in the arenas, I'd hoped Louise might feed her guys early and go home, but she decided to bring Adonis out to graze at the end of the barn and watch the ponies go around the end of the covered arena. It was a decision that would have consequences—mostly for little Allie Lewis, who wouldn't stop starting at Adonis and missed the instruction from Kennedy to transition downwards from canter to walk. Allie cantered her pony straight into the one ahead of her, piloted by the more attentive Sophia, and found herself flipped over a shoulder and flat on her back in the clay. While she was busy catching her breath, the pony did what any self-respecting pony would do upon dumping his rider, and took off. By the time he was caught, two other girls were brushing clay from their breeches and my own student was standing by her horse, holding his reins anxiously, while he spun and snorted, watching the little white pony wheel around us with Margaret doggedly shaking a grain bucket, trying to corner him with his own treacherous appetite.

"A lot of excitement today," Kennedy observed later, when the barn had emptied out.

I looked at the clock over the tack room door. It was ten 'til nine. "You know I don't like excitement," I said drily.

She stretched and sighed. "I think everyone had fun... except for Allie, Maggie, and Parker. But they all got back on and finished their lessons, anyway. And Adonis seems to understand what ponies are now."

"What a relief." I watched Margaret stomp past, broom in hand. "Margaret, please go home."

"I'm just putting this away," she said sourly, waving the broom at me. "And then I'm leaving."

"Come late tomorrow. Kennedy and I will help Anna feed breakfast."

"Fine," Margaret replied, not looking back. She disappeared around the corner and I heard the clatter of hooks as she hung the broom up in its spot on the wall. A few moments later her truck started with a muffled rattle, and her headlights were two beams of light picking out the dust motes in the half-lit aisles before she backed up and started down the driveway. "We can't keep doing this to Margaret. She'll quit on me."

"Where else would she go?" Kennedy asked, interested. "She's not going to find another barn around here to work at."

"She could go to the parks."

There was a pop in the distance, as if on cue. "You're right," Kennedy said, craning her neck to look down the aisle, towards the fireworks show just beginning beyond the tree-line. The parks: short-hand for the sprawling forty-some square miles of theme parks and hotels under the Disney name. They had dozens of horses there. "I guess Louise could give her a reference, if she wanted it. They'd trust a recommendation from her."

I looked at Kennedy sharply. Was that a wistful note in her voice? Wouldn't that just be perfect, for Kennedy to get me buried neck-deep in trail horses and ponies and horse show kids, and then go off to work with parade horses? Wouldn't it just?

A stall door slid shut and a few minutes later Anna came around the corner, hay in her brown hair and brushes in her tan hands. Kennedy's face lit up from within. I wouldn't have expected Kennedy to get that look on her face for anything short of a new horse. It took me aback, and I leaned back in the folding chair a little too far. It tipped swiftly and my head cracked against the concrete wall.

"Ow!"

Kennedy and Anna's heads both swiveled to look at me, and the dreamy moment between them was over. I felt bad for bursting their bubble. "I'm fine," I said hastily, and stood up, kicking the chair back into place. "I better just get to bed. Anna, I gave Margaret a late start in the morning, since she has to drive home."

Anna nodded. "No problem. Hey—what are you doing on Monday?"

"Monday? Nothing." I used to go to the grocery store on Monday, but now that we lived so close to civilization—now that civilization had moved so close to *us,* rather—I just ordered everything online. Sometimes encroaching suburbia wasn't *all* bad.

"Louise wants to take us to the park. She has an invitation from the equine manager to look at the horses she's sold them. Like, a thank you day. What do you think? Want to come?"

"The park?" I blinked. "Like, the Magic Kingdom?"

"Yeah," Anna said. "I think it would be fun."

Kennedy bounced out of her chair, sending it skidding behind her, and gave Anna a bear hug. "Let's take a picture with Cinderella!" she cried joyfully. "It's princess time!"

Anna ran a hand down Kennedy's mass of maroon curls, and smiled at me over her shoulder, rolling her eyes affectionately. *This silly girl,* she seemed to be saying. I shook my head slightly at her, smiling back, but inside I was simply fascinated. What a pair these two were turning out to be. Sensible, gentle Anna and brash, bold Kennedy. I could see them running a barn together, with none of the fireworks you saw from couples like Jules and Pete up in the backwoods of Alachua, or wherever they were now. Those two would never stop fighting. Anna and Kennedy, on the other hand, would complement each other beautifully. But what disciplines would they specialize in? I was starting to think Kennedy would never settle, while Anna was happy with hunters and jumpers.

It had been easy for me, I thought later that evening, stirring a chunk of sweet tea powder into a glass of water. I took the glass with me onto the porch and eased into one of the old rocking chairs my grandfather had set out here. A good eighty years ago, I thought, maybe longer. He sat out here and smelled the orange blossoms, and watched his foals play in the moonlight, and when I came along, he put me on my little pony and took me riding.

Except for our trail days here, though, I'd always been an English girl, a show-ring girl, plain and simple. I'd always known what I'd wanted.

Kennedy was different. You didn't leave a successful show career the way she had if it was your life's work. You didn't walk away from a lead role in a trick-riding show just to sit at a desk if your destiny was to play a princess under the spotlights. And you didn't look so wistfully at a row of future parade horses if your mind was made up to train show ponies.

I'd been trying to imagine a place for Kennedy in the new life I had to build, out beyond this equestrian center I'd thought would be my last stop in the world. But not knowing what my life would look like had made it hard to picture where she fit in. Being a trainer for so long, I was used to feeling responsible for the future of the younger horsewomen around me. Maybe, with Kennedy, that feeling was misguided. She wasn't here to be my student, after all. She never had been in my program. Kennedy, for all her outsized place in my thoughts, was an employee.

Headlights picked through the lacework of dark oak branches between my house and the highway; cars whizzed by as if it was rush-hour. Here in tourist-land, the visitors and the residents alike kept odd hours. I felt a sudden need to be alone in the night, just me and my horses, far from all this construction and the endless pursuit of plastic pleasures. I sipped at my lemony sweet tea, the same sugar-tart concoction I'd been drinking on warm nights since I was a pigtailed pony-rider, and imagined a smaller, quieter life than I had led before. All alone, I thought. A cat appeared from beneath the porch and sidled up alongside me. *Ginny.* "And you," I promised, dropping one hand to let the tabby push her hard-toothed face against my fingers. "And a dog. I need a dog."

Maybe I'd never be all alone on a quiet country acre again. I couldn't say, when I didn't even know what my next move was, where I'd be in six months. But, I thought, I really should get a dog.

Chapter Six

LET'S JUST SAY I'm not a theme park person.

There are crowds and then there are crowds, and that might not be the most illuminating statement in the world, but the crowds which descended upon the theme parks nestled amongst the swamps and oaks a few miles west of my farm were beyond any sort of rational description. The English language was not built to handle such masses of humanity. Shoulder-to-shoulder, toe-to-heel, wheeled and sneakered and flip-flopped and even platform-heeled, they blotted out the pavement, the curbs, the drains and whatever detritus they might have dropped along the way—park maps, lollipops, Starbucks cups still full of sticky-sweet coffee, popcorn, ice cream wrappers, pacifiers, ill-considered and unnecessary hoodies. All of it kicked beneath their feet and slid along the red-tinted concrete which, our guide enthusiastically informed us, had been specially chosen by Kodak for the best contrast against Florida's famous blue skies in family photos.

No one could have taken a family photo in *this* sea of bodies. I looked frantically at Kennedy, her dark maroon curls bobbing in the May humidity, and when she met my eyes with a questioning gaze, I simply ducked to the right, pushing past a flotilla of heavy plastic strollers and narrow-eyed Midwestern mothers, stopping only when I reached the relative calm of a false porch sheltered by elaborate white columns. I flattened myself against the yellow-planked wall, next to a plate-glass window wherein Donald Duck's entire family was showcasing a pastel array of candies, and resolved to just stay in place here until the morning crowd was finished pushing through, or Louise and the equine manager escorting us came back to retrieve me and take me home. One or the other. I had wanted to see the famous Disney horses in action, but deal with that pushing, shoving, sweating, sobbing mob again? There wasn't a horse in the world worth that.

In a few moments Kennedy, Anna, Louise and the concerned-looking equine manager, a trim man named Mark with streaks of salt in his peppery hair, were at my side, looking a little rough themselves after pushing through the sea of humanity to reach me. "Are you okay?" Anna asked, putting a tan hand on my arm.

"Perfect," I replied. "As long as I'm not being shoved down the street like a steer to market, I'm just fine. Come and get me when you're done."

Mark smiled nervously. "This is just a rush because of the morning parade ending. The horses will be back out in five minutes or so. I was just taking you down to the beginning of their show route..."

"Five minutes?" I found it hard to believe there'd be enough room for horses in this mob within five minutes.

"Oh yes," Mark assured me. He fiddled with the cuffs of his blue button-down shirt, which was definitely too warm for the morning. *Ah, the corporate life,* I thought. "Just watch what happens." He stepped back against the wall to let a particularly aggressive stroller-mama herd her brood along the sidewalk in front of us.

And wouldn't you know, the guy was right? The crowd was melting away in front of my eyes, their mass footprint ebbing like an outgoing tide. Suddenly I was aware of music playing, a cheerful piano medley which I recognized from some Technicolor-tinted musical I'd watched on a rainy Saturday years ago. I could see the photo-friendly red sidewalk in front of me, the darker pavement of the street a few feet beyond that. A horse-head hitching post materialized in front of me, its metal face painted a smooth dark green, seemingly waiting for a carriage to pull up so that the bustled and beribboned lady of the house might step out, open her parasol, and walk into the candy shop behind me while her driver looped the reins through the ring and went off in search of his own amusements. I sniffed, and a sugary sweet cotton candy scent floated into my senses.

I laughed, suddenly delighted with all the pieces that were falling into place around me. A family pausing for a photo looked at me with careful consideration, decided I was just giddy on the magic of the place, and went on with their picture. Mark watched them for a bare second before he stepped off the curb, took the mother's phone from her, and encouraged them all into a pose.

"Mark can't help himself," Louise laughed. "He's not even wearing a name-tag, the goofball. Those poor people probably think he's insane."

I looked at her, eyebrow twitching in question.

"Oh, it's just a Disney thing," Louise said. "They always offer to get everyone in the photo. That and picking up trash, those are the two things no one working here is ever above."

Sure enough, on the way back to us, the happy family waving goodbye in the background, Mark picked up a discarded Coke bottle and detoured to a recycling can on the street corner. *Good grief,* I thought. *He's an absolute Boy Scout.*

But it was kind of sweet.

"So we're going to watch the trolley show," he said as he came back. "It's one of the first things our morning guests get to see as they're walking down Main Street. Our trolley horses are absolutely amazing—they just stand still and let all this action, singing and dancing, go on around them. Flash photos. People shoving past. Fireworks in the background sometimes. They don't flick an ear."

Kennedy's grin stretched from ear to ear. She looked like a cartoon character. "They sound amazing!"

"They are," Louise sighed. "And the one you're going to see was one of my boys."

Mark laughed. "You already know who's coming?"

"I have my sources," Louise said coyly.

"Let's go to the end of the street and see," he urged us, and we picked up and walked down the now-broad and spacious sidewalk, past the cool air blowing from open doors of shopfronts, around an absurd line which apparently was just for Starbucks, and to the sugar-scented entrance of the ice cream shop on the corner. Beyond a broad circle of fountains and statues, the park's fairy-tale castle reached up to the blue Florida sky. All around us, piano notes tinkled like we were standing in the center of a music-box. Anna and Kennedy looked ready to melt into puddles from happiness.

Jesus Christ, I thought. This place was like a drug.

Then the music changed, and from the direction of the castle, a horse pulling a street-car trolley appeared. He was a dark, dapple-gray Belgian, with a wavy white mane and a diamond of pink skin between his white nostrils. He would be a gorgeous horse merely standing in a muddy field; in his shining black harness, adorned with gold-glinting hardware, he was simply stunning. The brightly-painted trolley behind him wasn't bad, either.

A small crowd gathered around as the horse pulled up in front of us and dancers in swirling full skirts and dapper suits hopped off and started performing to what I could only assume was music from another old musical. While they pranced and lip-synched, the girls' wigs bobbing with fat sausage curls, my eyes were drawn to the horse.

The driver, a young woman in a black and white conductor's costume, stood at the horse's head. A few others in the same outfit had arrayed themselves at strategic points nearby, guiding the people who weren't interested in the show into choosing routes that didn't involve walking right under the Belgian's nose. A few still made it past their waving hands and stage-whispered requests to keep their distance, but despite the rumbling stroller wheels passing dangerously close to the horse's hooves, the Belgian didn't move. He didn't flick an ear. After a few minutes, his eyelids fluttered and his nose dipped. He was falling asleep while the show whirled around him.

"What a champion," I murmured.

"That's what I do," Louise replied, her eyes never leaving the horse. "His name is Evan, by the way."

"Evan?"

"What? It's a good name."

I was used to show horses with titles, not names, but then again that's why I tried to give my horses barn names with personality, like

Ivor. I'd known someone once who called their horse Newsprint. Newsprint! What kind of name was that? "Evan *is* a good name," I agreed.

The song-and-dance show wrapped up, the performers hopped back onto the trolley, and Evan walked on up the street, the spare conductors walking in front of him, clearing the trolley tracks of oblivious families still trying to take photos with the castle perfectly centered behind them. It was an uphill battle, and the driver had to stop Evan several times while people simply refused to move until they were good and ready. I found myself gritting my teeth as a large family in matching red t-shirts ran in front of the horse's path to take photos, the conductor helpless to force them from the tracks. Evan stood and waited like a saint, but I wasn't that patient.

"I couldn't do this without resorting to a buggy whip," I told Mark. "You park people have some extra patience gene in your DNA."

Mark laughed, but it was a little hollow.

Evan stopped two more times for the show to perform around him, and each time he stood with the grace and manners of a prince among horses. Now I could see why Louise's horses were highly sought-after. With the dancers swirling around him, the loud music, and the constant barrage of clueless humans pushing their rumbling strollers right under his nose, anything less than sainthood wouldn't be good enough for this job. Evan had reached a serene state somewhere far beyond bombproof. He was theme-park-proof.

We settled down with coffees at a set of chairs around a metal-topped table in a little nook off Main Street, hidden behind a silhouette-cutter trimming away at children's shadows, and Mark and Louise chatted about what they were looking for.

"Parades are all about princesses now," Mark said. "And they can't all ride in carriages. You can't put Princess Jasmine in a carriage. It makes no sense. But we also don't have enough princesses who can ride. It's a real headache."

I glanced at Kennedy, who was looking attentively at Mark, waiting for him to continue. But his attention was focused on Louise.

"I have a couple horses who might fit the bill," Louise said. "I can send you video. Or you can come over—I'm right over at Seabreeze." She nodded at me. "Grace's barn."

Mark looked over at me. "I thought you were selling?"

"You're keeping tabs on me?" I asked tartly.

"Sorry," he said hastily. "Just farrier gossip."

I looked into my coffee and counted to ten.

"Business is booming," I heard Kennedy assure Mark. "We only have a couple empty stalls, and the lessons are non-stop every night."

"Well, that's great news," Mark said blandly. "It's good to know we still have horsey neighbors nearby."

Neighbors he'd never spoken to or visited before, sure. I lifted my head and smiled at him. "Come over for a cup of sugar anytime."

Our eyes locked, and I had a sudden prickling sensation climb up the nape of my neck. His gaze seemed to intensify, and I felt my lips part of their own accord.

"Mark," Louise burst out, "I'm sure I have *just* the horse for you. Look." She held out her phone with completely unnecessary urgency. Mark dragged his eyes away from mine. I buttoned up my mouth in a firm, thin line.

"Very nice," he agreed, looking at the phone. "There's just one thing… is he used to bagpipes?"

My eyebrows met my hairline. Anna and Kennedy gaped. Louise just sighed.

"Really Mark, can't you lead with that?"

Mark explained that the horses only worked at the park in the morning, and after that they went back to their ranch at Fort Wilderness, the campground resort at the edge of property closest to Seabreeze. "We do trail rides and hay-rides from there, and send out horses to do evening carriage rides at some of the historic-themed resorts," he went on. "But the theme parks are too wild in the afternoons to keep the horses out. Plus, it's hot out on the pavement."

I had no interest in staying amongst the hordes bouncing off each other in the park, so I accepted Mark's offer of a quick tour of the ranch, and followed him to a door hidden behind an advertisement for an old-fashioned livery stable. Anna and Kennedy saw me off with undisguised envy. Louise might be good for a free pass into the park, but she wasn't allowed to go behind the scenes without Mark as her escort. They'd had to choose between a day running around the Magic Kingdom, or going backstage with Mark and me, and the promise of meeting princesses had won the day.

"I'll see you back at the farm!" I called with a wave. Kennedy just shook her head at me, with a knowing look I chose not to try and interpret. She was I was just going to look at *horses.*

They weren't missing much behind the Victorian facades of Main Street; just a lot of industrial buildings and giant air conditioners clustered around a small parking lot. I snuck a glance into a shed with a particularly high roof, and saw a rainbow of balloons massed along its ceiling. At ground-level, a college kid in striped knickerbockers was fitting a new balloon to a helium canister. He turned a knob and let the gas whoosh in. The balloon filled in a flash and he let it join the colorful collection above his head with an exuberant rush upwards.

But that was the most interesting thing to be seen behind park walls. We passed a few cars and then Mark stopped at a white truck with that distinctive mouse-ear logo painted on the driver's side door. He opened the passenger tour and I clambered in, brushing aside some loose grains of sweet feed. This was firmly a farm truck, despite the corporate trappings. Hay-twine and double-end snaps and a stray halter decorated the bench seat. I felt right at home for the first time since I'd left the barn this morning.

We drove the couple of miles to the ranch in silence, the truck's radio switched off and neither of us really finding anything we needed to say. I glanced at Mark a few times; he looked content enough with the silence. I gave him a mental check-mark; people who didn't mind being quiet when there was nothing to say were a rare breed.

He turned down a lane, calling it a "backstage" entrance, and we drove through a cypress forest. There was no one else around—no cars, no kids, no strollers. The desolation was unexpected. "You'd think we were in the middle of nowhere," I said.

"That's the point of Fort Wilderness," Mark said happily. I could hear the affection in his tone... he clearly loved this place. "Believe it or not, there's a deluxe lakeside resort just about a quarter mile that way—" he pointed to his left, "and off to the right there's camp-sites and cabins, but we're careful to keep all the trees intact. Keeps the illusion going."

After driving a couple of minutes, Mark hit his brakes and pointed to a trail that crossed the road and disappeared into the forest on our left. To the right, I could see a long, low stable with a few paddocks behind it. "Our trail barn," he said. "They go out into the woods. It's a nice ride. You gotta think, a lot of the guests coming here have never been on a horse before and they'll never get on one again."

"That's sad," I observed.

"They come here for once-in-a-lifetime experiences," Mark said simply, and drove on.

The stables and paddocks where the carriage and parade horses lived were located near a cluster of buildings apparently built of logs, but despite the frontier-style facades, the barn was a big center-aisle with twelve-by-twelve stalls and a wide concrete aisle, built in a recognizable style that had dominated Florida equestrian centers for a few decades. He parked the truck in a service area and we walked around the front, where there was a warren of little pens filled with white and pinto ponies nosing at hay mangers—some here for pony rides, the others for pulling Cinderella's carriage in weddings or parades, Mark explained—and a big wash-rack where a girl in her mid-twenties, looking sweaty and miserable in jeans and a plaid button-down shirt, was scrubbing the feathers of an imposing Clydesdale.

"Jo," Mark said by way of greeting, leaning over the wash-rack's elbow-height railing. "How's Murphy today?"

"Better," she huffed, getting up from her knees. She shook soap-suds from her hands and the bubbles went flying. "If we could clip these feathers, this would be easier."

"You know we can't clip them," Mark sighed.

"I do know," Jo agreed. "But that won't stop me from complaining about it." She brushed dark hair back from her oval-shaped face with one soapy arm.

Mark watched her with an amused look, and she gave him a sassy smile in return—a little too familiar for boss and employee, I thought. *So it's like that.* I cleared my throat to break the intimate silence between them. "Why do we want to clip his feathers?" I asked.

"Cellulitus," Mark said grimly. "He's perfectly sound but it stocks up and gets scabs. All we can do is try to keep it clean."

"And if you clip it, you'll be able to see the scabs," I finished.

"Exactly. Bad show. We can't put him in front of guests like that."

"So, I scrub," Jo pronounced, and eased herself back down to her knees, feeling around in the bucket of sudsy water next to her for the brush she'd abandoned under the bubbles.

We walked through the barn aisle while Mark pointed out the finer points of the horses on either side. The first few box stalls had been replaced with museum exhibits: an antique steam calliope on one side, and a set of display cases and portraits featuring great moments in Disney equine history on the other. Further in, the horses' stalls had big, civilian-friendly signs bearing the horse's name and their daily diet. About six stalls in, a chain cut off access to the rest of the barn. Behind it, a giant fan sat in the center, humming as it blew a breeze down the aisle, ruffling my hair. Beyond that, more stalls stretched down the barn aisle, with grooms working on horses tied in the aisle. A sign hanging from the chain swung in the fan's breeze: *Cast Members Only.*

"We only keep the super-quiet horses out here where the guests can reach them," Mark explained. "Everyone thinks they have to touch the horses. You can put up ten signs and point cameras at them and threaten to call the FBI if they put a finger in a stall, but it won't stop them. So we just minimize the risk with horses who *probably* won't nip." He stepped up to one stall and tickled the chin of a tall gray horse who had put his head over his stall gate, looking for hand-outs. "We've been pretty lucky."

I looked around me, taking in the spotless barn, the friendly horse, the cheerful stall sign on his wall declaring that Pancho loved watermelon Jolly Ranchers for a special treat. I felt like I had wandered into a children's storybook. "This place is insane, Mark," I laughed.

He frowned. "How so?"

"You don't see it? You live your whole life in horse-show mode. Your horses are always sparkling, always perfectly mannered. Your barn is always on display for the world to see. Your grooms are apparently wearing uniforms?" He nodded. "Plaid shirts and jeans, sure, but still, when it's ninety degrees I bet everyone one of them would rather be in cut-offs and tank-tops. But they have to create this illusion of a ranch where all the horses are movie stars and the camera's always rolling." I shook my head, still grinning. "I don't know how you do it."

Mark looked disappointed in me.

I put a hand on his arm, which was pleasantly muscled under that blue dress shirt. "I'm not saying anything against you. I think you're actually accomplishing something I always reached for, but maybe I was never willing to go far enough." I thought of my perfect show-barn, the aisle always swept, the stalls always picked, the buckets always scrubbed, the saddles always polished. My barn was clean, but this somehow went a step above. This barn welcomed the public, then swept them away into another world. Mine was more like an homage to the traditions of our own secret society of equestrians. There were no translations tacked to the walls. You had to earn your place there.

"I *like* it, Mark. It's insane, but I get it."

I swept my eyes around the sparkling barn one more time, trying again to unlock the secret of this place's serene charm. Then my gaze met Mark's, and our eyes locked again, as they had in the park earlier. My breath caught in my chest.

His eyes were gray-blue, their expression thoughtful, as if he was trying to absorb the back-handed compliment I'd just given him, make it into something positive. That little smile he wore all the time, like a barrier between him and the guests he was constantly trying to please, had slipped away from his face, and I felt a sudden, unfamiliar urge to lean forward and see what happened if I got a little closer to those loosening lips. What sort of man might be hiding behind an unwavering smile and an obsessive attention to detail? Someone, I suspected, who was more passionate than anyone else I'd ever met.

Then there were hoofbeats behind us and Jo was standing beside us, the dripping-wet hooves of Murphy leaving platter-sized tracks on the concrete. "Did you want to take a look, Mark?" she asked, and when I glanced at her I saw she wasn't looking at him, but at me, and her expression was hard.

I took a step back. "Don't let me get in the way," I said, and I meant it in more ways than one.

Anyway, I thought later, waiting for Mark to get the truck and drive me home, he was probably only insanely passionate about his job. He hadn't seemed to have any particular affinity for Jo, despite her possessive looks. He hadn't seemed to notice the coy flirtation that crept into Louise's voice when she was trying to joke with him. And he wasn't wearing a wedding ring, so no one else had been able to break through to him, either. Deeply nerdy, I thought, and married to his job. Oh well. I had enough on my mind. I tipped my head back against the barn wall and let the hot sun soak through my closed eyelids. A mockingbird trilled car alarm songs from a nearby magnolia tree. A few moments later, he was there, jangling his keys, and our day out was at an end.

Chapter Seven

BACK AT THE farm for evening feeding, Kennedy was full of chatter about their day in the park. She threw hay with one hand and swiped through her phone to show me photos with the other. She talked about rides and shows and churros and ice cream sundaes that somehow, confusingly, were meant to look like cartoon characters. Then, in true Kennedy fashion, she came up with a dozen ways to improve the place and add horses to the mix. Her tongue tripped in her excitement as she described ways horses could make the world's most famous theme park even better, like for atmosphere in Frontierland and for conveyance at the end of a long summer evening.

"Imagine like, half a dozen of those streetcars, just taking people constantly up to the park exit, then going back to the castle hub for more. If you didn't have such huge gaps between them, people would know to stay out of their way! They wouldn't need that whole team of Cast Members to babysit each trolley, they'd move more people with tired feet, and they'd have more of that whole circa-1900 atmosphere they're going for. I don't know why Louise doesn't suggest it!"

"Maybe she will, now," Anna said softly, smiling at Kennedy in that new way of hers, an affectionate adoration that tugged at my heart. She had taken to looking at frothy, vivid Kennedy as if the other woman was a rainbow she'd spotted in a forest glen, and she was afraid the sunlight would shift and take it away from her before she could reach its end. "It's a good idea, and she said new ideas were the one thing they were really lacking over there."

I glanced down the barn aisle to where Louise was throwing hay to her own horses, her short, rather round figure silhouetted against the yellow evening sunlight streaming into the open aisle. "Does she have much pull with Mark and that whole crew?"

Kennedy shrugged, suddenly deflated. "I don't know. Probably not. She's just a contractor, at the end of the day. You probably have to be inside the team to really get your ideas heard." She clambered back onto the driver's seat and turned the Gator on, moving the little utility truck down another six stalls so we could easily get hay from its bed for the next set of horses. I stood still for a minute, watching her dark maroon curls bobble above her sturdy shoulders. There it was again—that premonition that Kennedy was looking at her next career move, and it wasn't training more show ponies for me.

That was a good thing, I told myself. It would help me downsize if I only had myself to think about, maybe Anna. *If* I decided to downsize, I emphasized, drawing a mental line under the words. Maybe I wouldn't go. Maybe I'd stay right here, finish what I'd started. Maybe if Mark could run a horse operation based on trails and carriages and hay-rides, I could make it a few miles up the road with lessons and camp and boarding. Kids still came with their parents on vacation, and kids were the lifeblood of most barns. Even mine, these days, though I'd never seen that coming. You never did know what you'd do to survive in this business.

A car door slammed in the parking lot and I left the girls to finish throwing hay while I went to see who had shown up so late in the evening. Mondays the barn was technically closed—no lessons, no grooms to help boarders who still showed up to ride. Only a handful of boarders came out to ride their own horses on Monday. For some reason, most of them preferred the clamor and tumult of a regular week-night, full of kids and lessons. For a while, the barn had been completely closed on Monday, even to boarders. I'd liked it because I didn't have to wonder what my boarders were getting up to when I wasn't around to supervise. If there was ever a group of people who shouldn't be left unsupervised, it was a gaggle of women at a show barn.

I was a little surprised to see a stranger getting out of a black Lexus by the time I'd rounded the corner to the parking lot. She was trim, neatly dressed in a suit—like a lot of my boarders were before they changed into breeches, actually—and I wondered if she was new to the area and looking for boarding. I ran a hand over my hair, hoping the humid evening didn't have every strand under three inches long standing straight up, and brushed some of the hay from the shoulders of my dark blue polo shirt. At least I had on one with a Seabreeze logo, so I looked like I belonged here; there was nothing I could do about my faded khaki shorts with the threads trailing from the cuffs. I wished I'd stayed in the house and left the girls to it, the way I usually did on a Monday evening. Then, at least, I'd be presentable.

"How can I help you this evening?" I asked, holding out a hand as I approached. "I'm Grace. This is my place."

The woman glanced at my hand for a moment before she grasped it. I felt all of her tarsals and metatarsals in that handshake; she was impossibly thin. A big gold engagement ring with a teardrop diamond setting dangled around her third finger like a ring at the end of a jousting lance. "Karen Lowery," she said in a strangled sort of voice. "From next door."

"From next door?" The only thing next door was the construction site.

"Bella Tuscany," Karen clarified. "The resort property?" She tipped her head towards the red-tiled roofs rising behind the thin line of pine trees that separated my half-dozen paddocks from the resort construction. "I just came by to talk with you about a few concerns. Is this a good time?"

I lifted an eyebrow. Who would think six PM at a barn was a good time to conduct a business call? *Civilians,* I thought. But Anna, Kennedy and the part-time grooms could handle the rest of evening chores between them. And maybe this wouldn't take that long. "Let's go up to my office," I suggested, and led the way up the creaking stairs to my eyrie overlooking the barn.

"Nice place," Karen said, glancing warily at the cushion of the chair I offered her before placing her black-skirted derriere on its aging vinyl. "You must have, what, thirty horses here?"

"Close enough," I said. "Boarders, school horses, a few of my own." I gestured at the photos decorating the bookshelves around the room. "I've been here a while."

"I'm sure," Karen replied, looking obediently, if rather glassy-eyed, at the old pictures. "I know things have changed a lot around here."

"That's an understatement," I said wryly, unable to stop the suddenly bitter twist of my mouth. "But," I said more lightly, "we're all just here to make people happy." I thought of Mark and his tourist-friendly barn.

Karen Lowery looked confused for a moment. "Well," she finally continued, "we know you've been here a long time, and we want to be good neighbors. That's actually why I'm here this evening. I do a bit of P.R. for the resort and I noticed we were getting a few concerns from visitors to our website, about having a stable next door? I'm sure you understand." She cocked her head slightly, dark hair cascading over her shoulder, and waited for me to agree with her.

The longer a person cocks their head, waiting for an affirmation they're not going to get, the more they look like a confused Labrador Retriever.

Karen was all but waggling her ears and panting before I finally answered her little head-tilt. "I'm afraid you're going to have to clarify that, Karen," I told her gravely.

"Oh!" Karen straightened her neck at that. "Well, there were just a few questions about the implications of living next to a stable, and we decided I'd better come and get the answers straight... you know, straight from the horse's mouth." She looked me dead in the eye and forced a laugh.

I leaned back in my chair and folded my hands, fixing Karen with a blank stare. This should be good. "What have you got?"

"Well, obviously there's a concern about liability should a horse get loose and end up on resort property. These are vacation homes, so owners are going to want to ensure their properties are receiving the best of care in order to keep their value up for rentals. Things like damaged lawns, pool screens, driveways—there's been some questions about just how much damage a horse could do running loose through their yards."

"Are you serious?"

Karen blinked at me. "What? I mean—of course, these are concerns being brought up by potential buyers and we have to form some talking points to reassure them—"

"What do they think a horse is going to do to their *driveway*? I can't answer that question until I understand what exactly they're talking about. It's a horse, not a jackhammer. And anyway no, I don't intend that my horses will get loose and run around their lawns and swan-dive into their pools. I have *fences*. In case you didn't notice, there's a perimeter fence around the entire property. Remember that gate you came through when you arrived? That's always closed for a reason." I realized I was leaning forward rather aggressively and settled back in my chair, trying to smooth my expression back into blandness. "If you need a talking point, tell them about the fence. Suburban types love fences. And tell *them* to respect my fence and stay on their own side of it. Then we won't have any problems."

Karen squared her jaw. "I don't think there's any need to be rude," she said tersely. "These are valid questions. Maybe horse behavior is crystal clear to *you*, but for the rest of the world, farm animals aren't exactly the norm."

"That's so wrong, I don't even know how to correct you properly. Can you tell me the next question on the list? Please make it interesting."

She uncrossed her legs, then crossed them again, and consulted her notebook. "What kind of noise level can neighbors expect from the horses?"

I looked at the ceiling. "Horses are prey animals, so most of the time they're silent to avoid being eaten by panthers. The swarms of kids running around on weekends, I can't say the same thing for. They get pretty loud."

"Kids?" Karen looked distressed at this new eventuality.

"Pony kids," I clarified, although to Karen this distinction meant nothing. "They get dropped off in the morning, they stay all day, go home exhausted. It makes their parents very happy. They get free Saturdays for brunch, and their kids go straight to bed at night. Another selling point for your clients—ponies make for sleepy children. Your clients *will* have kids, right?"

"I—well—some of them, certainly—"

"You're surely not putting in a water park for the peace and tranquility it will provide to your clientele?"

"It's not a very *large* water park—"

I snorted then. It wasn't a dignified snort, and I wasn't proud of myself for doing it, but sometimes when you're holding back a laugh and then someone says something truly absurd, it comes out as a big honking mule-sound and there's simply nothing to be done about it. Karen looked horrendously offended, and I couldn't quite blame her. But she was the one over here asking me if my horses were somehow going to trample her new flower-beds.

Things didn't get much better after that, and Karen didn't leave with a smile on her face. By the time the tail-lights of her Lexus had disappeared down the barn lane, the sun was setting and the barn chores were long done. I descended the staircase again and walked down the clean aisle, listening to the chatter of a couple kids hosing off their ponies in the wash-racks. It was nice having them around, I realized. The barn atmosphere had changed, and not for the worst. Back when it was just the herd of professional women trying to have their second shot at equestrian stardom, a niche I'd specialized in for so long it had seemed there was no point in changing, there'd been a lot of gossip and a lot of tears—typical show barn stuff—but not a lot of laughter. Now the kids were around with their terrible ideas ("Grace, what if we dye Toby purple with the whitening shampoo? Will you tell Mom it was an accident?" was a recent standout) and their constant giggling. I didn't even mind their yelling. I'd learned that when barn kids were quiet, it usually meant someone was whispering something mean into someone else's ear, and I had to send Kennedy to break it up.

I took a peek around the corner of the wash-rack and saw two twelve-year-old girls, Dawson and Melina, hard at work running sweat scrapers down their wet ponies' backs. While I was watching, Melina took her scraper and shook it hard at Dawson, who squealed and shook hers back. Water flew everywhere. The ponies, born and bred for these kind of barn shenanigans, dozed on their cross-ties. I shrugged and left them to it.

In the feed room, Anna was emptying bags of grain into the trash cans.

"You almost done for the night?" I asked her. "Want to get some dinner?"

"I'm going with Kennedy," she said, a pink flush sweeping over cheeks. She shook the last few alfalfa pellets from the bag in her hands. Their grassy smell filled the feed room and I was suddenly craving a big salad. "I'm sorry! I didn't think you'd want to."

"Don't apologize," I said, holding up my hand. "You go enjoy yourself. I'm tired anyway. I lost my day of rest by going to the park with you guys."

"You had fun, though," Anna said knowingly. "You liked Main Street."

"If the whole place was Main Street and horses, that'd be something I could get behind. The rest of it is a little over-the-top for me."

"And Mark," Anna went on in the same knowing tone, as if I hadn't said anything. "You guys seemed to hit it off."

I shrugged, although I was wondering just what Anna had seen between us. Our interaction at the park had been minimal; it wasn't until I'd gone back to the ranch, without Anna, that I'd felt a little... *interested,* let's call it, in Mark.

Or maybe I was wrong, and there'd been something there all along.

I wasn't around men enough to tell.

"One of the grooms at the ranch might be moving on him already," I confided. "She gave me that kind of vibe."

"The 'I'm doing my boss' vibe?" Anna folded up the empty grain bags and stuffed them all into the last one standing.

"The 'hands off or I'll kill you' vibe." I sighed. "It doesn't matter. I have enough to complicate my life right now without adding another human being to the mix. That woman that was here? Karen Something, from the resort going in next door. She really pissed me off. Apparently some of the people looking at buying there are getting scared off by the prospect of horses next door. Asking a lot of idiotic questions. I told her she was wasting my time and hers with these made-up problems people were emailing her with. You'd think no one had ever seen a horse farm before."

"That's sad," Anna said. "People are getting more and more

removed from horses. It's a shame we can't just stay here forever, even with all these houses around us."

"Just to spite them?" I didn't hate the idea. I'd always thought revenge and spite both had their places in an ambitious woman's playbook.

"Well, and to *teach* them," Anna laughed. "So they have the opportunity to have horses in their lives. If barns keep running away from suburbanites every time they get close, how can the suburbanites get to experience horses?"

I looked at her steadily for a moment. "Anna," I said finally, "These people come here for vacation at theme parks and concrete water parks. They don't *want* to ride."

From the barn aisle outside I heard hoofbeats on pavement, and the sound of little girls laughing. Anna and I were quiet for a moment, and I could only assume she was remembering when I'd told her the local kids wouldn't want to ride here.

Anna shrugged. "Maybe they'll surprise you."

"To spite them," I said to my imaginary dog, who was watching me with his imaginary ears pricked, looking over the battered arm of the (real) couch. I was in the kitchen, making a pot of spaghetti for one. "It's not a bad reason to do something crazy. And if it fails, I just leave. There's really nothing to lose."

I stirred pasta into submission and considered the prospect of staying. What was chasing me away, after all? Were those problems so insurmountable, or was I simply looking for the easy way out by refusing to fight them? Cooking spaghetti could lead to these sorts of ruminations. I'd made many strange decisions over a pot of boiling water. Once I'd bought into a Canadian Sporthorse stallion someone wanted to import and breed to Thoroughbred mares. We'd actually done pretty well with him, once we figured out he crossed particularly well with Arabs, not Thoroughbreds. Anyway, spaghetti had led me down some strange but successful roads in the past, and I wasn't about to turn its counsel away now.

Problems to consider, one: there was the noise of construction and the constant rock trucks blasting by the outdoor jumping ring. That wasn't going away. Two: there was the increasing isolation from the tack and feed stores which made farm life possible. That would not get better. Feed delivery was already expensive and would only go up. Three was more long-term but was always worth considering: the growing expense in taxes, city water and other utilities that would be seen as improvements to home-owners, but absolute money-pits to someone with forty-odd horses.

But all of these things could be worked around if I was willing to put in the effort. The horses could be ridden regularly in the jumping ring by staff until they were desensitized to the rattle and roar of the trucks, and turn-out alongside the construction site in the paddocks would help them get used to the earth movers and bulldozers and nail guns and the constant beeping of heavy equipment in perpetual reverse. The feed store's delivery charge was hefty, but I could spread that cost out amongst the boarders and they'd cheerfully pay the addition to their monthly bill if it meant they didn't have to start commuting out to the hinterlands of central Florida in order to ride their horses. Raising taxes in Florida usually took an act of God, and there were always exceptions to be pled for when you ran a legacy business in a changing community.

If I was willing to put up the fight, I could keep the farm going indefinitely. Certainly long enough to prove the developers wrong, and perhaps long enough to make me pull out of the contract to sell the farm at all.

Bowl of supper in hand, I went out to the living room and nestled into the soft, welcoming cushions of my old brown sofa. The little house breathed around me, its wooden planks expanding and contracting with the humid Florida evening.

"I can't give you up, can I?" I asked the living room, admiring the dark bookshelves, the vintage Dublin Horse Show poster on the far wall, the little old television huddled on the lowboy across from me. From beside me, my imaginary dog thumped his tail on the cushion. I glanced down at the empty space where he should be.

"And tomorrow," I announced. "I'm doing it. I'm getting a dog."

A dog would make things feel permanent.

Chapter Eight

MAX LOOKED LIKE a purebred Jack Russell, even though the animal shelter reps said he'd been found in the parking lot of a run-down mall in Ocoee and it seemed unlikely such an expensively-bred dog would be abandoned like that. But there'd been no microchip and no tag, and Max didn't seem too distraught about the loss of his previous family, judging by the way he leapt into my arms and licked my chin before I could stop him, so I signed the paperwork and slid my ten dollars across the counter and left the noisy shelter with a brown-spotted corporeal manifestation of my imaginary dog, still busily trying to get his tongue onto any inch of exposed skin he could reach.

There was a general pandemonium when I got back to the barn and Max leapt from the truck to the ground before I could grab his leash. He went barreling through the barn aisles with the sort of authority one would expect from an established farm Jack Russell who has been darting in and out of the kicking-range of horses for years. He showed off his talents in evasiveness, which had probably landed him in the pound in the first place, as the grooms shouted and chased him, a rare day-time boarder cooed after him, and Anna stood at the top landing of the stairs and looked down on it all, wonder in her face. I was suddenly very aware that the north and east edges of the property were ringed just by forest and not by fence, basically a wide-open, standing invitation for a Jack Russell to disappear into the palmettos forevermore, and when Max soared past Margaret on his second lap of the barn I screamed for her to stomp on his leash, which she did with great presence of mind.

Max hit the end of the leash and flipped backwards, turning a somersault before gracefully landing on his feet. He sat for a moment, panting and looking around him with pleasure, before Margaret leaned down and scooped him up. She had an amused expression on her dour face as she handed him over.

"Didn't have enough trouble in your life?" she asked.

"Never," I assured her, taking the dog in my arms. He panted up at me and gave my cheek a swipe with his pink tongue. "You're a mistake, but I love you already," I told him.

Anna came downstairs and accepted custody of Max so that I could get a ride in before afternoon lessons started appearing, and I hustled back to the house to change into breeches and a lightweight summer riding shirt while Kennedy tacked up Ivor for me. I'd thrown my day's schedule to hell by deciding to get in the truck and motor off to the animal shelter instead of coming down to ride the five horses on my book this morning. But a quick skim of the Petfinder site that morning while I'd sat over my solitary coffee had shown me my ideal dog was not going to be easy to come by. When Max's picture came up, I'd abandoned my mug and hustled out the door, determined to get him before someone else did.

"My mother always had Jack Russells," Louise said when she arrived at the barn, just as I was accepting Ivor's reins from Kennedy.

"Really takes me back. We had a barn full of them, and no mice at all. We didn't even need a barn cat."

"My grandfather had one for years," I admitted. "I guess I just thought the place missed having one running around."

Max strained at his leash, now tied to a screw-eye in the end wash-stall, desperate to follow me out of the barn.

"I totally agree," Louise said, watching him wiggle and writhe. "It's like having a resident gremlin."

I hadn't ridden Ivor in the outdoor jumping ring for weeks, and when the heat of the mid-afternoon sun hit me, I began to regret my decision before we'd even gotten to the arena gate. Riding outdoors in Florida between May and September was pretty serious business —you needed to plan for it, the way you needed to plan for an expedition into the Andes or a transatlantic crossing by canoe. May in particular was treacherous, because the days were usually cloudless, waiting for the stormy days of rainy season to come, but the heat and humidity were already at danger-zone levels.

Across the road and beyond the houses which had sprouted up on my grandfather's old orange grove, I could see a single fluffy cloud floating serenely in an ocean of unrelenting blue, and I tried to calculate its course to determine if it would block the blazing sun in the next fifteen minutes or so—because I really didn't see surviving these solar death-rays much longer than that. I squinted into the light for a few moments while Ivor tugged impatiently at the reins, far more interested in the grass growing too long around the arena fence, before coming to the conclusion that yes, the cloud had greater aspirations and yes, it would block the sun very shortly. I leaned down, my weight sinking into my right stirrup, and lifted the ring on the latch, pushed the gate open, and nudged Ivor inside.

Such good footing! The clay arena had settled under the baking sun and torrential rains it had been subjected to during its month of abandonment, and now Ivor's hooves cut through its top crust to sink gently onto the half-packed layers beneath. There was something I liked about a rain-softened and sun-dried arena even more than a furrowed, freshly-groomed one, and I let Ivor move forward on a loose rein, his black-tipped ears pricked and his head bobbing as he shifted his gaze to and fro, taking in the new surroundings. My brightly-painted Grand Prix course looked more inviting than ever after a month of riding to the dull brown schooling jumps we'd set up in the indoor. Those fences were lightweight and boring by necessity, since we had to put them up and pull them down constantly to allow for the beginner lessons and dressage rides. Now I wanted to bounce over the bright red-and-white striped poles of that latticed oxer in the far corner, and gallop right up to the base of the grass-green rolltop at the head of the arena...

A rock truck roared by, so close to the bushes lining the property fence that their leaves rattled against its steel body, and Ivor ducked hard to the right. My seat followed his movement easily, and I drew the reins back through loose fingers, squeezing them closed to stop him from bolting, but we were both a little more on edge when I returned him to the rail a few moments later. "And that's why we're out here," I reminded us both. "We have to perform just as well with trucks going by as we would in perfect silence. You, of all horses, should be ashamed of yourself, Ivor. You're a Grand Prix horse."

Ivor ducked his head against the bit and broke into a jig, snorting. Luckily, when you've got a horse with big movement, you can easily turn lemons into lemonade, and channeling Ivor's excess nerves into a fun, showy, forward trot was a pretty pleasant way to start working. He arched his neck, carrying the bit in his mouth like a hot coal, and gave me an extended trot the moment I opened my fingers, retreating to a bouncing collection when I closed them again. I felt like I was riding with live wires in my hands. It was still exhilarating, after a lifetime in the saddle, to ride a horse who was one hundred and ten percent on the bit and eager to move forward every time my leg touched his side.

There were still a few spooks to ride through as we moved into a canter and then started taking a couple of turns over a low vertical jump set up in one corner of the arena, away from the road, but after thirty minutes of riding I realized the sun had gone behind the ambitious cloud, now a growling baby thunderstorm, and we'd become so totally focused on our work, we hadn't noticed the heat or its slow fading. A cool breeze flitted across my sweaty face and flapped the sleeves of my damp shirt, and I pushed back my helmet brim as far as it would go, letting the storm-cooled air reach my forehead and ears. "We should jump a course," I told Ivor, "now that we've got the weather on our side."

"Do you need any fences moved?" a male voice called.

I looked across the ring and saw someone leaning against the fence. Ivor glanced over as well, his ears pricking as he focused on the newcomer. *Who the hell…* I squinted, and realized it was Mark, the equine manager from Fort Wilderness. Mark, with whom I had shared several memorable looks. Mark, who had waved casually when I'd hopped out of his truck on Monday and then presumably never thought of me again as he went back down the driveway. *Had* he, though?

A blush swept up my cheeks, undoing all the good of that cool breeze. Just like that, I was hot and sweating again. "Oh, the jumps are all fine," I said eventually, letting Ivor walk over of his own accord. "Thank you."

"Sorry to disturb you," he said, straightening up as we approached. "I just came over to talk with Louise about something and saw you riding. I'm so rarely at regular barns anymore, I had to come out and see you jumping."

"Not a disturbance. It's nice to take a break halfway." I circled Ivor near the gate. Mark looked much as he had yesterday, wearing a blue button-down shirt with the sleeves rolled up to the elbows, a pair of khakis, brown Blundstone jodhpur boots. I gave myself a moment to run my eyes over his face and try to work out what about him appealed to me so. His black hair was flecked with silver, but otherwise unremarkable. His face was tan and clean-shaven, his sunglasses were wire-rimmed and functional. He looked, I thought, like a particularly tidy vet. Well, that was not an unattractive look to me. He was looking inquiringly at me now. I'd let my gaze linger a bit too long. "I wasn't going to do a course today, but since the sun's gone in, I'm considering it." I said, coming back to business.

The cloud to our west rumbled helpfully.

"If it's still safe," Mark said pointedly.

I laughed. "That storm's at least five miles away, Mark."

"At the parks, our rule is fifteen miles," he said mildly.

"This isn't a big corporation. We don't have to follow big brother's rules. We ride until we're satisfied. And no one's been struck by lightning yet." I smiled at him, glancing sidelong as Ivor circled, and he returned the favor.

"Let's see some jumping, then," he replied, and stood back from the arena fence, his hands on his hips.

I grinned and picked up my reins, chirruping to Ivor.

I surrendered Mark to Louise once we were back in the barn, but when I glanced back at him, he was still watching us—*me*—as I led Ivor down the aisle to the wash-racks. It was nearly four o'clock and the car doors were starting to slam in the parking lot as children began to arrive for afternoon lessons; I heard Kennedy greeting her pony riders in the four-thirty beginner lesson as they trailed in, helmets already on their heads, ready to help groom and tack their ponies. The chorus of hellos and the whinnies of ponies as they were taken out to the arena one by one drowned out whatever conversation Louise was having with Mark, but I didn't need to know their business. Maybe I was less nosy because I knew they really would be talking business—draft horses, parade horses, training with swords, whatever it was they did in their alien world of entertainment and theme parks—and I'd just impressed Mark with my jumping. He'd be talking about carriage rides for tourists from Ohio or Alabama or New York, but he'd be thinking about *me*, soaring over the roll-top atop my big gray stallion.

Not that it matters, I reminded myself, unbuckling the throat latch and noseband of Ivor's black padded bridle. Mark had no shortage of women who were attracted to him. Typical horseman, I thought. There just weren't enough of them to go around. I wasn't going to get between him and that groom of his, either. She'd probably been cultivating their relationship for months, if not years. Chances were, it was already at least partially two-sided. For all I knew, he was playing it cool because they were at work and they'd already been dating for ages.

Still, even if Mark *was* taken, it was nice to feel I'd been noticed. I spent so much time in the company of women and young girls, I didn't often get the chance to impress a horseman.

Ivor shoved against me as I pulled off his bridle, and I smacked his shoulder hard, sending him backwards into the wash-stall. "Rotten," I told him good-naturedly. "You better not do that again."

Anna came around the corner with his halter in hand and slipped past me, sliding it over his ears and buckling the leather in place. "I've got him," she said. "There's someone here to see you."

"Who now?" I asked, perplexed. "Not that Karen again, for goodness' sake."

"Someone named Heather?" Anna shrugged. "She drives a nice car."

"Oh shit, Anna," I sighed. "That's the real estate agent. She's probably here to see if we're moving anytime soon."

Anna froze, her hand on Ivor's girth buckles. "Are we?"

I shook my head no. "But she doesn't know that. I better go tell her."

My office was freezing cold, despite the gathering storm clouds outside, and I shrugged on a hoodie I'd left hanging over my chair while Heather took a moment to look at the pony pictures on the bookshelves. She'd been up here before, while we'd talked about selling the property and the details of the contract, but now she acted as if she'd never seen the photos, the ribbons or the trophies before, all that ephemera of a life spent in the show-ring. I was already sitting in my chair before she dropped into the one facing my desk, looking a little mealy-mouthed. I realized she was stalling, and seeing the bustling barn couldn't have been a good feeling for a realtor who had expected to find me in the last stages of packing my tack.

"I haven't found anyplace," I said before she could ask. "So far everything has been too far away from my clients."

Heather's red lips drooped. She was a nice woman, about thirty-five and fond of black suits with white blouses that gave her a very business-like air, just the sort of person you wanted wheeling and dealing for you, but with a feminine touch, whatever that meant. She'd been immensely sympathetic in the three months or so I'd known her, always offering me more time, more tea, more sympathy, while I was trying to come to terms with the decision to sell the farm and then while she was trying to get me to actually commit to doing it.

In the end, I thought, that streak of niceness she has left in her is going to be her undoing... at least, on this deal. Because she'd been way too lenient with me, and if I needed to get out of this sale, I was going to be able to do it without too much difficulty. *Oh, Heather, you sweet thing,* I thought, watching her try to decide what to say next, whether she should sympathize or remonstrate, *I pity your next client, because I know I'm teaching you a lesson about good deeds going unpunished.*

Heather went for sympathy, something I was sure would be wrung dry from her soul before our brief relationship came to an end. "I know it's so difficult to find an equestrian property near here. Have you talked to them about how far they're willing to go? You might be surprised. I know in some urban areas people drive an hour or two to get to their horses. Some might even move to be closer to your new property. I know you guys are a family, and it can be a two-way street when a business has to move from a community..."

"Most of them are very adamant they can't go further than thirty minutes," I said, lifting my hands in a helpless gesture. "They have families, they have jobs, traffic is tough to deal with. A lot of these women are at their breaking point already. As for my after-school business? That would dry up completely. I can't move all of those kids to Saturdays. There aren't enough hours in the day, or riding instructors and ponies, for that matter. I'm finding myself in a more difficult position than I think either of us imagined when we entered into this agreement." My words surprised me, tripping so easily off of my tongue. You'd have thought it was a rehearsed speech, practiced in front of a mirror with a set of notecards.

Heather looked at her fingernails. I looked behind me, out the window at the busy barn below, the afternoon lessons and rides exploding into life. It was a gesture for her to do the same, to see the evidence in front of her eyes. We weren't going anywhere. We didn't have to.

"Are you going to back out of the deal?" she asked finally. "Or are you just asking for an extension to the six-month grace period?"

Grace, I thought. *How funny.* "An extension," I said, because I didn't want to give her the bad news just yet. "For now."

Heather nodded. Her face was shrewd. She knew. "For now," she sighed, gathering her bag. "Let me know."

Chapter Nine

MARK WAS WALKING down the aisle alone when I came downstairs, trailing Heather's heavy, high-heeled tread down the wooden steps. I waved her off and turned to see he was waiting for me, a tentative smile on his tanned face. That smile gave me a surprising lift of spirits.

"Did you have a good talk with Louise?" I asked impersonally, trying to push aside the heady feeling he gave me. I was too busy for feelings. I didn't have time right now for sweet little Mark, photographer of families and producer of magical memories, trainer of princess ponies and knights' chargers, apple of young grooms' and middle-aged trainers' eyes. I had a show barn to save, and we show people were ruthless, moving forward at a hand-gallop with our eyes on the prize table. We did not have time for romance with middle-aged men who still believed in fairy tales.

But Mark didn't really know me, and he didn't know any of that, and his smile had widened the moment I'd begun speaking to him. It was possible he wanted to talk to me as much as I wanted to talk to him, a thought that left me momentarily off-balance, suddenly undecided about that whole single-minded commitment to my career/embracing spinsterhood thing.

"I *did* have a good talk," he announced brightly. "Between yesterday and today I found myself in possession of a horse I don't quite know what to do with, and she's going to take him on, make him into a well-behaved citizen for me... if that's possible." He chuckled a little, rolling his eyes. "He's a little bit of a challenge."

I raised my eyebrows, all thoughts of romance out the window. "This challenge of yours is coming *here?* What kind of bronco are you sending to my barn? Louise promised me quiet, respectful horses who wouldn't make any trouble."

"Oh—no, no, no, he's not so bad, not really, not *bad* bad." Mark back-pedaled as quickly as his tongue could take him, nearly stumbling over the words. "He's just not Main Street-ready. He has some... some bad habits. He just needs a little straightening out "

Hmmph. I'd heard that before. People had sent me outlaws who bit, kicked and flipped over, assuring me only, with those famous last words: *he has some bad habits.* "Sounds great," I lied blandly. I turned around, started heading down the aisle, though I wanted to keep talking to him about anything except his stupid bad-habit horse. I wanted to talk to him about... oh, anything! What did people discuss when they weren't talking horses? The weather, the economy, the new tapas bar opening downtown? My mind was a blank, and that meant I needed to get the hell out of there before he realized I was nothing beyond my business, a walking bore, all show horses and riding lessons, all the time. "See you around, I hope," I said over my shoulder, looking back at him because I simply couldn't help it, and then hating myself for doing so.

But Mark was following me. He was following me! Right behind me, an eager look on his rather chiseled features. Did I really think his features were chiseled? His jaw very strong, his cheekbones rather impressive, his nose positively patrician, his forehead slanted and his dark hairline just an inch or two higher than it probably had been a few years ago? I ignored the thumping of my heart in my chest. None of this meant *anything.* I was getting all worked up because of some hormone surge, and he was was just trying to butter me up because he knew I was the type who would kick his rotten horse out if he caused any problems. This was all about Mark the theme park professional getting saddled with a horse he couldn't keep at his fairy-tale barn, nothing more.

I was going to put him out of my mind, and only think about the evening lessons. I had to assign horses for the six and seven o'clock lessons in time for Margaret and Anna to make their game plans for who would need to be groomed and tacked, who would be handled by the students, and when hay and grain could go out. On nights like this, when we were slammed with back-to-back group lessons, I liked to push grain until after lessons so that no jealous horses tore down the cross-ties or misbehaved during a lesson because they could hear other horses chowing down on their dinners. But that meant someone, usually Margaret, started haying and watering early, getting it all done so that we could just dump grain and head out for the night, instead of staying late getting it all done after lessons. The balance of horse care, lessons and training was really starting to become a problem. If I could find the budget, I needed to hire someone else. Or maybe, I thought, truly getting into the problem and forgetting Mark completely, I could get some of the older girls as part-time working students? Lizzie Standwell would be *perfect...*

I went into the school tack room to check the white board where lessons and horses were written out for the grooms. The board was next to the doorway, and I nearly tripped over Mark, who was close on my heels, when I turned around.

"Mark!"

"Sorry!" he burst out, stumbling backwards. "Sorry about that."

"Good heavens, what's the problem? Is this still about the new horse? He can come, Mark." I uncapped a marker and tapped it thoughtfully on the board, trying to decide if I should put Mary Carson on Bluebeard or Splash in her semi-private lesson with Lizzie. Both horses were forward, challenging rides. Mary was capable, but timid. Splash was the least likely to give her trouble. "If he's that difficult I'll just ask Louise to work him before the kids get here in the afternoon."

I wrote *Splash* under Mary's name and assigned Bluebeard to Lizzie, who liked a challenge and wouldn't mind wrestling the big roan Thoroughbred around in the outside ring. Now that I'd reclaimed the arena with Ivor, I was going to send all my more accomplished students out to get the horses used to it again. Lizzie, in particular, could get any of the horses through a spook and back into a working mindset.

Lizzie, I thought again, would be the perfect working student. Sixteen, aggressively ambitious, anxious to buy her own horse but unable to afford the price-tag of a made jumper. She'd been thinking about buying an off-track Thoroughbred, but board was still a little out of her reach. I could give her a break in board and help her find a horse she could train—

"I guess I'll be going, then."

I turned. Mark was still standing just behind me, his expression rather strained, his jaw tight. When I met his eyes, he held my gaze a moment, and the feeling he was trying to hide there was suddenly right in front of me.

We looked at each other for a long moment, and I could think of nothing else but him. I felt like there were secrets between us that were going to detach from our tongues and come free, floating towards one another and colliding, and I thought, wildly, *I have someone to talk to.* My lips twitched, heavy words pushing against them. Then, slowly, the world outside began to intrude again: the clock on the wall behind me ticking towards the next lesson, the horses neighing in a conveyor belt crescendo as someone walked down the aisle, a potential bearer of hay or grain or sweets. The whinnies grew closer—five stalls away, four, three.

"Someone's coming," I said softly.

He blinked like a person waking from a strange dream. "I should go."

He took a step past me and I reached out, grabbed his arm. He was all muscle beneath his blue cotton shirt and I was surprised to realize he was strong, despite his soft-looking life—he was still a man who could stack hay bales and push stubborn draft horses between carriage shafts and hold up a platter-sized hoof while its giant owner wriggled and shimmied and demanded to put it down. Like me, I realized, he could do anything tough except confidently manage human relationships.

"When's your next day off?" I asked, knowing the theme park people, even the professional-level ones, lived college-student lives, expected to work all hours and all days.

He looked up at me, confused. "Friday," he replied. "Friday and Saturday."

"Today's Tuesday?"

He nodded. "I have to get back for the evening carriage rides," he said regretfully. He looked at the board behind me, then flicked his gray-blue eyes back to me. "And it looks like you're busy until late, too."

"Just call me Friday," I said. "I have lessons in the evening. Then we'll get coffee. Drinks. Something."

Mark's eyes brightened, and a smile cut across the worried lines of his face. "I will," he promised, his voice warm. "I'll call you."

I squeezed his arm once, then let go, and he paused for a long moment, eyes on mine, before he turned and left the tack room, his hand already reaching into his pocket for his keys.

"Well," Anna said from behind me, where she'd been perched, unseen, on a tack trunk, for Lord only knew how long. Max trembled eagerly in her arms, dying to escape her and leap up against my legs, scrabbling for a kiss hello. "That was unexpected."

I shook my head at her. "That's pretty rich, coming from you," I said with a grin, and Anna blushed until we both laughed, delighted at how surprising and out of character we'd both begun behaving.

All evening, I thought about Mark, Mark's horses, Mark's barn. I was curious about how they worked, especially those evening carriage rides he'd mentioned, and I wouldn't mind finding out just what he considered a quiet horse for that sort of work—the sort of horse he *wasn't* sending to the barn. After the seven o'clock lessons were done, I left the girls to it, put Max in the bathroom, and headed for my truck. I'd go over alone and take a look at the horses in action. There was no harm in it, I told myself. I could always learn something about how horses and the general public mixed, something that I could bring back to my own business as I looked for ways to invite more people into my barn.

The ambitious little storm that had begun rumbling in mid-afternoon had finally broken over the farm late in the evening, rumbling and threatening before finally pushing through with a few exciting moments of torrential rain and blinding lightning. Now the humid sunset left behind was a lurid watercolor of yellow, purple and blue as I walked through Fort Wilderness's puddled parking lot. It was a vast pavement of minivans and rental cars and pick-ups with empty cargo trailers hitched to their rears. At the Fort, a security guard informed me at the front gate, you left your car behind during your vacation, the better to foster the illusion of disappearing into the frontier. The caveat to this was that most people didn't want to walk around the place as if they were living on the frontier, especially after walking miles in a theme park all day, so resort buses rolled by endlessly, ferrying guests to the theme parks and back again.

The buses discharged the returning guests in tired, sticky hordes, to stumble through the dark paths back to their cabins and campers and comfort stations with running water and air conditioning, to shower and sleep and do it all over again the next day. I had to hop on one of these buses to get back to the stables, so I hoofed it over to the bus stop, a cavernous structure made of brown-painted logs, and found an unoccupied bench a few feet away from the gangs of sweaty families with their mouse ears and their princess dresses and their pirate swords. I wasn't ready to throw myself in with their lot just yet.

There was a chirpy frontier tune playing from invisible speakers somewhere in the thicket of palmettos between the vast covered bus stop and the blacktop of the parking lot, leaping from *Oh Susanna* to *Dixie* to *Home on the Range* every few choruses. The children fussed, and the parents argued, and the grandmothers injected cutting comments every few minutes. A few minutes went by with this discordant soundtrack jangling in my ears, and I finally changed my mind. I wasn't going to ride that bus all the way back to Mark's barn. I pulled out my phone as I went back to my truck.

The carriage rides, I learned with a quick web search, were available at a nearby resort—this one themed to old New Orleans. It was just a few minutes away, and promised no bus rides between me and the carriage route. I decided to go for it. Maybe I'd just see the horses go by, and that would satisfy whatever this weird craving was, this need to see Mark's world in action.

But the parking lot at Port Orleans Resort seemed too quiet after the constant traffic back at the Fort. I had to park some distance from the hotel's front entrance, and though I could see the lights of the portico, it didn't seem like many people were out front. Maybe there wouldn't be any carriage rides here tonight after all. I started walking up anyway, then paused a little distance away, leaning against an oak tree, spying on the scene ahead. I spotted another bus stop, and more tired families straggling away from it. A tinkling ragtime tune emanated from another hidden speaker somewhere down in the palmettos.

Then I heard the unmistakeable ring of hooves on pavement behind me.

I turned. A big dark Clydesdale with shining white feathers, pulling a white open carriage, was making his way up the resort's main drive. The horse had reflective bands on his forelegs and the carriage had a blinking red light on the fenders, but otherwise the scene could have come straight out of the nineteenth century. Suddenly it all worked, despite the bus-stop and the endless lurching buses and the tired toddlers and the bickering parents. Under the street-lights shaped like gas lanterns, as the unseen jazz band played away, I could fall into the illusions Mark worked so hard to create every day, and it was breathtakingly beautiful.

The Clydesdale walked past me and the driver turned the horse towards the lobby's portico up ahead, giving me a slow nod as she went. I thought about following the horse and carriage up to the lobby entrance, where I could see a cheerful porch lit up by more faux gas lamps, and valets dressed in striped shirts and broad-brimmed hats busily opening doors and slinging luggage around, sending smiling, fresh new families on their way to the lobby. I wanted to see more of what this little terrarium of a world was like, but something held me back. Maybe it was just that this was Mark's world, and I didn't want to get caught snooping around his turf, if by some chance he should be here. Or maybe it was the pleasant little fantasy of letting Mark show all of this to me, and discovering it through his eyes. Or maybe, just maybe, it was the curl of jealousy and the quickened heartbeat that comes with a challenge—right here in my own neighborhood, Mark was *succeeding*. He was taking these tourists and putting them on horses for trails, or behind horses on carriage rides, and they were paying a premium for it. I wanted to know how he was managing it. I wanted to do it, too, in my own fashion.

I climbed back into my truck and drove home, through the dark pine woods that surrounded the resort and the farm, emerging within a few minutes onto my county road where the subdivisions and country clubs and timeshares and vacation homes slanted down to the newly poured sidewalks. The median was now lined with expensive palm trees. Two miles of sleek concrete and date palms and skinny Tuscan pines and then I was turning at my farm's sign, glinting in the headlights: Seabreeze Equestrian Center. I clicked the button on the remote clipped to the sun-visor and waited as the gates slowly parted to admit my truck. This was *my* world, curated by *me*. There, through the oak trees, was the porch light of my little house. There, further on, was the massive structure of my barn and covered arena, dimly lit by the nighttime lamps. My arenas to my left, white streaks of right angles that were jump standards and poles, ghostly in the darkness. Lightning, high in a faraway thunderhead, suddenly lit up the night and I saw it all at once in one electric-blue flash: my own little terrarium, my own little dream-world, my own little theme park, captured in a single snapshot which flared up against my eyelids every time I closed them.

What I'd done here wasn't so different from what Mark was doing just across the road and past those houses that had once been orange trees: working hard to create an ordered counter-balance to the chaotic world around us, a place where traditions and old values still mattered. A show barn recreated the best version of yesteryear every single day, with high-tech tricks and equipment that was only meant to strengthen our connection with the old-fashioned ideals we held so dear: a balanced trot, even knees over a fence, the recognition of medium, collected, extended, and working gaits; worn leather and metal buckles everywhere.

In the house, lit by mellow golden glow from my grandfather's old lamps, I paused to straighten the throw blanket on the sofa, putting in order its pattern of galloping racehorses. There was a scrabble on the wooden door of the bathroom; I walked across the creaking floorboards and turned the latch, delivering Max from his temporary prison. He burst from the bathroom with an athletic leap, tearing around the living room in a tight circle before he came back and set his hard little paws on my knees, his brown face with its inquisitive white stripe down the middle gazing up at me with undeserved devotion. I scooped him up in my arms and he licked my face with the sort of dedication most dogs would reserve for a pilfered cheeseburger. "Ugh," I told him, pushing his pointed nose away. "You're disgusting." But I didn't put him down. I carried him over to the couch and threw myself down on it. Max wiggled loose and settled onto the cushion next to me.

"Well," I said, "here we are. This is home. For as long as we can keep it that way."

Max panted and looked at the blank television.

I thought about going to bed, but there was still lightning flickering across the dark trees outside, and it would only take one blue-white glow against my eyelids to wake me up—and once I was up, I was up. "Fine," I said, getting up to uncork a bottle of Monday-wine, even though it was only Tuesday. "We'll watch the news first."

Chapter Ten

HONEY STRETCHED HER nose towards the ground, and I let the reins slip through my fingers, giving her all the space she needed, although my seat still remained defensive. If I glanced down, I'd be able to see the toes of my boots poking out in front of my knees. This little chestnut mare might be a nice trail horse, but I was pretty sure no one had ever taken her into the arena, especially when the scary rock trucks of doom were roaring by just a scant few feet away. Sometimes a dedicated trail horse could be suspicious of civilization, and Honey had already done a double-take when presented with the green monster of the roll-top. Not that I'd asked her to jump it, mind you, just to walk up to it. "You're a little bit of a hick, aren't you?" I asked her as she cautiously touched her nose to the artificial grass covering the roll-top. "Only used to ducks and trees."

I let her rub her nose on the jump for a few minutes, listening to her nostrils blowing as she inspected the false grass—how weird that must have seemed to a horse! While she came to her own conclusions about the jump, I cast my glance around, looking at the finches fluttering in the shrubs and palmettos that buffered the arena fence from the road, at a flock of white ibis nosing around in the shade of the oak trees that filled the stretch of ground between the arena and my house, at my little house itself, nestled invitingly on the other side of the farm driveway, at the cotton-ball clouds floating through the intensely blue sky, their undersides slowly turning gray as they grew too thick to allow sunshine to pass through them. A tiny breeze ruffled at a lock of hair that had fallen loose from my helmet and brushed alongside my cheek. "Rain in about two hours," I forecast, peering to the west, where past that line of distant cypress and pine, past the theme parks the trees hid from view, past the subsequent swamps and suburbs and sundry roads, the Gulf seabreeze was whistling onshore, stirring up the humid air and driving it upwards into storm clouds.

A rock truck grumbled its way past in the southbound lane, removed from us by two lanes and a wide grassy median, and Honey didn't flick an ear. *Good start,* I thought. "Let's see what happens when one goes right past your eyeball," I suggested. "Should be anytime now." I picked up the reins again, to move her away from the roll-top and back into motion along the rail, and Honey stuck her head out in her habitual trail-horse pose, her flat neck somewhere between racetrack pony and schooling-show hunter. I wasn't too concerned that she moved like a two-by-four with legs. With her good brain, she'd make a perfectly acceptable lower-level school horse.

Kennedy had been completely surprised when I'd asked her to tack up Honey in my close-contact saddle this morning. "Honey... the *trail* horse, Honey?" she'd asked, looking at me over my desk. The trail horses were hers to exercise during their down-time, but she always rode them in her Western saddle.

I held up the legal pad I'd been scribbling horse notes on while the grooms had been getting the morning feed done. "I think the trail horses can be repurposed as school horses with just a little schooling. But you're the one who works with them every day. What do you think?"

Kennedy took the list and ran her eyes down the names and notes besides them. "This is pretty accurate," she admitted. "Frank might be a little hard-headed to be a good kid's horse, though." She handed back the notepad and I jotted down her assessment.

"We might try him in some different bits, a martingale," I mused, doodling some options. "But he's in this afternoon's trail ride, so we'll try something out later in the week." I paused and consulted the lesson book where I kept every single horse appointment detailed in black ink. "Friday at eleven, that should work. Fills up my day. There's no trail ride that day, so please put down Remy and Honey for yourself on Friday afternoon before lessons. Give them both nice workouts in the outdoor arena if it isn't too hot. I'll have started them both out there by the end of today."

"So we're doing this?" Kennedy said skeptically. "We're turning the trail horses into lesson horses? For what? If we're moving, why do you want more students?"

"We're not moving," I'd corrected her briskly, and enjoyed the way Kennedy's mouth dropped open, the way her eyes registered perfect, unadulterated surprise.

I heard the crashing, squealing mayhem of a rock truck braking nearby and knew one was about to pull out of the construction site and into the northbound lanes of the highway. That would put the beast just feet away from the arena fence. I quickly angled Honey so that her trot would take us towards the roadway as the truck went by; I'd rather she was facing the snorting monster rather than have it take her by surprise in her rear-view mirror. My heels were deep and my lower leg was on. I was ready for anything—buck, rear, spook, or spin.

The truck belched black smoke over us before its shining red hood actually appeared from behind the scrubby oaks next to the arena. But its accelerating engine was already reaching pitches so loud it would have been impossible to carry on a conversation— even a relatively one-sided conversation with a horse. "Look at that truck," I said to Honey's pricked ears as her head came up, but they didn't swivel to catch my voice. The little mare flung on the brakes, skidding to a halt, and watched the beast roar past with her head held high, every sense on alert in case she should need to turn tail and flee the scene. I kept my hands at her withers, loops in the reins so that she didn't back up against any alarming pressure on her mouth and start a panic spiral, but as soon as the truck disappeared behind the pine forest neighboring the arena, she dropped her head and walked on, chewing at the bit as if nothing had happened.

"You're going to be okay, kid," I told her, and gave her a big pat on the neck.

Honey ducked her head and I settled back a little to let her stretch again, and that's when a colossal bang from the barn behind us sent her shooting across the ring, head straight up in the air, her gallop short and choppy like she was doing her best kangaroo impression, and all I could do was slide my hands up her neck, sit down in the saddle and dig my heels down once more.

"Sorry!" Louise called, waving from the back of an unfamiliar Clydesdale... or was this a Shire? Whatever his breed, this horse was utterly massive. Little Louise was dwarfed on him, her legs barely reaching midway down his barrel. He had a thick mane of black hair that should have flown smoothly down his neck, but currently stuck out in all directions, a river of forelock that was surely blocking his sight, and swirls of coal-colored hair rushing in cowlicks across his muscled body. Not to mention those white feathers, although this guy's ankles could use a good scrubbing. His hind feathers, in particular, were yellowed and in dire need of purple shampoo.

The beast snorted at the arena gate as Louise pulled him up, her thin reins looking woefully insufficient to contain a horse of his size. It seemed like a horse with a neck that huge should at least go in doublewide reins. I thought he could snap those laced hunter reins with a single jerk of his head. He pranced a little, platter-sized hooves fairly shaking the ground. "Sorry," she repeated. "He kicked the barn wall on the way out."

"You're riding in here?" I asked, trying to keep the dismay out of my voice.

"We'd agreed this was the best place for me to school, since you hardly use this arena," Louise pointed out, a slight edge to her tone, the observation *and yet here you are* implied but not spoken. She gave the Shire horse a nudge to get him closer to the gate, even though it was very clear she was never going to be able to reach down and get it open from such a height.

"That's true," I remembered. And just a few days ago, that had seemed like the perfect arrangement. Things changed quickly around here. For one thing, where the hell had this elephant-horse come from? "Well, I was just wrapping up, anyway."

"Maybe you could get the gate for me?" Louise smiled winningly.

One thing Honey's long history as a trail horse was good for: she knew how to side-pass to a gate and stand still while her rider bent over and unlatched it. I nudged her to the right, the gate in my left hand, and opened it up with a flourish for Louise and her big horse. They came through in a hurry, with just an inch to spare, and I snatched back my hand in case the Shire's massive hip caught the gate and smashed my fingers.

"I don't recognize that horse," I called after them, pushing Honey through the open gate and pulling it shut after us. "When did he come in?"

"Early this morning," Louise said airily. "I think you were in your office. I'm surprised you didn't hear anything!"

I was, too. Odd. I had a sudden memory of Max barking in the wee hours, waking me briefly. Was Louise lying to me? I didn't know Max anywhere near well enough to guess at what made the terrier bark, but I would guess a horse trailer lumbering by would do it, and there definitely hadn't been an arrival since I'd come down to the barn at seven-thirty this morning. But since Louise fed and cared for her own horses, and she was isolated at the end of the barn aisle, it was possible she'd gotten in a horse and no one had even realized it.

"This is the horse Mark wanted you to take," I realized. *He just needs a little straightening out,* Mark had said, clearly omitting what he really thought about the beast. Now I could see, as the Shire jabbed impatiently at the bit and pawed with first one massive hoof and then the other, that he needed more than a little straightening out. He needed a Come-to-Jesus, and soon. Louise was gripping the reins like they were ribbons attached to eggshells, and from her posture alone, I knew she wasn't the trainer for the job. Louise specialized in finding quiet, sensible horses for entertainment, and giving them the skills they needed to perform. She wasn't the person you sent your bad apples for correction.

I left her in the arena, because nothing good could come of trying to teach Honey about civilized life with that ill-manned oaf plunging around, tossing his head and occasionally stopping stock-still, flapping his face from side to side and swishing his tail while Louise kicked and clucked and cajoled to no avail. "Short day for you, my dear," I told Honey as we walked away from them. "But you did so well, I'm not worried about it."

I rode right into the barn aisle, rather than taking her down to the covered walkway and dismounting, then entering through the center aisle where the wash-racks were. Ordinarily I'd follow strict barn protocol, but there were no kids around to corrupt with my bad behavior, and I was curious about Louise's off-handed "he kicked the barn wall," explanation for that almighty bang that had spooked both Honey and me. Kennedy and Anna were there already, standing with hands on hips and brooding expressions. I pulled her up alongside Anna with a simple shift in my seat, silently congratulating the mare when she halted quietly. "What have we got?"

Anna stood back and pointed. My jaw dropped. A horse had done that? A *horse?*

"*Shit.*"

Louise didn't seem to be too put out by the giant hole her psycho Shire had put in the front of his (my) stall, even when I suggested to her that this was not the kind of horse she'd told me she'd be putting in my barn when we'd first come to an agreement. By the time she'd brought the monster in, sweating and red-faced (Louise, not the horse, as the horse did not seem the least put out by the attempt she'd made to get him working), Margaret had begun tackling the hole with her typically dour get-er-done spirit, nails in her mouth and a grim expression on her face as she hammered out the damaged boards and replaced them with some raw-looking lumber she'd found stacked in the hay barn. I watched her for a little while, thinking how I really didn't know what I'd do without Margaret; if I ever did move to a faraway town in a mythical horse country, I'd have to insist Margaret come too or I'd be stuck hiring a succession of burly men to take on all the tasks she did without even being asked.

"So, uh, this horse is kind of a giant," I said, watching Louise struggle to get him untacked without resorting to a step stool.

"He is," she panted. "But this is what Mark got stuck with, and now I have to bail him out."

"How did Mark end up with such a—" I eyeballed the huge horse, who eyeballed me right back with an expression of pure dislike. "With a Shire?" I finished, swallowing all the more appropriate descriptions I could have used: *with such a completely unsuitable horse, with such a brat, with such a total bastard.*

"Sponsors provide horses sometimes, or upper management acquires one because they think it's pretty, and he winds up with a random horse that isn't even close to ready for the program. Once it was a three-year-old Gypsy Vanner colt, halter-broke and nothing more. He'd never even been on long lines. I think Mark ended up telling them a story about Gypsy horses not being ready to ride or drive until they were five years old, then he sent it to me in Ocala and I spent two years getting him ready for parade life. It's just part of the deal when you work for a non-horsey company. The bosses can get bad ideas and no one is high up enough to stop them." Louise surveyed the Shire, who barely seemed to have broken a sweat despite the hot sun. She, on the other hand, was red-faced and dripping. There was a conclusion to be drawn from this.

But Louise seemed confident the first session had gone well, despite evidence to the contrary. "I think he'll be fine. He just needs to understand what *go* means. He has *whoa* down pat, believe me."

"That's surprising, judging by the hole in the front of his stall," I said drily. "It's not usually the lazy ones that destroy barns."

Louise laughed, which annoyed me. I hadn't told her a joke, I'd given her an opportunity to apologize to me. "That was actually him saying he didn't want to leave his stall. So yeah, getting him moving is going to be our problem. Princesses can't wear spurs and they definitely can't carry dressage whips. That's always one of my most interesting problems with the horses who are going to be under saddle... everything I do has to be something a non-rider in a gown and sequined shoes can do."

Louise's problems were too weird to even consider. For that matter, so were Mark's. I pushed away from the concrete wall of the wash-rack, ready to move on with my day. Behind me, Max strained at the lunge line attaching him to the tack room door, determined to join me wherever my travels took me. I paused to give him a head-scratch and a cookie from my pocket. "After Ivor, we'll go back to the house for lunch," I told him.

The clock above the tack room door pointed to eleven-thirty. I'd had Ivor on the board to be tacked and ready now, but he was still in his stall, nosing around for whatever was left of his breakfast hay. I pursed my lips at him. I had one constant rule from my grooms: I didn't care who tacked up my horses, but I *did* need my horses tacked up on time, or I'd never get through everyone who needed schooled that day. Finding Ivor untacked was a pretty serious offense around here.

I wandered the aisles, looking for someone to scold, but I didn't see anyone besides Margaret, hammering away at the stall near the quiet west end of the barn, and Louise, hosing off her Shire while he wiggled and wormed and did everything he could to avoid being a good boy. One massive hoof pawed the air dangerously close to her hand holding the hose, and I heard her gasp and jump back. *Please don't get killed,* I thought. Louise had seemed like a model boarder for the first few days, full of fun and practicality—a nice mix I could get behind—but this surprise Shire of doom was just not what I had come to expect in our brief acquaintance.

As I approached the feed room I heard arguing voices, and they were heated enough to make me lean back against the wall instead of barging in to demand my employees get back to work. Anna sounded like she'd swallowed one of those nails Margaret was pinching between her thin lips. I almost didn't recognize her voice, which was always so soft and kind, in this razor-sharp tone.

"You can't just act like this doesn't affect me, not now. The barn is full, there's students here at all hours, even if we weren't—*involved* —you can't just abandon me now. I need you here."

I nearly clapped my hand over my own mouth to stop my sharp inhale of breath from giving me away. Kennedy was really going to quit, right now? And she'd gone to Anna not as her girlfriend, but as her employee, to tell her? I might not be veteran of many human relationships, but even I knew this was a very bad idea.

"It's not like I'd be leaving you and going off across the country," Kennedy said, tone defensive. "We are talking about a couple of miles away. Honestly, I might not even do it. I just thought it would be a cool experience and that Louise could give me a reference. I just don't think I'm cut out to do pony hunters for the rest of my career, Anna! It doesn't give me any fulfillment. I love seeing people have fun on horseback and hunters is just... hunters is just so sad and boring. Half these kids are going to quit riding once they start competing because the competition is so mean, and the other half are going to *be* the mean ones causing all the trouble. I was wrong to come back to this. I need out."

"I think you're taking yourself a little too seriously." Anna snapped cuttingly. "They're children on ponies. You're teaching them to post the trot and not get run away with at the slowest canter possible. When you're taking them to Pony Finals, you can start getting high and mighty about morals, but now's really not the time. And I need you here," she went on, her tone softening unexpectedly. "I was so lonely. Ever since Grace made me barn manager, she leaves me alone to do my own thing, and Margaret barely talks to me, and Tom left, and you're all I've got..." I heard a catch in her voice and I bit my lip. I hadn't known she was so unhappy.

"I wouldn't be going anywhere, Anna, I just wouldn't work here during the day. I'd be here every night with you."

I hadn't known that either! So Kennedy was planning on moving in? To Anna's little loft above the barn? That would be very cozy. Also, I thought with a businesslike turn of thought that was more in character for me than I would generally care to admit, a second person living up there was not part of Anna's compensation package at all. That studio was open for a potential working student or assistant manager—which it sounded like Anna desperately needed.

"It won't be the same." Anna sniffed. "And," she said after a long pause, seemingly having gotten herself back together again, "totally aside from my feelings, there's still the issue that you're a pair of hands that we need here, and I don't know how to replace you when there's still a chance we could be leaving town. So no, you can't go and expect things to be the same, in *any* capacity, because you'll have completely screwed me over. I don't think you thought this through at all, Kennedy. You didn't consider anyone but yourself."

Kennedy didn't have a reply to that, and I wasn't surprised. Who could win an argument when her girlfriend was clearly holding all the cards? Anna was right: Kennedy's position as groom/trainer/riding instructor was hard to fill on a good day, and would be impossible without knowing for sure where the barn would be in six months. Just because I'd intimated to them that we would be staying on didn't mean Anna believed it to be true. I came up with lots of pronouncements that I cheerfully backed down on all the time.

The silence was becoming worrisome; I quietly retreated a few steps, then came around the corner with purposeful strides, my boots ringing on the pavement, as if I'd just arrived on the scene. "I need Ivor tacked up immediately, girls!" I announced, walking right past the feed room door without so much as a glance inside. If there were tears to clean up, I didn't need to observe it and make things worse for them.

I went into the school tack room for a Diet Coke and a cooling breath of air conditioning, smiling benevolently when Kennedy rushed past the half-open door with my close contact in her arms and Ivor's padded bridle over her shoulder. I could hear Ivor's steps in the aisle, presumably being led by Anna to the wash-rack. They worked really well together, a true team. No wonder Anna didn't want Kennedy rushing off for another job.

I looked down at the lesson book open on the tack room desk, all those names of little girls and their ponies clustered around the four and five o'clock hours. Those were Kennedy's lessons. She had eight kids in total riding with her tonight, bringing in a pretty sum for my accounts. It wouldn't just be a massive ding in Anna's barn schedule if our groom and instructor left in search of circus horse dreams. It would be a hit in the bank account. Right when I wanted to turn down a massive offer from developers.

"Impeccable timing, Kennedy," I muttered, tapping the lesson book with one finger.

But then again, Kennedy's timing always seemed terrible, and still somehow turned into something good and unexpected for the barn. Just look at the trail riding business—that had stemmed from her disastrous arrival as some sort of trail-horse messiah, and although the good times for the venture hadn't lasted, it had gotten the farm through some pretty rough months. Plus, it had opened up some new landscapes for both me and my students, after years of sticking to the sandbox and steadfastly ignoring the charms of riding out in the wilderness that still sprawled behind the equestrian center.

Now Kennedy's enthusiasm had brought Louise and her cavalcade of parade horses into my barn, and if the allure of a new lifestyle was drawing Kennedy's interest away from my staid line-up of lessons, ponies and lunge lines, I had to believe there was a good reason for our troubles waiting at the bottom of all this. The question was, what could it possibly be? Maybe we should teach the trail horses to be vaulting horses instead? Was there any potential in a vaulting team? I had pulled out my phone to look up *Florida horse vaulting competition* when the screen suddenly shifted from browser to black in my hands. A name and number appeared, and I nearly dropped the phone on the tack room floor when I read *Mark Redford.*

Chapter Eleven

I LOOKED AT the horses in front of me, their shining ebony coats criss-crossed by gleaming patent leather. It was a strange view for me; I was more familiar with almost any other angle of a horse. Even looking up at a horse's belly after a fall would look more normal to me than the prospect of sitting behind a horse, raised up on a wagon seat.

"I still can't believe this is happening." I shook my head, clutching at the side of the padded seat as one horse shifted his weight. His body, pushing against the harness, shook the whole wagon. "I haven't been in a wagon since I was a little kid at the county fair."

Mark climbed up onto the wagon box beside me, grinning as he took the reins from the plaid-shirted woman on the ground. Her name tag read *Stacy* and she had the friendly, rather vacant expression of a Golden Retriever glued onto her face. I had a suspicion this was the preferred look for all resort and theme park employees around here. Luckily, Mark seemed to be able to turn his empty-yet-caring *how may I help you?* look on and off at will. That seemed important to me, somehow. "How can you have missed out on so many carriage rides over the years?" he asked, shaking his head at me. "All those horse shows you've been at, all those horsemen you've known, no one ever took you out behind their horse?"

If he was insinuating I'd gone on a lot of dates with horsemen, he wasn't going to get a rise out of me. "I don't exactly frequent multi-discipline horse shows," I explained. "Only a handful of shows every year would bring together jumpers and driving in one show. Devon, for example."

"Did you ever show at Devon?"

"When I was a teenager. A long time ago." As usual, I found myself regretting the reference to my age, but then again, what about it? Every line I had, from my crows-feet to the creases on either side of my nose, Mark could match. Wrinkle for wrinkle, I thought, we were just two old horse-people out on a hay-ride.

Mark shook the reins out, tickling the draft horses' backs, and the two Belgians nodded their heads obligingly before setting off into an ambling walk. I watched the slack in the harness stretch taut before releasing back, losing some tension, as the wagon first jerked forward, then eased along gently, the momentum of the wheels interacting with the horses' weight pushing against their collars.

Their hooves clip-clopped with a nursery-school rhythm on the blacktop road leading to the lakeside pine woods. As we passed the little pioneer settlement, where the campground's restaurants and shops were installed within very realistic log cabins, the resort guests stopped in their tracks, pointing and cooing with amazement. I felt myself blushing a little, but Mark smiled and nodded and waved to the gasping princesses and startled toddlers, completely in his entertainment element.

Once we passed the rustic surroundings of the settlement, with its red-painted gas lamps hanging from wooden posts, and cactus gardens surrounded by post-and-rail fencing, the pavement beneath the horses' hooves was quickly replaced by plain old grass, and we were tracking through a scrub forest of longleaf pine and palmetto thickets. The grass track was perfectly worn—just trodden enough to look old, just overgrown enough to be smooth.

"How do you get this so right?" I laughed. "Is every single thing you do pre-meditated, right down to how much pressure the grass can take?"

But Mark didn't have any idea what I was talking about until I pointed it out to him.

"You might be even better suited for themed entertainment than I am," he said with a grin. "Now that I've noticed it, I'm always going to take grass condition into consideration when I'm planning how many wagon rides to put on the schedule."

I gave him a friendly shove. "I'm definitely not suited for this. Whatever *this* is." I looked around at the skinny Florida pines towering above us, the chestnut Belgians lumbering along the green road before us, and the blue sky arching over it all, a few lazy white clouds showing us their shadowy gray bottoms as they floated aimlessly by on the seabreeze.

"This is my work," Mark said. "To make you feel like you're in another world. Or at least another time. Is it working?"

"It's working," I assured him, and I gripped the edge of the bench beneath me and watched the horses' hindquarters moving in their familiar rhythm. As time went by, though, I found I was more conscious of Mark's leg alongside mine than of the beautiful summer day preening all around me.

Back at the barn, it was the suspicious Jo who silently took the horses' reins while Mark climbed down from the box and then helped me back to solid ground. I missed vacant, pleasant Stacy, but she must have gone on lunch break or something. I could feel the dislike emanating from Jo in angry waves as she led the team into the wide barn aisle, the wagon wheels creaking behind them. I watched her go, her slim body fierce in her tight jeans and blue plaid shirt, dark hair in a braid down her back, the perfectly-cast barn hand for a frontier-themed stable, and wondered just what her status with Mark was. Probably nothing, I told myself, because he was her boss, and there was no way a company of this size would allow relationships between staff and management. The bigger the corporation, the more strict the rules, the more segregated the employees were by title and salary. So maybe she had a crush on him, but that was nothing I could help, and nothing I should be ashamed of, since I wasn't getting in the way of anything real, of anything that had a chance of becoming real.

Then again, she looked so *mean* when she glared at me. She made me nervous, a nervousness I was really too old to feel from a girl of her age.

I glanced at Mark to see if he'd caught the silent exchange of glares, but he had already turned away from the barn and was surveying the rest of the property, his fiefdom of horses and props. In corrals a few dozen feet away, the white ponies who pulled Cinderella's glass coach in some of the resort's more opulent weddings were pulling at the hay in their mangers. A few little girls leaned against the fence rails, cooing and squealing and trying to convince the ponies to abandon their snacking in favor of pats and kisses.

"That's a non-starter," I said with a grin, and Mark laughed.

"I actually get complaints about how 'unfriendly' the ponies are." Mark used air quotes to emphasize *unfriendly*. "At our monthly manager meetings, my comment cards are always the ones that get the most laughs. *Horse sneezed on my child* is another one I get a lot. The food and beverage managers especially like that one."

"You should sell pony food from dispensers, the way city parks sell fish food," I suggested. "You'd save a fortune on hay if the kids just tossed them alfalfa pellets all day long."

"That's genius! You have upper management written all over you."

"How dare you," I teased. "As if I'd ever sell out and work for The Man. Or The Mouse, as the case may be."

Mark gave me a considering look. "I have a hard time imagining you working for anyone," he observed. "You're very much your own master."

"That's the truth. I haven't had a boss in more than two decades." *Ugh,* again with the references to my antique status! I had to stop bringing up my age if I wanted... what? If I wanted Mark to take me on a date, buy me dinner and tell me I was beautiful? I could have slapped myself, if I wouldn't have looked so weird in public. But really, what a strange thing to want, now, after several very cheerful decades on my own. There'd been a few half-hearted attempts at relationships over the years—a fireman who had helped save the barn from a wildfire a few years ago; a hunter-jumper trainer who was banned for drug violations a few months after I told him to get lost, thus confirming my suspicions that he wasn't nearly as nice as he was pretending to be; the owner of a neighboring barn who had moved to Ocala at the first sign of urbanization, years ago. But having a man around had always felt a little like having a boss around; someone who had opinions without being asked for them was my least favorite sort of person, and that seemed to be a primary trait not only of all men, but of the relationship state itself. You had to not only *accept* someone else's opinion, you had to actually *care* what they thought. It had been so long since I'd cared what another person thought about my business, I couldn't even remember the feeling.

I thought this might be it, though.

"I've been running my own barn for most of my career," I said now, not sure if I was showing off or just defining myself to him, a man who somehow both worked with horses for a living and yet had a corporate job and a 401K and paid vacation days. "I built the equestrian center on my grandfather's old farm. He bred horses and kept cattle and orange groves, a typical Florida farmer. I've always done show horses—all kinds, as long as they wear an English saddle. This used to be all horse country... you probably remember, if you've been here long enough."

"I've only been here ten years," Mark admitted. "Feels like my whole life, though. I moved here from Colorado."

"Colorado! I've never been anywhere out west but California. What was Colorado like?"

"Windy," he said, and shrugged. "Flat. Not really like the part you'd want to be from. Or visit."

"I imagined the Rocky Mountains," I told him, chuckling.

"I always imagined them, too," he said with a grin. "Much better than my reality."

"That's your thing then," I realized. "Your imagined world is always better than the real thing."

"Isn't it always?" A family walked past us, stroller bumping on the mulch pathway, a girl in a pink princess gown shrieking in disbelief at the presence of ponies. I felt a familiar ache on her behalf, the endless tragedy of a modern world where children and horses rarely intersected.

"I make the real thing better," I said. "People come to me to learn to ride, or because they want to own their own horse, and I make it possible for them." I turned to Mark with a sly smile. "I make dreams come true every single day, not just for a vacation."

But he didn't smile back. Instead, his face clouded. I realized my mistake instantly. "I'm sorry, that came off wrong."

"It's fine, don't be silly," he said, but his voice was distant.

"Mark," I said as he took a step away, "Mark, listen—" I put my hand around his elbow, and tugged him back to me.

Suddenly he was too close, his chest close to mine, his gray-blue eyes locked to my gaze. My lips parted without my permission, and his did the same.

"What you do is important," I murmured. "I'm sorry."

He kissed me, lips gentle and undemanding, and there was a scant second of confusion and elation before I was returning the favor.

The afternoon rides and lessons passed by me in a blur, as if I was walking in slow-motion while everything else was sped up ten times. I gave Gayle a jumping lesson, taught a new adult student named Arlene how to achieve a walk-canter transition, and took on the Wednesday evening teenager class that had recently graduated from Kennedy's care to my more advanced curriculum. I thanked Margaret for the excellent job fixing the Shire horse's stall, while the big horse inside glowered at me through the bars. I fired up the Gator and pulled down the evening bales from the hay barn while Kennedy and Anna finished cleaning up the last of the lesson horses, and, steady on auto-pilot, turned out the handful of horses who went out all night, sliding open their doors and strapping on their halters without ever really noticing what I was doing. And if anyone noticed I was sleepwalking through my work, they didn't say anything.

The sun had set by the time we were finished, a cloudless late afternoon ending in a lackluster finish of pale yellows and dark azures. A low grumble off to the east hinted at storms which had passed us by. Venus made a half-hearted attempt at evening star duties before giving up and dropping below the horizon. She was already gone as I climbed the steps to the creaking terrace where the doors to my office and Anna's apartments were, and settled down in a lawn chair overlooking the arenas, Max curled gratefully against my chest. There was just enough breeze up here to keep the mosquitoes at bay, and I tucked my short hair behind my ears to stop flyaway wisps from fluttering and tickling at my cheeks. I'd slapped myself more than once thinking my own locks of hair were bloodsuckers.

Only a moment passed before there were footsteps behind me, and then Anna was there, settling into the chair next to me.

"You must be tired," I said. "Don't feel like you have to keep me company."

"What about you? I thought you must be exhausted all afternoon, you were so distant."

Max strained to see Anna, leaning over my arm and scrabbling his claws against me until I winced, so I set him down on the patio. He wiggled over to her, his short tail shivering madly. Anna leaned down and rubbed his ears. "I really like this dog," she said. "I'm glad you got him, but now I'm tempted to get one too. Have you killed the no-dogs-allowed policy?"

I shrugged. "What the hell. As long as it doesn't chase the horses or bark at the clients. Life's too short to fill it with rules."

Anna laughed. "Now I think you're getting sick. You love rules."

"I'm just getting too old to care. Those are the stages of life: first you break the rules, then you make the rules, then you realize rules are ridiculous."

"The anarchy of middle-age," Anna suggested. "Perhaps it's not well-documented."

"Is that what this is? Am I still middle-aged?"

"I think you're middle-aged into your early seventies now," Anna said. "It's getting later all the time."

"You're going to live forever."

"Maybe." Anna considered the idea, her nose still buried in Max's fawn-colored forehead. "I could probably find a way to fill forever up. There are always more horses to ride."

"Most people say they wouldn't want to live forever," I observed. "I kind of like that you're up for the challenge."

"Are you?"

I thought about it a moment. Maybe life was never easy, but it was never dull, either. "Sure, why not?"

In the paddocks to our left, a horse whinnied, then another one replied. I recognized the deep, chesty rumble of Frank. I was going to try him in a Pelham and martingale on Friday. New tack, new job, new life. The only constant is change, I thought, and that's what makes life interesting enough to go on living it, forever, whether you're a horse or a person. But I got to decide what the changes in my life were—most of them, anyway, and that was the difference between me, sprawled up here on the ledge, and Frank, sulking down in the paddock. I decided to tell Anna that I'd made up my mind.

"So, we're absolutely not leaving," I said smoothly. "We're expanding the lesson program and we're going to turn all the kids that show up in these resort neighborhoods into pony kids. We're going to have camps that match up with school vacations from all over the country. We're going to offer evening rides and movies so parents can have date nights on their vacations. That's just the beginning. We're going to do everything it takes to stay part of the community, whatever this community is turning into. We're going to outsmart the developers at their own game."

Anna was silent. I looked over and saw her staring at me, her mouth open.

"What?" I snapped, irritated.

"I just... you should hear yourself when you're determined about something. You're scary."

"Scary gets more attention when you're a woman."

"Are you sure? The trail ride business was supposed to be a big shift from what everyone else was doing. And it didn't stick."

"It didn't *work*," I corrected her. "But that's because it was half-baked from the beginning. We should have seen that. It doesn't create a lasting business. Convention people come and go, they never come back. But next door?" I waved my hand towards the construction site, unseen in the darkness. "Vacation homes? They keep coming back. Sometimes they even stay full-time. And here's the part we both forgot when we argued about this the other day. Yeah, they're coming here for the theme parks. But kids love horses, Anna. They just do. They can go and look at them in the parades or sit behind them on those carriage rides, but here? They can really make those dreams come true."

Anna burst into delighted laughter. "That's true, Grace. God. That's so true. What a way to sell riding lessons. *Is your little princess's dream to watch a horse go prancing by, or to be the princess on the horse?* Done. Sold." She glanced at me. "Is that what's been on your mind all afternoon?"

It was my turn to laugh. "Oh god, I wish it was." That would have been so much simpler than the reality.

I waited for Anna to say something else, to change the subject to herself, to tell me about Kennedy and her wandering eyes, always catching a glimpse of something shinier in the distance. But the minutes ticked away with only the rising sound of peepers chorusing in the forest behind the barn, and an occasional jingle from Max's tags as he sniffed around the edges of the patio, poking his nose under the railings, chasing the scents of long-gone raccoons and barn cats. I began to wonder if Anna and Kennedy had worked it all out after I'd gone over to Mark's barn. Maybe the crisis was over before it had started.

Then Anna spoke up, her voice soft and distant. "Will the trail rides stay after all?"

"In some capacity," I said. "I haven't worked out what it will look like. But they're going on hiatus after the last convention group, either way. I may start them up again this winter, when the development next door opens."

I glanced over at her shadowy face, but her expression was hidden beneath a curtain of long mussed hair. I thought of saying something reassuring, then decided against it. This crisis with Kennedy was Anna's battle to fight. If she wanted my help, she would tell me. "It's almost time for the fireworks," I said instead.

"That's how late the sunset has gotten."

"There—" Anna pointed, and I looked just in time to catch the first rainbow of explosions pop over the distant western tree line.

I didn't often sit up here and watch all of the fireworks—it was a really long show, and this late at night, I was more interested in the contents of my freezer and how quickly they could be transformed into a full plate on my table—but tonight I sat beside Anna, clutching Max when he leapt back into my lap and leaned against my chest, confused by the constant crackling and rumbling in the air, and watched every single starburst.

Chapter Twelve

IF I EXPECTED Kennedy to come straight out and tell me she was trying to get a job with Mark, I was to be disappointed. She must not have been terribly confident in her plan, or I suspected she would have simply stomped out of the barn announcing that she'd had enough of my boring show barn. Subtlety was not her strong suit.

Still, her behavior towards me had shifted. Dramatic Kennedy, the princess of the dinner show, had to let me know with a thousand little signs and symbols how very angry and disappointed she had decided to be. Requests for extra training rides were met with a sigh, queries about the progress of young students were answered with a few perfunctory words: *fine, great, crap.* After she snorted at my instructions for prepping horses later that evening, I washed my hands of her and went to ride Ivor in the jumping ring without another word. I wasn't about to be provoked into firing her, and I knew Kennedy was in such a self-destructive mood that getting ordered off the property would delight her. Then, she wouldn't have to admit she wanted to quit the job she'd begged me to give her.

She perked up that afternoon, though. There was a trail ride in mid-afternoon, one of the last of the summer, and she was in a hustle to be ready early. I watched her prep with interest, noticing for the first time the elements of her entertainment background. Kennedy really was trying to turn this into an ultra-themed event, not far at all from the way Mark's barn was operated. The bright blue yoked western shirt came out of the tack room on a hanger, the slate-colored breeches she'd been wearing for pony schooling were switched out for cowboy-cut jeans, and her neat, zip-up boots suddenly became Western, all tooled designs and pointed toes. The horses were groomed and tacked up, six in all, and I was reminded anew that while most trail barns just put horses out in any old saddle and blanket, our horses were in saddles and bridles which, while old, gleamed with cleanliness and matched in color. Their age lent a rather realistic dignity to the scene. Likewise, the saddle blankets were brightly-colored woven Navajo blankets, not the fat fleece pads, dingy with use, that I remembered buying back when we'd gotten into the business. Somewhere along the line, Kennedy had transformed my good-enough trail horse string into a themed Western adventure, complete with costumes for horse and rider.

Well, that was the princess in her, I thought resignedly, watching as she put on a brown riding helmet with leather trimming I'd never even taken note of before. She might have given up the dinner theater, but she'd done so because the place had closed down, not because Kennedy was done putting on a show.

By the time the hotel van had arrived with the day's clients, I was on a bay boarder horse named Jimmy, who needed some emergency remedial work on halts—specifically, he didn't do them without a very good reason, and those reasons so far included hauling back so hard on his face he nearly flipped over backwards. After the best fix appeared to be jumping in front of him with a lunge whip as he careened out of control around the arena, my suggestions that he needed some training rides grew more urgent.

His owner, Phoebe, was a whip-slim marketing executive trying to overcome a twenty-five year riding gap between high school and present day, and she'd been reluctant to concede that this problem was out of her control. That is, until her last ride, when she had simply refused to even try halting him. She'd chosen instead to walk, trot, canter, trot, canter, jump, and canter some more. After an hour he still wasn't ready to stop of his own accord, and she was breathless, exhausted, and finally ready to put him into twice-weekly training sessions. If nothing else, I'd been impressed with her fitness that day, and I'd told her so—electing to look away when she tottered bow-leggedly towards her Mercedes afterwards.

For today's ride on Jimmy, I'd opted to use the covered ring, both because the sun was hot and because the PVC railing around it looked less like a jumping obstacle than the jumping arena's three-board fencing. We'd been trotting around practicing halts without too many incidents—whenever I felt the need to halt and Jimmy disagreed, I could ride him ride into the rail. A little while into our workout, I heard the trail horses' hooves ring out on the pavement of the parking lot, so I rode Jimmy over to the end of the arena for a look.

Kennedy, Anna and Margaret were leading out the horses, and the cluster of waiting riders in their jeans and t-shirts were appropriately delighted. If first impressions were everything, their reactions told me they'd been given far more than they expected for their corporate credit card dollar. There were *oohs* and *aahs*, there were selfies, there was even one instance of happy tears, slipping from the crinkled eyes of a blue-jeaned young woman who flung her arms around Honey's neck and gave the chestnut mare a massive hug while Kennedy looked on, grinning.

Bringing horses to the people is a *service*, I reminded myself, reining back on Jimmy as he shifted impatiently beneath me. "At least, nice, well-trained horses—unlike you," I added aloud. Offended, Jimmy shoved his nose forward and managed to whack his nasal bone on the PVC railing. The shock sent him scuttling backwards, half-threatening to rear, and by the time I had him back under control, the riders were mounted and the horses had settled into their nose-to-tail line, heading across the parking lot and into the scrub.

I practiced halts with Jimmy and considered Kennedy's future for the next thirty minutes, reflecting occasionally that I was spending, once again, an inordinate amount of time on that girl. There was no help for it. As much as I wanted to blame Kennedy for her job-hopping, I had to admit I held a lot of responsibility for Kennedy's decision to leave her nice, air-conditioned, well-paying desk job and come back to the horse business full-time. Sure, she'd wanted to do it, but I'd enabled her, and so she'd given up any job security she could ever hope for, along with affordable health insurance and an employer-matched 401K, which probably didn't matter to her right now. But at my age, you started to wonder how much better life might be with those things. A big hunk of that decision to re-enter the equestrian life full-time had been that she loved putting on the trail rides. The ponies had helped, and the kids had been great, but for whatever reason, the ponies and the kids just weren't as fulfilling for her.

If she felt like she needed to put on a show, I had to find outlets for her or she'd take that energy somewhere else. When push came to shove, I didn't want Kennedy going anywhere, and of course if Kennedy went, that would cause a rift with Anna.

Anna. She was a whole other problem, my sweet little Anna. I nudged Jimmy into a trot and let him stretch for a few rounds of the arena, as a reward for halting without acting like a total psychopath, while my mind shifted to my barn manager. She'd gone away for a few days and the place had nearly crumbled without her around. Somewhere along the road from my working student to my tireless assistant, Anna had, in her quiet way, taken over the barn's rhythms and tamed the chaotic notes that jarred any boarding stable's days, soothing the cacophony to a smooth hum. Horses were always fed on time. Ponies were ready for lessons. Boarders found less to fight about. The lesson book was always neat and the tack was always sparkling clean. Margaret complained less, and the thin line of her lips could occasionally be seen relaxing into a grim smile.

I'd been in the horse business long enough to know a good barn manager was worth her weight in gold. Besides the very real fact that I loved Anna like a daughter and didn't want to see her disappointed in love, there was the simple, practical reality that I needed her if I was going to push this business past the comfort levels we'd reached over the years. This past year had been dicey, adding the ponies, inviting children into an adults-only world, but it had paid off. The atmosphere was noisier, but more fun. The adult riders were less stuffy and nervous, and eager to help the kids out around the barn and in the ring. Anna's calm professionalism kept us all in harmony. We were building a community, and Anna was our mayor.

So if Anna needed Kennedy to stick around to keep her happy, I had to figure out a way to keep Kennedy around.

Jimmy flattened out on the long side of the arena, sticking his nose out like a lesson pony. His strides quickened and I was distracted from my barn troubles long enough to pull him back together with a stern half-halt. I bent him towards the center of the ring and made him trot a polite figure-eight, trying not to be annoyed when he bowed his neck inward and let his shoulder drift outside. "Your entire bend is a lie," I huffed. "*Someone* missed basic circles in primary school. Mama's going to be doing some changes of rein in her next lesson."

Jimmy fluttered his nostrils in an apologetic snort, and after a few more rounds of the figure-eight, I determined his bend had become less a lie and closer to the real thing. I decided to wait until I had him perfectly balanced, then get one amazing halt and call it a day. *Not yet, inside leg, push him onto the outside rein, now balance, lift his back, there it is—*

"Whoa," I said sternly, sitting deep in the saddle, and Jimmy screeched to a halt so fast the foam flew from his bit and splattered across my thigh, leaving white flecks on my navy breeches. "That's a *good* boy," I assured him, and relaxed my right fingers enough to give him a stroke on his sweaty neck without releasing the rein too much.

Jimmy stood still for a quivering moment, then broke forward as a series of bangs came from the west end of the barn. I was disappointed he'd walked out of the halt of his own accord, but it was hard to be mad if that was his only reaction to the sudden commotion. "I suppose Louise is finally here," I said drily, but Jimmy was too busy listening to the scrapes and thuds of hooves against a wooden wall to pay any attention to me.

Sure enough, a few minutes later the far end of the barn discharged a black and white mass: Louise, riding that awful Shire. I was just wondering where she had been mounting up—had she dragged a stepladder into his stall?—when the monster horse took one look at the advancing outdoor arena, decided against going any closer to the place where work happened, and made a plunging, spinning pirouette which quickly transmuted into a flat-out gallop. I reined back, and this time Jimmy had no issues coming to a halt. He *needed* to stop so he could concentrate on staring with all his might at the rocket ship heading for the barn.

A runaway Shire was a fearsome thing to see. Louise clearly had no desire to hit the ground from that height or velocity. She dropped onto his neck and clung there like a jockey—the size proportions seemed right, since the horse was a good eighteen hands tall and Louise was only about five and a half feet herself—and I heard enormous hooves slamming and skidding on concrete as he returned from whence he'd come.

Jimmy was so astonished he didn't know *what* to do, so he just stood still and snorted, staring back at the barn. Margaret went running past the central barn door, heading up the aisle, and a beat later so did Anna, a lead-rope trailing behind her, but then, like I was watching a colorized version of Keystone Cops, Louise and the Shire appeared going the *other* direction through the barn, and she guided him with some muscling through the central barn door and down the covered walkway to the arena where Jimmy and I were watching. She followed up this maneuvering with a series of whacks from a dressage whip. She'd already given up on her no-whip rule, then.

She doesn't really get this horse, I thought, studying the ashen expression on Louise's face as they entered the arena. But I knew who would. The queen of barn-sour horses, the savior of stall-bound Shires, was out on the trails right now.

Louise *needed* Kennedy.

Jimmy shoved through his contemplation and burst into a long-strided, head-bobbing walk which I had most definitely not asked for, so I was pushed out of my own thoughts and back into the immediate problem of wringing a little respect out of this great big bay warmblood, and by the time I'd dismounted I was back in trainer-mode for the first time in a few days—nothing to think about but the horses I had to ride and the lessons I had to teach. The existential problems of the people I had surrounded myself with went slipping away into the background.

The Shire pranced. The Shire reared. The Shire bucked. All this, because the Shire did not want a bath.

"I appreciate your waiting until lessons were done to try and work with him," I told Louise, speaking from a relatively safe distance down the aisle while the drama was playing out in front of my wash-racks. "But it's now almost eight o'clock and I would like for this day to be over. Anything you can do to sort of, call today a draw, and try again tomorrow?"

Louise had the flushed face of a woman who is overheated and angry and trying not to show either. Her short dark hair clung to her sweaty cheeks and forehead, and her breath was coming in quick puffs. The giant horse at the end of her lead-rope was also sweaty, as he had been all afternoon. Louise had been unable to get him into the wash-rack after her ride, and after allowing her half an hour's argument with him, I'd called a halt, as I'd needed all six wash-racks free for the returning trail horses. She had been forced to move on to her other, more sane horses, while I'd moved on to Ivor, Peaches, Serenity and then my evening lessons. Night-check was Anna's tonight, I'd remembered blissfully, giving Max a cuddle after my last lesson had wrapped up, so all we had to do was make sure the night horses went out and everyone had hay, and then it was all sofa cushions and cold drinks for me.

But once the last straggling student had followed her mother out of the barn, helmet clunking against her calves, Louise had determinedly pulled the Shire back out of his stall and marched him down the aisle, his hooves coming quick and spritely at first, then gradually grinding to a halt as he realized where Louise thought she was taking him. I admired her tenacity, but not her methods. The horse had already proven once today that he was well aware he was bigger and tougher than she was, and so far, Louise had made no move to show him she was *smarter.*

She was probably just tired, of course; sometimes the haze that descends on a rider after a long afternoon in the heat is just too thick to allow for critical thinking. I knew Louise knew how to train a horse. I just didn't think she *remembered* how right at this moment.

Max, his leash slipped through a belt loop in my navy breeches, bounced around my boots, his paws slipping and leaving orange smudges on the leather; I'd let him run around the covered arena while I was setting out the sprinklers for a quick soak of the arena before we closed down for the night. Now he was out of his mind with excitement, watching the Shire slide and shimmy around the center aisle, and I wanted urgently to get him back to the house where I could fill his belly with food and watch him slip into a cozy state of snoozedom which I could follow up with my own deep sleep. These hot days were wearing me out before summer had even properly hit the calendar.

Basically, I didn't want to be out in the barn anymore today.

Kennedy came into the aisle with Anna, the barn key-ring dangling from her fingers. "Everything's locked but the boarder tack room," she said. "We noticed Louise's tack trunk was still open—oh." They stopped in lock-step and watched the dance of the tiny woman and the giant horse taking place a few dozen feet away.

"She can't do that alone," Anna whispered. "She needs help or she's going to get hurt." But she didn't make a move to assist Louise, and I had a feeling even Anna didn't want anything to do with this eighteen-hand bundle of joy.

"I'll help her," Kennedy announced, handing the keys to Anna.

Anna turned big eyes on me as Kennedy marched down the aisle, holding up a hand so that Louise would pause in her endless dragging and circling and clucking. "What if that monster kicks her?"

I lifted my eyebrows. "What do you want me to do? Any horse could kick any one of you, to be fair. But she's had her eye on these drafties since the moment they came into the barn. I don't think you could stop her from getting involved."

Anna nodded miserably. "She's obsessed."

We watched Kennedy confer with Louise, then Kennedy took the Shire's lead while Louise went for a lunge whip leaning on the wall nearby.

"They're going for the tap-tap method," I said.

"Tap-tap?"

"Yeah, they're going to tap-tap on his hindquarters with that whip until he's so bored and annoyed he'll be dying to go into the wash-rack." I glanced up at the clock above my head. Eight-fifteen. "I can't stay out here for another half-hour while they bore this horse into behaving. Call me if you need me." I turned, Max spinning delightedly at my heels. "Don't worry about her, Anna," I added. "You're the caregiver; she's the trainer. It makes you two a perfect combination, as long as you don't expect her to mind her own neck as much as you do."

Anna's gaze was trained on Kennedy, who was leaning back on the lead-rope, alternating between gentle pressure and a slackened rope whenever the horse started to lean backwards. "I don't mind her training tough horses, I just wish he wasn't so big," she said softly. "Can't she stick to ponies?"

"Be careful what you wish for," I chuckled. "I've seen her take some good spills off my ponies."

The Shire took a step towards the wash-rack, his black tail swishing with irritation as Louise kept up the soft tap-tap-tap of the furled lunge whip on his hindquarters, and Kennedy dipped a hand into her shorts pocket, coming out with a small horse cookie, which she offered him with great solemnity.

"A trainer is only as good as her treats," I said as a final goodnight, and left them there to finish the job.

Chapter Thirteen

Friday afternoon, I took a nap.

It was so luxurious, I didn't even feel guilty when I woke up, a summer shower tapping on the window next to my bed, and realized it was already quarter to four and I had a lesson in fifteen minutes. I'd missed two rides, and I didn't care. The moment the noontime sky had started to cloud over, I'd known what I was going to do with my afternoon. There was something so delicious about a summer afternoon nap, lying down and pulling up the sheet while the thunder rumbled in the dark clouds, that I made a point of doing it once or twice each season.

And tonight, I had a date with Mark. So feeling fresh and alive after I'd finished teaching three lessons would be slightly less challenging now that I'd had an extra two hours of sleep. We'd originally planned for a lunch-date, but he'd ended up having to go into work to meet a farrier and go over some special shoeing situations, so our first non-horse-related date had been postponed to the evening... which gave it a pretty special feeling, I had to admit.

I pulled an old sundress, dove-blue and swagged with small white birds, out of the closet from amongst the show jackets and shirts which took up most of the hanging space, and tossed it over a chair in the corner. There'd be just enough time for a quick shower, and a towel-dry of my hair before he arrived to pick me up. "He's picking me up tonight," I reminded Max, who was still trying to convince himself to get out of my bed. "I'm going out with a *boy*."

Friday afternoons bustled around the barn—quite a few of the adult boarders snuck out of work early to spend extra time with their horses before the Saturday morning rounds of birthday parties and gymnastics and soccer matches took their toll, while out in the arena, Kennedy had two action-packed novice lessons with six kids in each session, all of them vying to be the most dangerous young rider of their class. Last week, one of them had very nearly jumped Splash out of the covered ring *on purpose,* which was another reason I needed sensible, tough riders like Lizzie riding him a few lessons per week. The smart horses were easily spoiled because bad behavior was so much more fun than being good, and all I needed was Splash learning he could jump out of the arena every time he was pointed towards the rail and not expressly told he should turn when he got to it.

"Ah, I was just thinking about you, Lizzie," I said, reaching the tack room and finding the teenager pulling down school saddles from their racks, stacking them against her upper thigh. "You're helping get ponies ready?"

"Yeah," she said, throwing me a grin, braces glinting in the fluorescent light. Her white-blonde hair was pulled back in a fraying braid, two shades lighter than her tanned skin, and her Ariat riding top was one I'd seen Anna wearing last spring. The donation of clothes: a sure sign a student had been adopted by the barn staff.

"Anna and Kennedy are always swamped on Fridays, so they said I could help."

I loved that phrasing. *They said I could help do their jobs.* Someone was ready for her working student status. "Are you going to be here all weekend?" I asked.

"Yeah, if that's okay. My mom says it's easier to just drop me off in the morning and not worry about me all day."

"Perfect," I told her. "I'm sure we can keep you busy."

Lizzie looked pleased and hustled out of the tack room with two saddles under each arm. She had to go sideways to get out the door.

I opened the lesson book and wrote in the margin of Saturday *talk to Lizzie about working student responsibilities.* My part-time staff had just increased by one.

Evening came quickly.

The sundress was donned, Max was fed, and there was a truck pulling up in front of my house. This was happening. Mark was here. I ran my fingers through my short damp hair, watching in amusement as a few corkscrew curls sprang to life behind my ears. If I brushed my hair, they'd disappear, so I left them alone and turned away from the mirror. *This is who I am,* I thought. Tanned and lined and worn from a life in the sun, but in pretty damn fine shape and certainly good to kick for a few more decades.

Mark knocked at the door and Max literally fell down trying to get to the door before me. I was still laughing at the dog when I opened the door and saw Mark standing in the slanting golden light of late evening, looking fresh and dapper in a short-sleeved linen shirt worn loose over khaki slacks and a pair of loafers. It was a little disorienting at first, I was so used to his modest, professional button-down shirts tucked in and belted firmly above some rather unflattering jeans, like a veterinarian at a pre-purchase exam. I caught him staring at the same moment I realized I was, and it occurred to me that he rarely saw me in anything but breeches and a polo shirt. "Look at us!" I said delightedly. "We clean up so well, no one will ever know the truth."

My voice reminded Mark about simple niceties like movement and speech and blinking one's eyes. "We'll be undercover equestrians," he agreed, taking my hands in his. I had barely registered what a possessive gesture this was when he leaned over and laid a soft kiss on my lips.

I felt my cheeks flush warm as my heartbeat quickened, and I took a quick, shaky breath as his lips left mine, but his face remained close, his eyes intent. "You look lovely," he said softly. "We can go incognito whenever you want."

"And here I thought living a life in Spandex meant there was no mystery left," I said mischievously.

Mark burst into laughter and I felt the atmosphere around us lighten a little. I breathed a little more deeply. I wasn't quite ready for so much intensity. Not that I didn't want that promising gaze fixed on mine, skin brushing skin with an electric tingle. But let him wine and dine me a bit first. I didn't go on a lot of dates.

I was only a little surprised when Mark turned the truck down the road that led through the back part of the resort property. One thing I knew about these theme park people: they lived their life on the resort, spending all of their free time enjoying the same amenities they worked to bring to life for their guests during their working hours. The employee discounts helped, and I had to admit, if you considered the other choices available to us in this tourist side of town, going to an elaborately-themed resort restaurant was much better than a chain steakhouse filled with tourists who hadn't gotten back to their hotels to change out of their sweaty theme park clothes yet.

"Where are we going?" I asked.

"The Boardwalk," Mark replied, turning his head a little to smile at me. "You've been there, right?"

"Nope," I admitted. "I really haven't been anywhere on the resort."

"You live five miles away! How is that even possible?"

"I usually turn right when I leave, and go north. Towards Winter Garden." There was still a small tack shop in Winter Garden, and the sprawl there had been largely residential, so there were normal services like garages and grocery stores. The commercial spaces up there hadn't been completely abandoned to the swarms of tourists who had taken over everything south and west and east of the farm. "There's nothing down here for me, most of the time."

"It is really expensive if you don't work here," he allowed. "Or if you're not on a vacation you spent the past five years saving up for."

We passed out of the dark woods that ringed the campground and entered the more bustling core of the resort. There were more cars here, and resort buses, and big purple signs announcing exits for various theme parks, shopping districts, and resort hotels. I felt a little stirring of excitement at the sights. Anyone would. Something about coming here made everyone feel like a kid.

I glanced at Mark, noting the way his biceps were highlighted by the folds of the Cuban-style linen shirt. Maybe not a *kid,* precisely.

We pulled up in front of a brightly lit hotel foyer, and a young guy in knee breeches and a flat cap came over to open the door and help me down. I was more used to climbing out of a truck than walking into a luxury hotel, but I accepted the gesture as if it was an everyday occurrence. There was a ragtime number playing from hidden speakers, piano jangling.

"Should I be wearing a flapper gown?" I gestured at the hem of the sundress, brushing around my shins. "I feel like everyone was raising the hems of their dresses while I was stuck out on the farm."

Mark laughed and extended his arm to me as the valet drove off in his truck, the windows reflecting the popcorn lights spelling out BOARDWALK over the portico's archway. "Now that's getting into the spirit of things! Next time I'll find a pair of shirt braces and a fedora and we'll do this right."

Next time, I thought, taking his arm. We were sprinting right out of the gate. I smiled at the young woman in the doorway, an iPad draped over her arm in odd juxtaposition with her striped blouse and old-fashioned blue skirt, and made our way into the hotel lobby.

"Usually I wouldn't walk through the lobby," Mark said softly, "but there's something here you have to see." He led me around a corner and pointed towards the ceiling.

I looked up—and gasped. The chandelier hanging overhead was like nothing I'd ever seen—four golden plunging horses with fluted globes of light rising above their backs. But wait, not horses...

"Hippocampi," Mark said. "It's one of the most beautiful things on the entire property."

"Just one of?" *Hippocampi* was a new word to me, but I supposed it must mean merhorse, because these horses had fish tails as lovely as any fairy-tale mermaid's. They were beautifully detailed, harnessed in elegant trappings like carousel horses. Their necks bowed in noble arches, as if being held back by unseen reins. Their forelegs were extended, one hoof slightly curved back, as if they were leaping from the sea. I could imagine the foam and spray bursting around the horses, nearly catch the scent of salt in the air. "It's magnificent. Would you consider stealing it for me?"

He burst out laughing. "I imagined many things you might say to me after seeing this chandelier, but that was not one of them."

I shrugged, grinning at him. "I see something I want, I simply scheme for the best way to acquire it. And something tells me I can't afford this."

"Come on, you. Before you get me fired." Still laughing, Mark pulled me down a hall paneled with white wainscoting and tall windows, then down a broad staircase. We emerged into the night through a pair of heavy doors and I paused to take it all in. We were in the courtyard of the hotel lobby—when I looked up, I could see the hippocampi chandelier sparkling through a high window—but beyond the square of grass in front of us, there was a broad lake circled by a promenade. Popcorn lights strung along the promenade beckoned, boats hummed through the water, and people strode along beneath the balconies of old-fashioned hotel buildings, gabled and arched and turreted with fanciful disarray, like an old seaside resort.

"There's really a boardwalk," I said, astonished. "This is supposed to be like New Jersey?"

"Yes... just a much better Jersey Shore than the one which ever existed," Mark agreed.

"The one people remember. That didn't exist."

"The nostalgic, rose-colored glasses version."

Once, I wouldn't have seen the value in that. Now, the poignancy of wanting to revisit lost places was far more relevant to me.

By the time we'd finished dinner and wandered the Boardwalk's promenade with a cup of ridiculously rich ice cream, the fireworks shows had ended and the day was ending for most of the resort guests. The music was still playing, but the crowds were thinning and the families were disappearing, one by one, into the hidden courtyards of the hotel. Lights were winking out, more and more balconies growing dark, but Mark was walking me towards a shadowy pathway along the water, and I was in no mood to insist he take me home quite yet.

At dinner we'd talked about the usual things: horses, feed, bitting, farriers, all the things I knew about and was happy to hold court on for hours. Mark knew them too, but in everything we discussed, his perspective felt a little different. He had grown up out west, riding every horse he could get a halter on, and then gone to California. He'd gotten a job driving the trolley horses in Disneyland, done some movie and parade horse training, and eventually moved out here to take the manager job when it opened up. His job was the kind of position that came available once every couple of decades, the kind that no one left once they were lucky enough to snag it. He'd never had a traditional equestrian job, never been a working student, never run a commercial boarding barn. We were like members of the same species, but two different families.

Which might be for the best, I reflected.

The pathway ran down alongside a canal, behind the humming air conditioners of the serene hotel buildings and a hidden pool where splashing and screaming were still competing with the carnivalesque music playing in the background. The water slide looked like a wooden roller coaster. A few steps, and we left the sounds of vacation-land behind. Peeping frogs took up a chorus in the trees, and a nocturnal quartet of ducks ducked and dove in the canal.

"Ever see yourself anywhere else?" I asked him.

"Never," he said without hesitation. "You?"

"All the time," I sighed. "But never with enough conviction to make it real. I love my farm."

"They haven't made it easy on you." He squeezed my hand. "Myself included, probably."

"If you ever start giving riding lessons, give me a heads-up so I can get the hell out of here, okay?" I laughed, to assure him I was kidding... mostly. "Every time I'm ready to sell out, something stops me."

"What stopped you this time? Assuming you *are* stopped. I know you'd gone under contract."

"How did you know that?" I withdrew a little, letting air drift between us. A mosquito whined near my ear and I swung at it.

Mark hesitated before answering. "It came up at a strategy meeting," he admitted, with the air of conferring a state secret. "We have quarterly management meetings to make sure all the departments are in alignment. Cabins, campsites, watercraft, food and beverage—all of us department heads in a room. When we talk strategy, naturally we have to take local competition into account. I have to make sure we're offering the right number of trail rides per day, charging the right amount, that kind of thing. We charge *more,* don't get me wrong, but it has to make sense."

"And if we're finally run out of business, that's definitely going on the meeting agenda," I prompted.

"Well, yeah... that's important, too."

The ducks went skimming past, in a sudden hurry to leave the canal; they took off with a great deal of splashing and quacking. Behind us, I heard the hum of a boat engine. I glanced back—yet another resort ferry. This place must have dozens of them.

"Picking up guests at the Studios park," Mark explained. "That's where this path goes. Most people are too tired to walk back at night."

"Amazing to think this is the clientele I'm chasing." I rolled my eyes.

"Are you?" Mark's voice was studiously casual. "I thought you only did corporate accounts?"

I glanced side-long at him. He was facing straight ahead. It was too dark to see his expression. "You know what, Mark, I'm not sure we should talk about business."

He stopped and turned towards the canal. It was dark and the waterway was wide, a ribbon of black with a cluster of oak trees on the other side, no doubt masking more hotel utilities and parking lots and the endless machinery that went into making nostalgia a billion-dollar business. His hand still held mine, but his grip had tightened. I thought about alligators and wished we could keep walking, at least to the nearest lamp post, where a pool of orange light might keep the monsters away.

"That's fine," he said after a moment's thought. "Yes. That makes sense."

We walked on, but the conversation never recovered.

Chapter Fourteen

THE SATURDAY UPROAR was in full swing, and I was hiding in my office in hopes of avoiding it. Ponies and horses and kids and adults everywhere, the weekend help making Anna and Margaret pull their hair out, dogs barking because at least two moms per weekend thought the no-dog rule didn't apply to "just hopping out for a second while I drop off Bethany for her lesson" and, now, an endless clanking and banging from the construction site next door, where apparently Saturday work was *de rigueur.*

I tapped my pen on the legal pad in front of me. I'd been jotting down ideas as they floated into my brain, looking for interesting new ways to attract vacation business. The one I couldn't get away from, no matter how much I wanted to, was keeping trail rides—and making them even better.

I needed to compete with Mark's operation.

While I was definitely interested in keeping the good thing Mark and I had going, I wasn't the sort of person who could shrug off a good business idea. More than anything else, I wanted my barn to succeed.

What I needed now was a good look at the way his trail operation worked. A little light espionage was in order, as I'd never even been over to the trail barn. I'd opened the map on my phone and zoomed in on his barn areas. I knew the trail barn was a short distance from the draft horse barn, through a patch of trees, and that it backed up to a pine forest. That would be where the trails were.

The wagon ride earlier in the week, and our date last night at the Boardwalk, had really opened my eyes to the kind of experience they were selling over there. If I wanted to compete in even a small way, I had to go further than throwing Western tack on a string of horses in the aisle of a modern English show barn. Maybe that had been my biggest mistake all along. Kennedy themed her trail ride experience, but the *venue* wasn't themed.

I flicked my pen across my legal pad, sketching out a hitching post, a line of horses in some sort of three-sided shed, a crude dash of lines to indicate a steer skull hanging on the wall. A Western trail barn, maybe, just for this purpose? There was space over near the hay shed. The horses didn't have to live out there... it could just be a staging area for scheduled rides. I considered my drawing, adding a few embellishments for added realism: a few quickly sketched horses, scratches of ink for straw around their hooves, a cowboy hat hanging from the end of the hitching post.

The door was flung open and Max nearly fell out of the guest chair he'd been napping in. He woke up strong, barking furiously, until he realized the intruder was just Anna. Her face displayed an expression just a few notches below panic. I dropped my pen. "What? Spit it out!" I barked when she just stared at me without speaking.

"You're *drawing?*"

I flipped the legal pad over, hiding my sketches. "I'm working."

"Thought you better know that Louise is going to ride Sampson in the outdoor ring."

"Sampson?"

"The Shire."

"I didn't even know he had a name. Did I? Maybe I did." I honestly couldn't recall.

"Well, there's a six-student lesson starting in ten minutes and she's tacking him up right now." There was a bang below us that made the office floor shudder, the perfect punctuation to her words.

"Like hell she is," I growled, getting up from my desk.

Anna scrambled after me as I marched down the stairs, Max barking after us in indignation at being shut in the office.

People started calling for me the moment I appeared in the barn aisle, boarders who all arrived on Saturday morning with something to say about the way their horses had been cared for Monday through Friday, while they'd been in offices and we'd been out here sweating over their four-legged children. I turned around and cut around the outside of the barn, entering the far aisle where Louise's horses lived without acknowledging my roaring fans. Indeed, the only sound at this corner of the barn came from the actual roaring fans, metal fans bracketed into every stall's corner, blowing with all their might on the famously heat-adverse draft horses.

Louise was in Sampson's stall; the big horse was tethered to the back wall by a short chain. Rather pettishly, I wondered when *that* screw-eye had been added. She was lifting her saddle high above her head, trying to get it over the horse's mile-high back without banging it against his tall withers.

"No," I said through the stall bars. "Nuh-uh. Untack him. It's not happening."

Louise nearly dropped the saddle on her own head. "What? What's wrong?" She had to jump away from the horse, who moved threateningly towards her the moment her focus was distracted from him. "Knock it off," she said to him, unconvincingly.

"I've got Kennedy teaching six kids out there in a few minutes. You're not taking this monster out around them. If you want to ride him on Saturdays you're going to have to do it first thing in the morning."

Louise's cheeks colored. "Look, we don't have any kind of contract saying when I can and can't ride these horses. I have just as much rights as any boarder here."

I shrugged. "You think I wouldn't tell any boarder here she can't ride her horse? This is *my* barn. You pay for the privilege of keeping your horse here. Every other privilege comes from me."

Louise changed tack. "Grace, come on," she said wheedlingly. "Mark needs this horse ready ASAP. You wouldn't want Mark getting into trouble at work because this horse isn't in the July Fourth special, would you?"

"Don't bring Mark into this," I snapped. Was she talking to him about me? Was he talking to *her* about *us?* I thought of my drawing upstairs, my surreptitious satellite app surveillance of his trail barn. Of course everything was going to get complicated and weird. Last night had ended quietly, a bit of a whimper compared to the bang I'd been hoping for—not like *that,* get your mind out of the gutter! But if I'd been hoping for a bit more than a goodnight kiss, I'd gone to bed disappointed, and spent more time than I was proud of lying awake, wondering how much of our short dating life had been corporate spying and how much was really about attraction. I shook my head to get myself back on the problem at hand. "If your horse is a disruption to every other rider, your horse stays in his stall until the barn is quiet. That's just the way my barn works. One person doesn't get to ruin a Saturday ride for every other person here."

"Fine," Louise huffed, coming out of the stall. She set her saddle against the stall wall and closed the door behind her, leaving Sampson tied inside. He shuffled his big feathered hooves in the shavings and watched her, craning his neck against the awkward angle of the wall tie. "But you can't pretend Mark's not a part of this situation, Grace. This is *his* special project horse. He wants this horse in his barn, not over here getting fat because you won't let me work him. You better believe I'll be telling him that *you're* the one slowing the process down."

I shook my head. "Tell yourself that, Louise. But we both know you aren't getting through to this horse, no matter how many times you manage to ride him. I'm not the problem here."

I set off down the aisle, Anna scuttling in my righteous wake, ignoring the huffing sounds of insulted horse trainer in the background.

Kennedy and Lizzie were in the cross-tie bays, presiding over the tacking up of school horses. The gaggle of mostly twelve-year-old girls was running around with brushes and splint boots and saddle pads, in a happy state of panicked euphoria. Lizzie plucked a set of bell boots from the hands of a pig-tailed redhead in shocking pink breeches. "Reed doesn't go in bell boots," she scolded, "and you know that!"

"They're so cute," the girl—was it Kaitlin? There were two or three Kaitlins on Saturday—"come on, Lizzie, they won't *hurt*."

"Never use anything you don't absolutely need," Lizzie proclaimed, with the implacable authority of a sixteen-year-old who considered herself an expert in her subject. "You never know if you'll do more harm than good."

"Fine," maybe-Kaitlin huffed, clearly bested, though not convinced. She returned the bell boots to the school tack room.

I sidled up to Kennedy. "Lizzie seems to be working out?"

"So far so good," Kennedy said. "Of course, she's only been a working student for an hour."

"She doesn't even know she's one yet. I just told her to help you with lessons today and then come see me at lunchtime."

Kennedy cracked a smile despite the ongoing offensive of dark looks and short replies she'd been waging against me. "I love it. On trial and she doesn't even know it."

"There's no reason to tell a teenager everything," I shrugged. "Goes to their head."

I left the students to their pandemonium and continued around the corner, where in the other set of cross-ties, Phoebe was tacking up Jimmy, the bay gelding I'd ridden for her yesterday. He pricked his ears at me and sidestepped quickly. Phoebe's hand slipped from the billet she'd been tightening and she ended up hitting her own nose.

"Dammit, Jimmy! Jesus!" Her voice was muffled from behind her clenched hands. "I think you broke my fucking nose!"

"Sorry about that," I said, taking her hands down so I could get a look. "No blood. You're fine. I think Jimmy would prefer not to have a replay of yesterday. We had a pretty long ride."

"Whatever you did to him, he deserves it," Phoebe said darkly, giving Jimmy a black look. "Sometimes I don't think this is working out. Every week it's another thing. He's regressed since I bought him."

Since Phoebe hadn't bought Jimmy from me, I felt perfectly comfortable in agreeing with her. "He might have been a little green for what you wanted," I suggested. "But let's see how he goes today, and if you're happy with it, we can talk about next steps." Next steps being, adding Jimmy to my training program along with half my other adult clients' horses. Everyone was happier when they could come out after work and get on a horse who had been schooled professionally all week—the rider was happier, the horse was happier, my bank account was certainly happier.

Phoebe had been reluctant to hand Jimmy over to me, but now that we'd gotten the initial ride in, I sensed an addition to my weekly rides was imminent. If he was awful today, it would be because he needed more work. If he was wonderful, it would be because I'd given him such a good school. Win-win. "I'll meet you in the arena," I promised, and moved on.

The next stop on my walkabout was the hay barn, where I could see Margaret had dragged one of the weekend grooms. They were at the top of a mountain of hay bales, tossing bales down to throw for lunch. Margaret expertly tossed a bale into the back of the Gator. Nadine, watching her, gaped. "How do you *do* that?"

"Practice," Margaret said gruffly. "Now you try." She noticed me standing at the corner of the shed. "And don't hit the boss."

Nadine pushed back her dark braid, grasped the strings of a hay bale, picked it up, and heaved. The bale crashed against the side of the Gator and burst open, the strings falling slack as the flakes spilled out like a broken accordion.

"Oh, shit," Nadine said, looking crestfallen.

"Go and pick it up," Margaret waved her down the pile, then made her way down to me. "What's going on, boss?"

"Just doing a lap. I had to stop Louise from riding that horse in the outdoor during the twelve-year-old class."

Margaret shook her head, but her stoney face told me she was not at all surprised.

"Care to look at something with me?" I asked, an idea popping into my head.

We walked out of the hay shed and I turned along the side of the big metal building, looking at the empty strip of ground that ran up to the last paddock, about forty feet away. It was a patch of scrubby grass and some out of place palmettos that ran up to the trees and fence separating us from the development next door. Just waste ground, really. "Could you see a three-sided shed going in here? Just deep enough to to put the trail horses before and after a ride went out?"

Margaret considered the empty space in front of her. "I don't see why not," she said eventually. "There's nothing here to disturb." She looked at me. "New scheme?"

"I've grown to like the intrigue. And I'm trying to figure out how to cash in on all the vacation home people that are going to be here in, I don't know, six months?"

"Have you told Kennedy?"

"Told her what?" I fastened a level glance on Margaret. "What has she said to you?"

Margaret was unashamed. "What hasn't she said? All she does is talk about how bored she is, and what a mistake she made in ever getting out of the dinner show business, and how she's tired of teaching spoiled rich kids how to ride ponies that she's already trained to go like clockwork."

I raised my eyebrows. "She said all that?"

"That's all she says. That girl gets obsessed with one problem and makes it into the end of the world. You remember what she was like when she first came here."

I did. Trail rides for all the show horses. Trail rides to liberate my poor imprisoned show-ring riders. Trail rides even if riders got hurt and horses ran away and husbands got mad. She'd upset the biome of the equestrian center within twenty-four hours of entering its system. Eventually, we'd all adapted, but things had been touch-and-go there for a while.

"Margaret, would we be better off without Kennedy?" I looked down at the sandy ground, kicked at a chunk of asphalt from the parking lot. "Are her mood swings a problem for the barn... I don't know, for the barn morale?"

Margaret considered this for a moment. "She is certainly a pain in the ass," she said after a moment. "But everyone likes her. And when she's not having one of her identity crisis-es, she's good at her job. Better than Nadine," she added, for the benefit of the groom who was creeping out of the hay shed, wondering where we'd gone.

"Hey," Nadine said, stung. I waved my hand at her, letting her know to dismiss the comment.

On the other side of the trees, a mechanical banging started up, giving us all a shock. "What do you think *that* is?" I yelled over the din.

"Weapons of mass destruction," Margaret grunted, and went back into the hay shed, Nadine at her heels like an eager spaniel.

I stood there a few moments more, listening to the racket and wondering why on earth they'd started working on Saturdays. Maybe they were behind schedule and needed to catch up if the first phase was going to open in December. Or maybe they'd heard I'd told the realtor to extend my grace period, and they were under orders to smoke me out of here.

But inside the barn, the extra banging wasn't so bad, and in the covered arena, I barely noticed the noise. Phoebe walked Jimmy in a circle around me at one end; Kennedy's lesson was careening around at the other end, and a few boarders were using the outdoor rings again, emboldened by my recent decision to revive outdoor riding. We were the very picture of a successful modern riding center, I thought. If someone from the development came over right now, they wouldn't see a trainer who was running scared and a riding instructor who had lost her purpose; they would see happy horses, happy riders, and happy grooms—and that was the perfect view, if I was going to make them see us as allies, rather than enemies. I had an idea, and fixing my relationship with that prickly P.R. woman was key to its execution.

Monday, I thought. Monday I'd go over there.

Chapter Fifteen

I STROLLED DOWN to the barn on Monday morning to check in with Anna. It was her Monday to get through barn chores with the weekend grooms, Nadine and Ricky, as help. Kennedy and Margaret had the day off. So did I, technically, but I felt like poking my head into the feed room, just to be certain no drama had cropped up overnight. Plus, Max had woken me up early, anyway. Now, Max trotted at my heels, looking insanely happy with himself, as Jack Russells tend to do first thing in the morning, when all the scents of raccoons and armadillos and stray cats are fresh and bursting from the dewy grass.

"You don't need to be here," Anna observed from the feed room, where she was unpacking supplement packs from the shipment we'd gotten Saturday. In the fuss of all-day wall-to-wall lessons, weekend things left undone unfortunately had to be moved to Monday, the Barn Day of Rest. "Something up?"

"Just Max," I said with a rueful laugh, nodding at my high-caliber canine. Max poked his nose behind a metal trash can that housed high-fiber, low-sugar feed for the ponies and let out a short bark. His tail was wagging madly. "Get the mouse, Max," I suggested encouragingly. Max dove behind the trash can, claws scrabbling on the brushed concrete floor.

"He hasn't learned your Monday sleep-in schedule yet," Anna smiled. "Or he doesn't care?"

"Yes," I said. "That one."

I watched her stack supplement packs on the shelf over the feed bins for a minute longer. Then she took a box knife and broke down the box they'd come in, neatly slicing through the brown tape and folding the cardboard flat, which she slid behind the actual garbage can in the corner, ready to be added to the recycling bin for pick-up on Wednesday. She ran the barn with quiet precision, careful to place everything in its place the first time, exactly as I would have done it—because I'd done all her training.

Sometimes the degree to which I'd customized every inch of this farm to my own desires absolutely amazed me. For years now, I had been building my own giant terrarium, placing each shrub and each model horse exactly where I wanted it. It was funny to think that until a couple weeks ago, I'd been planning on giving it up instead of just rearranging the pieces inside. "Anything I should know about today?" I asked eventually.

"Everyone is bright-eyed, happy and cleaned up their grain," Anna replied. "I would say you've earned a drama-free day. Go and enjoy it."

"I'm going to pay a call on the Bella Tuscany people today." I leaned my head back against the wall and looked at the upper shelves. There'd been a few stray cobwebs yesterday, but this morning they'd been swept away.

Anna stopped her work and fixed me with a serious look. "What are you going to do? Please don't get into a war with them. If you're really dead set on staying, then we all have to make nice and get along."

"I'm going to offer their residents a special deal on riding packages, for starters."

"Riding packages being..."

"Pre-paid riding lessons. Packs of three, six and nine. No expiration dates. Vacation special. Perfect for beginners who've always wanted to ride or intermediate riders who want a mini-clinic from Florida circuit professionals." I trotted out the marketing copy I'd jotted down in my notes, ready to present to what's-her-name, the woman who had come over last week with her list of complaints. Karen, that was it. I was going to convince Karen that her rich vacation home buyers were also the perfect match for my equestrian center, and together we could both benefit from our previously unfortunate shared property line. "Riding camps during school vacations. And possibly more recreational offerings, too. Trail riding, by appointment. Parties. That kind of thing."

"That is..." Anna thought for a moment. "That is a really good idea," she decided, looking impressed.

"It'll be better if it works."

"That's almost always true, right?"

"Good point." I sat on a trash can and patted my lap. Max appeared from behind the feed bins, no rat in sight, and sprang onto my legs, his tongue reaching for my chin almost faster than I could tilt my face away.

"You trained him to jump up fast."

"He came this way," I admitted. Max had evidently been someone else's lap dog first. The thought was depressing. I pushed it away. *Mine now, sucker!* "I felt a really strong urge to come down here this morning, to be honest. Maybe it was just to remind myself that it's worth whatever happens over there today. The last time their rep was here, they seemed pretty aggressive. I don't know if they're going to want to partner up. I'm going to have to be persuasive."

"You're persuasive," Anna assured me. "Scary-persuasive, when it's worth something to you."

Her words touched a chord in both of us, and together we looked around the spotless feed room, the shining stainless steel trash bins with their specialized mixes and rice brans and alfalfa pellets, the big deep freeze, long disconnected, which held textured feed in rat-proof magnificence, the shelves of supplement packs and bins of neon electrolyte powder, the white board with the horses' names and their feeding regimens written neatly on straight lines we'd inked with a tape measure to keep everything ramrod-straight. All the work and love that had gone into this little room, just ten feet by ten feet, represented everything on a grander scale out there: the deeply-bedded stalls, the pristine aisle, the bays of cross-ties and wash-racks, the raked walk to the covered arena, the riding rings with their tidy fences and groomed footing. This place was a temple to the sporthorse. I had built it.

"I think it's worth it," Anna said, breaking the silence.

"I think you're right."

The office at Bella Tuscany was all earth tones: ochre-swirled marble columns, terra-cotta tile, beige drapes held back by golden ribbons. The view outside the tall, arched windows was painted in earth tones as well: the main palate being that red-orange clay from Lake County, ferrous-tinted and thicker than our precariously shifting white sands. The clay always signified construction in these parts. It was alien soil, brought in by the truckload—hence the constant rock trucks rolling past the property—and now it loomed up in vaguely obscene mounds of earth. A false landscape of rolling hills was being built on our flat, swampy land, to fool the vacationers into feeling like they were someplace more exotic than Central Florida. As if you'd ever need a place more exotic than Central Florida, with our tempestuous weather and ever-growing collection of snakes, lizards, birds of prey, and butterflies. We had everything in place for a wild time already, but sure, recreate a storybook version of Tuscany on it instead.

I swallowed down my annoyance at this misguided place-making —walking in with a bad attitude wasn't going to help me today— and asked the young woman behind the massive marble reception desk if Karen was in.

The receptionist, who had been eyeballing me nervously from the moment I'd walked in, asked if Karen was expecting me.

"Not today," I said. "But in general, I'd say, yes."

"I... okay." The receptionist tried but ultimately failed to care that I didn't have an appointment. I liked this about her. "Let me call her."

She picked up a phone and from down an echoing hall I heard a telephone ring, the lift of a receiver, the voice saying, "Yes?" I grinned at the receptionist, who just looked embarrassed. She tugged at her red ponytail with one hand. "Karen," she said softly, trying to minimize the echo of her own voice traveling down the hall. "Someone to see you, are you free for a moment?"

"Did you ask who it was?" Karen's voice was impatient.

The receptionist cast her eyes up at me.

"Tell her I'm from the farm next door," I whispered

conspiratorially.

Her eyes widened. "She's from the farm next door," she repeated. "Oh God."

I bit back a laugh. The receptionist waggled her eyebrows at me, suddenly on my side, and I was nearly choking by the time she'd put down the phone and nodded at me.

"Second door on the right." She pointed. "Grab a drink from the fridge if you want one."

I had a suspicion it was her job to walk me to the office and offer me a beverage on the way, but something told me my carefully-curated ensemble of navy-blue breeches, high-tech riding top in white and blue stripes, and clean field boots was still relegating me to the service entrance. I decided to live it up anyway and grabbed a Diet Coke from the glass-fronted fridge in the luxurious waiting area, saluting the receptionist with it before I plunged down the hallway.

Walking past framed photos of the neighboring theme parks—although none of the Fort or Mark's trail barn, to my disappointment—I found Karen waiting inside a small office overstuffed with dark, Victorian reproduction furniture which gave the place a stodgy feel. I'd gotten so used to the IKEA look in every store, restaurant and professional office which had opened in the past five years, that the swags of heavy curtains over the window and the bulbous swellings of the desk and chair legs were a surprise. In the center of all this faux luxury, Karen seemed to be crouched like a little girl, her new page-boy haircut not really helping matters.

"Karen," I said, standing in the doorway so she could fully take in my ensemble. "You got a haircut. Welcome to the short-hair club."

Karen touched the little point of her bob and smiled uncertainly.

"It's a change, that's for sure," she said with a wince, and that's when I knew I had her where I wanted her. Too nervous to put on airs, she would have to meet me on equal terms, instead of as the troublesome farmer-woman from next door, asking for favors.

"You'll like it." I started inside, then paused, as if something had just struck me. "Your receptionist was nice enough to offer me a drink, and a horse trainer never turns down something cold. You want something while I'm up? Your coffee looks empty."

"I—" she looked helplessly at her empty mug. "A water would be great, thank you."

I ducked back out of the room and snagged a water bottle from the fridge. The receptionist didn't look up from her phone.

"Here you go," I said. "Your girl out there isn't too busy, huh?"

"Well, it's slow when you just have a few models built," Karen said defensively. She took the water and opened it while I was sliding into one of the over-stuffed chairs, upholstered in floral fabric reminiscent of someone's grandmother's house. "But we need to be ready for walk-ins. Summer vacation's in full swing. People come and fall in love with the area, so they start driving around looking for options while they're still on vacation. Here we are, in case they're swept off their feet."

"So next summer you'll be in full swing, everything open?"

"Almost. The water park won't be finished. But one of the golf courses, all of the condos and the first wave of villas."

I suppressed a shudder at the thought of all that activity next to me. Time to embrace the change, time to be a force for good. "I think we could be good for each other, Karen. That's why I'm here. Having a world-class equestrian center right next door isn't a negative. It's a definite positive."

Karen blinked at me. I slid the brochure I'd mocked up across her desk. It was very basic, just square photos and text dropped into a template program I'd found online, but it told a story. A story mostly about smiling children with expensive taste and access to nice ponies.

She unfolded the paper and studied the photos. The lines about my qualifications. Our history at shows. Ribbons. Award money. Championships. Horses for sale and lease. Summer riding camps. Intensive mini-clinics. Spring break. February break. All of it—whenever they wanted horse time, I was there, waiting to sell it to them.

Karen nodded, taking it all in. Then she tapped the line on the back—*Bella Tuscany Discounts.*

"Exclusive, or do you offer this to all the neighboring properties?"

"Exclusive." I leaned forward, put my elbows on the desk in a conspiratorial manner. "Are you interested?"

"We have a program you might like." Karen put down the brochure and opened a drawer in her desk. She riffled through some papers and pulled out a glossy, heavy-weight flyer. "Preferred providers," she explained, handing it over. "You provide exclusive rates and perks to our residents, and we provide shuttle service and advertising."

"What kind of perks are we talking?" I ran my eyes down the list. The theme parks were on here. Water sports like kayaking and parasailing. Airboat rides and wildlife safaris. Mark's business was here too. *Carriage rides, pony rides, trail rides, private events — all with our signature touch of magic.* I narrowed my eyes at the words. He hadn't told me about this.

"A private lounge would be ideal," Karen said thoughtfully. "A couple places have offered that. It's been very successful in drumming up business at other properties I've done that with. I think people go just for that perk sometimes. Some comfortable couches, waters in the fridge, maybe some fruit, a shower—it doesn't take much, honestly."

I raised my eyebrows, thinking. A lounge wasn't a half-bad idea, actually. I had benches and chairs in the tack rooms, but they were always spilling over with kids these days. "I might be able to manage something. Is exclusive a must? I'm thinking of my boarders, if I suddenly offer an amenity that I've never had for them before."

"It would help. But if you don't have a lounge at all yet, something is better than nothing. People still want to feel like they're on vacation, you know? They want to feel pampered. Especially if they buy here and are used to concierge services for every little thing."

I nodded. They would be annoying, I thought. But more annoying than some of my boarders already were? Probably not. "I'll look into it. It's a good idea."

"That's fine. Let me know," Karen said. "No rush." She flipped through the brochure again and paused. "Western trail rides? What's your price point?"

I named a figure I knew was twenty percent less than what Mark's business charged. I'd looked it up online, specifically for this meeting.

"Really? The Disney barn does trail rides, but they're expensive and they're not offering a discount on it. With you right next door, charging less... could be pretty attractive to our residents."

"They're not known for discounts."

Karen sighed. "You're telling me. I can't even get a contact over there to *talk* about it. My boss told me when I started working on partnerships that no one from the parks would be willing to talk to us, but I was still shocked at how insulated that place is. I met with the barn manager but he couldn't give me any special deals. All I got from them was permission to use their marketing copy for their recreation that's open to the public—the horses, golf, tennis. You don't know anyone there, do you?"

"I'm kind of seeing the barn manager," I admitted.

Karen's eyes bulged. She leaned across the desk. "Girl, are you here to undercut your boyfriend?"

"Well, boyfriend is a strong word," I considered.

"But everything else is a yes?"

I grinned.

Karen grinned back. "Well, I'm glad you're here."

"Well, that was my goal," I said. "I know we could have started on a better foot before, and I apologize for that, but... what do you think? Can we be good neighbors with good fences?"

Karen looked a little embarrassed to be reminded of the way she'd scolded me in my own office last week. "I... I really didn't know what to think when Alison said you were out here. I assumed you'd come to yell at me some more. And..." she picked up the brochure and glanced at the photos again, "maybe I deserved that. Because you clearly have a strong business here and know what the community is looking for. Better than I do, when it comes to this sort of thing—obviously!"

"Don't worry about it." I stood and held out a hand. Her manicured red nails flashed as she grasped my considerably rougher palm. "My email's on there. Let me know what you need from me and when. If you have any other ideas about what your residents might want, I'm ready to work with you."

When Karen smiled, I could see it was genuine. "I'm really glad this is going to work out," she said, with feeling.

"Me too," I said, and I meant it.

Chapter Sixteen

I WENT HOME with a spring in my step, feeling emboldened by Karen's enthusiasm for my ideas. It was time to put things into motion... six months could pass in the blink of an eye, and I really only had the summer months to concentrate on this project before the show season would arrive and demand my full attention. If I wanted to be ready to hit go in January, I'd have to have everything in place by October at the latest, including trained staff who could handle the new resort programs without having to come to me for everything.

The toughest things would be the physical ones—building out a lounge and a Western Trail barn. I had my sketches to start with, but I still thought I could learn a thing or two from the masters of themed spaces. Shucking off my field boots at the door, I made up my mind. I went into my bedroom, opened my closet door, and took out a pretty sleeveless blouse patterned with small trotting horses, and a pair of light khaki capris.

For several days after our date, nothing had passed between Mark and I except for a few texts—*it's been so busy, I know right,* those sort of texts. I didn't think things had ended super-well that Friday night, but I also didn't think we'd closed any doors. As a trainer, I could easily accept that he was simply too busy to talk to me over the weekend. Initially, I'd figured we'd pick back up whenever we could, try again... but now I decided to just give him a surprise visit. I wanted to see him again—even if we were destined to be rivals. I wanted to know more about his business—even if I was hoping we could be more than friends. I gave Max a rub on the head, apologized for being out all day, and hopped into my truck.

I went out of my way and into the tourist district first, so that I could bring him a coffee—iced, on account of the soaring midday temperature—and then set about wheedling my way past a groom I'd never met before, who didn't want to let me past the chain dividing the guest area of the barn from the working area. I could see Mark's office door, invitingly open, just a few feet away. I pointed this out to the groom.

"But Mark's not *in* the office," the groom, a stout and unforgiving woman named Mel, told me. She crossed her arms over her chest, which was doubly aggressive here, where only positive body language was allowed. "You can wait here and I'll see where he's at."

"I'm happy to come with you. I brought him a coffee and the ice is melting." I waggled the sweating cup at her.

She gave me a look which suggested I should have brought enough for the whole class. "I can't have you walking around the barn without his permission," she said sternly. "Those are the rules."

"Fine." I didn't love being ordered around by a groom, but she clearly wasn't going to give in, and there was nothing to gain by starting a fight with Mark's employees. Anyway, if they were loyal and didn't allow anyone to break the rules, that was so much the better for him. "I'll just wait in the office," I suggested, as if the offer was on the table. "Thank you for going to find him, I know you're busy."

Mel's expression informed me that I had *no idea* how busy she was, despite the lack of horses or tack or even wheelbarrows in the barn aisle to suggest she was doing anything at all, and that she was being extremely lenient in allowing me past the chain at all, so I'd better not double-cross her by wandering around. Duly chastised but inwardly triumphant, I meekly retreated into the little cluttered square that was Mark's office.

Once inside, I had to smile; the wall-space that wasn't hidden by schedules and spreadsheets thumb-tacked to the plain white walls were decorated with fading photos which clearly spanned years of the ranch's history. Grinning grooms climbing from fences onto unsaddled Clydesdales; Mark leading a trail ride from atop a white-splashed pinto horse, a ridiculous cowboy hat on his head; a little girl in a princess dress giving a dappled grey Percheron a kiss on his lowered nose, and, most impressively, Mark in full royal regalia, complete with a white feather drooping from a velvet cap, driving an open carriage drawn by two white horses right down Main Street USA. The occupants weren't visible in the shot, but I suspected they were fairy-tale royalty... or a large mouse in a tuxedo. I lingered over the photo, which had to be at least fifteen years old, thinking how odd it was that he'd been right down the road all this time, while I'd been taking my clients to shows and importing prospects from Europe—he'd been here, leading trail rides and driving princesses through theme parks. All this time, I'd thought the theme park industry had stolen something precious from me, and from Florida, but maybe, in some way, they'd been doing the same thing I was—connecting horses with humans, creating incredible memories, and... yeah, and making money at it along the way.

It was unsettling, but it also gave me plenty to think about.

After looking through the photos, I turned my attention to the schedules with interest: spreadsheets with rows for horses at the trail barn, horses for the carriage rides, horses for hay-rides and parade duty and weddings. There were an impressive number of moving parts; no wonder he sounded stressed to death the few times I'd spoken to him while he was at work. He had dozens of horses of all shapes and sizes, and dozens of employees as well.

I heard footsteps outside and hastened to sit in the sagging chair by Mark's computer, not wanting to get caught looking over his work papers. I must have jostled the mouse, because the monitor lit up and I was treated to a lock screen featuring a professional shot of one of the black Percherons, head held high in front of the park's castle, his black bridle trimmed in brass and looking very dapper indeed. Holding his reins and slightly out of focus in the background was Mark, wearing the 19th-century trolley-driver's costume I'd seen in the park a few weeks ago.

"Now, *that* photo-shoot was a nightmare," Mark said from behind me. "A million degrees and crowds everywhere. They wanted a midday sky, otherwise we would have done it at sunrise with no one around. We had to get security to keep guests out of the shot."

"It was worth it. The sky is beautiful." I spun around in his chair and smiled at him. The very sight of his face made me feel warm and cozy inside, like I was in my favorite place in the world, as long as he was in it too. "A lot like it is out there right now. I love those fluffy white clouds we get this time of day."

"It's just a matter of time until it rains, though." Mark came in and leaned down, pressing a soft kiss on my lips. A little current of electricity ran through me, and I resisted the urge to stand up, push against him, get a little rambunctious right there in his office. We were definitely moving beyond the awkward end of our date. But we weren't teenagers, and I'd come here on a mission that couldn't wait. I'd schedule some frisky time for us later in the week.

"I brought you coffee." I held out the cold cup, dripping water on the floor, and wiggled it so the ice rattled invitingly.

"Is this bribe-coffee?"

"How well you know me," I laughed. "I was wondering, can you take me to the trail barn?"

His fingers were touching mine as he took the cup, and he'd been looking as if he was enjoying the intimacy, but for just a moment he hesitated, his face clouding. Then his smile came back. "Come to steal my secrets, then?"

"I shouldn't have to steal them. But you're too tight-lipped to give me the goods." I grinned at his surprised look. "Come on, big boy, you have how many trail horses over here? Twenty? I have six, and I'm retraining them to be used in riding lessons. I'd say there's room in this town for both of us."

Mark took a drink of his coffee and regarded me thoughtfully. "I'm not sure there is," he said after a moment of consideration. "I'm not sure there's room in this town for *me.*"

"What are you saying? The trail rides aren't going out full?"

He rattled the ice in his cup, slow circles, drops of water cascading to the floor, splashing my paddock boots. "It's June, it's hot. Summer isn't our best season."

"Mine either. But I was concentrating on convention season."

"They're never much for us. We do better with the longer family vacations."

"See? Plenty of room for two barns." I didn't mention that convention season hadn't been particularly good this past spring. Let him think everything was going perfectly well. Then he'd be less suspicious of my intentions, and we could concentrate on building our relationship, not fighting over customers. "Come on, Mark, I want to see your barn. I'm interested in your work."

Mark sighed and smiled at me. "Okay, okay. Hop up, little lady, we'll take my golf cart."

We zipped away from the draft barn and down a paved walk through the woods beyond, squirrels fleeing our path and chattering at us from the oak tree branches overhead. Off to my right I spotted the huge lake the Fort fronted, and heard the old-fashioned whistle of the ferry boat sailing to the dock, laden with families. "I can hear those boats from my place," I said over the rattling of the golf cart. "On foggy mornings, it sounds like they're right outside my barn. I've always liked them."

"They're nice," Mark agreed. "All of the background noises here are kind of comforting, makes it feel more real... more substantial. It's easier to feel at home when the place feels like it has its own life outside of you, like it would keep on ticking over even if you were gone for years. People always want to feel like they have a home to go back to, and that really isn't the norm anymore, is it?"

"But that's kind of the point of everything here, right? To make it feel like some kind of imaginary, best possible version of home?"

"You're right. I didn't know you were that familiar with the place." Mark sounded impressed, like I'd passed some test I hadn't even known about. "The funny thing is, everyone wants this version of home no one has even been alive to experience. The Fort, Main Street—people feel at home in these places, but they're mock-ups of more than a century ago. It's kind of a collective unconsciousness kind of thing."

"I've read a thing or two that wasn't about horses. There's a lot of interesting blog posts out there about place-making at the parks. They don't talk a lot about the Fort, though." And this was the place-making I was most interested in.

"We're usually relegated to 'hidden gem,'" Mark said with a chuckle that ended in a sigh. "Which sounds great to everyone but the finance team."

The trees opened up before us and then we were in a clearing with a collection of grassy paddocks clustered around a long, low barn with open sides. Inside, I could see a line of horses who seemed to be clustered close together. I was a little confused until we turned into the barn aisle and Mark stopped the golf cart. To the right there was a row of empty, open-sided stalls, perfect for catching the breezes and housing uncontentious horses who wouldn't fight through the bars all night long. To the left, there was a long hitching post with hay-nets tied at intervals, and a good twenty horses, mostly between fourteen and fifteen hands, standing tacked in Western gear. A groom in the usual plaid shirt was mucking one of the empty stalls. She waved and continued with her work. A digital clock had been mounted strategically in the aisle, where only employees would see it, counting down the minutes until the next ride. There were thirty-three minutes to go.

"Wow!" I exclaimed, hopping out of the cart. "Now this is efficient."

"Thank you." Mark gave the nearest horse a stroke on the neck.

"My design, although it's almost ten years old now and there are definitely things I'd change about it. But all in all it's worked well."

We walked down the line and Mark told me tidbits about the horses as we went. Most of them picked up their heads and looked for attention, ears pricked and eyes bright; a few backed up a step when I approached, flattening their ears. "I suppose that's just what happens when a horse is a tourist attraction," I observed as a rusty black draft cross folded his ears flat at my approach and pulled away from my hand. "Some of them are going to be bitter about all the attention, some are going to eat it up."

"I try to find the horses who will eat it up." Mark produced a tin of mints from a pocket and the horse changed his expression instantly, moving forward and shoving his neck against the hitching rail in a bid to get at the rattling tin. Mark gave him one, and then was obliged to start handing them out to everyone else. "The ones that don't thrive, I pull out of the schedule and put into our adoption program. You can't force a horse into this lifestyle."

I hung back for a moment, thinking of the Shire back at my barn, and watched Mark move down the line, handing out mints to the remaining horses. He talked to Louise regularly, if she was to be believed; he had to know that Sampson wasn't working out, and yet she'd been at the barn before me on Sunday, waging her daily battle with him in the arena when I'd come out onto the porch with my coffee, wondering why I heard hoofbeats so early in the morning. If any horse was being forced to try and fit into the theme park lifestyle against his will, it surely had to be Sampson.

Well, that wasn't my battle to fight. I focused instead on the tack he was using on the trail horses, noting the slim therapeutic pads and the light nylon saddles on top of them. I was surprised Mark's attention to authenticity didn't extend to insisting on leather saddles, although I had to admit they would be much heavier than these. Most of the bridles were leather slip-ear headstalls, hanging from hooks on the support poles every six horses or so. I fingered the brass identity tags clipped to each one. "They all have their own bridles? Do any ever get misplaced?"

"Oh, definitely. But they all go in the same bit, which keeps things simple. If I can't send out a horse with just a light curb, something the rider can manage to turn and halt with, but still have slack in the reins, then he's just not the right fit for this program." Mark ran his fingers through the rich forelock of a good-looking palomino at the end of the line; the horse nudged against him. That color and sweet disposition were a killer combination: he was clearly a fan favorite. "You're probably looking at the quietest, most simple collection of horses in the world, to be perfectly honest."

I smiled and gave the little pinto in front of me a pat on the neck. Imagine being Mark, or any of these grooms, surrounded by the most quiet horses in the world. Talk about losing touch with reality! They said some of the employees at the theme parks were here to escape the real world, but I couldn't even imagine spending my equestrian career amongst horses for whom a spook, or a spirited canter, would be considered not just wildly out of character, but grounds for dismissal.

"Mark, don't you ever get *bored* with these horses?"

The thought burst from me without pausing for permission from my brain and better judgement; as soon as I said it, they both let me know I shouldn't have.

Mark's hand was still on the palomino's head, his fingers curled into the horse's forelock, but they had stopped moving. His expression was closed. The only one unperturbed was the palomino, who waited patiently for the scratching to continue, his eyes closed, his lower lip hanging blissfully.

"I'm sorry," I said quickly. "That was rude. I'm just so used to crazies all the time, you know, performance horses full of alfalfa and protein, not getting the rides they need from their owners—seems like every time I turn around, someone else needs a tune-up ride." I forced a laugh, hoping he'd join in.

But Mark just looked down at the palomino, and after a moment, his fingers resumed their slow movement. The horse sighed, nostrils fluttering, his half-closed eyes showing his utter content. "It seems like you find these horses to be less than yours," Mark said finally. His voice was quiet, his tone flat.

"Less... no, I don't... I just meant because they're so *good,* I'm just used to a little more chaos." I babbled a little, gripping the hitching post in one hand, digging my fingernails into the smooth wood. "It just feels... like the calm would be confusing, after all that."

Mark sighed and looked up, our eyes meeting. I wanted to push down the line, past all those nodding horse heads between us, and wrap my arms around him, apologize for hurting his feelings and for using him to get a look inside his trail business and for doubting his motivation in getting Sampson into the program, but I didn't know *how.* I didn't know how to shove aside restraint and let emotions run the show—that was the opposite of how I'd lived my entire life. I couldn't just change my stripes now, no matter how much I might want to.

"It's fine," Mark said. "I shouldn't have taken it so seriously."

That's how you know when you've struck a nerve—that line, right there, it tells you everything is *not* fine. "What you're doing is incredible," I told him. "Who knows how many people have their first equestrian experience here and go home to become horse people because you put them on the right horse?"

He smiled reluctantly. "We get cards sometimes, and repeat guests... there's a girl named Emmie who has been coming every year since she was ten. She's sixteen now and rides Training Level eventing. I have a picture of her and her mare in my office, actually."

"Show it to me?" I gave him a wheedling grin, while I tried to think if I'd seen the picture during my careful study of his photo collection. Maybe Emmie Eventer was in a drawer somewhere. "And maybe we can meander over to the snack bar and I can buy you an ice cream to make up for being stuck up."

"Well, when you put it like that... your golf cart awaits, princess," he said with a flourish, and we walked back down the line, the nickers of mint-hungry horses following us.

Monday nights, nothing happened around the barn. A couple of owners did ride on Monday after work, quietly driving in, grooming their horses themselves, and schooling in their own separate arenas before cooling their horses and heading back to wherever their everyday lives took place. There was an agreement between us for these Monday rides: they wouldn't bother the grooms with anything that wasn't an emergency, and they would sweep up after themselves if the spaces they used were already clean for the night.

The quiet of a Monday-night barn gave me a welcome opportunity to walk around the barn and take stock of what spaces I could use to execute the ideas I'd drawn up. I'd been sketching more and more design concepts onto my legal pad since I'd come back from the Fort. While Mark's barns and public spaces were unquestionably Western in theme, I thought I could pull off a sort of country shabby chic that walked the line between disciplines and still spoke to non-equestrians and equestrians alike, as something indisputably horsey in nature. Instead of a grinning steer skull nailed to a wall, a small, subtle set of antlers could work. Instead of hanging up a Navajo saddle blanket on the wall, I could put up a wooden shelf to display some faux bronze horse sculptures—mares and foals, perhaps. I thought I could accomplish quite a lot of decoration with a few hundred dollars at HomeGoods, looking over the lists and sketches with satisfaction. Now I just had to decide where all of it should go.

The school tack room and boarders' tack room were set up perfectly as they were, with just enough space for tack trunks and saddle racks and bridles hanging along the walls. If anything, I needed another boarders' tack room, this one fitted with lockers. I made another note; if we had more day guests here, the boarders would want the security of lockers. I could empty the stall at this end though, I thought, have someone throw up some drywall and a ceiling, put glass in the window and an A/C unit, and boom... I'd have a small lounge. Was twelve by twelve big enough, though? I tapped the pen against my chin and studied the space, while the horse inside watched me, chewing thoughtfully.

No, I decided, walking back up the aisle. The horse whinnied after me, in case I'd forgotten to give her a treat, which of course set off a chain reaction. Half the horses in the barn and all of the horses out in the paddocks started neighing as well, and Max began to quiver with indignation, barking in his staccato voice until I figured Anna would be running downstairs to see what trouble I'd gotten into. Then I noticed her apartment window was dark, though it was barely eight o'clock and the sun was still up. There was no way she'd gone to bed so early. I stepped into an empty stall and glanced through the window into the parking lot—her car was gone. *Well*, I thought. Then she won't notice if I were to check out the extra apartment.

I flicked on the lights and surveyed the dusty, dismal little apartment. No one had lived here since that event rider, Jules Thornton, had been an apprentice last summer. I'd meant to get another apprentice and instead, with the uptick in junior riding shifting my responsibilities and those of the staff, I hadn't gone through with it and the apartment sat empty. The kitchenette was hung with cobwebs, and the lumpy brown sofa against the opposite wall looked somehow lumpier than ever. The beige carpet looked like an abandoned lawn that had been trampled into hard, flat dirt. But it was cool—even as I stood here the air conditioner clicked on and hummed for a few minutes before subsiding, keeping the temperature just south of eighty degrees. I was glad I'd left the air running; this place would have gotten moldy without the circulation.

"You'll do," I told the apartment. "Get ready for a makeover."

I dropped the legal pad onto my desk in the neighboring office before I went home for the evening. The sun was setting in a dramatic face-off between yellow and purple, billowing clouds creating a scene straight off a fantasy-novel cover, and I paused to take it all in for a moment, breathing in the hot Florida night. It was dry and still, even the tree frogs silent, waiting for a signal from the rain gods that they should take up their summer song, and I felt like the farm was holding its breath, waiting to see what Grace was going to do next.

The headlights of Anna's car had appeared in the driveway as I went up the steps of my porch. I stopped and watched her drive by, but she didn't turn her head, didn't notice me there. I'd have to talk to Kennedy, I thought. Before I made her angry; before she did something selfish that broke my Anna's heart.

Chapter Seventeen

MONDAY'S ADVENTURES WERE satisfying, but the next afternoon, Anna handed me a shopping list and told me I'd forgotten to go to the tack shop.

"I was supposed to go to the tack shop?" Apparently in my old age people were instructing me to go shopping and it wasn't registering. I peered at the shopping list. "What's all this?"

"It's extra supplies we need for the show this weekend. We're taking some ponies we haven't had off-farm yet, so we need a couple new sets of shipping wraps, a head bumper, some other stuff..." Anna was watching my expression grow more confused. "You forgot about the horse show, didn't you!"

"I—yes?"

"Okahumpka Horse Park. Schooling show. Our rig plus a couple of boarders shipping themselves. You did the entries last month after everyone begged you for a fun show."

"Oh right." I remembered now. "Was I drunk? Why would I agree to this?"

"Maybe. Maybe it was the night Ellie Anderson brought over all that homemade sangria and we sat on the patio and watched the thunderstorm?"

"That was a fun night." Just a random Saturday evening, afternoon lessons canceled because it had stormed so violently I hadn't thought it was safe to ride even in the covered ring, and a few boarders had hung around after the storm had blown into the distance. A couple of them had been headed to a picnic but *it* was cancelled, too, so they'd brought up their coolers and an impromptu barn party was born. "A fun night I am now regretting."

"You have time to go the tack shop between one and four today," Anna announced, looking over my lesson book. "But not again for the next month."

"Fine, I'll go." I pocketed the list. "Watch Max, will ya? And where's Kennedy? I wanted to talk to her about the new plans."

"She was going somewhere for lunch," Anna said vaguely. "She said she'd be back for lessons."

"She's supposed to ride two horses before lessons." I frowned. "I hope she isn't blowing work off."

Anna bit her lip and said nothing.

The tack shop was about half an hour away, just enough space for the resort properties to turn back into residential suburbs and then give way to few leftover cattle ranches and orange groves, hanging on by their teeth. It was small and a little overpriced, but I tried to pick up essentials there every month, just to help the owner carry on. Irene was a sweet little woman of about fifty who had worked part-time in the shop until her daughter went to college on an equestrian scholarship, and then ended up buying the whole thing when the old owner decided to retire. If she regretted buying a boutique store which only serviced a disappearing population, the majority of which was addicted to saving money by ordering their brushes, breeches and boots online, she never let anyone know it.

"Grace!" she sang out as I entered the shop, the door's sleigh-bells jingling behind me. "I haven't seen you in weeks!"

"Hey, Irene. I wish I could stay longer, but I'm on a tight schedule today. Apparently I agreed to go to a schooling show this weekend."

Irene cocked her head, brown hair falling into her eyes. "In June? That doesn't sound like you."

"I may have been under the influence."

"Ah. Makes more sense then."

We studied the list together and then Irene led me around the little shop, pulling out everything I needed and stacking it on the counter. "Any word on a new farm working out for you?" she asked conversationally.

"No. I have to tell you, Irene, I've been talking to the resort people and I think we're going to try and work together on some programs. Instead of me clearing out and heading north."

Irene pulled a set of dark blue shipping wraps out of a cabinet and handed them over. "Really? Trail rides still or something else?"

"More than just trail rides. I'm working out the details." I counted the shipping wraps. "Do you have one more set? I can always use more. The ponies trash everything."

Irene bent over the cabinet again. "How is Louise Brinker working out?" she asked.

I raised my eyebrows. "You know about her? Who told you?"

"Just the grapevine. I know she's been at a dozen barns around here over the past ten years."

My eyebrows actually went higher. "Excuse me? How have I never heard about this woman?"

"She comes and goes. Here we go, one more set." Irene added another set of plastic-wrapped shipping boots to the pile. "She's one of those types who makes a great impression at first and then it all comes falling apart."

I should have known. *Most* horse-people seemed to fall into this category. They showed up with their great stories and their impressive photo album and their nice horses, and then somehow they turned into pumpkins after about two weeks and became nuisances with no manners and nasty horses. "I think one of the horses she has right now might actually kill her," I said, then regretted it, because as much as I liked Irene, this gossip would be bestowed upon the next person to walk through that door, jingling those bells.

Irene looked unsurprised. She unearthed a head bumper from beneath a stack of saddle pads with her usual unerring instinct for locating the less popular items of her store's stock. I didn't even know which horse this was for, just trusting that Anna and Kennedy had become aware of one of our horses' penchants for throwing his head up and banging it against the trailer roof during a previous outing and had made note of the problem. "She's very good at training tricks, bomb-proofing, that kind of thing... *if* the horse is uncomplicated. But usually, that's the kind of horse she's picking out for parades and so forth. Why's she even trying to work with a dangerous horse?"

"I don't know," I admitted. "Apparently someone really wants him in a July Fourth parade."

Irene shook her head. "Probably someone so high up, they wouldn't even know if she got killed trying to make it happen."

* * *

Kennedy wasn't back yet when I returned with my load of shopping. I looked at Frank, nosing through his shavings in search of hay, and then at Wishes, who had been naughty in his last lesson and needed a tune-up. Both were on Kennedy's work-list for today. Clearly neither were getting schooled today. Where the hell had she gone?

Anna was saying nothing; either she didn't know or she was defending her girlfriend. I didn't love this swap in allegiances, Anna sticking up for a member of staff instead of being clear with me, the boss, about what was going on. Then again, if Kennedy was where I thought she was, Anna couldn't be very happy about that.

I texted Mark, wondering if there was any way he'd tell me if he had one of my trainers in his office, glibly explaining all the ways she'd be a great employee for him to bring onto the team. My message went unread, though that meant nothing. He'd ignore a text during an interview, but there were a million other reasons as well—he was on a trail ride with guests, he was in a budget meeting with his bosses and everyone was looking grave, he was overseeing a parade with his horses performing in it.

I tossed Max in the truck with me and drove him back to the house before the afternoon mayhem descended and he went out of his mind—he'd been a little crazy the past few days, and I could do without the drama—then I walked back to the barn to prep for evening lessons. There were already five or six kids in the barn; school had let out at last, after some extra days had been tacked onto the calendar to make up for hurricane days last fall, and I could hear general hilarity coming from the boarder's tack room. I settled into the school tack room on the other aisle, opened the lesson book, and started writing horse assignments on the board. After a while, the giggles faded and I heard boots pelting down the barn aisle. I shook my head at the noise. This would be my first summer with a clutch of pony kids hanging around all day. Another reason I needed Kennedy's help.

I was nearly done with assignments when I heard truck doors slam in the parking lot, then Kennedy's voice coming down the aisle. "She's still at the house, I saw Max's face in the window."

"She doesn't always bring him down," Louise replied knowingly.

Louise and Kennedy, conspiring! I put down my pen and cocked my head, hoping to better catch their conversation.

"Well, either way, I'm going to have to tell her by the end of the night. If you want me at the new barn to get things ready in two weeks."

I felt my jaw slacken, my mouth drop open, my fingers begin to tingle.

"Look, I told you if you can stay on part-time, that's better for both of us at first. I might not have enough work to keep you busy right away. And she's very reliant on you. And," Louise's voice softened. "There's Anna to consider."

If Kennedy had a reply to that, I didn't hear it. Their footsteps moved away, heading for the opposite aisle, where Louise's horses were stabled.

Once I knew they weren't going to pass the school tack room, I picked up my pen again, started to write a horse's name in the column next to a rider's. The letters were jagged; I looked at my hand and saw it was trembling. All of me was trembling, actually, a tremor born from the adrenalin of overhearing a clandestine conversation, and from frustration, and from hurt.

She was just going to abandon me, and head off with Louise! Bad enough that Louise was clearly in the process of acquiring a new barn to base her business out of, without giving me the courtesy of thirty days' notice. But to take *Kennedy,* who thrived on constant movement and hard work, who would go crazy at a barn with five or six horses as soon as the fresh excitement of learning to teach tricks had passed her by? It wasn't just a slap in my face that she'd scouted Kennedy like that, it was disservice to the young woman herself, who was going to realize in just a few weeks that she'd made a big mistake.

Knowing Kennedy as well as I did, she was planning on burning her bridges with me in a big way on her exit. She'd regret that, too, before much time had passed.

I picked up my phone again and texted Kennedy. "Just got here, can you please come to the school tack room? Something to tell you."

Kennedy appeared in the doorway a few minutes later, looking rather pale. "Hey, I'm sorry about skipping out—"

"Come in," I interrupted. "We can talk about that later. I just wanted to update you on plans for this place before the afternoon got crazy, okay?"

I sketched out the resort program plans for her, starting with the Western Trails concept and continuing with the mini-clinics, vacation season riding camps, and the lounge. "It's not going to happen overnight, but we can really transform our business and do something no one else is," I said by way of conclusion. "If you want to own Western Trails and make it yours, I know you can come up with something really fresh that hasn't been done before."

Kennedy was silent. At first I thought she was stunned by the good news, coming right before she'd almost made the mistake of giving me her notice. But then I saw the sullen set to her jaw, the way her lips were pursed, as if she was so annoyed, she couldn't trust herself to speak.

I couldn't trust her to speak, either. I got up hastily and went for the door. "You just need two more horse assignments," I said on the way out. "Go ahead and fill those in for me. I'll see you later."

Upstairs, safely locked in my office, I could let my outrage spill over in the form of angry tears. Damn that girl! Why did she do this—get so mulish and stuck in her head even when the right answer was staring her in the face? She didn't want to go off with Louise and teach horses to bow on command or walk politely while people waved banners around their heads or their riders brandished swords. She wanted to do *everything.* She wanted to go on trails and she wanted to ride tough horses and she wanted to teach. Kennedy wasn't a specialist—she was too scatterbrained, too easily distracted, too hummingly amazingly *alive* to settle on just one thing in life. If I handed her the Western Trails business that would be just one thing on her plate, which would always be overfilled as long as she worked for me, but it would be a bigger portion than the corporate trail rides had ever been, and it would be something she could build up and be proud of, her own creation.

From my window over the barn, I watched her leave the school tack room with bridles over her shoulder and saddles perched on her hips. I saw her stop to talk to Anna, give her a little kiss, keep walking down the aisle, Anna watching her go. I saw a little girl come pounding down the barn aisle to give her a hug, wrapping her arms around Kennedy's legs. I saw them go together to halter a gray pony, Kennedy showing the girl how to slip the leather halter strap behind the pony's ears.

I glanced to the left. In the other aisle, Louise was grooming one of her Belgians, reaching up to get the brush onto the horse's tall back. Too tall for Louise—the woman who asked for too much, and didn't know when to call it quits.

My phone buzzed and I lifted it, turning away from the scene below. Mark, saying he had been stuck in a budget meeting all afternoon. I smiled despite the tears still smeared across my cheeks —well, I'd guessed right about one thing, anyway! He asked if I wanted to get a drink after lessons tonight. *It's non-stop tonight,* I typed back, regretful I had to turn him down. *I don't think I'll have the energy.*

Maybe it will storm, he replied. *Don't you have to cancel if there's too much lightning?*

On cue, I heard a rumble of thunder. *That jerk!* I laughed aloud. He was looking out of his barn aisle at the sky I couldn't see, watching my evening suddenly free up. *We'll see,* I replied. *Try me at seven.*

Chapter Eighteen

"How did I let you people convince me to show in June?"

There was a chorus of laughter, mostly led by the pony kids, who were still too young to feel heat. So far their summer vacation had consisted of them riding around in the sun until their cheeks were fire-engine red, spraying each other with hoses while they washed down their ponies, and then lounging around the boarders' tack room eating those cheap tortilla chips, the ones that come with "$2 only" already printed on the bag, and bag after bag of mini-donuts, until I chased them out and told them if they wanted to hang around my barn all summer they'd have to do some work.

"Fine, let's get everyone's numbers and get you mounted." I left Anna and Kennedy to supervise the grooming and tacking, and marched over to the secretary's tent with a fat wad of paper in my hand—Coggins tests, release forms, receipts from pre-paying online.

Okahumpka Horse Park was one of the few places in the region where you could brave the summer sun to enter your insane students in unrecognized short stirrup and low jumper and junior/senior equitation, all of those bread-and-butter schooling show classes. A lot of my kids were looking forward to their rated show debuts in the fall, since they'd just started riding in the past year or so and I'd seen no need to trundle a load of ponies and kids around the state so they could forget their diagonals and miss half their distances. There'd been lots of whining over the winter as I took the adults on the rounds of Venice and Wellington and Ocala, hitting a few big jackpots with my jumper Ivor on welcome nights and even a pair of Friday night Grand Prix classes that were, frankly, a little out of my comfort zone. But Kennedy had happily stayed home to mind the children, and I could now see, to fall in love with the barn manager, so she'd borne the brunt of the complaints.

Still, I couldn't put off their show-ring careers forever, and even some of my adults, like Gayle, who should have known better than to want to show in June, had been pleading with me to bring the crew to this schooling show. Maybe they'd gotten me drunk specifically to get me to agree to it. Either way, here we were.

"I've got the crew from Seabreeze Stables," I told the secretary, a red-faced woman named Sasha whom I remembered from many previous years of schooling shows and dressage tests here at the little horse park.

"Nice to see you, Grace," she said drily, as if annoyed I had felt the need to give my barn name.

"Force of habit." I shrugged. "It's been a minute or two since I've been to a show here."

Sasha leafed through the ream of paper I'd handed her, plucking out the various forms and laying them in their correct trays. "Twelve horses! Did you bring two trailers?"

"Four. Some of the parents have bought their own."

"You gotta watch those horse show moms when they have their

own trailers," said a man lounging nearby and watching proceedings. It was a guy named Otto, I remembered after a second of searching my memory, a local hunter trainer from the east side of Orlando. "Too much freedom, they start bouncing from barn to barn!" He laughed, then wheezed. "I got empty stalls too, you know!"

We laughed along, Sasha and I, *hahaha those students, they're wily ones, have to watch them!* and then I took my pile of numbers, grabbed a few extra safety pins from the red plastic cup on the folding table, just in case any disappeared between the trailer and the show-ring, and waved goodbye. I sweated back to the trailers, all lined up in a little row as close to an oak tree as we'd been able to get them. Kennedy and Anna had overseen the distribution of brush boxes and, along with some of the adult riders who were more capable, were making sure everyone got their mounts brushed clean of travel dirt without getting kicked or smooshed between the horses. It was tough without stabling—once you got used to having a nice set-up at rated shows, with a tack stall and a grooming stall and every horse with his own box, going back to tying horses to a trailer and hoping no one freaks out or throws a fit is kind of nerve-wracking.

I grabbed saddle pads and started distributing them to riders, then started pulling out the saddles, matching them up with their horses and tipping them pommel down on the grass, cantle against the trailer. "It's almost ten o'clock already, let's go everyone who is going in short stirrup, your class will get called in about half an hour!" In the distance, a loudspeaker squawked with the winners of the first Walk-Trot class. It was one of those shows with a long roster of beginner classes, starting with Hunter in Hand and proceeding to

Cross-rails, so the traditional hunter classes were mid-morning affairs.

I was helping with bridles when another truck and trailer pulled up near our compound. At first I didn't take any notice of yet another competitor's arrival, just letting it pass by in the corner of my vision, but when the horse inside let loose with a series of banging kicks, I paused in the middle of tightening a noseband and looked. I recognized the four-horse gooseneck trailer with its extra-high roof immediately—it was Louise's rig.

Anna caught my gaze from over the back of Wonder, two ponies down from me. Her eyes were huge. "Did she bring that Shire here?" she gasped.

"Anna, if she brought that Shire here with all my kids at their first show, I will murder her."

"Murder!" The kid next to me, working the pony's throat-latch into place, looked up in astonishment.

"Yes, Nora, I will murder her," I snapped. "But don't tell anyone or the police will know who did it."

"Got it," Nora agreed, and went back to wriggling the keeper onto the throat-latch strap.

Good kid, I thought. "You're all set here, Nora. Anna will get you mounted in a minute. Circle under the tree with the other kids and then we'll go to the warm-up together."

"Got it," Nora said again, and I slipped out from between horses to see what Louise thought she was up to.

I caught her as she got out of the truck, paperwork in hand. "Louise. You didn't say you were coming today."

"I brought him to get some off-the-farm experience." Louise thumbed through her papers, muttering as she took stock of each form. "He's been going so well," she added.

If you considered a freight train with no brakes going well, I thought, my jaw tightening. Things had *not* been going well with the Shire. I was getting so fed up with the horse's incessant kicking, bolting, neighing, shoving and every other sort of bad behavior, I was almost reconciled to the probability that she'd be leaving without notice in the next few weeks, breaking her rental contract without any thought to how her sudden absence would cut into next month's budget. I did want rid of her at this point. Louise had gone from annoying sideshow to three-ring-circus of drama in a remarkably short period of time, even by horse-people standards. Plus, there was the whole Kennedy situation. She hadn't said a word to me about leaving or staying, but she'd certainly managed to go around the barn doing chores and teaching lessons with a haunted expression. Anna didn't look happy, either.

Come to think of it, the only person connected to Sampson and Louise who wasn't looking down in the dumps was Mark.

We'd gone out last night, even though I knew I'd be getting up early for the show this morning, and would regret the lack of sleep. There'd been dinner at a huge, touristy Irish-themed pub, with dancing and fiddle music and a foaming black pint of Guinness served by what was apparently a genuine Irish lass named Niamh. Then there'd been a walk around a moonlit lake, with more laughter and chatter. We'd talked about horses and our past and our present, but not much else—no politics, no plans, *no pressure,* I'd thought on the way home, letting my face slip into a blissful smile.

It was the perfect relationship for someone like me. Mark didn't know what we were doing; I didn't know what we were doing—I just really, really liked him and he seemed to really, really like me. I was happy to take things slow with him: Colorado Mark, firm and upstanding mountain man Mark, salt-of-the-earth Mark, treat a lady with respect Mark.

So if keeping his idiot Shire around meant I saw more of him, well, there was always a bright side to everything, right?

Besides, Louise wasn't Mark's property. I could be straight with her and not worry that I was somehow interfering with his plans for the horse. If he didn't like the limits I was forced to set on Louise's training program, he should find a better trainer for his crazy horse.

"Listen, Louise," I said seriously, "a lot of my kids are at their first show today. I need to keep Kennedy and Anna's attention one hundred percent focused on them, because I need all the help I can get. So if you have any issues with this guy, please understand, we can't help you."

Louise nodded, her head cocked slightly, an eyebrow lifted in apparent confusion, as if she was wondering where I'd gotten the idea she'd ever need help, like she didn't need one of us to help her with that bloody horse every single day, like she wasn't trying to steal Kennedy from right under my nose, when I would have been happy to lend her Kennedy to fix this horse if she'd only asked for the help.

"And I need you to keep your distance from my kids and their horses. Warm-up ring, over here at the trailer, anywhere. No coming over to say hello, no riding anywhere near them."

She nodded again, letting a bored expression fall over her round face.

Fine, I thought.

"Good luck," I said, and walked away, leaving her with a lead rope in her hands and a kicking Shire in her trailer. *Good luck to all of us.*

* * *

"Left rein, left rein, left rein, oh good girl, now just keep him on the rail."

"You're talking to yourself."

I looked to my right and saw Mark smiling at me, and my heart, which had been squeezed tight by the strain of having three of my pony riders in the ring at the same time, lifted with a sudden stunning buoyancy. For a moment I just drank him in—*oh, look, it's Mark!*—taking an idiotic pleasure in the simplicity of his features, his kind eyes, his silly Mickey Mouse ball cap which I supposed I was just going to have to get used to. "What a surprise," I managed to say finally.

He put his hand briefly on my shoulder, gave my arm a companionable rub, before taking it back and placing it carefully on the hot black fence rail in front of us. "Louise called and said she was bringing Sampson. Since I knew you were coming too, I thought I'd come cheer everyone on." He glanced at my conspicuous lack of show attire. "I kinda thought you'd be riding."

"In a summer schooling show? Mark. Please." I laughed, then turned my eyes back on the ring. Nora trotted past, her eyes up and her heels down and her shoulders back and her diagonal dead wrong. "Sit two beats," I hissed, and Nora cast me a panicked glance before she did as she was told. "These are my green beans," I said in a normal tone to Mark. "Very first horse show."

"They look great," Mark observed. "So calm! How did you do that?"

Melanie came up on the rail next, so close her boot was nearly scraping the wood. "Little inside rein and give yourself some room," I told her. "Just close your fingers until he's off the fence." She gave no indication that she'd heard, or indeed that she was even breathing, but as they progressed down the arena, I saw Figment come off the rail a few feet. "Good girl," I said to myself. To Mark I threw a sidelong grin. "They're not calm. They're just too terrified to do anything so they're riding on auto-pilot. And they all know how to ride, so that's the best possible outcome."

"Clever trainer," Mark chuckled.

"And where is your pony?" I asked, finding I had some space between students. The judge asked them to walk and Nora, Melanie and Sarabeth all managed to comply without too much head-shaking and drama. "Off nibbling buttercups in the shade?"

Mark looked around. "I have no idea actually. But she isn't taking him in a class until after the lunch break, she said. Adult equitation under saddle?"

"That won't be for ages. There's still a junior jumper class after the lunch break and that one's always at least half an hour long. Every kid wants to do it, even if they just trot all the fences."

Mark smiled. "Then I guess I get to hang out with you."

I felt a thrill at the sentiment, although he wasn't really going to get to hang out with me. Follow me around, more like. The judge called for the canter next, just as I'd warned the girls she would do after a walk, and I groaned as Sarabeth picked up the wrong lead. "Sit down, trot, and fix it so the judge knows you can do it!" I told her clearly as she approached. She winced and did as she was told, picking up the right lead in the corner of the arena.

It went on like that for the next couple of minutes, lots of hissing instructions and panic-stricken glances cast at me by my students; then all the kids went to the center of the ring so the judge could make up her mind about placings. "This is when we wait for the tears," I told Mark. I picked up my ring-bag, stuffed with Gatorade and granola bars. "Want to help me with triage?"

"Of course." Mark took the bag from me and smiled.

Luckily, there wasn't too much triage—Sarabeth managed to eke out sixth ("that's because you *fixed* your lead," I told her, "rather than just riding around on the wrong one") and Nora and Melanie got white and pink ribbons, respectively. Nora was admiring her white ribbon as she dismounted and obediently took the Gatorade bottle I held out. "I think this one's prettiest," she said.

"You've never had the curse of the white ribbon before," I told him. "Sometimes, you get on a fourth-place streak and it seems like you can't win anything else for months."

"I wouldn't even mind." She clipped the ribbon to her pony's bridle, where it fluttered prettily alongside his black-tipped mahogany ears.

"Pink's better," Melanie argued, and I decided there was no point in telling them otherwise. If they wanted to think their ribbons were all the best color, that was better than tears over the blue ribbon disappearing with a pigtailed girl on her buckskin pinto pony. That was a flashy little pony, now that I thought about it. I wondered idly if he might be for sale. Schooling shows could be interesting places to find diamonds in the rough.

Sarabeth didn't bother dismounting, sticking to the saddle as she admired the bright green of her ribbon and dug her free hand into the box of granola bars, eagerly attended by her pony, who had nearly turned himself inside out trying to see what she was eating while still on his back. "Obviously I'll give you some, Romeo," she told the pony, pushing his head back from her stirrup. Her mother arrived to take over refreshment duties, giving me a minute to look over at the ring. The ring volunteers, a quartet of horse show dads with red cheeks, had nearly finished putting up the line of fences for the Hunter Hack class.

"They're calling your next class in a second," I said. "Mel, Nora, back in the saddle." The girls scrambled up and Sarabeth's mother ran a towel over their paddock boots, brushing away ring dust that had settled on the brown leather and bringing a shine to their toe-caps. "Thank you, Amy," I told her gratefully. "You're already the top horse show mom."

"That's just my first class," Amy laughed, throwing the towel over her shoulder. "But thank you."

In the melee of getting the girls back through the in-gate with the other competitors in the class, I completely forgot about Mark, and it wasn't until they'd lined up to take turns jumping the five-stride line of fences that I realized he wasn't by my side anymore. I climbed up the six steps of the little grandstand, then turned and scanned the show-grounds, a big sunny green of trailers and horses and humans milling around, and finally saw Louise's unmistakable horse in the distance beyond our trailers, walking around with his head straight up and Louise looking like a tiny bee clinging to his back. The person standing nearby was Mark.

"Don't get yourself into trouble out there, Mark," I muttered. Maybe Mark was a capable horseman, used to outsized draft horses, but he was also a bit too much of a gentleman to let Louise take the brunt of any bad behavior the Shire threw at her. I could imagine he'd rush in under those dinner-plate hooves to take the reins if the horse went up in the air, and I didn't want to think about what could happen to him then.

Just then, a gust of wind came up.

It was a lone breeze, a flick of moving air that seemingly had no reason, no cause, and no follow-up. It came blasting through the arena first and knocked over the standards of the hunter hack line just as the first pony was trotting up to it. The pony spooked and backtracked in rapid reverse, the child on board toppling over his shoulder, a frustrated squall leaving her lips as the reins were plucked from her fingers and the pony took off in the opposite direction. The deviant breeze shot past the scattering horses, ruffling my hair and snatching a few ball caps as it went, and socked into the white-board with the afternoon's courses taped to it, knocking it over. Then it tackled the tents set up nearby—the secretary's tent, the tack vendor's tent, the tent belonging to the hippie-type lady selling horse cookies she'd made in her kitchen the night before, and *that* tent it decided to whip up into the air. *Straight up* into the air —I'd never seen anything like it: an invisible column of air, a tornado with nothing in it but some leaves and, at the very top, that white, four-poster tent, with a painting of a smiling horse holding up a cookie on it.

I looked back at the ring and saw the ring steward had caught the runaway, and the kid's trainer was consoling the fallen rider. The rest of the horses in the ring were still lined up, ears pricked, watching the slow-motion disaster of the flying tent. My kids were sitting pretty, heels down, shoulders back, ready for anything. I turned again.

The tent went soaring over the show-grounds and flung itself into the ground a good hundred feet beyond my trailer. There were no horses at my trailer; I did a quick headcount of horses in the warm-up ring and saw the rest of my students clustered close to Kennedy and Anna. The only horse over by the trailers was the Shire.

I never saw what he did—the big oak tree we'd parked near hid that. I just saw him after the fact, galloping, riderless. He beelined straight to the fence along the road and let it turn him, then he spun back and went hard in the direction he'd come, confused, his white legs flashing, his black body soaring with more speed than a horse his size should have had.

And then Mark was in front of him.

I nearly jumped off the little grandstand, I was in such a hurry to stop him, but he was far away, not even within earshot, so even if I'd screamed, and maybe I did, who knows, he never would have heard me. Even if he had, my screams never would have stopped him. His body was at an angle to me and I thought he was holding something, but I didn't know for sure, all I knew was the Shire was going to kill him. There was no way that horse would stop.

It was a drama playing out for just a few people—the other two observers here at the top of the grandstand, the handful of people close enough to the open field to see what was going on. For everyone else, heads and horses and trailers and trees would have blocked their view. They might have heard the rumble of hooves, might have heard shouts of *Horse! Loose horse!* from the distance, and tightened up their grip on their reins and lead ropes, but they wouldn't have seen Mark standing in front of that towering horse, and they wouldn't have seen what he did—even I couldn't see it— but then the horse was slanting, slowing, plunging, halting.

Mark took the reins.

Behind me, immune to the drama in the distance, the Hunter Hack class had started back up again.

I let out a long, shuddering breath. The other spectators on the top looked around, and our eyes met nervously before we turned back to the ring. Nora picked up her reins and nudged her pony forward to take her turn over the fences, and as she went, the fluff of cottony cloud directly overhead unleashed a downpour of massive cold rain drops. Puffs of sand rose up in mini-explosions as each drop hit the arena footing, and I realized it had been the birth of this cloud that had precipitated the gust of wind.

Chapter Nineteen

MARK HAD STOPPED the horse with a shavings fork, I found out later. He'd held it out in front of him not with the points out, like an angry villager joining a mob, but sideways like a staff, making it into a long and threatening rod which, in turn, made him into a much wider and more dangerous of an obstacle than your average puny human. He told me the story while I drank from a bottle of Gatorade, holding Splash's reins while Lizzie was in a nearby Port-a-Potty, and wishing there was something stronger than electrolytes in the sports drink.

"You can't ever risk them getting out back at the Fort, or at another resort, or *definitely* not in a park," he explained. "There's just no other option—you get out there and you stop that horse."

"I see," I said. "Well, I was a long way away, like I said. It looked really bad from where I was."

"It could have been," he acknowledged quietly, and that's when Lizzie emerged from the Port-a-Potty, still buttoning her breeches, and asked for a leg-up.

The sudden rain shower had passed, blowing west and billowing up into a luxuriously pillowy thunderstorm, its white heights blinding in the midday June light. The temperature was creeping towards ninety, with a swampy humidity that stuck to the skin and made the mere act of thinking a challenge. Once junior jumpers ended, the children's part of the day wrapped and Anna was free to ride her horse in some adult classes. Louise, reunited with the Shire, was still planning to do the same. All I wanted to do was go home and collapse in front of an air conditioner vent.

I gave Lizzie a hoist onto Splash and she kicked her boots into the stirrups. I held the reins while she got situated, watching her serious face as she straightened out the kinks in her reins and adjusted her stirrups just so. Of all my juniors, she was the only one I'd considered taking to the rated shows over the winter season, but she wanted to do jumpers and Splash could be a speedy, technical ride. Now she looked down at me and a grin lit her face. She was deeply tanned and cool as a cucumber, the quintessential Florida horse show kid.

"Go get it," I told her in lieu of actual coaching, because she'd explained once that last-minute course instructions made her forget everything she'd memorized beforehand. I released Splash's reins and stood back.

I watched her ride over to the in-gate to check with the steward about her ride. He nodded at her question and held up three fingers in response. "Three riders ahead of her," I told Mark. "Want to climb up to the top and watch?" I pointed to the grandstand.

"Let's," Mark agreed, and we climbed up the rattling steel grandstand, to the spot about fourteen feet up where I'd recently watched what I had thought was his impending demise.

"So this is quite a gig you've got," he said when we'd settled onto the metal bench. A young rider was cantering a heavy-set Appaloosa around the ring, cheerfully demolishing the course. "A lot of students to keep track of, and horses too."

"It's not usually this hairy," I laughed. "At the big shows we have stalls, tack rooms, an extra groom. Lizzie, the girl I just sent out, is my new working student, so she'll be an extra pair of hands when she isn't showing. I usually stay at the in-gate and the warm-up ring most of the day, and call over on the phone when it's time to send up another horse. Today has been a reminder of what life used to be like, though."

"Before you went to the big shows?"

"Yeah. Some trainers, this is their entire career, and I'm sure plenty of them are happy with it. But I've always preferred the big shows. It's a whole lifestyle. If I can't be at my farm, I like to rebuild a nice, orderly version of it at a show-ground."

"See? It's all about order. We have a lot in common." Mark laughed and put a hand on my knee, shaking it familiarly.

The Appaloosa refused the final fence with what appeared to be a dogged devotion to tradition, simply stopping in front of the little brush box and pole as if he'd forgotten what to do when confronted with such a thing. The girl on his back resignedly gave him a kick and a slap with her crop, and he stepped over the brush box (although not the pole—that fell between his legs) and jogged away to close out the timer. There was a scattering of applause from the crowd, most of whom seemed to be regulars who knew the Appaloosa and his quirks.

"No," I said. "This is definitely not my scene."

"You're ambitious," Mark observed. "You're not going to quit this anytime soon, are you? You still have things to accomplish."

"You know, that's funny." A tall teenage girl on a slab-sided

Thoroughbred entered the ring, an old saddle pad scrunching behind the knee-roll of her battered saddle. I sat up a little. Something told me this kid was going to ride her racetrack reject like a bat out of hell. "I used to think I was ready to retire. Like it was all getting to be too much stress. Like I was tired of going to shows, tired of the fuss and the expense and the students. But I had a good winter, I made some money, and I've got all these students who want to do something with their riding, not to mention the sheer fact that I built this equestrian center and I'm proud of what I've done... and I don't know if I'll ever be able to give it up. I might have to drop in the traces, you know?"

The Thoroughbred in the ring broke into a ragged canter, then a hand gallop, and careened down to the first fence, his head carried at giraffe height. He got a close distance at the very base of the fence and sprang straight up, four legs curled under him like a deer fleeing a hound. His rider sat steady and centered, eyes forward, chin set, hands quietly hovering a few inches above his withers. I liked the way she held contact; most kids at this level threw their reins away over every fence, like they were jumping maxed-out Grand Prix fences.

"And then you see girls like this," I added, keeping my voice quiet as I didn't know where her trainer was in this scatter of spectators, "Determined. She's going places. I'd like to help her."

"Well, I can't deny that makes me happy," Mark said. His hand was still on my knee—no, it was on my thigh now. When had he done that, the sly dog? I glanced at him. He wasn't looking at the girl in the ring, he was looking at *me*.

"Why? What difference could it make to you? If anything, if I retired I'd be around the farm more. As it is, I'm gone half the winter."

"Because I'd heard you were selling up and moving away, and I didn't want you any further away than you already are."

"I'm five minutes away from your barn."

"Exactly."

The rider was urging her horse full-tilt at the fifth jump, an oxer facing the in-gate. He took a flyer and must have jumped twice the width of the fence, landing with a grunt on the other side and bolting forward as she hung onto his left rein with grim determination, dragging him around to the next fence. She had no notion whatsoever of strides and distance. I was fascinated by her. Unless she crashed, she would definitely win the class—getting the time and leaving the poles up with pure grit and instinct.

Next to me, Mark had moved his fingers from my thigh to my hand, pressed against the steel bench as I leaned forward, watching the teenager in the ring, and I felt the warmth of his touch spread over my skin. I widened my fingers a little, gave him room to snake his in between them, and we watched the teenager finish the round, wheeling through the sandy arena at a hundred miles an hour, the far-and-away fastest round—and clean, too.

I had everyone safely loaded by late afternoon, and the parents who had hauled in with their own trailers, gleaming and new and unblemished by hooves and teeth, were the first to leave. The nervous drivers went bouncing down the lane as slowly as possible, their SUVs groaning slightly with the actual work they were being asked to perform for only the second time in their suburban careers. Back at my own rig, six-horse-strong and shiny in the sunlight, a line of sweaty pony and horse faces blinked at me from behind the bars of their windows. I usually trailered with everyone wearing fly masks, to keep dirt from blowing into their eyes, but it was so awfully hot I'd decided I couldn't burden them with another sweaty irritant. We'd take our chances.

Kennedy was still packing up saddles in the tack room; Anna was gathering the water buckets the kids had left in piles over at the closest hose-pipe. I picked up a stray hoof pick left on the fender and reached up to the barred window above me, giving Wonder a tap on his pink nose with it. He wrinkled his nostrils and snorted at me. "Give us a minute, guys, I know it's hot," I told the horses apologetically, then turned. *"Seabreeze kids!"* I shouted. "Everyone in the truck!"

The kids who were left over from the SUV parade came crowding over like a pack of Labrador puppies and went wiggling up into the back seat of the truck, climbing over each other and squealing. There were ribbons in their hands and their garter straps had been replaced by rainbow-colored socks, pulled up to their knees over their beige jodhpurs. A few of them had bags of horse cookies from the organic horse cookie baker, who had recovered her battered tent and set up shop again after the drama during the hunter hack. I took a minute to consider the chaos I'd invited into my life, and how much fun it seemed to be having. Then I turned to make sure we'd absolutely picked up everything.

"That's it," Anna said, tossing the last few buckets into the tack room and shutting the side door. "Ready to go?"

"There's no *air conditioning!*" someone shrieked from inside the truck cab.

I looked around. The only trailer left nearby was Louise's gooseneck, abandoned in the sun. Neither she nor Mark nor the

Shire were anywhere to be seen. I supposed it was close to time for their class. The junior jumpers had taken forever, and it had pushed everything much later than usual. Anna had abandoned all thoughts of showing under that sweltering sun, but Louise had stuck around.

"Hop into the truck and pull the trailer up under the shade," I told Anna, tossing her the keys. "I'm just going to run back to the ring and let the others know we're leaving, and then we can go."

"The *heat!*" a child shouted, as if I'd forced them into the truck and locked all the doors.

"And turn on the air conditioning before someone calls the police."

Gayle was standing over at the show-ring with Patrice—not a good pair, I thought, since Gayle was sweet and impressionable and Patrice was... Patrice was not the good rider she thought she was, making this a friendship which could lead to disastrous advice sessions. I placed myself between them and draped my arms around their shoulders. "Ladies," I cooed, interrupting what was left of their conversation. "Are you staying? We're getting ready to take the horses back."

"We just want to watch Louise," Gayle explained. "Her class is coming up next."

In the arena, six adult riders, wilting from the heat, were waiting for the judge to make her final decision. Jackets had been excused but one hold-out was still wearing her navy-blue hunter coat, urged to maintain tradition by an overly eager trainer. Her beet-red face was the perfect compliment to the blue, I thought. With her white ratcatcher collar in the middle, she could be in dress rehearsals for a Fourth of July parade. She could go as a rocket pop, or the Empire State Building. "Aren't you glad I didn't make you bring jackets?"

"I would have died," Patrice said. "I honestly can't believe I let Gayle talk me into this today! It's too hot for this nonsense. I think you have to be born in Florida to handle riding in the summer."

"I could not agree more." I winked at Gayle, who had wanted to come as much as the kids and now wore a slightly hurt expression. "But some of my students have become truly die-hard horse show brats."

"I might take the rest of the summer off," Patrice admitted. "I'm just not used to this weather. In Philly—"

I tuned out. Listening to the snowbirds complain about Florida heat was almost as boring as listening to them compare how bad their winters had been back up north. Sure, life would be better if the ambient temperature was a steady 72 degrees, but that wasn't the reality, so could we please just move on? Sometimes I wondered where all the Florida natives had gone, or if there had only ever been a few dozen of us all along, and we'd been fooling ourselves into thinking there was this entire population of people who understood the seasons and pull of this hostile, gorgeous place.

The judge made up her mind, or maybe just got tired of standing in the sun and pointed out a random order of finish, and the adult riders filed out of the ring. All of them looked rather defeated, even the ones who had pinned in the top three. It was a bit much, I thought, since they all got ribbons in a six-man class, but June horse showing will do that to you.

"Here comes Louise!" Gayle said excitedly. "Sampson looks gorgeous, doesn't he?"

I stepped back and let Gayle and Patrice gush over the Shire. I didn't think he looked gorgeous. He looked wiped out—and I was kind of impressed that Louise had managed to get the best of him, physically, anyway. Mark was standing next to Sampson at the in-gate, his hand on the horse's left rein as if he was leading them to the ring, and I wondered how involved he'd been in the current taming of the Shire. He'd disappeared after Lizzie's jumper round had ended with sixteen faults, and I'd been forced to rush over and turn it into a technical discussion before her mother over-sympathized the situation into tears and frustration. Lizzie was too good a rider to let one bad day get in her way. By the time I'd gotten everything under control, Mark was nowhere to be seen.

Now he was standing back to let Louise nudge Sampson into the ring, where the pair took up their place alongside the rail. As the Shire passed us, I stepped away from the fence, eager to keep those massive hooves far from me, but he didn't offer to kick or buck or even crow-hop—none of his favorite antics. He was puffing, his breath coming so hard I could hear him even after they'd moved off down the rail, and his veins were standing out like a relief map on his neck and hindquarters. Yet his eyes, which should have been gleaming with excitement, were dull and glazed.

What had they been doing, galloping the beast in circles until he was ready to collapse? Not to say that wasn't exactly what Sampson might need to get his head out of the clouds and onto his rider, but in the middle of a hot June day? At a horse show, no less? That crossed both lines of ethics and lines of equestrian etiquette.

A breeze tickled the sweat at the back of my neck and I reflexively looked up and east, noting the cloud that was starting to raise up beyond the trees along the main road. "It's going to storm," I told the ladies. "I need to get on the road before the weather gets all Florida on me. The road out ponds up the minute it starts raining."

"But Sampson! Don't you have a minute to see what he does?"

Patrice's eyes glittered with suppressed excitement and, I suspected, a touch of malice. Had the barn ladies been rooting *against* Louise all this time? Here I thought they'd been getting their heads turned, and all the while it had just been another source of gossip for them. Well, that wasn't so surprising. The only thing at a show barn more popular than the horses was the gossip.

"Take a picture for me," I said. "But I don't think he's going to do anything." That horse was too knackered to put on a show now.

I lifted a hand to wave to Mark as I walked past him, but he didn't see me. He didn't look away from Sampson and Louise.

I heard the crowd *ooooooo* but I was already too far away to know what happened, and I decided not to stop, not go back and satisfy my morbid curiosity. I just hoped no one had gotten hurt.

Chapter Twenty

THE WEEKEND FELT endless. Between the show on Saturday, and lessons on Sunday, I felt like I'd been run through a full washer/ dryer cycle by lights-out Sunday night. Luckily, Monday was an actual day of rest this week, with no extra chores or state visits on the schedule. The weekend grooms would feed, turn out, and clean stalls alongside Margaret. The rest of us were welcome to sleep all day, if we so desired.

Still, I woke up up restless on Monday morning, and found myself wandering back and forth between kitchen and bedroom. Max's toenails clicked behind me, as he patiently trotted in my wake across the old wooden planks. I wanted nothing more than to shut my brain off and climb back into bed, but I'd woken up fretting over the project that had kept me up late last night.

There had been a buzz in the barn yesterday, a rumor spreading quickly amongst the adults and kids alike. People kept asking me: were we moving barns, was I going to close this one and take the business someplace more rural, more remote? One little girl was actually holding back tears when she confronted me, helmet on head and reins in hand, to demand why I was going to ruin her life by closing up the barn.

"I'm not," I told her. "Don't believe everything you hear. Barn gossip is notorious for being far from the truth."

"I don't know what *notoriously* means," she assured me, giving in to a luxurious sob. "I'm only *seven.*"

Putting out fires all afternoon made Sunday, already a beast of a day, absolutely exhausting. My ambitions for the farm made it even worse. After the day finally came to an end, when I should have simply collapsed into bed, I'd gone up to my office and studied my notes instead, reading through the pages I'd scribbled with ideas for decor and riding programs again and again. I'd finally flipped open my dusty laptop and typed them into something resembling order, ironing out all the problems I could along the way.

The problem I came to again and again, the problem I just didn't want to face, was Mark.

I hadn't seen him after we left the show on Saturday. I knew he was off work that evening, and thought he might have texted, but my phone stayed quiet all evening, and I was too tired to care... well, *almost* too tired, anyway.

I had my suspicions about his radio silence. He'd done something he was ashamed of on Saturday, something he didn't want to talk about with me. I told myself I was being paranoid to think such a thing, but I knew I wasn't. This was the horse business. We were professionals who were subsidized primarily by amateurs and braggarts, trying to cover our bills in a business that paid its investors in scraps of fabric and good feelings. We'd all done things we were ashamed of to make sure our checks to the feed store would clear.

Drugs, I thought, whenever I let my mind worry at the question.

He'd drugged the horse. It would describe the dull glaze of Sampson's eyes. And what if he had? What was the problem? Well, it made the horse an unpredictable danger to himself and others, in a myriad of ways. Just sticking the vein—just depressing the plunger—just pushing that cocktail of chemicals into the horse's neck: this was a recipe for an explosion. You simply didn't know how'd they react. I'd seen horses go into seizures. I'd seen horses go from simply high-strung to utterly high-wired, panicked and strung-out, crouching in terror at every sound and leaping at every falling leaf. Not usually, of course... but the problem existed. Reactions happened. People got hurt. Horses got hurt.

Then, there was the potential of the opposite happening. Dulled reflexes and slowed cognition could turn a simple stumble into a rider-crushing topple to the ground.

I couldn't blame a trainer for occasionally resorting to drugs when a horse was out of control and there were no simple solutions, but the right answer for a Shire at a schooling show who was potentially on the rampage amongst a crowd of children? That was to shove his wooly arse straight back onto the trailer and get him home for the Come-to-Jesus he so sorely needed. Not taking a chance with so many others present.

I *could* blame a trainer who had just realized a rival down the road was planning on undercutting him on his bread-and-butter, and who needed to keep his bosses happy at all costs, and decided that getting the horse into the ring that day was more important that anything else.

When that thought darted into my brain, unbidden and unwanted, I'd closed the browser window and shut my laptop. I'd been looking at reviews for his trail rides, making notes on what people mentioned they liked (the cute cowgirl costumes on the guides, the wildlife that was pointed out to them, the feeling they'd gone back in time) and what they disliked (the heat, the smell, the prices). Two of those things, I'd been thinking, I could influence. How often did Mark have the trail barn really thoroughly cleaned? Did he use enough shavings? I hadn't taken note during my brief visit. Well, I was new to corporate espionage, I'd told myself. I wasn't going to get everything right on the first try.

By that time, Max had fallen asleep against the back wall, just behind my chair, and I'd nearly stepped on him when I roused myself at ten o'clock and crept down the creaking stairs and out the open barn aisle, avoiding walking past the sleeping horses, who were always ready to wake the dead for the chance at an extra flake of hay. I'd dropped my clothes on the floor and wriggled between the sheets to try and snatch a few hours without dreams.

So by all rights, I should have slept late on Monday, given all the extra drama, given that single late night in a lifetime of early bedtimes.

Instead, I pulled on riding clothes and went to the barn.

"Hey buddy," I said to my gray stallion, who puffed his nostrils at me through his stall bars.

Ivor was delighted with my unexpected attention, rumbling his happiness with a deep-throated nicker every time I rounded the corner with another item of tack. This happened rather often, as I rarely tacked him up myself, and kept forgetting things and having to go back to the tack room to seek them out. Front and back boots of black neoprene and vinyl, a space-age saddle pad somehow designed to cool him off more efficiently than if he'd had nothing on at all, a black jumping saddle I'd treated myself to after one of our

Grand Prix wins over the winter, a matching breastplate-bridle-ear bonnet trio because he'd taken to shaking his head over imaginary flies—bit by bit I assembled the perfect riding kit, until finally he was ready to go. I stepped back and looked at him, a masterpiece of black and white, all muscle and grace and big floppy lips that never stopped chewing on whatever part of me he could reach.

"Gorgeous boy," I told him. He nipped at my shirt-sleeve and then darted back, ears swiveling, eyes bright. "Awful boy," I amended.

Anna texted me as I was leading him out to the mounting block. *Did you need help?*

I sent her back a quick *no thanks, enjoy your Monday* and dropped my phone into the pouch I'd clipped onto my saddle's back d-ring. This ride was just for me.

We warmed up with a leisurely trot in the covered ring, my eyes drifting occasionally to the sky outside, the shifting white clouds with their gray underbellies growing more and more numerous as the day heated up and the Florida swamps began to seep into the atmosphere. We'd have to hurry it up if I wanted to get out there at just the right moment—I was craving that sweet spot between sunny blue sky and crashing thunderstorm. I nudged Ivor into a billowing canter, his back rising to meet me and his neck arching in front of my hands, and we bounded around the arena for a few laps before I judged him steady enough to take out of the arena. Ever since this winter's grand prix campaign, Ivor had been more prone to fits of the sillies than before. And even if I wanted a joy ride, my good sense was too strong to let me take him out on the trail without making sure his bucks were already out of his heels.

"You ready now?" I asked him, and he flicked his white tail, the end brushing my boots. "Good," I replied. "Me, too."

We walked decorously across the parking lot and through the framing palmettos that marked the trailhead. I kept Ivor at a steady walk, reins long, as his hooves hit the white sand of the old trail running through the scrub. The sun was blinding on the sand; then it wasn't, as a cloud ducked in front of its white-hot glare for a moment, plunging the palmettos and longleaf pines rising in high, lonely stands into a quick moment of somber gray. From somewhere distant, the air seemed to wobble a little—a rumble of thunder nearly too far away to hear, shaken out from the skirts of a cloud still hidden by the horizon. Ivor tipped his black-tipped ears forward, backwards, side to side, watching the sky, the quiet palmettos, the lizards skittering across the trail in front of us.

I lifted my hands and my pelvis and my heels and my heart and Ivor plunged into his joyful canter.

We sped up the trail, the one I'd galloped with my grandfather, the one I'd sworn off once but just kept coming back to, the one left here by ancient tribes, cutting so deep into the palmettos they'd never grown back, the one the crackers of old Florida had ridden in search of wild cattle to drive to Spanish ports, the one that brave, half-crazy settlers had driven their wagons down, looking for a gator-free patch of ground to build their new life upon. Florida had an ugly history but no one could deny that everyone who had fought over these cypress swamps and sun-drenched forests and storm-tossed lakes had been a lethal combination of brave and mad, and my own forebears were in that mix. There might be an ugly future in store, too, but mine was bright. As for everyone around me, they were going to have to find a way to live with my singing, soaring prospects. Poor Heather, when I told her I wasn't going to sell after all. Poor Kennedy, when I told her I wanted an answer and she had to re-evaluate, yet again, what she wanted from her life. Poor Louise, when Kennedy stayed with me and she had to figure out how to run her barn alone. Poor Mark, when I undercut him on prices he had no control over. And lucky me, lucky lucky *lucky* me, for the chance to share this crazy corner of the world with strangers and civilians who had no idea what they were getting themselves into.

Central Florida had been reshaped into a wonderland of amusements and fantasies, but I was the one who was going to make sure there were still horses in it, always.

The dark underbelly of the clouds swept over us, crackling with electricity, and we had to turn back before we could get to the gator pond, but that had been my goal all along. We galloped towards home with Ivor's hooves pounding the packed-sand road, with the cold wind and the rumbling thunder in hot pursuit, under long-legged egrets winging their way home and a circling, screeching red-tailed hawk who didn't seem to know what he wanted, but would damn well make sure everyone knew he was displeased with the world. By the time the saucer-shaped lip of the storm's gust front had crawled over the barn, we were walking across the parking lot, empty except for the little collection of horse trailers, our breath coming fast and our eyes sparkling with the thrill of just being here, just being a pair of Floridians in love with our place in the world.

I untacked Ivor as the rain drummed down on the roof high above us, a deafening roar that was as much part of Florida, in my mind, as lazy beach days and wearing flip flops in semi-formal settings. His bridle and breastplate were sopping with sweat; I hung them up on the designated tack-to-clean hook in the tack room before I hosed him off. When I came back to the wash-rack, I stopped for a scant second, my steps arresting and then restarting like an engine which sputtered to stall but thought better of it. Mark was there, tickling Ivor's chin while the stallion clapped his big silly lips at him, trying to catch his fingers.

"Are you teaching my stud to bite?" I asked, pretending Ivor was a horse of great manners and gravity.

Mark turned, wisely bringing his fingers out of reach before he took his eyes off Ivor. "Something tells me he came pre-programmed with that information. I thought you didn't ride on Mondays?"

"I don't," I said, picking up the hose and unwinding a few lengths from the hanger. "Today I did."

"Any special reason?"

"No." And there really wasn't any. I'd just felt like it, that was all. He hadn't worked on Saturday, because of the schooling show. Mark certainly didn't need to know I'd been up late last night thinking of ways to beat him at his own business model, and that it had left me feeling restless and unsettled today. "Just felt like going for a gallop. Don't you ever feel that way?"

"I do," he admitted. "But I don't get the opportunity to do anything about it. Our horses never go faster than a jog."

I stopped unwinding the hose. "Mark! Are you telling me you haven't even cantered in—in how long?"

"It's been a while."

"Months?"

"Years."

I stood staring at him, my mouth agape, until he got

uncomfortable. "Don't look at me like that. I run a business aimed at giving tourists a nice, safe cowboy experience. You run a top show barn. The only similarity is our hay bill."

"I doubt you feed as much alfalfa as I do," I laughed. "You can get away with cheap-ass coastal."

"Good point."

I moved a little closer, mindful that Ivor was watching, ready to pounce if either of us came within nibbling range, and gave Mark a one-armed hug that didn't quite let our bodies touch. "It's nice to see you."

"Is that all I get?" He puckered his lips.

"Ugh, I'm drenched in sweat. That's all you get and you should thank me for it. Now move so I can hose off this horse."

Mark obliged, and I added the hiss of the water ricocheting off the concrete floor and walls to the rain pounding on the roof above. Ivor loved a good shower, and he leaned into the water pressure. I always had to set the nozzle to the highest jet to please him, while most of the other horses made it clear they preferred the more gentle shower option. Ivor was an extremely tactile stallion; he gloried in every sort of touch.

"What made you come over?" I asked while I was running the sweat scraper across Ivor's flank, his thin skin rippling in response. "If you know I don't ride on Monday? It was Sampson, wasn't it."

"I wanted to check on him after the show." Mark pushed off from the wall he'd been leaning on. "In fact, I haven't yet. You completely distracted me." He snuck under the cross-tie, ducking Ivor's eager mouth, and laid a gentle kiss on my damp cheek.

I paused momentarily; we hadn't really been casual kissers up until this point, saving them for more purposeful moments, but I supposed that was what we were now—someone had to make the first move, and it definitely wasn't going to be me, the queen of spinsters. Then I went back to squeezing the water from Ivor's coat. The rain had slowed down to a quiet hum, although the thunder was still cracking nearby, and I spoke in a normal tone when I asked, hesitantly, "What happened to him on Saturday?"

I didn't have to shout to be heard, and I knew it, but Mark still didn't answer me. I looked back, and he was gone already.

"Shit," I muttered, stroking the sweat scraper under Ivor's dripping belly. Ivor picked up a hind leg experimentally and I absently whacked him with the scraper in response. "Why doesn't he want to tell me what he did?"

When someone wasn't bursting at the seams to tell you their training story, the real answer to *what happened* was rarely anything you wanted to hear. Of course, we'd all done things we were ashamed of, I knew that, I did, and yet—it was hard to believe quiet, kind Mark had done something to Sampson he didn't want me to know about.

I didn't actually know him very well, I reflected. Just because I'd never seen him lose his temper, or peeked inside his barn's medicine cabinet, didn't mean he wasn't capable of troubling behavior.

Time to end that line of thought. There was no point in pursuing it.

"It's time for *you* to go back to your house and eat your hay," I told Ivor, who was chewing on the cross-tie now. He slapped the pavement with one foreleg in apparent agreement, and I was careful to slip the chain of his lead shank over his nose before I took him out of the wash-rack. He was just entirely too full of himself these days.

* * *

I purposely left Mark alone at the far end of the barn and busied myself cleaning Ivor's bridle and breastplate. I made a ritual of the job, filling a little bucket with warm water, stripping the sweat first and then rubbing in thick yellow saddle soap, then letting it dry before I sprayed oily conditioner on a separate tack sponge and lacquered the whole thing until it gleamed. I dunked his bit, a Pessoa with a fat French link in the center of the mouthpiece, in clean water and rubbed it with a tea towel. I buffed my saddle with conditioner as well, bringing out the shine in the black leather. Finally I tackled my boots, slipping each one off and wriggling my sweaty sock-clad toes on the cold linoleum while I scrubbed at the accumulation of horsehair and sweat which clung to the inside of the heels.

I killed all the time I could, and still Mark didn't come looking for me.

The rain stopped falling, the thunder moved out of earshot, and still I waited.

I came out of the tack room at last, my feet shod in an old pair of clogs, boots left in the tack room to wait for my rides tomorrow, and when I walked down the center aisle and peered down the row of stalls where the drafts lived, I saw no one.

He'd gone without saying goodbye.

"Well," I said aloud.

The pony across the aisle looked at me through his bars, whuffling a hopeful greeting through his nostrils.

"No," I told him. "No more hay right now."

So I went back to the house, where at least Max was waiting for me. As the oak trees overhead drip-dropped on the tin porch roof, I opened my laptop and began a new document.

Exclusive Extras, I typed at the top. *Bella Tuscany Friends and Families.*

I paused, hit enter a few times.

Western Trail Experiences.

Chapter Twenty-One

MARK SEEMED HAPPY to leave things hanging for the rest of the week, and I was hardly going to be the one to call him first, so I left things hanging, too.

And boy did they hang there—dirty and distressing, like a roommate's laundry that's always in your way. I couldn't do a thing without wondering what Mark was up to, wondering how his horses were today, wondering why the *hell* he didn't send me a text or drop by or call me to tell me he never wanted to see me again because he was a massive shit or because he'd somehow found out I was chasing a deal with Bella Tuscany that was going to carve, however tiny, a crescent out of his annual profits. No matter what his reasons, he should have wanted to end the limbo state he'd left things in. Or perhaps I should have wanted it to end more than he did.

But my nerves were so on edge, I didn't even have the courage to look up his number on my phone, let alone press on the phone icon, let alone type a message. If I messaged him, I thought, it would be once I was over this teenage drama and the only thing I would be able to say then would be: *Hey Mark, you're an asshole, love, Grace.*

I had butterflies in my stomach all of the time, as if I was looking at the diagram of a tough Grand Prix course while holding the reins of a very green horse, so I didn't feel like I could eat. This was a distress to Max, who had quickly gotten used to sharing every meal with me. Over the course of four days I think I ate six pieces of toast, half a bowl of spaghetti and some chicken tenders that Kennedy forced on me because she thought I looked peaked. I drank Vitaminwater all day, hoping that whatever mysterious chemicals were in it would at least provide me with enough nutrition to get through my days of riding and teaching without fainting dead away, a Victorian maiden in a Gothic novel.

It was awful, realizing I'd fallen for a guy and that I didn't know if he'd fallen for me. And then: recognizing that he probably hadn't, if he wasn't even going to call me. He'd kissed me on Monday and here we were on Friday and, what, I got nothing? I found it hard to fathom that entire populations of humanity lived this way, willingly falling in love all the time, seeking out relationships, even trashing the relationships they were already in because they wanted more of *this,* this endless drawn-out drama, which they apparently thought was *exciting* and *passionate* and made them feel *alive.*

Could I just go back to being cheerfully emotionally dead, please? It had served me well for several decades of adulthood. I hadn't asked for some metamorphosis into a person with a heart at this rather late stage in the game.

Of course, if Mark did want to be with me, didn't that make this great silence even worse? It would mean he was avoiding me because he was ashamed of something he'd done with Sampson. I hadn't gone down to the horse's stall the rest of Monday, afraid whatever Mark had found there had encouraged him to get the hell out of the barn before I discovered his transgression and confronted him. Even though I'd seen the horse on Tuesday, our paths had crossed only briefly, when Louise arrived and did her usually dramatic routine to get him to the cross-ties and tacked up. I'd been in the tack room, doing the horse assignments, by the time she went out to ride. In that brief moment I'd walked past the cross-ties, I hadn't seen anything incriminating on him—no marks from whip or spur, no cuts on his mouth or face. His shoes were all intact and he didn't have any new scrapes on his hooves or fetlocks which would indicate he'd been stepping on himself in an effort to get out of a frightening situation. He looked a little thinner, but he'd done a lot of galloping and work he wasn't fit enough for on a hot summer day. The excess stress and strain could take a noticeable fifty or hundred pounds off a horse overnight, to be packed on again nearly as quickly.

I had nothing—*nothing*—to go on and nothing to hope for, either. Well, that wasn't quite true. I had my pride. Snuggle up with that on a cold night! But we didn't have many cold nights here.

Anyway, he'd left first. He'd kissed me and then he'd left without saying good-bye. No one could have expected me to reach out to him.

Well, the trail horses were going nicely, anyway, I told myself briskly. I'd called Kennedy and Anna into the office on Tuesday after morning chores and showed them the Western Trail Experiences outline I'd worked on all of Monday afternoon.

Kennedy had been confused at first, taking the sheet of paper but not really looking it over. "No one lives over there yet. What will the horses do in the meantime? There's nothing else on the schedule for them now."

"They're still going to be all-around lesson horses, like we've been prepping them for," I said, leaning back in my chair and giving it a little side-to-side swivel. "We'll evaluate again when this gets rolling. We have a lot of prep work. I was hoping you'd do it, Kennedy. This can be your project. Western Trail Experience Manager, what do you think?"

Kennedy frowned, digesting this information. She didn't know I had overheard her plans to take off with Louise—suddenly, I wondered if Louise had said something to Mark about the secret barn plot, and that was yet another reason he wasn't speaking to me. What if Kennedy surprised me by not taking the job, and instead went with Louise *and* told Mark everything I was planning? I rolled this unpleasant idea around in my mind while Kennedy leaned over and began whispering in Anna's ear.

"Well you have to *ask* her," Anna hissed in response to whatever hushed nonsense Kennedy was pouring out to her. "She's right here. Can we just do this?"

I raised my eyebrows. "You kind of have to, now."

Kennedy shifted uncomfortably in her seat. Her cheeks, usually pale, flushed pink; it clashed rather horribly with her maroon curls. Anna gave her a nudge. "Fine," she said at last. "Grace, can I move into the empty apartment?"

Anna bit her lip. Her gaze, trained intensely on me, was puppy-dog pleading. *Dammit,* Anna!

I spread my hands and looked at them helplessly. "That's kind of a problem, girls. I was thinking we could make that over into a rider's lounge. We're going to need one, and I'm not sure where else it can be done so cheaply."

Kennedy sighed gustily. "You *see,*" she told Anna, ignoring me completely. "I told you this wasn't in the cards. If she'd wanted me to live here, she would have asked me along time ago."

"That wasn't the reason," I interjected. "This just came up. The woman over at Bella Tuscany suggested it as a perk for members. I never asked you to move in here because you already have your own place. If you'd asked me…" I closed my mouth. No point in making her feel she'd squandered her best chances with me. "I need it for client space," I tried again. "These people have certain expectations, they'll want some resort-style amenities."

"So what, we're just resort recreation staff now?"

"No," I snapped back, stung. "We're making the best of a bad situation and we're catering to the customers that we're being given. This is the reality now. We have to accept it. If the new neighbors are only here a few weeks out of the year, then we'll have riding opportunities for them during those weeks. If they want to go for a trail ride, we'll give them a trail ride. If they want a lounge to shower and eat a snack before they ride the resort shuttle back to their villa, we'll give them a lounge. The cost is almost nothing and the payout is… well, it's everything. It's keeping the farm open. It's our best shot at staying relevant, without getting kicked to the curb and told to take our rustic selves out to the country with the rest of our kind."

Both of them blinked at me for a moment—I suppose they hadn't been expecting me to get quite so passionate and deliver a stump speech.

Then Kennedy got up and left the room.

The door banged shut behind her and Anna and I looked at each other steadily while her footsteps went down the creaking staircase next to the office—something else I'd have to replace, I thought, if there were rich tourists clumping up and down on their way to the lounge.

"Anna," I said, "what is going on?"

"She wants to leave," Anna sighed, her chin wobbling. "She wants to train those theme park horses. And I just want her to stay. I'd do anything to get her to stay."

Anna leaned forward until her forehead was resting on the edge of my desk, and took a few deep, sobbing breaths. "Oh, honey," I said helplessly, because even if I'd know how to comfort her, I knew the words wouldn't come right now, not while I was dealing with my own miserable love affair.

We schooled the trail horses all afternoon. Honey was going so well, I asked Anna to pop out and drop some of the fences in the outdoor arena to cross-rails, and then I hopped the little mare around the course, jump by jump, trotting over them at first and then even letting her take a few at a canter. She bounced over the jumps happily, her ears pricked, with more spring in her step than I'd ever felt before. "Don't like it too much," I warned the mare with a chuckle, "because I still need you to be chill trail horse Honey, too."

Kennedy, riding nearby on Frank, must have heard me, but she didn't even look our way. She just trotted the big horse around the arena, round and round and round in an oval without a start and without a finish. I watched her for a moment from the center of the ring, annoyed, and then called out, "Are you trying to bore that horse to death?"

Kennedy shot me a death glare from under the brim of her hard hat. "Not exciting enough for you? Maybe you want a little drama?" She picked up her reins and sank her heels into Frank's sides.

The Appaloosa grunted and shot forward, his ears pinned and his tail flagged. They flew around the arena, Kennedy's seat riveted to the saddle like she'd been stuck there with glue. Sand scattered through the air when they hit the turns, Frank's big hooves shoving through the footing. Kennedy's hands had gone Western; only one was gripping the reins, and she held it high above the pommel of her jumping saddle; the other one was held at her side, waist-high, clearly just being used for balance whenever she sent Frank skidding around yet another tight turn.

They went around the arena three times, picking up impressive speed on each long side, and then, for good measure she jumped him over a couple of the cross-rails, Frank easily clearing the little fences without needing to scramble to find his stride. I filed that information away for later. Even with my temper rising, I could rationally observe the signs of a sensible jumper.

She pulled up in front of me, Frank's mouth gaping against the bit, and gave me a fierce glare. *"Well?"* she snapped. "Does he look bored to you now?"

"You did *not* just do that, sweetheart," I said flippantly.

Kennedy narrowed her eyes in response. *Yes I did,* she challenged me silently. *What will you do about it?*

"Get off him," I said, keeping my tone even and calm. "Walk him back to the barn. Get Anna to cool him out. Take the rest of the day off. Don't worry—you won't be paid."

"I have *lessons* tonight," she hurled at me. "What are you going to do—teach the beginners? I thought you were so above that."

"Kennedy," I replied softly, "get off of my horse."

Kennedy dismounted. She slowly, deliberately, ran up the stirrup leathers and loosened the girth. I sat on Honey with a loose rein, watching her. If she thought she was going to antagonize me with good textbook horsemanship, she was more far gone than any of us had realized. She turned and took Frank out of the arena, her boots sinking into the red clay. I resisted the urge to call out a saccharine-sweet *thank you!* But only just.

I turned my attention back to Honey, who was hot and blowing from our jumping workout. She was still just a couple of weeks into post-trail horse life, and the afternoon sun was pitiless. I had been hoping for a few rain clouds to cool us off, but so far the cotton-ball cumulus were sparse and the sky was a relentless French blue. "Sorry, mama," I told her, urging her back into a walk. "Let's go cool off in the covered arena."

Anna joined us in the covered arena a few moments later, sitting on the huffing, puffing Frank. She had her feet out of the stirrups and her legs drawn up over the saddle flaps, in an effort to protect her bare legs. She'd been working in khaki shorts all afternoon, doubling down on one of the constant barn manager projects she'd invented to constantly bring the facility to a higher state of cleanliness and functionality. Anna was surpassing her schoolmaster on a regular basis now.

"Do you want to tell me what happened?" She brought Frank alongside Honey and the two horses, old friends, exchanged a few friendly nips.

"Kennedy decided to show me how pissed she is at me by taking it out on Frank," I said simply. "So I told her to get out of here for the rest of the day."

"I gathered as much." Anna sounded unusually sarcastic. "Are you guys going to get through this, or I am witnessing a breakup?"

I gave the question its due consideration. Barn breakups were part of the business. Very few partnerships lasted more than a few years, and explosive dissolutions of happy trainer/employee relationships were almost to be expected. I was not one for drama, despite the show barn trainer stereotype, but I did draw the line at roughing up my horses, and poor Frank had not been ready for that kind of treatment. Even if he'd been fit enough to gallop flat-out around the outdoor arena at one o'clock on a June afternoon, there was no excuse for giving a trail/lesson horse any bad ideas about what to do the next time someone carelessly kicked him in the ribs. Ideally, the most he should have given Kennedy when she thunked her heels into his sides was a mild-mannered jog.

"We can't break up as long as the two of you are together," I said eventually. "It would be too awkward for everyone, and I'm not losing you. I'll never find another barn manager like you."

"Well, you might, but you'd have a few years of schooling ahead of you," Anna said with a snort. "If I'd ever gone off to ride with someone else, who knows what awful ideas I might have picked up. But seriously, I don't know if I'm thrilled to learn you're going to keep Kennedy around just to keep me happy. This feels awkward."

"Oh, don't worry. She's going to stick around because she wants to. She just doesn't know it yet."

"Don't you think I know that?"

I grinned at Anna. "Are you keeping things from me? What has she told you?"

Anna blushed and ducked her head. Her pony-tail spilled from under her hard hat, hastily put on back in the barn, and covered her face. "She wants to run the trail business, but she says you change your mind a lot. She doesn't trust you at the moment. She'd already made up her mind to go off with Louise. But now Louise is wishy-washy, too." Anna lowered her voice. "Louise said she can't pay her right away."

I shrugged. "That's typical." I ran a hand along Honey's neck, testing the length of her chestnut mane against my fingers. Her locks were nearly a palm's-width, far too long. "Can you pull manes next week? Start with the trail horses and work your way through to the ponies. You can get some kids to help if you want."

Anna was quiet for a moment, as if she wanted to keep arguing about Kennedy. But I was finished, and she knew me well enough to understand that when I changed the subject back to work, work was all I was going to talk about. "I can do that," she assented. "I'll grab some of the older kids and show them how."

"Perfect. Be sure to include Lizzie." I turned Honey towards the center of the ring, dropping my stirrups. "I'm heading in for lunch. I'll be back at four for the beginner hour."

I caught Anna's look of confusion as she realized I was teaching Kennedy's lessons, instead of canceling or trying to pass them off to her. *Yes, Virginia, I can teach the beginners,* I thought with a secret smile. I'd been teaching children longer than Anna and Kennedy had been on this earth. You always needed the next generation if your business was going to survive—that was one lesson I'd learned the hard way.

I had a couple of hours before lessons, and still no appetite. I looked in the fridge and I thought about Mark. I looked in the pantry at my rows of cans and I thought about Mark. I looked at Max, asleep on the sofa without much interest in whether I stayed or went, and I shrugged, slipped my clogs back on, and went out the door.

I was halfway to the Fort before I realized I should have changed out of my breeches; I was going to be conspicuous in riding clothes. I snort-laughed at the absurdity of looking out of place at a barn because I was wearing breeches and a cool-tech riding shirt with snaffle bits all over it, but that was part of the insanity of Mark and his life, right? His make-believe horse wonderland, a stable swarmed by tourists in shorts and cartoon mouse t-shirts? The turn off the county road was already looming in front of me, that back entrance by the warehouses and the employee ball-fields, the side of the theme parks which the tourists never saw. I shrugged, accepting myself for the sore thumb I was, and turned the truck down the tidy road. Everything here was neat as a pin and carefully landscaped, even though we were essentially on the backside, where things could have just as easily been industrial and trashy.

The canopy of live oaks overhead gave way to pines as I turned onto the resort road, and then I was pulling up to the rustic guard shack, I was smiling to the security guard as I showed him my ID and explained I was going to the horse barns, I was pulling into a parking spot and hustling across the pavement before a bus-load of guests came tumbling down onto the bus-stop and crowded around me. Maybe if I didn't want to be seen, I should have let the wave of families and grandparents and strollers full of toddlers wash around me, carry me up to the barns and beyond with them, but right now I only had one thing on my mind, and that was finding Mark and getting an answer.

Where have you been? What did you do? What are you hiding from?

Fine, I wanted three answers, then.

Few of the families dandling along the path were actually heading to the barns; they were going to their campsites and cabins for a rest, or to get a late lunch after a long, hot morning at the theme parks. They passed the pathway to the draft horse barn without a glance, streaming on towards the pioneer settlement ahead where the saloon beckoned with cold beer and the restaurant beckoned with fried chicken. I didn't really blame them. I wasn't much interested in horses on a hot afternoon, either.

But I turned down the path anyway.

The mulch pathway dawdled between little paddocks where the ponies lived, inviting me to pause and say hello, but the sun was hot and my temper was up. I walked right up to the chain strung across the aisle and leaned around it, craning my neck to see inside the office door just beyond.

I saw the back of Mark's head, a phone cradled on his shoulder, his back hunched over in front of a widescreen computer monitor. There was a spreadsheet open on it, with horse names and human names listed across the top; half-hour blocks running down the left. The night's carriage schedule, I figured.

"Right," Mark was saying, "what I'm telling you is we're one hundred percent open. So tell your guests about us. Call us and we can put the charge through when we book, and they can walk right out and get into a carriage." He paused, listening, and I saw his shoulders lift and fall, as if he was exasperated beyond all measure. "You're telling me you don't know how to book carriages? You're a concierge, you can book everything. Who told you that? Let me talk to your manager. I'm not trying to report you or anything, I just need to figure out something so we can get bodies in these carriages."

I slid back to the civilian side of the aisle. A groom came out of the harness room, arms laden with leather—of course it was Jo, it couldn't have been anyone but Jo, it would never be anyone else but Jo—and she eyeballed me with barely concealed venom. I got the impression she'd like to throw down that pile of hugely expensive harness, dart across the aisle, and wrap her tanned fingers around my neck, but she just hung everything carefully from the hooks on the wall, then went to pull out a horse from one of the interior stalls. She slid open the heavy door and greeted the black Percheron who stuck his nose through the opening with professional courtesy. I took the opportunity to sneak down the aisle, ducking into the carriage horse exhibit to stay out of sight and gather my thoughts.

Was it possible Mark had disappeared because the business wasn't performing? After all, this was now mid-June. Summer vacation was supposed to be high season. If he was sending out horse and carriage combos without any reservations, and no one at the hotel sites where the horses worked even knew how to book them, it didn't just sound like he was having a bad night... it sounded like the entire operation was in trouble.

I heard voices down the barn aisle and crept to the doorway edge. Mark was talking to Jo, his back to me, but Jo was facing my direction. I edged back inside, out of her sight. "It looks like you were right," he was saying, and even from this distance I could hear the resignation in his voice.

"They're not even teaching them to book us, are they?" Jo sounded triumphant. "That's what I thought. All this time you thought the drivers weren't selling it, and the managers are telling you no one wants it, and the fact is they're telling people they can't book at the resorts, that they should have called us earlier in the day to reserve a carriage. They're *screwing* us, Mark. This is deliberate. And I guarantee you they're doing the same thing with the trail rides."

There was a pause. The Percheron next to Jo shifted; I heard his shoes ringing on the concrete. "Be still," Jo scolded. Then, in the same brusque tone: "Mark, they want to close us down."

"They don't want to close us down. The new parade horse—"

"Means nothing. They'll let us keep the parade horses. Special Events loves them. Weddings makes a fortune on them. But the other twenty draft horses? The trail barn? How much are they a year to feed, Mark? They want rid of them."

"Jo—not out here. We can't be talking like this in guest areas."

"Fine." I heard the rattle of a brush box. "Go talk to the managers. Go make them a flyer that explains how to book. But I'm telling you, the VPs want to shut it down, so you better make it a cute fucking flyer."

"Jo!"

"I'm sorry, I'm sorry, but there's no one in here."

"Still. My god."

I smiled a little at how horrified Mark sounded. As if Jo was the first person in the history of the world to swear inside a barn. This fake little world, so precious. And, it seemed, in danger of being lost. Poor Mark.

Still, there was some reality for you, right here in the heart of Wonderland. Was there ever a barn in the twenty-first century that wasn't five minutes from being shut down?

Chapter Twenty-Two

I MADE IT out of the barn without being spotted again—at least, not by Mark. A family coming through the pony paddocks saw my breeches and boots, and decided I must be an employee who was here to answer all of their pressing questions about ponies. I guessed the Western theme all around them went right over their civilian heads. I gave in and answered a few of their urgent queries—yes, horses lay down and no, that doesn't mean they're dying; yes, horses like to eat people food and no, you shouldn't give them any of your corndog; yes, they can see through those masks and no, they're not sunglasses although funny you should say that, because they do actually work as UV blockers but that's not their purpose.

Then I abandoned them to their fate and scampered back to my truck, hoping Jo wouldn't mention I'd shown up. But why would she? Jo would be happiest if Mark forgot my name. Jo would love to monopolize his attention with her conspiracy theories so he'd never have time to call me again.

Jo would absolutely adore knowing my plans for Bella Tuscany.

I, however, wasn't ready to give up that easily. Sitting in the truck back at the farm, I sent him a text. *Dinner at my place? You must be having a hell-week or I'd have heard from you at some point.*

That was perfect, I thought. That gave him an out. He could say yes, he was having a hell-week and he was sorry and leave it at that, or he could even tell me everything that was happening and trust me with his problems. I'd never particularly liked other people's problems, having plenty of my own, but I thought I wouldn't mind helping Mark with his.

After all, one thing I wasn't offering the Bella Tuscany lot was carriage rides.

I stopped off at the house to pick up Max, waiting for me on the living-room couch with an aggrieved expression on his pointed little face. We'd already headed back to the barn, listening to the thunder rumble in the east as storms decided to make a late-afternoon appearance, before he texted back. *Would love to. Sorry to be a ghost.*

I love ghosts, I typed, then rethought things and deleted it. *I like ghosts. Last lesson ends at seven. Come find me.*

There was already a roast with garlic, orange juice and a few other spices bubbling in the slow-cooker. Yes, I could cook when necessary. And a simmering Cuban dish like ropa vieja was much easier than it looked, giving me a few extra brownie points in the "this woman can do everything" category.

Maybe I'd even have the appetite to eat it, once he materialized in my life again.

"Check your diagonal! Your other diagonal! Izzy, get your pony out of Rufus's tail! What are you going to do when Rufus kicks Star? That's what I thought! Okay everyone, say whoa and walk." My voice was so hoarse I had to get them down to a safe gait so I could take a break from all the shouting.

The circle of children around me came to various, head-bobbing, tail-wringing versions of a downward transition. Sometimes it was very hard to believe that someday they'd all be capable riders who were able to sit deeply, think *whoa,* and get a quiet, polite trot-to-walk transition. Probably in just a couple of months, for the precocious ones. Good riding crept up on you. "That was really nice, guys," I lied. "I think we're going to be adding cross-rails to this lesson very, very soon."

Izzy, a tiny six-year-old, turned eyes like a startled lemur's upon me. "You mean... *jumps!*" she shrieked in television actress fashion. "Actual *jumps!*"

"I do," I confirmed. "If you manage to keep your heels down and not drop your inside rein just because you're looking at me."

Izzy quickly evaluated her position and corrected her errors. At her age, she was going to look a little odd in the tack until she grew another foot or two, but there was certainly no reason she couldn't be as perfect as possible. That, my friends, is what riding is all about.

"Better," I told her.

The evening progressed quickly, with a nice purring thunderstorm nearby to provide cool breezes, shade, and the occasional flash of lightning which made everyone squeal and created a few spooks which I chalked up to a learning experience for the unsettled riders. June, July, August, and September would all be filled with close calls and sudden storms, and long, growling afternoons and evenings when the thunder just wouldn't quit, so the sooner everyone got used to riding through Florida's fits of temper, the better.

As soon as the last lesson began to cool down their horses, I fetched Max out of the lesson tack room, where he'd been lounging with a gaggle of students under strict orders not to let him out unless someone was attached to his leash with duct tape. "I'll see you all later," I called, waving my hand. Hopefully no one was going to wait around to ask questions after the lesson, because I was done for the night. I'd already told Anna and the crew they were on their own. Anna had enlisted a battalion of children to start washing off ponies and when I passed the wash-racks, the swarm of activity around all of those soapy ponies was almost more stimulation than I could handle. Sometimes this place truly felt out of control.

I had to admit, though, that all this mayhem was better than imagining the barn empty, filled with cobwebs, waiting to be torn down and replaced with rows of Italianate mini-mansions.

I had just enough time to shower and run a towel over my wet hair before Mark arrived, Max noting his footsteps on the porch steps with a series of staccato barks. The dog ran into my bedroom, skidding on my wet footprints, and ran in a few anxious circles in front of me before he sat down and barked some more.

"Good boy," I told him. "But be quiet now."

Max, newly invested with his authority as a good boy, went back to the front door and barked some more. I dropped a loose green sundress over my head, pushed my wet hair back with a plain black headband, and went to meet my date in my bare feet, drops of water still beading my toes.

"Am I too early?" Mark asked, between pushing down Max and trying to get into the house without falling over the Jack Russell. "What—an enthusiastic—dog!"

"He's just a couple weeks out of the shelter," I explained. "No manners yet. Plus, I kind of want him to attack men entering the house—no offense." I scooped up Max in my right arm, and extended my left one for a friendly hug. I turned up my cheek as Mark came in for the embrace, but the kiss he placed there was so inexpressive, I couldn't tell if it was a domestic *hello, girlfriend* kiss or a European *hello, female member of the species* kiss.

This is why it's best to reserve your affections for dogs and horses, I told myself, slinging the wriggling dog onto the sofa and accepting the bottle of wine Mark held out, looking at the label as if I had any opinion on it besides the quality of the artwork. It was a very nice label, with a watercolor of a tall bay horse, standing in a field of daisies.

"Did you buy this because of the horse?"

Mark grinned. "Maybe?"

"Thank god. I don't know anything about wine besides what they put in front of us at exhibitor parties, and I'm pretty sure that comes out of gallon jugs."

"Would it be terrible if I were a wine expert?" he asked teasingly.

"It would be annoying," I said. "Mainly I'm going to find it terribly annoying if you're an expert in anything I am not. It's my age."

I bit my lip and went to the kitchen, shaking off the nagging worry about mentioning my age. I had to admit middle-aged dating felt very graceless, something which couldn't be done without looking a little bit foolish—and I didn't relish feeling foolish in front of anyone. But when, I argued with myself, had I ever engaged in any human relationship that hadn't left me feeling a little ridiculous? I had nothing new to complain about here. If Mark wanted a kid hanging off his shoulder, he had Jo waiting for him back at the barn. He was here because he wanted to be. I got down my wine glasses, feeling quite relieved I'd thought to wash the second one and it wasn't dusty with disuse, and poured. "A screw top," I called from the kitchen. "How thoughtful."

Mark held up his hands. "I figured your fingers ache as much at the end of the day as mine do. Corkscrews are torture to me these days."

See, *that* was the joy of dating someone your age. So we could complain about aches and pains together. I bet he couldn't have told Jo that his arthritis was acting up. "Good thing it's red," I said, coming back into the room. "I have ropa vieja in the crockpot. I'll throw together some rice and we'll have a feast in no time."

"Can you sit for a little bit first?" he asked suddenly, looking a little anxious. "I mean, I'm in no hurry to eat. I had a late lunch today."

"I can sit." I sank into the cushion next to him, holding up my glass so the wine wouldn't tilt right out while I found my balance in the deep sofa. "Is everything all right?"

Mark was running the stem of the wine-glass back and forth in his fingers, a nervous tic I didn't have a good feeling about. "I feel like I owe you an explanation for the radio silence this week," he said. "Since we saw each other a few times last week... this week felt odd."

"It did," I agreed carefully. "Leaving without saying anything to me on Monday felt odd, too, if we're being honest with each other."

"I—" Mark paused, took a sip of wine. Then a slightly longer one. I was getting alarmed. "About Sampson..."

I leaned over and set my glass on the coffee table, suddenly not trusting myself to hold it.

He watched my movement and then his eyes flicked up to meet

mine. "The thing is, I absolutely have to get him into the July Fourth parade. There's no way around it. He needs experience in front of crowds, but the park can't be the first place he gets it, so he needed to get through that show day without... he needed to have a good experience."

Well, beating him wouldn't have given him a good experience, so that wasn't the big secret. "What did you do with him after he ran away?" I asked, perplexed and slightly annoyed that he wouldn't just come out and say it.

"I tranq'd him," Mark said, his tone guilty. "Like I said, I just wanted him to get a good experience in the show-ring, so he wouldn't associate crowds and fuss with bad behavior. After the whole incident with the tent, I knew we didn't have a chance for a normal day, so I told Louise what I wanted to do and she agreed it was the best idea. But I knew—I knew we shouldn't have. When he went to his knees..." he trailed off, looking miserably into his glass.

"He went to his *knees?*" Of course, that was what the crowd had been gasping over as I'd been walking away. Seeing an eighteen-hand monster like Sampson nearly flip over must have been the shock of the show series.

"He stumbled and he couldn't catch himself. Honestly, if you don't keep these draft horses balanced while you're riding them, they'll do that. Their shoulders are very top-heavy."

"Don't defend it. You shouldn't have put someone on him." Mark looked hurt, but he needed to hear this—so I kept going, annoyed riding instructor voice switched back on. "And you definitely shouldn't have taken him in the show-ring. Look, I know it's done every single day but that doesn't make it safe for anyone involved. He could have fallen and taken Louise down with him, or another horse and rider pair—he's so huge, he could kill someone." I paused. It was odd, the way Mark knew I'd find this news upsetting; after all, the hunter classes were full of horses sliding along on varying degrees of chemical relaxation. But I considered tranquilizing horses for riding not just cheating, but incredibly dangerous for the horse, the rider, and the other horses and people in their wake. People *died* this way. Whether it was because their horse stumbled and didn't have the reaction or motor control they needed to keep themselves on their feet, or they had a bad reaction and went into a seizure, or even had heart attacks and dropped dead. There was simply no place for a half-zonked horse in the show-ring—or under a rider. "Mark, that horse is a problem. And he isn't better since the horse show, so I'm sorry, but whatever you were trying to teach him... it didn't work."

"I know," he sighed. "Louise told me. She told me that day she didn't see him being ready for the parade. But I need her to understand, this isn't my call. I *have* to have him ready. There are some requests which are just that—they're requests. And there are some requests which are actually orders." He took another deep pull of his wine; his glass was half-empty already, and I'd barely touched mine. I was going to have to feed him soon. "The horse came from a sponsor and the sponsor wants the horse in the parade. The VP is all over me to make sure it happens and the sponsor is kept happy. We're talking a million-dollar deal here. This July Fourth event is huge—there's going to be a film crew, a TV special airing that night, a live-stream that's going to get a million eyeballs on it... everyone is kind of freaking out and Sampson is key. If he's not in it... well, are you hiring grooms?"

I ignored his joke, although mentally I thought, of course I'd hire

Mark to groom for me any day of the week. That wouldn't get weird at all, right? "You're actually saying you'll get fired if Sampson isn't in this parade? I mean, that sounds a little extreme, and really not at all like a big company. I thought corporations had rules about these kinds of things. Surely you have to have more transgressions than one missed parade with one crazy horse."

Mark laughed. "Sure I do. But have you ever worked for a big company? Someone's always got more sway than they should on paper. And when it comes to paper, my business doesn't look so good compared to all the other units. We're not theme park merchandise. We're not even hotel rooms. The entire ranch is more about perception than profit. We have horses because horses fit the theme of the resort, not because they make a lot of money. And that didn't used to matter. But now... things are different now."

It was my turn to take a drink and consider my next words. I couldn't tell him I'd been there today, that I'd overheard his half of the phone conversation with the hotel manager. "I know how that is," I said after a moment of thinking. "I've reinvented this place twice in the past two years, and I'm about to do it again. The horse business is changing, Mark. We can't just get by the way we always did. There just isn't enough money to go around anymore, and that counts whether you work at a resort or a regular barn."

I explained the way I'd run Seabreeze for years: counting on the stereotypical doctor's wives with disposable income, buying horses they couldn't ride and paying me to keep them show-ring ready, showing up ring-side at Wellington in their newest pair of custom boots to get vaulted into the saddle and coached to a blue ribbon on the horse I'd prepped for them. It was a good model for a long time, if you didn't mind the rather bad taste all of that pandering to the rich could leave in your mouth.

"And then the neighborhood changed, and the sport seems to be changing too, and it just wasn't working anymore," I finished. "So I tried trail rides, and that wasn't enough, so I tried going after the juniors, and that's working better. I'll keep thinking of new things. I'll keep changing it up." I didn't mention the resort deal. This wasn't the time to bring it up. I wasn't sure if there would ever be a right time.

"Like boarding parade horses?" Mark managed a grin. "How's that test run going?"

"Don't even ask me that," I said, shaking my head. "You should have told me about her."

"I've never had her as a tenant. I've just gotten horses from her. I guess I thought she could make a parade horse out of anything. I didn't give her enough credit for finding the quietest horses in the world."

We sipped our wine in silence for a moment, then I got up and took the rice out of the fridge. I busied myself for a few minutes heating and spooning and stirring and yes, tasting a little—chef's prerogative!—and tried to decide if I believed Mark had told me everything. All that guilt, not calling me for almost a week, running out of the barn without so much as a goodbye, was because he'd stuck a needle in a horse's neck at a show? Maybe this guy was too innocent for the likes of a show barn, I thought with a little smile and head-shake. Or maybe all that pixie dust floating around his barn office was masking the real world a little too well.

When I came out with plates in hand, Mark was fiddling with the old iPod dock by the television. It had been a gift from the boarders one Christmas and I rarely used it, but now he was dropping his phone into it and coaxing my small set of speakers to life. "I hope you were expecting Victrola-quality audio," I called. "I think those were made by a company called Boze."

He convinced some jazz to squawk to life, then turned it down until the sounds were more like music and less like pelicans fighting over a hot dog. "Dinner music," he said. "Unless you hate jazz? I'm given to understand there's a certain jazz divide in this country."

"I like it fine. I like anything I don't have to pay a lot of attention to. My mind is usually occupied with other things."

Mark brought our wine glasses over to the table, then fetched the bottle and gave us refills. "Horse show entries and fence heights and vaccination schedules and farrier appointments?"

"Something like that." I grinned. "Can you relate?"

"A little." He shrugged and grinned back at me. "No matter what we do with them, we're both in the horse business."

I held up my glass. "To endless trouble?" I suggested.

His glass came up to mine. "And boundless delight."

My lips rounded into a surprised smile, which is probably why Mark felt compelled to lean over and press a kiss on them instead of taking a drink. And that, my friends, is how Mark spilled a glass of wine over me on the occasion of our first dinner at my place.

Chapter Twenty-Three

I HAD A little bit of a habit of taking control of everything around me, whether it was my business or not. So when I called Kennedy late that evening, after Mark left, it wasn't because I needed her desperately to come and ride the trail horses the next day. I mean, I could have used her help, naturally, but I was happy to let her stew a little longer and come to her own conclusion about what to do with her life. I'd been ready to help her right up until she took her anger out on Frank. Involving horses in one's little temper tantrums was where I drew the line.

Mark's troubles, though, I was happy to take over. And that meant using Kennedy.

"Kennedy, I want you to get Louise to give you a job," I said as soon as she answered her phone. "Get that Shire horse of Mark's sorted out for her and then we can talk about your next move."

There was silence on the other end of the line, long enough to make me wonder if I'd hit the wrong contact in my phone. I took it away and looked. No, it definitely said *Kennedy* on the screen. "Kennedy? Hello?"

"I'm here," came a small voice. "Why are you doing this?"

"Doing what? Getting you what you want? Because I want something out of it, too. Obviously."

"Did you... did you fire me yesterday?"

"In a manner of speaking, I suppose I did." I hadn't actually given it a lot of thought, but I supposed telling her to get off my horse and leave my barn and not come back was probably easily interpreted as a job termination. "I was angry. I still think you're great, don't get me wrong. I'd actually take you back if you apologized nicely enough. But the point is, you don't know if you want to work for me. I know what you're up to with Louise. Don't just go off with her. Trial it. Tell her you can fix Sampson in the next two weeks, then do it."

There was a short pause, then a rueful laugh. "So you just want me to expedite getting that problem horse out of your barn."

"Yes and no," I said. "Mark needs him fixed, and I need Mark to be happy. And I'm pretty sure you know that even if we're fighting right now, I want you to be happy, too. Oh, and there's Anna. Anna's happiness is paramount to me, and when you're not here, she's upset. Plus I don't want Louise getting killed on my property, for insurance reasons. Kennedy, there are *so many* very good reasons to get you riding for Louise ASAP."

"Grace?"

"Yes, Kennedy."

"Are you drunk?"

I glanced at the slosh of wine left in the bottom of the second bottle, which had been on top of my fridge for a few weeks, just waiting for an evening like this. "A little," I decided. "But sometimes, Kennedy, that's exactly what you need to get things done."

I wandered through the living room, picking up things which had gotten scattered about while Mark was here. A bra here, a dress there. Yes, it had been a fine evening for wine, and a fine evening for jazz, and a fine evening for making new connections. Such a fruitful evening, all in all! That's why I was feeling invigorated enough to call up Kennedy and make her see the light. "So do we have a deal? Come over tomorrow around ten and we'll both tackle Louise together. Get ready to ride that beast. You can handle him, right?"

"The Shire?" Kennedy, the pony queen, sounded amused. "I can handle him. Louise is just too timid. She's used to handling the nice guys, taking quiet horses to the next level. I've ridden enough bullies... I can handle this one."

"That's what I wanted to hear. Good girl, Kenn."

"Thanks."

"And Kenn?" Apparently I was calling her *Kenn* now. That probably wouldn't survive until tomorrow morning, luckily. "You can have the other apartment. We'll just convert my office into a lounge. I can move my things into the school tack room. I've been spying on the barn help from above long enough. Now I'll just listen from around the corner."

"What?"

I was suddenly ready for bed. Max was curled up on the sofa, fast asleep after the excitement of having company over. I settled down next to him. "Just remind me that I told you so tomorrow, okay?"

Kennedy wasn't tall, a fact made glaringly obvious once she was mounted on an eighteen-hand horse with a wide barrel. Even with her stirrups lengthened to account for Sampson's anticipated bad behavior, her heels were still a good foot higher than where they'd be on a medium horse. I was reminded of Carol Lavell and Gifted, the dressage duo from the early nineties. Carol had looked like a precocious toddler who had stolen her father's carthorse and taken him to the Olympics.

"Guess you were built for ponies," I told her with a grin.

Kennedy grinned back; she wasn't a bit scared of Sampson, which was what I'd been counting on. She'd fearlessly trained our little collection of feral ponies into useful school and lease ponies, and she'd been riding every kind of horse, in every kind of tack, since she was a kid—with nothing too awful happening to her. Kennedy still had that immortal glow which most of us lose somewhere in our twenties. I hoped she got to keep it a lot longer. Definitely past this ride, anyway. "Ponies, Shires, what's the diff?"

Sampson crossed his forelegs and crab-stepped across the covered arena, his massive hooves and their gowns of white feathers stirring up red dust. It was exactly the kind of move he pulled on Louise every day, and Louise, well aware she was not immortal, had not been willing or able to push the issue as far as it had to go. Sampson didn't need to be chided or corrected with a gentle but firm hand, unfortunately. Sampson needed a true Come-to-Jesus session.

"You're sure about the covered ring?" I asked as Kennedy started popping her heels against his burnished black sides. "The jumping ring is smaller."

"Too many distractions," Kennedy said, grunting on the last syllable with the force of trying to push Sampson forward. "I've just got to keep his head up and sit deep." She brandished her whip, flipping the bat with the easy confidence of a jockey on her way to the winner's circle.

I got out of the ring in a hurry then, hustling over to the gap where the covered walkway connected the barn and sliding the

PVC pole across the entrance. If Kennedy was going to go ahead and pick the fight Sampson had been itching for since he'd arrived here, I wanted to be on hand—but not in the way.

You wouldn't think a little jumping bat would connect with a huge Shire's brain the same way it would with a more reasonably-sized horse, but when Kennedy got sick of going sideways and dropped the stick on his hindquarters, he jumped like he'd been bit by a rattlesnake. The leap was impressive—could Shires actually be trained in airs above the ground? I wondered fleetingly—but maybe not as impressive as Kennedy's legs, locked into place even as her seat lifted out of the saddle slightly with the air-time Sampson was achieving. He landed and immediately launched again, shoving his head viciously against the bit in an attempt to free his head and get in a good buck, but Kennedy was braced against him with every muscle she had, and a good bit of grit besides. The second his front hooves hit the ground again, she slammed her heels against his sides and sent him flying forward. "Get—*up!*" she growled, her voice deep and menacing. "Get *up* there, *now!*"

Sampson got up. He got up into a rolling hand-gallop that shook the earth. But Kennedy wasn't a trained princess for nothing, I thought, impressed. She sat back into that thundering motion like a Saxon warrior-queen, like a shield-maiden of Rohan, like nothing I'd ever seen in real life before, and swayed her body to influence Sampson's body through the turns at the top and bottom of the arena. One, two, three, four, *five* times they rounded the arena, and by the time Sampson's strides were slowing and his nostrils were flaring red, everyone else in the barn at midday—that is to say, Margaret and Anna and Louise and a couple of boarders who didn't have to work—were all standing behind me, keeping a respectful distance from the PVC pole separating us from the arena, just in case it had to be slid open in an emergency, or in case Sampson came barreling through it.

"He'll slow down to a trot now," Louise said confidently. "I've gotten a nice trot out of him after a blow-up like that before."

I didn't bother pointing out that Louise had never ridden Sampson through a blow-up like that—she'd always sidestepped the conversation, easing him out of his crab-walking and crow-hopping with a lot of gentle urging into an unbalanced, inelegant canter that soon fell apart into a nose-first jog. Kennedy was far from finished with this lesson. "She's not going to let him stop cantering until it's her decision."

Louise glanced at me. "He's not very fit. She won't push him until he gets hurt, will she?"

I gave Louise a sardonic look. "He looks pretty fit to me."

Sampson went thundering by a sixth time, his breath pounding out of his nostrils every time his front hooves hit the ground. Kennedy was sitting back in the saddle, her whip cocked out a right angle from her hands, giving it a wave in the air every time his stride faltered.

I turned around and gestured for everyone to go back to the barn. "The show's over, and it's going to be harder for Kennedy to concentrate on getting him going if she has a peanut gallery watching her every move." Anna cast me a pleading look, but I shooed her away with everyone else. "There's nothing to see but a big horse running in circles."

Louise was starting to wring her hands. "Should she still be galloping him? He's breathing so hard."

"She's making sure he knows that he's on her time now, not his," I said. "But I think you know that. Come on, Louise, what happened between you guys? I know you've been training horses like Sampson all your life." I was being generous, giving her an out.

She didn't take it. Louise shook her head slightly, looking spooked. "Not like Sampson."

"There's never been another headstrong Shire out there? I find that hard to believe."

"Maybe there has been... but there's something, I don't know, something *raw* about him. Like he's really half-wild. Like he might really try to hurt someone, instead of doing it by accident. I've ridden *horses* like that, but never a draft. Certainly never a Shire. Although," she admitted, "I haven't trained many Shires under saddle. Maybe one or two." Her eyes drifted from the galloping horse to meet my gaze. "I might have bit off more than I can chew. But you know... there's the whole Mark thing."

Maybe my eyes widened a little, maybe my jaw tightened just a bit. But that was it. I'd been poker-faced for too many years to allow something little like *the whole Mark thing* to give away my surprise and dismay.

"The whole... the whole Mark thing?" I asked carefully. "Like, you've trained so many horses for him, you don't want to disappoint him. Oh, I get that," I rolled on, deciding that my best course of action was to pretend I believed professional goals were at the heart of Louise's motivation. "But those are the owners who are the most understanding. Well, clients, in this case, but you know, I'm sure he gets that this horse is a special case or he wouldn't be giving you so much trouble—"

"I've been trying to get Mark to notice what a great job I've done with his horses for years," Louise said tightly. "And after the last one went straight to the parks and started performing like a superstar, I really thought I'd gotten his attention. Then this horse came." Her voice turned bitter. "And he's made me look like a fool in front of Mark over, and over, and over."

"Which is bad for business, I get that," I gabbled, but I was just grasping at straws now.

Louise looked at her boots, rubbed one toe over the other, brushing away at the red clay from the arena. "It's bad for way more than business, Grace. At least, for me." She laughed bitterly. "I imagine it doesn't mean a thing to Mark."

Christ, I thought, was *everyone* in love with Mark? Okay, a good-looking man with a steady job and a way with horses was a little bit of a unicorn, as the kids were saying these days. But finding out every single horsewoman within five miles was obsessed with the man *I* was seeing was not exactly welcome news. I wasn't looking to complicate my life any more than was absolutely necessary. Extra rivalries outside of the normal barn politics and horse show drama? That was a strict no thank you.

In the arena, Kennedy had brought Sampson down to a head-tossing trot. He wasn't tired enough yet. She had a ways to go before he was ready to listen to her without a fight. But she was getting through to him—purely because she was the first person to get on his back and not take his shit. "You'll be able to ride Sampson around like a little lamb in two weeks," I predicted, turning back to Louise.

She shrugged. "Super," she said tonelessly.

I realized then that Sampson didn't mean a thing to her as a horse. He was a means to an end—a way to get Mark's attention and admiration, not a project horse to be understood and fixed on his own merits. That was sad, but when a lot of horses went through your hands over the years, it was understandable, too. "He's really nice, Louise," I said, pushing back from the arena fence. "It's a shame you never took the time to figure out what he was looking for."

I was already on my way back to the barn when I realized that Louise could have taken my words two very different ways. I looked over my shoulder and saw her staring at me, her expression hard, and I knew she'd definitely taken it the wrong way. I hadn't been talking about Mark, but there was no way she was going to be convinced of that now.

Chapter Twenty-Four

Suddenly, the calendar was out of date.

I flipped the page to July and looked at the blank spaces waiting there with quiet amazement. Many of them would stay blank, thirty-one days of peace. July was usually my quietest month. No horse shows. Kids and adults alike disappearing from the barn for weeks at a time, whisked away on summer vacations. This was when the fathers swooped in and demanded their wives and children take a break from the horses. There were cruises to take, mountains to hike, and European cities to explore. In every one of them, my clients would be looking for any horses they could find. Police horses, dozing by government buildings. Carriage horses, trotting through traffic. Trail horses, nose to tail on a wooded trail. Island horses, splashing through surf. They would squeal and ask if they could touch the horses. Their husbands and fathers would sigh and take their pictures with the horses, as requested. They would give up saying, "but you have a horse at home you can see every day!" after just a few attempts.

Fathers and husbands nearly always seemed mystified by this attraction to horses, a species they'd somehow relegated to women's work. When I told people this had been my grandfather's farm, they assumed he'd been a cowboy. A gentleman farmer who raised oranges and cattle and racehorses and maintained, for a time, a membership with a hunt some distance away in the Ocala hills— that was hard for people to balance with their vision of Florida, once a tropical frontier. They found it hard enough to imagine someone's grandfather wearing breeches and boots for recreation and not out of necessity. They found it doubly confusing in a modern context, when equestrian life was intensely female.

This relentless femininity probably explained why I found myself the recipient of hot, disapproving glares every time I entered Mark's barn. Jo was the worst of them, her gaze somehow palpable on my back when I walked down the aisle with Mark, but as I found myself dropping by more and more often—not for corporate espionage, that part of my business plan was concluded—I encountered plenty more female employees in plaid shirts and Wrangler jeans who looked none too pleased to see me.

"You think?" Mark asked when I brought it up, over drinks at the Boardwalk on a sultry Saturday night, fireworks crackling nearby. "No. You're just imagining things."

"I shouldn't have said anything," I sighed, tossing him a fond smile. "Now you're going to think about it all the time, and you'll end up so smug I'll have to smack you."

"I won't!" Mark had protested, but he was already considering it, weighing his own experiences with his staff against what I'd told him of their hard looks and dismissive comments whenever I was around. I could see the satisfaction in his smile when he looked down at his drink and swirled the copper-colored bourbon in its glass. I'd rolled my eyes and took a deep pull from my Negroni.

After a few nights out like this, the posh cocktail menu was looking less alien and more inviting. I'd started branching out, trying a new drink each time. This one, sharply bittersweet, might be my favorite.

I thought about the herbal bite of that drink now, pulling the lesson book towards me and looking at the day ahead. I'd marked out a half-hour to do saddle checks with Anna; billets and stirrup leathers needed inspection for wear, with offenders removed from circulation and dumped in the back seat of my truck, there to wait for me to remember to take them to the tack shop and drop them off for repairs. There were a few horses to ride before their owners showed up for evening lessons, tune-ups to make sure the horses remembered their duties as amateur packers.

But before anything could be worked on around the barn, Louise and Kennedy were coming to load up Sampson and take him to Mark's barn for the afternoon. The parade was in four days, and although they'd decided not to move him to the barn permanently yet, he would have to be tacked up and shipped over to the park from there. So the next few days would be dry runs, to get him used to the surroundings, the grooms, and the performer who would be riding him.

If they could get a performer who could ride him, I thought. He was going nicely enough for Kennedy, and they'd taken him to schooling shows the past two weekends, traveling two hours last week to find a property foolhardy enough to run a show in late June. Kennedy had reported he was nervous but rideable. "And he didn't try to kick anyone," she'd added.

So Sampson was showing improvement, just as I'd promised, but a schooling show wasn't the streets of the world's most popular theme park, on one of the busiest days of the year, with cameras swinging nearby to live-stream it to the world outside, under a new rider he didn't know. When I'd put this plan together, I'd been confident Kennedy was the only one who could get him even close to prepped for the parade… but that didn't mean she could have him one hundred percent. There simply wasn't enough time to get a horse completely ready for such mayhem.

"I didn't expect you to come along," Mark said. He stood back from me, his hands folded behind him in his manager's *may I help you* stance, and cocked his head a little to indicate the little cluster of men—and a single woman—in professional clothes standing in the shade of the barn, conversing intently and looking anywhere but at the horse trailer pulled up in front of them.

I hopped down from my own truck, parked in an employee space. We were on the back side of the draft horse barn, accessible only through an interior road, and this was where all the detritus of an equestrian facility was stored neatly, away from the eyes of guests wandering the equestrian wonderland front of house. Pallets stacked with bags of shavings, a fleet of wheelbarrows turned neatly against the back wall, a large plastic barrel filled to the brim with knotted hay string. You really got a sense of the scale Mark was working with when you saw all of the equipment and necessities for daily horse care stacked within one small paved courtyard. My barn had as many horses as his, but somehow it all felt more natural and attainable than what he had to keep going here, this illusion of horses who did not make messes and did not require constant care, but just ate their hay and waggled their ears at the guests to make them smile.

"Kennedy asked me to," I said, pocketing my keys and glancing over at the trailer, where I could see Sampson's pricked ears through the vent along the side. "Just in case. She doesn't know if Louise can handle him if he does anything stupid."

I saw Mark look nervously back at the group of professionals. "Who are they?" I asked.

"The general manager of the Fort, the VP of brand strategy, a couple other execs. No one I'd usually want around when I'm getting in a new horse, naturally." He looked a little green, now that I looked more closely.

"You know what? Let's not even give Louise the chance to screw this up." I smiled at his inquisitive expression and waggled my fingers at him. "Leave it to me."

Louise was standing by the trailer's back door, nervously fingering a leather stallion lead, while Kennedy fumbled with the latches. Sampson had loaded well enough back at the barn, probably thinking he was going to another schooling show where he would be given piles of carrots in exchange for trotting around an arena—a pretty good deal for a lazy draft horse—but neither woman had looked as confident as the big horse had as he strolled into the trailer. Kennedy was white as a ghost under her crown of dark red curls, and Louise managed to look pale beneath her tan as well.

I'd pulled Kennedy aside and asked her if she was going to come back to work for me once the Sampson situation was concluded, and she'd nodded yes, her face suffused with gratitude. Working with Louise day in and day out was no picnic, as I'd expected. Of the new barn, nothing had been said and I didn't ask—perhaps the idea had been postponed until Louise had gotten Sampson out of her hair. Or maybe Louise didn't have the rent money anymore than she'd had the money she'd promised to pay Kennedy when they ran away together.

"Kennedy," I murmured, sidling up beside her. "Tell Louise I'm going to get the horse down and show him to the execs. She can be the presenter, I'll be the groom."

Kennedy glanced back at me. "Seriously? You'd do that?"

"Are you kidding? Let's make this horse look like a star. The sooner he's gone, the better." I grinned.

Louise didn't dispute the idea and handed over the lead shank. As I stepped into the trailer to hook Sampson and get him out, she was already at Mark's side. Together, they headed over to the suits to give them a run-down on the horse they'd all come to see. Sampson was looking at me over the divider; all I had to do was drop the bar in front of him and lead him out—no backing, no complications. It should be a simple task, but he was so tall, looming over me like no other horse had ever done, that I couldn't help feeling a little nervous.

I took one look back as Sampson shifted his massive hooves, the sound reverberating around the metal confines of the trailer, and saw Mark out in the harsh daylight, looking in at me. His face was pinched with a worry he couldn't suppress, even now when he should have been playing the proud, confident papa. Was it worry for his career, or was it for me, wedged into a dark, close space with a horse he couldn't trust? I wondered if we should have tranquilized Sampson for his big reveal, but it was too late now. I touched the horse's jowl, a quick stroke to say hello, and then threaded the chain through his halter's noseband. His chin was above my head. His neck was quivering. I felt a dread in my stomach I hadn't experienced in years.

What did anyone need with a horse this big?

"Behave," I whispered, but he was staring out into the blinding midday light, and his ear didn't so much as flick in my direction. All at once I knew I was holding a fully-fueled rocketship by one thin strip of leather and a few links of chain. I gave the shank a little tug, heard the clinks as the chain slipped through the brass of the halter rings. He lowered his head a little, blew hot breath on my shoulder. "Better," I said, in my full, firm, trainer's voice now. "No silliness, now."

I dropped the bar and as one we walked forward, the trailer shaking with his tread.

I already knew he'd jump out the second we got to the ramp, so I was prepared for the leap, the leather racing through my fingers. I closed my fist the moment he hit the ground, the knot at the end of the shank an anchor settling into deep sediment, and he spun around, his body wheeling and his hooves slipping and scraping on the pavement, nose up and eyes focused on me, knowing I was the one in control of the pressure across his nasal bone.

When his motion skidded to a halt, I stepped down from the side of the ramp and gave him a proprietary stroke on the neck, letting the chain links pop through the rings again, clinking cheerfully as they stopped biting into his nose. "Good boy," I told him, though it was only half-true. There'd been no need for him to jump the ramp, he'd just decided to be an asshole because he was young and large and had been allowed to revel in this knowledge for too long. "Thank you."

Overly excited but also deeply aware of the chain on his nose, Sampson pranced beside me as I led him on an exhibitor's walk in front of the suits. I spared Mark a glance and saw his forehead crumpled with worry, his fingers clenched in front of his belt, and I had a moment's pity wash over me, then splash against a little irritation that he'd be so certain this horse had any power over me. Maybe for a moment, back in the trailer, he had, but now we were out in the open and I'd already taken him to task for one foolish move. There was nothing Sampson could do to me now that I didn't allow him to do. He was just another big horse in a lifetime of big horses.

Louise went on detailing Sampson's finer points to the suits, who had questions such as "will he keep growing?" and "but how much does he eat?" and I did not envy her the task. Finally, she stopped talking and everyone watched us in silence as we circled the parking area, Sampson's rippling neck arched and his hock-length tail curving away from his hindquarters in a black waterfall. I wasn't willing to let him stand still and build up his nervous energy into another leap, so we just kept going. I brushed sweat from my eyes and wished for a thunderstorm.

"Well, we should take him inside," Mark said finally. "Grace, can you bring him into the third stall here, and we'll let him settle for a little while before we start tacking him up? The rider will be here around two."

We stood back and watched Sampson circle the stall, putting his nose up to the top of the walls, snorting at the scent of strange horses. Louise had Kennedy explaining some trick riding secrets to the execs. The female exec looked terrified of the entire situation. The men looked either bored or confused. There was no trace of interest in the group. I suspected everyone was thinking of where they'd like to have lunch.

I found myself alongside Mark without having meant to seek him out. We stood a few inches from each other and the slight distance was tantalizing. I rocked back on my heels and smiled sidelong at him. He smiled back, with a hint of promise in his eyes. I felt a pleasant liquid sensation somewhere in my middle.

"Grace, are you staying for the ride test?" Louise called, snapping me back to the real world.

I glanced at my phone. "No," I said regretfully. "I have two horses to ride before four. And then lessons. I better hustle." I gave Mark an apologetic look. He'd call me later, tell me how things went. Maybe he'd come over. Probably, judging by the way he was looking at me right now, he'd come over.

The woman was looking at me with sudden interest. She'd taken off her blazer and it was draped over one arm; sweat was pooling in little dark spots on her sleeveless ivory blouse. "You have horses near here?"

I felt Mark tense, though we were still not touching.

"I have a farm just behind the resort property, on the county road. You turn left at the ball-fields, away from town, and I'm right there."

Several eyebrows went up.

"I drive by that place every day," one man said. "It's hard to see what goes on back there, behind all the trees and hedges. You have a lot of horses?"

"Thirty-some," I said. "Mostly boarders and lesson horses, some trail horses."

There was a general air of astonishment. The woman flicked her eyes to Mark and held his gaze for a long moment, hostage to her professional disappointment. I remembered Mark had monitored my trail business for the Fort strategy meetings, but clearly it didn't get any higher than the Fort management. These guys were much,

much higher, and they were looking between Mark and I as if the wool had been pulled over their eyes. Had they really thought they were the only game left in town? I wished I'd just slipped out quietly. I wished I hadn't said anything.

"Better go," I said hastily, and left without meeting anyone's eyes.

Kennedy came into the school tack room while I was grabbing a water between lessons, her face red from heat and her curls tousled and flat. She threw herself down on a tack trunk and leaned her head against the white wall, sighing at the coolness locked into the cement. I had the window air conditioner unit roaring like a race-car engine. Through the glass, I could see a dark cloud scudding closer and closer, putting the six o'clock lesson plan in jeopardy. We were supposed to jump in the outdoor arena tonight. Anna had set up the fences for me while I'd been at the Fort, playing show groom with Sampson.

"What happened?" I asked, capping the water bottle and tossing it into the recycling bin under my desk.

"The test ride was a disaster." Kennedy closed her eyes. "They want me to do it."

"Do what?" I debated a second bottle of water. I'd have to stop halfway through the lesson for a pee break. I left it in the fridge and closed the door. "Not, ride in the parade?"

"Ride in the parade," she confirmed. "I ended up riding him all over the place tonight. After their performer left in tears, I got on and took him through the whole property. Louise said not to but I couldn't let him get away with it. I made him follow a trail ride. I made him follow a hay-ride. I made him stand and watch the band play outside the saloon. He finally settled down. But there's no way that performer is coming back to ride him again. Mark said it's got to be me." Kennedy opened her eyes and looked at me with something like panic. "There's going to be tens of thousands of people there."

"Not all along the parade route," I said, considering the logistics. "In the park, certainly, but they won't all be lined up to watch you. Just a couple thousand, I'd bet. And you were a princess, this should be old hat for you."

She shook her head at me. "This is nothing like being a princess."

Chapter Twenty-Five

KENNEDY WAS RIGHT, of course. I didn't have any princess experience myself, but I knew that whatever she'd done in that dark dinner theater, riding under the spotlights, had been nothing like this.

The park was a sea of humanity, and the couple of peeks I'd taken around the backstage entrance had been enough to convince me that there were simply too many people on the planet. The wide walkways, designed to move fifty thousand people in a single day comfortably and without congestion, were a gridlock of strollers and grim faces. Children were crying and parents were bickering. Against a decorative iron fence leaned a young woman, her face blissful and vacant, her clothes pastel and flowing, existing in a tiny sphere of her own obliviousness, taking selfies with the staggering spires of the castle in the background. A patchwork of fluffy white cumulus drifted overhead, occasionally dappling the chaos in a desperately welcome shadow. There would be storms tonight, violent and late into the night. Orlando's July Fourth storms were the stuff of legend. Maybe it was all the gunpowder in the air, all the aggressive patriotism and posturing stirring up the atmosphere.

Maybe it was all the extra heat from barbecues, the bursting plump centers of hot dogs releasing their steam into the roiling clouds. Maybe it was just midsummer.

The horse trailers were parked alongside an access road within the park berms, and grooms were unloading them and getting to work hitching up the carriage horses, tightening the girths on the saddle horses. A few performers had arrived already, shrouded in light linen robes and cowls to keep their costumes and wigs clean. They looked like sky-blue monks with serious make-up addictions. Thickets of banana palms and shrubberies hid us from the various rides scattered around, but we could hear the engines of boats humming past, the rattle and whistle of the steam train, the endless drumming of the guest area's background music throbbing from speakers hidden in the bushes.

My life had gotten stranger in the past couple of months, I reflected, taking in the scene. It was nice to know your life could always get a little stranger.

Sampson had been over here every day for the past three days, and he stepped off the trailer now with an air of expectation. He knew the routine now. He would be tied to the trailer, he would be saddled, he would be ridden up and down the road for an hour while the steam whistle pierced the air every time the train chugged past. Kennedy would stroke him and tell him he was a genius. Then she'd ride him to a parade gate and let him gaze out at the crowds. He had already experienced a few short glimpses of the hordes he'd parade before today, and she'd been happy with his reactions.

Yesterday morning, not long after sunrise, she'd ridden him into the park and down the route before the turnstiles opened. There had been early morning breakfast guests in the park already and she'd been obliged to dress to the nines, pulling out her full hunter show regalia and polishing her boots. Sampson, she'd reported, had loved it. "He still isn't quiet enough for a performer to ride," she'd explained, "but I think he's going to be a hell of a parade horse someday."

The lack of experienced equestrians who could also face-double for movie characters was something I'd never pondered before, but now I could see Kennedy was a rare bird, a still-young woman with decades of training experience and the ability to carry a face pancaked with make-up into a crowd and not just call herself a princess, but sell it to every person there.

A woman beckoned to Kennedy and she reluctantly detached herself from Sampson's retinue of grooms, three ranch hands (including Jo) who had devoted themselves to keeping Sampson happy throughout his inaugural parade experience. "Let's get you into costume," the woman told her. "Ready for this?"

Kennedy ducked her head in a nod and smiled. The woman hustled her off in the direction of Main Street.

"There goes your girl."

I turned to find Mark at my shoulder. "Seeing everything handled by someone else is very weird for me," I admitted with a laugh. "At a horse show, I'm the first and last word in everything."

Mark kindly didn't point out that I was only here because I wanted to be, but he let his gaze trail over me with amusement, and I knew he was thinking it. I doubted he knew the role I'd played in getting his horse here today, or he might have thought differently. I'd gotten Kennedy onto Sampson, because I wanted him to be happy—that was, quite simply, the only reason the horse had made it this far, to the backstage of a theme park, waiting to be draped in royal regalia. That it made Kennedy happy, and Anna happy, was just a happy coincidence. I could admit that now.

"Mark! Mark? Come over here." It was Louise, waving and beckoning from near Sampson and the grooms. "Let's get him tacked up, Mark."

"Maybe she could say your name a few more times," I snickered.

"Stop," he chided, but he was shaking his head, too. "She's been all over me the past few days. I think she wants an award for getting Sampson here."

Mark still didn't believe that Louise, Jo, and half the other women working in his barn were in love with him. I let him go without complaint, secure in the knowledge of his own lack of self-awareness. Sometimes these character flaws were really for the best.

As the minutes until the parade ticked by, the access road grew crowded with floats and performers. The engines of the floats grumbled as they made their way past us, shimmering confections that were half sculpture, half stage sets on wheels. A flat-bed trailer arrived with a glass pumpkin coach, and a team unloaded it near the trailer where the white ponies were squabbling with one another. Their grooms hastily descended with harness buckles flying, and got the six ponies hitched in what had to be some sort of land-speed record. I heard the music out in the park pause, and an announcement was made in a booming ringmaster tone. I glanced at my watch—the fifteen-minute warning! This was about to happen. I spun around to look for Kennedy just as she appeared from a gap in the thick palm groves across the road.

She was swathed in tartan and leather, a golden Celtic broach gleaming on her chest. Her own curls had been replaced with false ones, so many of them, spilling down her shoulders and bouncing off her back. She looked at me with big eyes, somehow made larger by strokes of eyeliner and mascara. They looked alien on her. "So this is the princess version of you," I called. "Impressive."

"There are so many layers," she gasped. "I've never worn this much for riding. We weren't exactly going for historical integrity with the dinner theater costumes."

Both of us turned our eyes to the midday sky, thinking the same thing: she was going to roast out there.

"At least it's waterproof mascara," Kennedy said after a moment, and we laughed.

"Kennedy?" Mark was calling. Beside him Sampson stood with his ears pricked, a fantasy version of a medieval charger, bedecked in green swags of cloth, black watch plaid, and an elaborate saddle. I noted the deep, anatomically curved seat of the saddle with satisfaction. Kennedy would feel like she was in a dressage saddle up there. She'd be safe enough... if all that fabric didn't get in her way.

"Off you go, princess," I told her, and gave her shoulder a squeeze. The costuming woman frowned at me, but didn't say anything. The drapes of plaid still fell from Kennedy's shoulders in elaborate folds after I let her go. It would take more than an encouraging hand to muss what the professionals had pinned into place.

The front of the line had started moving, and floats and carriages were beginning to inch forward, moving for a few minutes, then stopping for a few more. We were in the queue, already in parade formation. Sampson was flanked by two grooms, like a racehorse being led to the track, and during the stops they walked him in circles to keep him from growing anxious.

"Why the stops?" I asked Mark. "Shouldn't a parade just keep going?"

"Show stops," he said. His dark shirt was showing patches of sweat, and his forehead was pinched with worry. I wanted to tell him not to worry, that Kennedy wouldn't do anything she wasn't positive she could do, but honestly, I wasn't sure that was the truth. "The parade has intervals where the entertainers do dances, interact with the crowd."

"What will Sampson do during those once he's out there?" The grooms were not going onstage with Kennedy. She'd be on her own out there, although of course there were back-up crew, including Mark, in case something went wrong. "He can't stand still for five minutes with all those people and that uproar."

"She can still circle him. There'll be enough room." But Mark was looking progressively closer to a nervous breakdown. Ahead of us, Sampson swished his tail and stamped one hind hoof just hard enough to leave a white scrape on the pavement. He was growing irritated already. The parade gate was close enough now for us to hear the music clearly. It hit a crescendo and the parade began to creep forward again, sweeping us along in its lazy currents. I didn't think there'd be another show stop before Sampson's unit made it through the gate. The bagpipers and Highland dancers already beginning to work through their choreography.

"I better go," I said. We'd agreed I'd hop in a golf cart with Louise and have a parade tech drive me up to the other gate at the park entrance, where we could watch the parade wind its way through Town Square and back to the access road. "You'll be onstage in a few minutes."

"Wait," Mark burst out, gripping my wrist urgently. "Walk with me."

"What? I can't go out there." Then I realized there was no reason I couldn't. Mark had told me to wear all black so I'd blend in with the other backstage parade techs. I had on black breeches, a black polo shirt and my field boots. I looked exactly like I should be out there on a horse unit, keeping an eye on my charge.

"The only thing you're missing is an ID and a radio," he said. "But no one's going to question you. This is my call. Please come."

I ran my hands over my hair, wishing I'd brought a hat—both to keep the midday sun off, and to cover up what was probably a sweaty mess up there. Thousands of people, I'd assured Kennedy, thinking it had nothing to do with me. "How do I look?"

Mark managed to crack a smile, and for a moment he didn't look quite so close to a heart attack. "Like a professional."

The music swelled and then seemed to subside, and I realized there was a pause while the soundtrack switched from the pirate theme of the unit ahead to the reel of our Scottish unit. The bagpipers began to play in a skirl of music that brought Sampson to a startled halt, his tail swishing. The grooms urged him along, and I saw Kennedy's heels, nearly obscured by plaid fabric, come back to touch his barrel. The tension dropped from his hindquarters and he stepped forward again, his strides coming willingly. His head raised as the people beyond the parade gate became visible for the first time, and I could see the interest in his expression as he turned his head from side to side, absorbing the audience's presence. This horse was born to be a star, but it had taken the right rider to bring it out of him.

There was still plenty of work to be done, but Sampson's debut was happening right now. I squeezed Mark's elbow and we passed through the parade gate and into the crowd.

Chapter Twenty-Six

SAMPSON TURNED HIS head to avoid the hose water, pinning his
ears, but Jo was relentless, getting the soft spray between his eyes
and ears, rubbing with a sponge at the sweaty marks across his poll.
She was standing on a step-ladder in order to do it, bringing home
to me again the insane challenges of working with a horse who was
at least twelve feet tall from hoof to nose—when he chose to be. But
this was what the people wanted to see, and they had loved every
second of Sampson's performance out there today.

The day had been a triumph, even if there had been a few
terrifying moments. The first show stop, just minutes after we'd
gone onstage, had sent Sampson into a tailspin—literally. He was
just showing the interested crowd what a canter pirouette looked
like when Mark and I latched ourselves onto either side of his bridle
and brought his forehand back to earth. The crowd *oohed* and there
was a ripple of applause for us, the death-defying horsemen in black.
I'd glanced up at Kennedy and seen her princess smile still in full
force, one hand on the reins, one hand waving to her loyal subjects.
Only her white knuckles betrayed the death-grip she had on the
reins, the nerves she had to be choking on.

At the next show stop and all the others, Mark and I simply stepped up and walked Sampson in a circle, avoiding the Highland dancers as they swooped and kicked through their complicated reel, allowing Kennedy to greet and call out to children in the crowds as she passed them. It turned out to be a pretty good system, getting us through the parade with a minimum of temper tantrums and absolutely no cable news-worthy incidents.

Twenty-five minutes after it had all begun, we finally passed through the Town Square parade gate, walked decorously past the white line painted on the ground which indicated where one officially passed beyond the sight-lines of any observers onstage, and let our shoulders droop with exhaustion. Kennedy had kicked her feet out of the stirrups, and they dangled there along Sampson's sweaty barrel, clad in preciously tooled leather booties that hadn't even been visible during her ride.

Now she was wearing shorts and a tank top, leaning against the barn with a water bottle in her hand, looking absolutely shattered. She wanted to go home, shower, stick her entire body in the freezer if that was what it took to cool off, but Mark said a casting manager from the entertainment department was coming by and he wanted to meet her. Kennedy acquiesced, a gleam coming into her exhausted eyes, still glam with dark eyeliner. I watched her surreptitiously and wondered who would run my Western Trail Experience if Kennedy went back to full-time princessing.

"Look at that horsey!" A mother picked up her toddler and held the little girl up as if that would give her a better view of Sampson from six feet away. "He's so BIG!"

"BIG!" The toddler agreed. "BIG HORSEY!"

"Do you want to pet the big horsey?"

Jo's jaw tightened. She put down the hose and picked up a sponge from a bucket of soapy water, giving no indication she'd heard the mother and daughter behind her, but I knew she was ready to give the mother a lecture if she brought her daughter any closer without permission. It must be maddening working here, I thought for the millionth time, trying to keep people from willfully hurting themselves and creating dangerous equines at the same time, by treating living horses like they were large stuffed animals in a shop display case.

"Come on, we'll pet the horsey." The mother took another step, cradling her daughter against her shoulder.

"NO!" The toddler shrieked, her face contorting with terror. "NO HORSEY NO TOUCH HORSEY NO NO NO!"

I burst out laughing and immediately ran into the barn, ducking into the exhibit on carriages to hide from the mother's glare. The toddler was crying now, completely broken at the realization that her own mother had been willing to take her close to that monstrous horsey of doom, but her sobs faded and were replaced with the exhibit narration which had snapped on as soon as I passed the electric eye in the doorway. I let the tape play through while I looked at the old harness on the walls and recovered myself. By the time the tape had finished, there were voices just outside. I realized the casting manager had arrived and found Kennedy.

"It would be for special events," a woman was saying. "Holidays like today—Christmas, Thanksgiving, movie releases, that kind of thing. You'd be on call, but you'd have plenty of notice. We always need princesses for those, and people love them on horseback. What do you think?"

Kennedy's voice was confident. "I would love to."

I smiled, tipping my head back against the wall. Across from me, a painting of a six-horse hitch prancing in front of the castle rippled with color. Horses, I thought, were a thread that ran through humanity. You could pave over the farms and build pleasure palaces, but everyone still clamored to put horses in them. You couldn't have a Wonderland without horses in it.

It felt unreal to be back at Seabreeze by three o'clock, as if the midday parade and the cool-down at the barn had never happened. I took Ivor out for a hack around the covered ring as a shower blew through, raindrops drumming gently on the roof like a warm-up act for the weather we were sure to get later. A million years had gone by this week, this summer, and I was thankful we were done with the upheaval of the parade. July's doldrums could set in now and I'd welcome every quiet, boring day, and let every cancelled lesson become a compelling reason to pick up a book, lean back in a chair, close my eyes for a nap. Just for a moment, I was going to relax.

My phone began to vibrate against my thigh, and I fished it out of the stretchy pocket of my breeches and wedged it under the harness of my helmet. "This is Grace," I answered absently, watching Ivor's black-tipped ears waggle with every stride. He was relaxed, too. *July*, I thought again.

"Grace! It's Karen, from next door?"

"Hello, Karen," I replied warmly. Karen, my unexpected ally. "How are you? Working on a holiday?"

"I hope you don't mind my calling you on a holiday! I just got the most intriguing request and I wanted to run it by you."

I wiggled the phone so it was securely wedged into my helmet and put my right hand back on the reins. "What's up?"

"Well, we got a call from this travel agent who does equestrian holidays. And what she's suggesting is a total family experience in Orlando. Lessons for the family members who ride. Trail rides for everyone. Catered dining with a riding demonstration for entertainment. The idea is they do the horse thing for a few days, they do the theme parks for a few days, so everyone in the family feels like they got included in the vacation. You think you could put something like that together?"

"How soon?"

"Next month? End of August? The agent wants to do a test run and then she'll build it into a package. She's really big, Grace." Karen lowered her voice, as if she was telling me a secret. "I looked her up and her credentials in this kind of thing are major. African safaris on horseback, people dropping tens of thousands of bucks for a week. I love all of your ideas, but this is taking things to the next level."

July, July, July, I thought tenderly, watching my quiet month slip through my fingers and sail off on the rain-scented breeze. "Let's do it, Karen."

Chapter Twenty-Seven

A MONTH OF hammering, a month of power tools, a month of the sharp smell of paint. Combined with the crunching and clunking of home construction on the other side of the paddocks, even my dreams were filled with noise. One night I woke up in terror, certain I was about to be crushed by an avalanche, and found that my thermostat had broken in the opposite way most thermostats break and my air conditioner had industriously chugged away at bringing the house to a cool sixty-two degrees. My capacity for combining loud noises with ambient air temperature was interesting, at least.

Karen's travel agent had tipped my summer on its head, and sent all of my plans into overdrive. If Mark had come to the barn during July, he certainly would have had questions about what I was up to, with renovations going non-stop upstairs and down. The new lounge, which I'd decided would be open to both boarders and Bella Tuscany guests, had to be ready for the test visit. So did the Western Trail barn, and I decided to enclose the end two stalls across from the school tack room as well, converting them into a new tack room with lockers where guests could store their riding gear for the entirety of their stay. The school tack room itself got a little makeover, making space for my bookshelves and desk from my old office, which had been turned over to the lounge.

But he never found a reason to visit the barn that July. Sampson ended up staying on at the Fort, settling into a stall on the private end of the draft barn, where no guests could bother him. Kennedy and Louise went over once a day so that Kennedy could school him, theoretically under Louise's direction. They came back after lunch and Kennedy settled into working for me once more, schooling the trail horses, schooling the ponies, teaching the kids. She brought some things over to the empty apartment next to Anna and started spending more time up there, prepping to give up her lease and move in full-time. Louise rode her quiet Belgians and Percherons, teaching them to halt squarely, to arch their necks, to bow, to stand still for interminable amounts of time. Any talk of moving barns had dissipated. Kennedy said the lease had fallen through, and I'd left it there. If it hadn't been for the renovations, July would truly have been the quiet month I'd been longing for.

Mark came over and stayed a few nights, never going further up the driveway than my house. I kept the plans for the lounge and the barn out of sight, and said nothing about them. It was conversation I didn't know how to have with him, so I decided I wouldn't have it.

Finally, two days before August, the lounge was ready for its big reveal. I hadn't allowed anyone behind the curtain yet; even Anna, whose apartment shared a wall with the lounge, hadn't seen what was going on inside. I led a troop of clients and boarders up the stairs, which hadn't been replaced yet and groaned with our collective weight. These were definitely next, I thought.

"Your new, luxurious barn lounge awaits!" I announced, pulling aside the curtain the workers had left hanging there with a theatrical flourish.

Behind the old canvas was a brand-new door, elegantly painted in a dark dove color, with an opaque glass panel in the middle. Painted in gold letters, arching over the top half of the glass panel, were the words "Rider's Lounge." It had a pleasing, turn-of-the-century feel I liked. When I'd chosen the typeface with the designer Karen had sent over, I'd emphasized I was going for more of a late Victorian feel than a Wild West one. "Think top hats and hunting and Downton Abbey," I'd suggested. "We'll have some Western props, and of course the trail rides will go out in Western tack, but it's always going to be an English barn."

"The English theme feels more expensive, anyway," the designer had assured me, pushing back his bleached blonde locks with one manicured hand. "When you want big bucks, you bring in elegance. Rustic can only get you so far—it's actually a very limited audience."

It must be, I'd thought, or Mark's elaborately themed ranch would have been raking in the profits instead of just hanging on.

Anna was the first to push open the door, turning the heavy brass latch and stepping inside what had formerly been my cluttered, dusty office. "Oh my god," she said. "What did you *do?*"

There was a rush after those provocative words. Margaret was close on Anna's heels, followed by Karen and the handful of boarders—Gayle, Jen, Phoebe—who happened to be in the aisle when I'd been gathering guinea pigs to test the lounge on.

Judging by their gasps of rapture and squeals of glee, I'd say the space was testing out quite well.

I stepped over the sill and into the air-conditioned comfort of the lounge. Gayle was already lying flat out on the red chaise lounge in the far corner, her boots carefully hung over the edge so as not to mar the upholstery. Anna was tracing the elaborately curving frame of a hunting print hung above the long red couch along the wall just to the left, her mouth a round *o* of surprise. Phoebe and Jen were inspecting the kitchenette space to the right, their boots clicking on the dark laminate flooring, which looked just like reclaimed barn boards. Karen stood in the middle, her hands clasping her purse to her chest, gazing around the space with obvious pleasure.

"Well?" I sidled up to her, reaching up to turn on the ceiling fan. It was dark wood, too, with a frosted globe light that echoed the nineteenth-century feel of the gold letters on the door. The furniture was really all from IKEA, but its modern lines of dark frames and bright red upholstery somehow worked to give the room a retro-modern feel. "The designer you recommended was really a genius, right?"

Karen shook her head, but she was smiling in delight. "I knew Philip was talented, but this is really incredible. And he did this on a budget? I don't believe you."

"I'm guessing you guys paid him a lot more for those model homes." I chuckled. "Sometimes you really have to challenge someone to get their best work."

"Well, you're the riding instructor," Karen laughed. "I guess you know how to get the best out of someone. I'm kidding, of course— the models are great, and decorated just the way we need them to be. But I really love this on a personal level... I think it's perfect for a lounge, simple and comforting."

"And easy to clean," I added. "Everything can be vacuumed or hit with a dust mop and a bleach wipe." I caught Anna's eye. "Anna, it's up to you to determine housekeeping duties."

She grimaced. "Thanks, boss."

Gayle had hopped up from the chaise and was examining a series of horseshoes nailed to the wall at eye level, each one surrounded with a small gold frame. "Is one of these from my sweetie?"

I glanced over the horseshoes. "The middle one," I lied, taking a guess at the shape of her mare's hooves. Gayle clapped her hands and announced she was definitely doing this in her own living room.

I stood back and let the little crowd mill around the lounge, watching the delight on their faces. Who knew this was what they'd wanted? Had *they* even known? We'd been happy for so long with folding chairs, or perching on top of tack trunks. But maybe barns were changing. I was rarely in anyone else's barn these days, not since the local horse business had moved away. Rated horse shows were a different story, with everyone competing for the most opulent decor in the stalls designated as offices, lounges and tack rooms—but that was showing off, part of the horse show culture. I'd never been one of those types that brought along a chandelier, a sideboard and a hunting print. It was a *horse* show, not a barn show.

But this was nice. I opened up the refrigerator and surveyed the lines of water bottles and soda cans within, the bags of carrots stowed in the crisper. Pretty soon it would be full of forgotten cups of yogurt and abandoned salads, but right now it could have been a fridge in a model home... just like the ones next door, and set up to woo the very same clients, too.

The chattering was starting to get to me—Gayle was in one of her noisy raptures again, and Phoebe wasn't much better. I took a Diet Coke out of the fridge and went back onto the deck. The boards creaked under my feet. "You're next," I told the weathered planks. The new landing would be broader, with room for a few picnic tables—to take advantage of the view over the outdoor rings just beyond the barn. This was where the travel agent would dine during the exhibition ride. Kennedy and I were putting together a pas de deux, and then she'd show off with some trick riding.

"New barn, new me," I murmured, and took a long drink, until the bubbles were fizzing in my nose.

The stairs behind me creaked and squeaked, and when I turned around Mark had appeared. I felt a stab of apprehension; he'd spoken with Karen before. She'd said she'd met with the barn owner, back when I'd gone to her office to first propose our partnership. Would he recognize her, two months later?

"What's going on in there?" he asked, inclining his head towards the open door and the bubbling chatter floating out. "Do I smell fresh paint?"

"Just redid a space for the boarders," I said dismissively. "A lick of paint and some new couches. The room was going unused and I have a lot more people running around here than I used to."

"I had no idea! Let's see it." And Mark took my arm, guiding me back to the lounge door. "I came to take you to lunch, but I demand a full tour in compensation."

I wondered if there was any chance Karen had locked herself in the bathroom and was planning on remaining in there for the next ten minutes or so. Surely in that space of time I could get Mark through the lounge, back downstairs, and maybe safely in his truck, driving away with a promise that I'd come and meet him shortly. But when we went inside, Karen was leaning over a sofa, running her hands along a pretty wall-hanging of white tiles, painted with a hunting scene. I'd gotten the idea for it directly from Mark's waiting room at the trail barn. Only there, the scenes were of cowhorses, tied to a hitching post and waiting for their cowboys, lariats coiled alongside their brash Western saddles.

She looked over her shoulder and saw us, and her smile widened in surprise... and maybe to cover her dismay. "Mark!" she exclaimed. "What on earth are you doing here?" Her voice was strained, and I balled my fists behind my back to cover my rising panic. He definitely wasn't supposed to know about the Bella Tuscany deal— at least, not yet.

Mark was looking at Karen with undisguised curiosity. "I was going to ask you that, but you beat me to it." His eyes flicked past her and fastened on the tile-work. He looked at it for a long moment. The room had fallen silent, everyone watching this new, unexpected drama in action.

"That's nice," he said after a moment, perhaps aware that everyone's eyes were upon him, although only two other people in the room could possibly know why. He looked at me once, quickly, and then his gaze shifted away, as if he couldn't bear to meet my eyes. "Pretty room," he added, nodding to the boarders. "You're lucky Grace takes such good care of you."

He backed out of the lounge, stepping over the door-sill, and a moment later I saw his shadow passing the front window. The steps put up their usual protest as his boots went drumming down them.

Karen and I exchanged a horrified glance. The boarders were looking at us with undisguised curiosity. "Who was that?" Jen asked, and Gayle replied that she didn't have any idea.

Anna was beside me suddenly, tugging at my elbow. "You should go after him," she hissed. "Explain what's going on before he gets the wrong idea from somebody else."

"What's the wrong idea, Anna? The truth?" I laughed bitterly.

There'd never been any other ending to this game I'd been playing. The only unknown factor had been *when* Mark would find out I was setting the barn up as a rival to his.

"So you're just going to let him leave?"

I went out onto the deck and Anna followed, her hand still pulling at my arm. I brushed her aside. I heard the slam of a truck door, heard an engine roar to life. Anna would have run after him, heart on her sleeve, but I wasn't like Anna. I'd never been, or I wouldn't have managed all these years on my own. I would have settled down with some show jumper decades ago, and we would have had a colony of Jack Russells and a glass of champagne waiting at every exhibitor's tent, and we would have gotten sick of each other after a while and started training out of different barns, and it would have ended in a divorce years after we'd stopped talking to each other. I could see that version of my life as easily as I could see the real one. I'd never had a deep relationship with anyone, not because I hadn't wanted one, but because I'd never met anyone who called out to my good side. If I had a good side anymore, I'd shown what was left to Mark—but that hadn't stopped me from hurting him, and I didn't feel any regret for having done it—just for the fact that I'd had to do it.

"If he'd wanted to stay, he would have," I told Anna, and she blinked at me, uncomprehending. I gave her a pat on the shoulder, and went downstairs, leaving the women with their new lounge.

Chapter Twenty-Eight

AUGUST IN ORLANDO makes you revisit every decision you've ever made that could have brought you to this time and place. The sky faded from the heat by noon, its rich blue base bleeding away and leaving only merciless white glare in the sky. The storms came late, too late to cool the afternoons, and lasted for hours. The lightning skated hundreds of miles across the sky, leaving behind blue-white spiderwebs which might have been far away or right overhead; it was impossible to tell for sure, and the thunder rumbled late into the night with the same disdain for geographical context. It was impossible to know when it was safe to go outside again, so people gradually abandoned their safety rules, internalized after constant preaching from meteorologists on TV and social media, and just went about their chores and hobbies and dog-walks and jogs without waiting for storms to pass into the distance. There was an "if I die, I die" air to August in Orlando. We'd made it this far into the rainy season, so it seemed unlikely the lightning would get us now.

In this spirit I cantered Ivor around the dressage arena, with Kennedy darting around us on her Quarter Horse, Sailor, while the sky growled all around us and lightning occasionally lit up the somber darkness to our south, to our west, to our north, to our east. The farm was in a pale gray circle of thin clouds which seemed bright as a sunny day when compared to the deep blue-black of the storms surrounding us. But it wasn't raining at this exact moment, and lightning seemed to be mostly further than five miles away, so we were taking this moment to practice our pas de deux routine.

Tomorrow the Chester family arrived, Mr. Chester and Mrs. Chester and Baby Chester (well, she was twelve), and the test visit for Ariel Chester's Orlando Family Magic package would officially be underway. They would be staying not at Bella Tuscany, as none of the condos or villas were ready yet, but at a rental home a mile or so down the road. Karen would be escorting them here after they'd been settled in, attended to by their personal concierge, and had some time to float in the pool—weather permitting, of course. Then it would be our turn to show off what we had. Little Kiera Chester rode hunters, so there'd be a lesson from Kennedy for her while the adults enjoyed a glass of wine by the arena and watched their little darling show her stuff. Then there would be a catered dinner on the new deck upstairs (so new there was still sawdust on the ground below it) while Kennedy and I put on a show. The next morning they'd all go on a Western Trail together, first posing for a picture with their trusty cowhorses, and then to have lunch by the gator pond or at the lounge, weather-dependent, before being carted off to the theme parks.

It wasn't a lot to ask of us; Ariel had suggested most trips would involve two or three lessons, at least one trail ride and lunch. The dinners, she thought, would be a more rare event. "That's good," I'd admitted during one of our many phone sessions, "because this is a working barn, and I don't know how often I can clear the patio and outdoor rings for this sort of thing."

"We'll make it worth your while," Ariel had said with a chuckle. "Private dinners have a serious up-charge in this business."

I was happy to let Ariel make the arrangements and set the prices. This was going to be her exclusive offering to clients. We'd just accept the bookings, make sure they had a good time, and collect the cash.

"Let's practice the changes of rein again," Kennedy huffed, pulling up beside me. Sailor was out of shape. I'd suggested another horse from the school program, but no one else knew bridleless work like Sailor, and that would be Kennedy's big finale after our pas de deux. "I want to be sure we're crossing the center line at the same time. You can really see it from the patio. It's like watching a dressage test from a drone."

Thunder rolled across the sky to the east, sounding like someone was rolling a boulder through the parking lot behind the barn. "Was that closer?" I asked. "That sounded closer."

"Didn't even see any lightning," Kennedy said, looking around. She squinted up at the sky. "I can't even tell which way these clouds are going. It's like they're going in a circle around us."

"The eye of the storm. Did someone throw a hurricane and forget to invite us?"

Anna appeared in the barn entrance. "Guys? Why are you still out there? It's about to storm like hell. Kennedy, come here."

Kennedy gave me a twisted smile and walked Sailor towards the barn obediently.

I wasn't so willing to give in. I waved my hand in the general vicinity of the sky. "It's looked like this for an hour."

"Just *please* come in—"

There was a deafening crack, like the world had split in two. I must have closed my eyes, but I could still see the red flare imprinted on my eyelids. Instantly Ivor was standing on his hind legs and I was leaning forward through the sheer force of instinct, my arms reaching around his neck as far as they would go, and I even though I couldn't hear anything I was aware of screaming, somehow, like a ghost of a sound was seeping into my skin, washing through my bones and plucking delicately at my raw-ended nerves.

Then we were on four hooves again and Ivor was in motion beneath me, galloping, and I opened my eyes and blinked just as we entered the barn, people running to stop him, and I slid off of him as Margaret took his reins and held him, snorting and kicking out at his own tail. I stood still for a second and then reached out, touching his frizzy mane. "His hair is standing on end," I said, disbelieving. I turned around, terror wrenching at my heart. "Is Kennedy—"

She came into the barn, muddy, limping. My hearing came back suddenly and I heard hooves outside, Anna calling *whoa whoa whoa.* A figure dashed by in the center aisle, shaking a feed bucket on her way outside. My ears were ringing and I staggered backwards, suddenly consumed with pinpricks in my legs and feet, my fingers and arms.

Margaret passed Ivor's reins to Lizzie and caught me before I hit the ground. "Easy there," she said in her grim, stalwart tone— unflappable Margaret, the queen of every crisis, I thought adoringly, before I gave myself back over to the ringing in my ears and the prickling in my nerves. "Hospital? Or chair?"

"Chair," I managed to spit, because going to the hospital on a

Sunday afternoon sounded worse than any ailment that could send me there, and because I was sure that despite whatever had happened to me, the worst *hadn't* happened. If I'd been struck, I'd be dead. I wasn't dead, therefore, I would be just fine: the horseman's mantra.

Margaret shuffled me towards the school tack room, and settled me into my desk chair. Kennedy was close on our heels, escorted by Ricky. I remembered seeing Nadine run by with a feed bucket, and wanted to ask if they'd caught Sailor yet, but my tongue was suddenly thick and uncooperative.

Margaret handed me a red can of Coke with a straw. "Drink up," she commanded gruffly. "Sugar and caffeine will fix you right up."

Kennedy accepted a can, but pulled out the straw. "I'm fine," she said. "I just got dumped in the mud. We were halfway to the barn already." She took a drink and grimaced. "Are you sure we can't have Diet, Doc Margaret?"

"Has to be regular," Margaret said firmly. "I don't make the rules."

I heard a siren's wail with sudden clarity, as if it had just flipped on inside my brain. "What's that?" I managed to say.

Margaret glanced out the door, leaning to see down the barn aisle. "Tree's on fire down by the jumping arena," she reported without emotion. "Fire department just got here. They didn't need to bother. It'll be out in a minute. Everything's too water-logged to burn much."

I nodded and put the straw in my mouth. The Coke was sickly sweet, coating my tongue like cough medicine. I felt like I should care more that a tree was on fire, or that the fire department was driving around my property, almost certainly leaving black muddy grooves in my grass with their massive tires, but there just wasn't enough of me intact to react properly right now. I wiggled my toes inside my boots. The pinpricks were retreating slowly.

Ricky stuck his head in the door. "Sailor's fine. Nadine has him in the wash-rack. She's going to brush the mud off because of the lightning around." A rumble overhead punctuated his words; he pointed up and grinned before dashing off again.

The Coke washed around in my stomach. I wanted to put my head down and sleep. I opened a magazine instead, fumbling a little with the glossy pages, and forced myself to concentrate on the typed letters. *Holly Jackson and Never Say Die have another great weekend at Charlottesville.* "I used to know Holly," I mused. "Her mom and I rode together for a while."

Margaret and Kennedy watched me for a moment. I looked back at them, one to the other, puzzled.

"That's all," I said finally. "There's no story."

Kennedy burst out laughing. She laughed so hard she had to put down her Coke. She laughed until Margaret actually began to chuckle, and then she went on laughing until her laughter turned into big sobs, and she bent over on the tack trunk and covered her eyes and cried while Margaret thumped her resolutely on the back and I just blinked at the scene, completely taken by surprise.

"Are you... okay?" I asked cautiously, once the episode seemed to have passed. Outside, I could hear the idling of a big truck which must have been the firefighters, pulling up to talk to someone in charge. There were a few patters of rain on the roof, then a few more, then a regular drumming began to rattle on the metal.

Kennedy hiccuped and wiped her face with her fingers, leaving smears of dirt on her cheeks. I remembered last month, when she'd been a princess, her face white and pink and contoured by an expert's brushes. She looked nothing like herself then. A little mud on her cheeks, that was the Kennedy I knew. "We almost died," she sighed. "On horseback, sure, but… that was a little too close, and by too close I mean it literally could not have been closer."

I opened my mouth to tell her I felt bad about that, but just then Anna burst into the tack room, tackled Kennedy and proceeded to alternately sob over her and demand that she apologize for staying out in the lightning. I glanced at Margaret and cocked my head, asking if I could leave my chair yet. Margaret shrugged. Once I'd proven I wasn't going to drop dead, she'd lost interest in me.

We went out into the barn aisle, where Nicky was having an enthusiastic conversation with a fireman, and the handful of students and boarders who had shown up despite the weather were gathered in little clumps, chattering excitedly about the incident. The rain outside formed a white curtain at the barn entrance, hiding the woods and the hay-shed in the distance. If they'd waited, I thought, the rain would have just put out the tree for them.

"Hello there," I said to the fireman, putting out my hand—the tingles were gone now—and smiling at him. This wasn't my first run-in with the local fire department. "Thanks so much for coming out."

Chapter Twenty-Nine

NEAR-DEATH EXPERIENCES are supposed to unravel your brain, straighten out everything you've been confused about and show you the path you were meant to tread. As an equestrian, I'd had a few of them already. But this one was hitting a little closer, if you'll pardon the pun. I could expect to take a plunge from a horse, end up under hooves at just the wrong angle, crack my helmet, crack my skull, crack my neck—but walking away from a close encounter with an explosion of electricity, so close that my nerves were fired up and I lost track of my senses—that was a serious contender for scariest close encounter yet.

Anna and Margaret were a united front of no-sirree when I suggested Kennedy and I get on with our day. Anna took Kennedy upstairs to her apartment and made her lie down; Margaret told me I wasn't getting on another horse today and looked as if she was strongly considering putting me into bed with her own strong hands. Instead of trying my luck, I obeyed her commands, waited for the worst of the rain to pass, and then dawdled down the lane to my house, Max at my heels.

The tree by the dressage ring had been a small laurel oak, and now it was a charred stump, with some blackened branches scattered around in the ring. They'd have to be picked up tonight or tomorrow, and be tossed into the woods. As I'd expected, there were now dark, muddy tire marks marking the green grass between the lane and the ring, and the fire truck had taken out a length of white chain on its way into the arena, so that would need to be repaired before tomorrow night as well. Plus, the arena would have to be dragged to erase the deep tread marks left in the clay. I made a mental list, thinking rather sadly of my lost Monday. This would be a long week coming up. Maybe I really should take a nap right now, while I had the chance.

But you couldn't walk away from a near-death experience and simply slip into a nap. I lay beneath a thin cotton sheet, Max at my side, and carefully picked apart my life, starting with my childhood and working up to the moment Mark had walked down the stairs and left, exactly one month ago. I hadn't spoken to him since. Kennedy reported back on him after her daily rides at the Fort for a while—Mark was very quiet, Mark was working very hard, Mark looked worried all the time—and then the reports became redundant, and I told her I was over him; she didn't have to keep me up to date anymore.

"Max," I said eventually, "I'm going to have to go over there. Unless you stop me. Do something to stop me. Bar the door. Trip me."

Max stretched, sighed, went on snoozing. Max lived life without regrets. It was the Jack Russell way.

"Mark is in the trail barn." Jo glared at me, and I knew she'd thought she'd seen the last of me. I wondered if she'd made a move on him yet. "He's closing up. The weather isn't going to clear."

"I think you're right," I said, just to be friendly, although there was no point. Jo turned her back on me, leaving me on the wrong side of the chain strung across the barn aisle. But there was no gate across the pathway to the trail barn, and though the rain was still pattering down, its pace had grown lazy and the thunder had moved on. I backtracked down the barn aisle, past the slumbering draft horses and a dripping-wet family examining the carriage exhibit, and took a shortcut through wet grass towards the woods beyond.

Mark was alone in the trail barn, taking off saddles and leaning them against the wall beyond the hitching line, tossing damp saddle pads into a pile nearby. The horses were pulling at hay-nets and looked content, but they'd clearly been standing there for quite a while. There was some serious mucking out to be done. They must have been inside all afternoon, tacked and ready in hopes the weather would allow a ride to get out. I made a mental note to go over weather clauses and cancellation policies with Karen, then shook my head to clear the thought. I wasn't here on business, and if I could stop thinking about my farm first and everything else second for just a few minutes, I might have a shot at something more.

Maybe.

I went into the barn and stood in the shadow of the mulch-covered walkway. The closest horse reached out his nose and blew at my palms for a moment, then went back to his hay. Mark was working with his back to me, six horses standing between us. He was bent over, untying a cinch. He stood up, pulled down the saddle, ducked under the hitching post with it. When he was halfway up again, he saw me, and he froze for a scant second, confusion sweeping across his features before he shook his head, stood upright, and leaned the saddle against the wall beside the others.

"Mark," I said, and then I realized I didn't know what I'd come to say. I hadn't planned any words on the way over. I'd just known I needed to come.

He picked up the saddle pad and tossed it over with the rest. "I didn't expect to see you here again," he said, turning his back to me again.

I listened to the rain drumming on the low metal roof for a moment. "I missed you," I said finally. "This wasn't how it was supposed to go."

"How was it supposed to go?" He still hadn't turned around. He ducked under the rail, started on the next horse's saddle. He was closer to me now. With every horse he'd come closer. In a few minutes, we'd be standing right next to each other. My heart skidded recklessly at the thought. "Was it supposed to be a happily ever after?" he asked harshly. "Because Fantasyland is across the lake over there. And you have to pay to get in."

"Maybe it's too soon to talk about happily ever after," I said, "but I think it's too soon to end it all over a misunderstanding."

"What's the misunderstanding, then?"

"That I was with you to get inside your business model."

He snorted. "Much luck to you with it. May your entire life be as insecure as mine has become."

"I run an equestrian center in a tourist town. I run an equestrian center, end of sentence. I've never known a day's security."

Another saddle hit the wall. Another saddle pad on the ground, rolling over, showing its fleece underbelly to the roof. "They didn't know about you for so long. We kept it at the Fort. Upper level didn't know there were horses left around here. Then it comes out. Then they want to know everything. I wouldn't tell them. Jo did. Jo found out everything she could—your pricing, your clients. The Bella Tuscany deal. They hit the roof, Grace. They wanted to know why I hadn't cut a deal with them first. I told them it had never been our position to discount and cater to outside resorts. They said I wasn't even doing my job getting business from the internal resorts, and that if I didn't start hitting budget targets, I could start shopping for a new job. I've been here ten years. I planned to be here another twenty. Now, I don't know."

"I'm sorry," I said, genuinely horrified. But I remembered Mark's struggle on the phone with the concierge a few months ago. They hadn't even known how to book the carriage rides for the guests staying at the resort. This went deeper than discovering competition existed just down the road. Jo had thought it was a conspiracy to close the ranch down. I wondered if she wasn't so crazy after all. "But there has to be a way to fix this—"

"There's *not*." Mark swung under the hitching rail again. He didn't bother setting down this saddle nicely. He pitched it to the ground. The saddle horn dug into the mulch and tore up the sand underneath. "Not with you right there, offering the same experience for less money."

I swallowed down an angry retort. A fight wouldn't help us now. It was a shame; I was good at fights. But he had to get past this so we could start talking about his next move. I was sure there was an answer right under his nose—here, with twenty internal resorts, he shouldn't have to worry about who got Bella Tuscany's business! I took a deep breath and spoke in the most calm tone I could manage.

"Mark, if we couldn't coexist here, we were doomed from the start. Because if my barn closes, I'm gone. I can't stay in Orlando. There's nowhere left to go here. If you'd wanted me to stay, you'd need me to succeed. And if I want you to stay, I need you to succeed." I paused; he still looked angry, he still looked like nothing would ever bring him back to me. "I *need* you to succeed," I said softly.

Mark's shoulders sagged suddenly. He looked from me to the horses. There were just two left between us, two dark-colored Quarter Horses with quiet expressions. The perfect trail horses. "Let's ride," he said suddenly.

I opened my mouth to say I wasn't supposed to be on a horse, Margaret's orders, but stopped myself. "Yes," I agreed, suddenly desperate to be in the saddle, legs wrapped around a horse, the only place where life made perfect sense. "Let's ride."

The early evening air was almost cool, a little trick Florida played every now and then to make us think the end of August was the end of summer. I tipped my head back to look at the black tree limbs criss-crossing under the gray ripples of cloud, and a single cold raindrop fell from a pine branch overhead and balanced itself on the tip of my nose before rolling off and disappearing into the wet leather of my saddle. Pippa, the little dark bay mare I was riding, reached out for a mouthful of some tall Florida mystery-grass growing alongside the trail, and I let her do it without a second thought. Ahead of me, Mark swayed companionably with the motion of his horse, a bay gelding called Marvel, but though his hips were loose, his shoulders were still rigid with tension.

We'd been riding for nearly twenty minutes in silence. The trail wound close to the waterfront, the big expanse of lake just visible at times through the cypress trees along its shore, and I could hear the whistle of the ferry-boats out on the water, and now and then, a squeal of laughter from a child, amplified to startling strength by the sopping-wet air. I wondered when he was going to pull up, turn back to me, say something. The tingling had come back to my toes, and I'd dropped my stirrups to try and give them some relief.

In a little clearing, just a wide spot between the palmettos and pines, Mark reined back and Marvel obediently came to a halt. I brought Pippa up beside him. She dropped her head to graze. The bit in her mouth was so light and narrow, I decided to let her do as she liked.

Mark chewed at his lip. "I missed you," he said finally.

"I missed you. I should have called you, or come over. I shouldn't have left it up to you."

"I thought you'd stolen from me. Not *things,* just... when I saw the decorations up, I realized what you were doing, and it... I over-reacted. You were right when you said we both have to win." He looked at me. I was working my fingers now, stretching them and squeezing them together rhythmically. The pins and needles had come back while I'd been holding the reins. "What happened?"

"Nothing," I said. "Well—I was almost struck by lightning earlier. I guess the voltage affected me some."

"Earlier *today?*"

"About two hours ago? A little more than that, I guess."

"But—*Grace.*" Mark leapt down from the saddle, dropping Marvel's reins, and clutched at my leg, reached up to my waist. I let him pull me down from the saddle and clutch my body up against his, his chin tipped down to look at me, his eyes grave with dismay. Behind me, Pippa cropped at the wet grass, unperturbed by my sudden dismount. He took off his helmet and tossed it to the ground. "You could have *died*."

His kiss was deep and desperate, and I felt my arms tighten around his neck, my fingers curl into his hair, the pins and needles forgotten. If my near-death experience had failed to unravel my brain as much as I would have liked, it certainly seemed to clear things up for Mark.

Chapter Thirty

"I'm too old to learn new tricks," I grimaced, clutching the neck-rope Kennedy handed me as Ivor wriggled beneath me. "Can't you make Anna do it?"

"Anna is busy," Anna informed me, marching by with a stack of linens I'd never seen before. "You want a gourmet dinner, you gotta have white tablecloths. The caterers won't bring their own, not after last time, so it's laundry time to get the plastic smell out of these."

"Last time wasn't *that* bad."

"No one ever explained to them how their tablecloth ended up in the front paddock, being used as a chew toy by Frank and Honey."

"Well, we never figured out how it got there," I said, crossing my arms defensively. "Anyway, it was our test run. Things happen."

Lizzie swung her legs alongside Splash's barrel, her calves and heels never touching his sides. Being sixteen meant being just as comfortable bareback and bridleless as she would be with all her tack, and she had been happy to take on a role in the evening dinner show when Kennedy had gotten called in to work a parade the same night our first paying guests were due. "You're going to love it," she assured me, nudging Splash into an energetic walk and circling Ivor and me. "You'll never want to ride with a saddle and bridle again."

I pushed myself back from Ivor's shark-fin withers. "I seriously doubt that, young lady."

"He'll be fine," Kennedy assured me. "I've been working with him all week. It's just seat and leg. Dressage without the saddle in your way. The rope is there as back-up in case he gets carried away, because, well, he's Ivor."

Nevertheless, I wished there was more of a barrier between the dressage arena and the outside world than a length of plastic chain strung a few inches above the ground. Today, at least, I could practice this bridleless game in the covered ring, with a big firm fence to contain any shenanigans. As Kennedy pointed out, he was Ivor. He liked to get carried away.

How did I reach this point in my life? I asked myself, riding Ivor's swinging walk over to the rail and turning him deftly with seat and hip. The evening entertainment, riding a pas de deux without tack. In my white full-seats, white shirt, and gleaming black dress boots, I would look like I'd simply misplaced my saddle and bridle, and decided to enter a competition anyway. Or like a waiter who'd stolen a big gray horse.

Kennedy turned on the music and there was a swell of violins. Ivor swiveled his ears around, picked up the beat from the routine Kennedy had been riding him to all week, and broke into a high-stepping trot. *Oof.* I should have insisted on the saddle. This horse's withers were no joke. Originally, there'd been saddles for everyone, but as the show had evolved in Kennedy's rich imagination, bits and pieces of tack had slowly vanished.

"Splash *loves* this," Lizzie announced, cantering past without a care in the world. "It's like he just discovered his calling."

"You have a show in two weeks, miss," I called after her. "Don't get any ideas about running away to join the circus!" A typical day of riding with Kennedy, I thought. Enthusiastic to a fault, so she got everyone worked up about her latest crazes.

It was a good thing I loved her.

I found my seat at last and settled into Ivor's swinging gaits. We cantered side by side with Splash and Lizzie for a few rounds, getting used to matching our strides, and then Kennedy started the song over again and we went into the routine, dancing through serpentines and mirrored movements on either side of the arena. It was a pretty little show, a touch regal for the tourists who thought themselves cosmopolitan and upper class, a touch of whimsy for the ones who were here for princesses and magic castles. I'd never aspired to the level of musical freestyles, so this was my first taste of choreographed riding. Matching Ivor's cadence to the beat was surprisingly addictive.

We halted nose to nose at the very end, and Lizzie grinned at me from between Splash's pricked ears. "Piece of cake," she boasted.

"We'll see how it goes outside," I grumbled. "And at night, with shadows for extra fun." But I had to give in and grin back at her in the end. It *was* fun.

"Bravo!" Mark was leaning on the rail, clapping his hands. "We should hire you to perform at the park."

I shook my head at him. "Not a chance. You've already poached my star performer, you're not getting the understudies, too."

"A private performance," he suggested, smiling as I rode over to him. He put his hand on Ivor's warm neck, scratched him in the itchy spot under his mane. Ivor preened and did everything but climb over the rail and into his lap. "Take those boots off and show me your tempi changes."

"Don't be suggestive in front of my working student, Mark." I waggled my eyebrows at him. "Dressage innuendo is so nineteenth century, anyway."

"I'm out of here," Lizzie announced dramatically, and sent Splash springing away. Ivor watched him longingly.

"No more," I told him, and dismounted. "If I'm going to survive tomorrow night, I have to save my seat bones now."

"I guess that means me, too," Mark remarked to Kennedy, who tittered appreciatively.

I rolled my eyes at the lot of them and took Ivor into the barn, dragging him by his neck-rope when he hung back to watch Splash canter past.

The warm October afternoon held the slightest hint of cool autumn air in its breeze, but the brief ride had still brought sweat up where Ivor's back and my thighs had rubbed together, and I led him into the wash-rack for a shower. Mark followed and I noticed he had Max on a leash, trotting at his side.

"Thanks for stopping at the house," I said. "How did you know I didn't have Max?"

"You said you were going to practice the ride. You told me yesterday," he added, in response to my puzzled look. "I figured you wouldn't want to risk Max running through the arena."

"You figured right. Thank you." I gave him a puzzled glance. "Don't you have your open house tonight?"

Mark shrugged. "The grooms have everything under control. And the catering managers are kind of going crazy, and someone from employee relations is planning on taking video of *everything* for social media... I guess I just wanted to get away from it for a few minutes."

Ivor stood on the hose resolutely, causing the water to hiss in distress from around the spigot. I shoved on his shoulder. "I'm always happy to be your escape," I told Mark without turning. "But I think you should be there."

The open house had been in the works for the past month, and it would be a shame if Mark didn't get full credit for its success—though of course with so many people involved now, chances were good he wouldn't. He deserved every accolade, though, because the entire concept had been Mark's—and mine, if we're being honest here, though I'd planted the idea into his mind so quietly he'd be hard-pressed to identify me as the one who'd come up with it. It wasn't that putting on a catered party for the resort concierge teams, the ticket-sellers, and anyone else who could convince resort guests to head to the Fort for a trail ride or a carriage ride was such a revolutionary idea. It was simply that a place with so many moving parts was often myopic and missed the low-hanging fruit dangling right in front of its eyes. Plus, giving people free carriage rides and barbecue while a folk band howled old cowboy tunes was a surefire way to build goodwill at a job site where everyone willingly dolled themselves up in polyester reproductions of old-time pioneers, Victorian servants and riverboat queens. By the time the bonfire was good and hot and the s'mores fixin's were passed around, everyone there would be a brand ambassador for the Fort's equine recreation.

Having liberated the hose from Ivor's big fore-hoof, I busied myself hosing the gray stallion down. When I ducked under his neck to get to the horse's other side, I saw Mark watching me, a wistful look on his face. "Say it," I told him.

"I need you to come with me," Mark said.

I moved behind Ivor, training the water on his hindquarters, and allowed myself a secret smile. "Of course I'll come with you," I said. "We're in this thing together."

When I came back around, Mark's head was tilted. "This thing?" he asked curiously.

I was present enough to turn the hose off before I spread my arms, indicating, roughly, *everything.* "We're reinventing all of it. Everything they told us we couldn't do, this business they told us we couldn't run here anymore—it's going to work. *We're* going to work."

He grinned. "Grace, has anyone ever told you you're slightly scary when you're on a roll?"

I leaned over the low wall between us and gave him a pert kiss on the lips. "Stay scared," I told him. "This is just the beginning."

Your Next Read

LOOK FOR AN update to the Show Barn Blues series in the near future. In the meantime, get a preview of the award-winning novel *The Hidden Horses of New York* below.

Set in Florida, New York City, and Saratoga Springs, NY, this novel follows a trio of young dreamers who believe they can change the way the world sees horse racing forever. Narrated by Jenny, the daughter of a hardscrabble Thoroughbred breeding and racing family, it's a story about hope, dreams, and the price of love.

The Hidden Horses of New York
Chapter One

Jenny jiggled the lead-shank to distract the three-year-old colt tugging at the other end, and tried to ignore the phone buzzing in her back pocket. Her mother's gaze, sharp and unforgiving, caught hers from across the saddling ring, and Jenny felt the force of her warning: *don't touch that phone while you've got hold of a horse.* It was one of Andrea Wolfe's most ferociously-enforced rules. Once, she had taken a rider's phone right out of his hands and thrown it with the power and grace of a pitcher. The phone had landed in the cattail-choked drainage ditch running along the inside of Sugar

Creek Farm's training track and was never seen again.

"Settle," Jenny hissed at the colt, who rolled one wild eyeball at her and flared his nostrils, tossing his head towards her face. For an instant her vision was a blur of black skin, ringed inside with red. The colt's sleek coat was graying out slowly, his neck and body spangled with white-ringed dapples and his mane a cloud of black. Jenny remembered when he'd been born, a fox-colored colt blinking owlishly through spectacles of pale hair, a dead giveaway that this pretty little chestnut would grow up to be a gray.

Jenny jerked back to the present and gave the lead-shank in her hands a tug to remind him not to get so personal. The colt straightened out and they kept on walking in their tight circles, using every inch of the space they'd been allotted. The walking ring of Tampa Bay Downs was tight; the little crowd of spectators pressing in so closely that Jenny was sometimes afraid even the rail keeping them back from the horses was still not far enough away to protect them from a kick. As a rule, hot-blooded young Thoroughbreds were not malicious. But they were in a hurry to get moving, and indiscriminate with where their flying hooves ended up.

Jenny's phone was buzzing again, furiously rattling against the thin chest pocket on the flowing blue blouse she'd paired with her race-day khakis. She desperately wanted to answer it, wanted to see her friends' silly faces and hear their stupid voices so much, and she was crazy to find out what had happened with their final presentation, if Professor Mulvaney thought their idea was any good or if they were just a bunch of idealistic kids (which Jenny did not think was a bad thing, not yet). They needed his buy-in if they were going to get anywhere. Lana's father had been determined on that point. He wasn't giving them a dime otherwise.

The loudspeakers crackled as if they were clearing their metallic throats, and then the feed from the track's resident commentator took over the sound of jingling metal and thudding hooves. He was standing near the paddock with his back to the horses, a small burly man in a three-piece suit that strained at the arms, wraparound sunglasses and gel-stiffened blonde hair competing with his swirling tribal neck tattoos for attention. Jenny always thought he looked like a cross between a professional skateboarder and Guy Fieri. He spoke, with a thick Long Island accent, about past performances and speed figures and jockey win percentages. When he got to Mr. November, he just said: "this one is the favorite for a reason, but if you want to beat him, try the three and the six," and then continued on with the next horse.

Jenny ran a hand along Mister's hot neck. They weren't going to beat him—not the three, not the six, not any of the other horses circling the paddock. His dark eye met hers, and suddenly Jenny forgot about her phone, and the conversation she was missing in New York right now. This happened before every race. Jenny would live entirely in the moment for the next fifteen minutes: the moment she handed Mister off to the outrider, the moment she caught him after his race, the moment she led him into the winner's circle.

Today was Mister's day.

She smiled at him, the sounds of the horseplayers dissipating around her.

Then he ducked his chin backwards and tried to bite her, his eyes bright with mischief, and she was wrenched back to reality. *"No,"* she huffed. "You're *bad.* Don't do it again!"

Mister pushed hard against the bit in his mouth, grinding his teeth. The movement tugged at her joints, made her wince as she pulled back. He was so ready, so painfully ready. Why wasn't it time to mount up yet? She looked to the center of the ring. Her mother was there, talking to the jockey, a slim-hipped young man who was having a very good year. It had been easy to convince him to ride Mister in the colt's first big stakes challenge. Everyone knew the colt was peaking. No one knew it better than Jenny. Because while the line for *owner* was always filled in with "Sugar Creek Farm," Mr. November's real owner had always been Jenny Wolfe. He was the last good thing she'd done before she'd gone away to school, and the one good thing she'd returned for, over and over again. Bred by Jenny, foaled by Jenny, halter-broke by Jenny, started under saddle by Jenny. She'd done it all over winter holidays, spring breaks, summer vacations, and long weekends. She'd hurried home from a cold, snowy New York to a warm March evening when his birth seemed imminent, despite her mother's tired reminders that there was no telling when the mare might actually foal. And early that morning, as a storm blew through the open rafters overhead, her colt had been born.

The new foal had blinked at her from his damp bed of straw and then promptly bit her, all gums and tiny milk teeth closed tight on her hand, and Jenny had laughed and told him, "you're the one, you're my Mister November," and he'd been Mister every day since then.

Jenny's mother had disapproved of naming a wobbling newborn colt for a race three and a half years (and a solid mountain of luck) away. "There are thirty-six foals due on this farm alone, thousands all around Ocala, and you're pinning all of your Breeders' Cup hopes on this one?"

But Mister was *Jenny's* hope, not the farm's hope or her mother's hope. And she thought Mr. November was a fine name for a colt she planned to point at the world racing championships, held in November each year. "Plus he looks like a Mister," Jenny added. "With those little spectacles of his."

"Those will be gone in two months," her mother snorted, but she left it alone after that.

Three years ago, Jenny thought, her hand still on the taut muscles running along Mister's arching neck. Three years ago, he'd stood no higher than her waist. And now he was this big beast, this monstrous colt with muscles toned into the airstream lines of an Art Deco locomotive, coat spangled with white stars like the iron-gray sky the morning before a hurricane, taut skin and flowing raven mane and dark, intelligent eyes that landed on Jenny the moment she entered his field of vision and never left her until she was gone again, back to wherever Jenny went when she left Mister behind.

"Riders up!" the ring steward called, raising his clipboard in the air like a ceremonial flag. As if released from taut strings, the jockeys and trainers dispersed in every direction, flowing toward their mounts in a wave of bright pageantry.

In her pocket, Jenny's phone buzzed three times—then stopped again. They were learning, she thought, tugging Mister in a circle for the jockey.

Mister was not the sort of horse who stood still for mounting, despite Jenny's best efforts to teach him good manners. She'd come home last summer and ridden him each morning, teaching him to be a racehorse on the white-fenced oval back home in Ocala. It hadn't been enough. Jenny's mother had snorted that a body could hardly expect some rude *New Yorker* to teach manners to a two-year-old colt, and Jenny had protested even while inside she felt a glow of pride at being called a New Yorker. There was something about belonging in the city that was beginning to call to her by then, a realization that the alien streets and endless traffic and soaring towers were somehow as richly intoxicating as the green hills and ancient oaks and molasses-scented feed rooms of Ocala, and she had already begun to wonder if she was going to stay on after school was over.

Now, she was just waiting for the chance.

Her phone was still and silent, but she felt it rumbling against her hip, a phantom vibration with every step. Her whole life was waiting to begin, and she'd find out what came next in minutes... if she could just get Mister out to the race course without bloodshed.

She kept walking the colt, slowing his stride infinitesimally (infinitesimally was all Mister would tolerate) as her mother held out her palms alongside the colt, waiting to help Manny spring into the saddle. Mister, watching him with a sideways ear, tensed his muscles, his steps shifting into a hopping-skipping jig, his hindquarters weaving sideways as he hit Jenny's unforgiving hands on the leather and chain binding them together and he ran out of room for all of the energy flowing through him. He held back for a moment, and Manny put his hands on the saddle, his knee into Andrea's hands, and jumped onto the colt's back.

"Watch him in the gate," Jenny's mother spat out, falling back from Mister's swinging haunches before he let a hind hoof fly, heedless of what might be in his way. "Don't let him twist and carry on or he'll miss the break." It had been Mister's undoing in all but his last start this year. It was the reason he was still in Florida in

May, when everyone had expected him to go to Kentucky. He just hadn't had the brain to go with his speed yet.

Jenny thought his brain had finally caught up.

"I got this, Miss Andrea," Manny said, his voice confident. Jenny glanced up at him and he grinned back at her.

"I'm glad you're riding him," Jenny told him.

"Yeah, me too." Manny laughed and adjusted his stirrups. Mister was still trotting in slow motion, but the jockey wasn't bothered. The only thing that would have gotten his attention was if the horse reared or bucked. Spine flat? All systems go. "I like this boy. He got a lot of spirit, but he not stupid."

They gave up their circle, and started toward the gap in the track fencing. The outriders were waiting on their track ponies, the retired racehorses and bored quarter horses watching the younger horses' antics without interest. Track ponies had seen everything before, twice over. Jenny slid the chain free of Mister's halter, and began to unbuckle the strap behind his ears, preparing to turn the colt over to the outriders. Manny wouldn't be asked to control Mister alone until the bell rang and the gates sprang open.

A darkly tanned woman with a long bleached ponytail flowing from the back of her helmet leaned down from her rangy horse's back, and, just as Jenny slipped his halter free, the outrider slid a slim leather strap through the ring of Mister's bit.

She timed it perfectly; Mister was never free for a moment.

"Let's go, old man," the outrider told her mount, and the horse broke into a shuffling jog while Mister hopped alongside like a big gray bunny, shaking his head furiously against the outrider's taut hold on his bridle. As he sprang away, a gob of white foam slopped from his bit and onto Jenny's shoulder. She brushed the saliva away without looking at the damage done to her blouse, wiping her hands on her race-day khakis, which had seen much worse. For one long, frozen moment she just watched Mister cavorting at the end of the leather thong. He flipped his head, propped his shoulders, blew loudly through his nostrils. No one paid him any mind. The outrider was ignoring him, the pony horse was ignoring him, even Manny, perched above his withers, was ignoring him. Refusing to acknowledge his foolishness was the only way to deal with Mister's mischief-loving heart; the moment you got on his case about something, the colt escalated things to a scale that quickly got dangerous for everyone.

Jenny thought about how much she loved him, and how much she had missed him while she'd been in New York, and how much more she would miss him if she went back for good.

Then her phone buzzed again, breaking the spell, and she pulled it out of her pocket just as her mother came hustling up. "Let's go, girl. You're standing in the track like a crazy person," Andrea commanded. "They're trying to put a race on, if you haven't noticed."

She hit the green button on her phone's screen, her heart between her boots, suddenly afraid of whatever news was waiting. Yay or nay, go or no go, it was all going to be a disaster for half of her.

"JENNY!" the people in her phone shrieked in a chorus, and her heart rebounded like a balloon freed of its string, soaring up into the endless blue of the Florida sky.

"GUYS!" she yelled back. *"HOW DID IT GO?"*

Jenny's mother shook her head and hustled away, pushing through the crowd. She was heading for the spot near the winner's circle where she always watched races. Jenny hung back in the walking ring as the remaining horses danced past her, bound for their own outriders, and held up her phone to get a good view of her friends.

Aidan crowded Lana for optimal screen time, his broad smile taking over Jenny's entire display. She couldn't help but let her grin slip into something deeper, a more all-encompassing smile that probably put her heart on her sleeve for a few revealing seconds. She wondered how her hair looked, if her dark waves were hanging lifelessly thanks to the humid May evening. She imagined just how red her cheeks were, how sweaty her upper lip must be. Aidan looked cool and collected, his walnut-brown hair falling in its habitual wave across his forehead. Lana, pushing her way into the frame, was as flawlessly made-up as ever, and Jenny shrank from the comparison Aidan must be making between the two of them.

Then she caught herself, pushed the thoughts away, and and produced a toothy, friendly grin. "Stop shoving Lana, Aidan! Haven't you ever heard of chivalry?"

"It's called being a gentleman, *learn* about it," Lana screeched, pushing him back, and as Aidan tumbled off his bar stool she could see they were at Fargo, a dive bar on the Lower East Side where they'd been celebrating good grades and good days for the past few years. Jenny waved at the bartender, an aging hipster boasting a glorious lumberjack beard, but he couldn't see her. "JENNY," Lana roared, swiping back white-blonde hair from her face, where it was always falling with orchestrated abandon, *"HE LOVED IT. HE LOVED IT!"*

The bartender spoke up without lifting his gaze from his lemon slicing. "Yo, stop yelling, Lana, there's no one here but you guys. Let me enjoy some peace and quiet before the evening hits."

"Sorry, Mike," Lana whispered, and she crossed her eyes at Jenny, making a gag-me face. Lana thought Mike was secretly in love with her. Lana thought every man was secretly in love with her, and most women, too. "Professor Mulvaney said the entire plan was a fantastic idea. He said it made him think differently about horse racing! And he *never* even thinks about horses period!"

Aidan pushed his face back into view. "If we can get through to people who aren't even interested, think about the actual equestrian community. This is really it. We're going to build bridges. We're going to connect people like never before. This is going to change everything."

Jenny took a deep breath, feeling a rush of excitement tingle from her nose to her toes. This was it, then. One step closer to going back to New York. They were going to get to work, just as they'd planned. Now all they needed was Lana's father to finance them.

Then she felt someone tap her on the back. She turned to find a hectored-looking member of staff, holding a manure fork in one hand. "Miss, can you clear the paddock?"

Jenny looked around and instantly felt guilty. No one else was left. She looked around at the screen in the infield—the horses were cantering up the backstretch, heading for the chute at the far corner of the track. All of the spectators were either finding spots to watch the race or inside, getting their bets in.

"I'm getting chased out, guys," she said. "I have to call you back."

"NO!" Lana shrieked. "We have to see the race! Keep us on."

"Live-stream everything," Aidan suggested. He turned his head slightly. "Mike, come watch this. Get a taste of what we're going to offer with our new website."

Jenny could practically hear Mike rolling his eyes, but the bartender finally put down his paring knife and came around the bar. Her heart melted a little, just to know he was pretending to care. So he really *did* like them! She knew he had always thought she and her friends were just a bunch of spoiled college kids, and to a certain extent, he wasn't wrong. Even though she and Aidan didn't have a spare penny, being friends with Lana, who was generous with her father's money, meant living like a trust fund kid... well, part-time, anyway. For Jenny, at least, the experience was still dizzying—even after three years of Lana's luxurious hand-outs, spendthrift shopping sprees, and expensive meals out. Maybe Aidan and Jenny's inability to accept nice things as their lot in life, and Lana's open-pocketed approach to friendship, was why Mike still treated them with a sliver of respect, instead of eyeballing them with the same distaste he reserved for the other college students who came swaggering into the dark little bar. She decided to put on a good show for him.

"Okay, guys!" Jenny flipped the camera view, held out the phone, and began touring her little audience through the paddock as she headed for the gate out to the apron. She gave it a slow swing for a panoramic view, trying not to bounce the phone too much with each step. If live-streaming from around different racetracks was a key aspect of their audience engagement plan, the art of not making viewers seasick was going to be the most important skill in her toolbox. And commentary, she reminded herself, realizing she'd been silent for the first ten seconds. "So, this is the paddock. Over here is the barn where we saddle up. If I'm quick we can get a look at the shoe board, that's pretty cool, it shows bettors the shoes that are allowed on the horses—"

Jenny's patter was momentarily interrupted as she tripped over a grooming tote someone had abandoned on the walking path, and Lana and Aidan shrieked with laughter. Their howls rang from her phone and she wondered how two people currently located in Manhattan could be so loud all the way down in Tampa. Technology was a mystery she accepted as her master without understanding it at all, sort of like a medieval peasant at mass.

"Oh, sorry, Jenny!"

She turned at the sound of an actual, non-digitized voice and saw Luis, a groom from the Lawson barn. She liked Luis; had known the guy since she was just a kid. The Lawsons were neighbors back in Ocala, and rivals here at Tampa, and aggressive, unpleasant humans in both towns. But Luis had always been nice: a middle-aged, soft-faced man with a shy smile and a sweet way around horses. He stooped down to retrieve the grooming tote, his horse's halter flung over one shoulder.

"No problem," she told him, letting the phone dangle from her hand, forgetting temporarily about the live-stream. "You've got a good horse in today. Good luck!"

"Good luck to you," Luis said, grinning. "Your Mister, he's a crazy one, huh?" He was ready to settle in for a chat.

The phone protested Mister's innocence. Luis looked at the screen with interest. "Your friends are upside-down," he observed.

"Whoops!" Jenny righted the phone. "So that was Luis, he's a groom of another horse here—"

"Well, *this* is totally inappropriate," a familiar voice growled, interrupting her commentary. Jenny looked up from her phone, alarmed. Luis had already scampered for the fence, ducked between the two lowest bars, and disappeared into the crowd gathering along the rail.

Jenny swallowed, trying to push away a wave of anxiety that would surely show on her face. She didn't want to give Brice Lawson any hint that he frightened her. The middle-aged trainer was a big, forbidding man, with broad shoulders strong enough to snatch a runaway racehorse out of stride and a frowning face that always found fault with Jenny's horsemanship. If she was breezing a horse on the main track, he'd find a reason to complain about her to the stewards. If she was walking a horse before a race, he'd protest she was taking up more than her allotted room on the path. He and his wife, Laura, behaved in the same roughshod way with her parents, always pushing their jockeys to claim fouls on Wolfe horses and blowing up over petty nuisances on the backside. It was all the stuff of racetrack legend now. The time Laura Lawson had run over Andrea's tomato garden next to the barn. The time Brice Lawson had called animal control to remove the Sugar Creek grooms' hens. The time the both of them had moved a Sugar Creek horse, in the dead of night, to another barn so that they could steal the stall for one of their own shippers. The Lawson-Wolfe feud had been going on for as long as Jenny could remember.

She made to chase after Benny, but Brice moved between her and the fence.

"Three minutes," the track announcer intoned, his terse voice echoing from the loudspeakers. He was talking to the bettors, but it felt like a countdown for Jenny, as well.

"I have to go," Jenny said desperately. "My mother is waiting."

"You better keep away from my staff," Brice demanded. "And stop videoing the paddock. This is for horsemen only. You have no business sharing it with your little social media following."

This—*this* was the problem. Jenny felt an unusual courage rise up in her chest, the same feeling that got her around tracks on top of young horses she ought to be afraid of, the way she was afraid of everything else in the world. It was the courage that got her through four years of school in the city, and helped her talk to Aidan and Lana back in freshman English, and gave passion to the thesis statement which would become their website. If these old school horsemen and their fear of cameras didn't sink everything before it started! Their suspicion of everything tech, their shortsighted denial of everything good about transparency and branding and carefully curated insights into the worlds of their horses that the public was so anxious to see for themselves. They wanted to keep everyone on the other side of the rail; they thought of race-day visitors as bettors and could not conceive that anyone would drag themselves out to a racetrack to see beautiful, powerful horses for the sole purpose of just that, without any financial gain or sporting itch to be scratched. They refused to let any light in, and as a result their sport was dying in the dark. She saw it so damn often, and she was enraged by it.

"There's nothing to *hide,* Brice," Jenny insisted, waving her phone around the empty paddock, ignoring the shrieks from the speaker as she gave her viewers back in Manhattan a wild ride of their own. "Why do you need so much privacy? Why can't people look inside? We act like our shed-rows need security details to keep out the fans, so the fans get discouraged and do something else with their time. They're just horses, Brice. They're just horses running in circles. We don't have anything to hide." She paused, took in the fullness of his anger as he stood before her, clenching his fists at his sides, and wondered if Brice Lawson was really so cruel and stupid that he'd hit an assistant trainer in the paddock before a stakes race. She didn't care—not yet. That was the glory of Jenny when her blood was up. She was a different person until the moment was gone. "What do *you* have to hide?" she asked softly.

There was an *ooooooooh* of approval and shock from the New York audience, and then Brice moved suddenly, like he was going to grab at her, and Jenny sprang away, turning on her heel and running for the paddock fence. She slid through the bars and went pelting through the thinning crowds at the back of the concrete apron in front of the grandstand doors, her waves of dark brown hair bouncing through the haze of cigarette smoke hanging over the crowd. The people around her spoke with accents almost entirely Long Island and New Jersey-bred, making her feel like she was back in New York, maybe out at Aqueduct or Belmont for a stolen day of photography with Aidan, but the concrete ran out too soon. Tampa Bay was a comically small track compared to the New York racing machines, but it had a big heart for its racing family. She knew almost every groom leaning on the wall behind the winner's circle, and most of the trainers as well. She had known them since she was a child.

Her mother gave her an annoyed look. "What took you so long? They're in the gate."

"Bathroom," Jenny lied. She glanced over her shoulder; no Brice had appeared through the crowd of blue-haired bettors.

"Uh, Jenny?" A voice at her side, oddly low to the ground, asked. "Could you like, pick us up?"

"Oh, sorry!" Jenny lifted her phone; she'd completely forgotten about her little screen crew. "Hey guys, did I give you motion sickness?"

"I put the phone down on the bar when you started running,"

Aidan laughed. "That was quite a speech you gave that dick in the paddock. Was he that guy Brice you told us about?"

Jenny laughed and put her finger to her lips. "Shhh, you'll get me in trouble! But yes, that was him."

As the horses broke from the gate and the announcer began to call their positions, Jenny went on gazing at her phone, listening to Aidan congratulate her. She hadn't realized it was possible to miss a person this much. She'd been in Florida for four days, and now she was drinking Aidan in like a lost lover she hadn't seen in decades. His lean face and sand-streaked brown hair falling over his forehead and his dancing green eyes and his big-toothed grin, so carelessly thrown her way for the slightest agreeable thing she did—bumping him gently on a rocking subway car, catching his shirt in one hand when he pushed too far ahead of her on a crowded sidewalk, bringing him an iced coffee when she came up to the studio to work on a project or quietly study beside him. He always looked delighted with her, as if he didn't know that she did these things for herself, as naturally as breathing: she could not have stopped herself from brushing against him every time the F train screamed its way through the labyrinthine tunnels of lower Manhattan, or let him get away from her in a crowd, or not buy two coffees as habitually as she had once bought herself one, knowing when he'd be nearby and that he'd always be happy for a fresh jolt of caffeine. These gestures were part of her very being.

He was looking delighted with her now, but she couldn't even hear what he was saying anymore. The air around her ears was roaring, there was noise all around. She looked up, and blinked, and gasped. She spun the phone around, held it above her head. *"Look!"*

Mister flew past, his gray dapples flashing as he thundered down the center of the track, Manny's face pressed close to his fluttering mane with his whip hand high. Only a flashing second of her horse was visible, then the rest of the field came pelting after, one flicker-frame of horse and then another, disappearing into the distant clubhouse turn.

"I have to go," Jenny gabbled into the phone, but Aidan protested.

"Just take us with you," he said. "Give us a view of the winner's circle when you can. We'll wait."

Jenny nodded, heart too full to speak, and dropped her phone into the pocket of her khakis. She had a fleeting thought, as she followed her mother to the gate onto the track, of Aidan's face pressed against her ass. But she shook it off. It was time to catch her horse, and lead him into the winner's circle.

Her new stakes-winning colt, Mr. November.

You can find *The Hidden Horses of New York* in ebook or paperback from your favorite bookseller.

Acknowledgments

WRITING A NOVEL is never easy, or even fun, but we do it anyway. I would never finish a single story without the support of my husband, Cory, who organizes my life so well that I have no excuses. My barn family, equine and human, give me so much happiness and plenty of things to write about, so thank goodness for Jess, who answered my Facebook ad asking for a nice horse to lease with the unappealing question "would you be interested in riding a pony?" I'm still relieved, a year and a half later, that I lied and said yes.

Horses in Wonderland's settings are drawn from my many years working at Walt Disney World Resort, managing the legendary Grand Cypress Equestrian Center which used to share a boundary line with the resort, and also working as a mounted member of the New York City Department of Parks and Recreation. I'm thankful beyond words for the people who gave me encouragement, assistance, and opportunities in these incredibly unique workplaces.

This year was especially challenging thanks to a demanding work schedule and many weeks of travel. The generosity of my Patreon supporters really made Horses in Wonderland a one-year project instead of a two-year one (or worse, I might not have ever finished it). To all of you: Heather Voltz, Emily Hamblin, Cindy Sperry, Rhonda Lane, Jenny, Lindsay Moore, Emily Nolan, Barbara Hawkins, Brinn Dimler, Tricia Jordan, Lori King, Zoe Bills, Sarah Seavey, Cheryl Bavister, Rose Taylor, Orpu, Amy Jungk, Diana Aitch, Megan Devine, Liz Greene, Mara Shatat, Caitlin Harrison, Kathy, Kim Keller (hey wait, that's my dad!) and Elena Bryant (hey —that's my sister!) I'm so grateful for your support, financial and otherwise! Thank you for reading Horses in Wonderland as I wrote it, sharing your critiques and ideas, and making it a better book. Let's do this again!

At the end of the road, when I have a final edit staring at me, my beta readers step up and get me through the final furlong. Massive love to Rachael Rosenthal, Emily Justice, Kathleen Edwards, Liza Sibley, April Jo Williams, Kelsi Sloan and Michelle Harper for making time to read and assist me! And if you like the cover, thank Michelle—she made me change it! Thanks, Michelle—it's gorgeous.

And shout-out to my writing chums who keep pushing me with their great work (and helping me distract myself on Twitter)—Mara Dabrishus and Mary Pagones, you two are the best.

Finally, thanks to Jean at Taborton Equine Books, the bookseller who gets me out of my house once a year or so and puts me in front of readers. She even gave me my own page at her website. Go buy your horse books from Jean!

About the Author

I CURRENTLY LIVE in Central Florida. While most of my books are set in Florida, I also love writing about New York City, where I worked with racehorses and mounted police horses. Between recounting tales of both city life and country life, I feel like I'll always have enough to write about.

I write fiction and freelance for a variety of publications, but my favorite topics are travel and horses. In the past I've worked professionally in many aspects of the equestrian world, including grooming for top eventers, training off-track Thoroughbreds, galloping racehorses, working in mounted law enforcement, on breeding farms, and more.

Visit my website at nataliekreinert.com to keep up with the latest news and read occasional blog posts and book reviews. You can also subscribe to my newsletter and get a free book just for being a fan!

For installments of upcoming fiction and exclusive stories, visit my Patreon page to learn how you can become a member: patreon.com/nataliekreinert

www.ingramcontent.com/pod-product-compliance
Lightning Source LLC
Chambersburg PA
CBHW051214190726
48288CB00006B/1954